You never know . . .

Liza sat down on the couch and unlaced her dirt-spattered gardening shoes. "Do you agree that we should start meeting again for classes?"

"Sure," said Claire. "I mean, that's what I'm here for. Especially if you think it'll help people feel better."

Liza tugged at a muddy shoelace. "Why not? It couldn't hurt. People don't have to come if they don't want to."

Meredith appeared at the door holding a tea tray. *"Voilà,"* she said, though it was apparent from the cookie crumbs around her mouth that she had a head start on the Lemon Crunch cookies. "Oh, I had to sample them to see if they were safe," she said in response to Claire's look. "You never know who might be trying to poison you . . ."

MORE MYSTERIES FROM THE
BERKLEY PUBLISHING GROUP...

CAT CALIBAN MYSTERIES: She was married for thirty-eight years. Raised three kids. Compared to that, tracking down killers is easy ...

By D. B. Borton

ONE FOR THE MONEY	TWO POINTS FOR MURDER
THREE IS A CROWD	FOUR ELEMENTS OF MURDER
FIVE ALARM FIRE	SIX FEET UNDER

ELENA JARVIS MYSTERIES: There are some pretty bizarre crimes deep in the heart of Texas— and a pretty gutsy police detective who rounds up the unusual suspects ...

by Nancy Herndon

ACID BATH	WIDOWS' WATCH
LETHAL STATUES	HUNTING GAME
TIME BOMBS	C.O.P. OUT
CASANOVA CRIMES	

FREDDIE O'NEAL, P.I., MYSTERIES: You can bet that this appealing Reno private investigator will get her man ... "A winner."—Linda Grant

by Catherine Dain

LAY IT ON THE LINE	SING A SONG OF DEATH
WALK A CROOKED MILE	LAMENT FOR A DEAD COWBOY
BET AGAINST THE HOUSE	THE LUCK OF THE DRAW
DEAD MAN'S HAND	

BENNI HARPER MYSTERIES: Meet Benni Harper—a quilter and folk-art expert with an eye for murderous designs ...

by Earlene Fowler

FOOL'S PUZZLE	DOVE IN THE WINDOW
KANSAS TROUBLES	MARINER'S COMPASS
IRISH CHAIN	SEVEN SISTERS
GOOSE IN THE POND	*(Available in hardcover from Berkley Prime Crime)*

HANNAH BARLOW MYSTERIES: For ex-cop and law student Hannah Barlow, justice isn't just a word in a textbook. Sometimes, it's a matter of life and death ...

by Carroll Lachnit

MURDER IN BRIEF	A BLESSED DEATH
AKIN TO DEATH	JANIE'S LAW

PEACHES DANN MYSTERIES: Peaches has never had a very good memory. But she's learned to cope with it over the years ... Fortunately, though, when it comes to murder, this absentminded amateur sleuth doesn't forgive and forget!

by Elizabeth Daniels Squire

WHO KILLED WHAT'S-HER-NAME?	WHOSE DEATH IS IT ANYWAY?
MEMORY CAN BE MURDER	IS THERE A DEAD MAN IN THE HOUSE?
REMEMBER THE ALIBI	WHERE THERE'S A WILL
FORGET ABOUT MURDER	

Who Killed Dorian Gray?

CAROLE BUGGÉ

BERKLEY PRIME CRIME, NEW YORK

WHO KILLED DORIAN GRAY?

A Berkley Prime Crime Book / published by arrangement with the author

PRINTING HISTORY
Berkley Prime Crime edition / July 2000

All rights reserved.
Copyright © 2000 by Carole Buggé.
This book may not be reproduced in whole or in part,
by mimeograph or any other means, without permission.
For information address: The Berkley Publishing Group,
a division of Penguin Putnam Inc.,
375 Hudson Street, New York, New York 10014.

The Penguin Putnam Inc. World Wide Web site address is
http://www.penguinputnam.com

ISBN: 0-425-17553-7

Berkley Prime Crime Books are published
by The Berkley Publishing Group,
a division of Penguin Putnam Inc.,
375 Hudson Street, New York, New York 10014.
The name BERKLEY PRIME CRIME and the BERKLEY PRIME
CRIME design are trademarks belonging to Penguin Putnam Inc.

PRINTED IN THE UNITED STATES OF AMERICA

10 9 8 7 6 5 4 3 2 1

Author's Note

The characters in this book are fictional and are not meant
to represent anyone living or dead.

Acknowledgments

Thanks first of all to my editor at Berkley, Christine Zika, for her invaluable help in shaping this book; thanks also to Sergeant Clayton Keefe of Woodstock for his help in answering many questions about police procedure; to Katherine Burger for introducing me to the arts colony at Byrdcliffe; to my agent Susan Ginsburg at Writers House; to Chris Buggé for the nifty books on forensic science; to Anthony Moore for his research help; and to Marvin Kaye for his continued support of my literary endeavors.

For Katie and Suzie, in memory of
our childhood in the country

Chapter 1

Claire Rawlings heard her phone ringing as soon as she stepped off the elevator. She turned the key in the lock and entered her apartment, nearly tripping over her fat white cat, Ralph, as she fumbled for the light switch. She reached the phone just as it stopped ringing.

"Damn," Claire muttered, throwing her bag of manuscripts on the living room couch, along with a stack of mail. Her answering machine was in the shop. The worst part of it was that now she couldn't screen her calls, but would have to pick up whenever the phone rang. Lately Claire had taken to screening her calls; even though it summoned up feelings of Protestant guilt, she was becoming more protective of her time.

Ralph wound around her legs, purring seductively, his fur tickling her ankles.

"All right, all right," she muttered, going into the kitchen. She opened a can of Liver 'n Onions, holding her breath as she spooned half the can into Ralph's bowl.

"There—live it up," she said, putting the bowl on the floor beside the stove. She went back into the living room and picked up the pile of mail from the couch. She tore open the letter addressed to her in Meredith Lawrence's sprawling, feathery handwriting, then picked up the satchel of manuscripts and went into the bedroom. She dumped the bag in the corner by the bureau, tossed off her office pumps, and lay on the bed to read Meredith's letter.

Dear Claire,

It's a wonder that the youth of America doesn't rise up en masse *and declare a mutiny against adults. Since I have been here, I have been forced to a) sing stupid songs; "Camp Songs," they call them, but I call them Hitler Youth Songs; b) learn a variety of utterly useless tasks, such as How to Tie a Slipknot, or How to Paddle a Canoe Without Tipping Over; and c) worst of all, eat horrible food, prepared by genetically engineered Neolithic Cafeteria Slaves.*

Good Lord! Save me from the well-meaning programming of my father, who I am beginning to suspect wants to mold me into Hilde the Magnificent Hun. Or perhaps he just wants to be rid of me for a while, to enjoy the sexual favors of the Wicked Witch of Greenwich. (She must be good in bed, because Lord knows she's not good for anything else.)

What am I to make of all this frenetic activity here at Camp Wallawalla? I wish someone would give these people some Ritalin! All I want is to curl up in the corner with a tome of the writings of St. Augustine, or Dostoevsky or something. However, I am forced to hide my books under my bed for fear one of my cabin mates—all of them Nazi clones—will find them and have me sterilized.

I must go—there is the bell summoning us to another Youth Rally. Wish me luck—or better yet, get me the hell out of here!

Yours,
Meredith

Claire put down the letter and lay on her back looking at the ceiling. She stared at a water stain in the shape of

Texas, which was turning brown at the edges, and thought about the strange girl who had come into her life so suddenly last fall.

Meredith was so different from other children. With her precocious intelligence, her almost universal disdain for her peers, and her troubled home life, Claire feared that the girl was headed for difficulties. While Claire admired Meredith's attempt to weaver a protective web around herself, using her fierce intelligence and wit, she also worried that sooner or later the strain between Meredith and the rest of the world would begin to take its toll. Until then, Claire could only watch and try to be there in whatever way she could whenever Meredith needed her.

Ralph's head appeared at the side of the bed. He jumped up on the bed next to Claire, put an experimental paw on her stomach, and looked at her for a reaction. When she did not push him away, he tried a second paw; still getting no reaction, he crept slowly onto her stomach, purring defensively. He turned in tight little circles, finally settling on her rib cage, his head on her sternum. Eyes half-closed languorously, he kneaded her flesh with his claws, digging through her thin linen shirt.

"Ow," said Claire, lifting his claws from her skin. Ralph dealt with this interruption of his routine by licking himself, finally dozing off with one paw on Claire's neck. The soft weight of the cat was soothing, and Claire felt herself slipping into sleep as light from the setting sun crept across the slats of her venetian blinds. She dreamed that she and Meredith were running through a ravine, pursued by Jean Lawrence, Meredith's stepmother, and a host of Connecticut matrons dressed in golf clothes.

The sound of the phone ringing jolted her into consciousness. She sat up abruptly and picked up the receiver.

"Hello?"

"Claire, it's Liza Hatcher."

"Oh, hi, Liza."

Liza Hatcher was a former colleague from Claire's early days as an editor for Waverly Press. Unlike Claire, Liza had aspirations to write, and was working on a novel at the time, which she eventually had published. She left Waverly at about the same time as Claire, and Claire ran into her a few times after that at parties, but then lost track of her. Claire had heard from someone recently that Liza had become a lesbian.

"It's been a while, hasn't it?" Liza spoke with a cultivated Southern accent, thick and smooth as hot syrup.

"Yes ... what have you been up to?" Claire said, regretting once again the absence of her answering machine. She liked Liza, but had grown increasingly impatient with chitchat. It occurred to her that this was perhaps Meredith's influence.

"Well, I'm still writing, of course, though it's harder these days to get anything published, you know."

Claire glanced at the pile of unread manuscripts in the corner of her bedroom. She hoped Liza wasn't calling to ask her to look at a book.

"Tell me about it."

"I have a proposition for you which may or may not interest you."

"What is it?"

"Well, for the last couple of summers I've been holding writing seminars at an arts colony called Ravenscroft. It's up in Woodstock."

"Sounds wonderful."

"Yes, it is. It was built as a residence for painters, but lately they've been admitting writers, too, so there's an equal mix of painters and writers each year."

"How nice." Claire's stomach began to rumble. *Get to the point, Liza.*

"What I was wondering is whether you would be interested in coming up next month in a professional capacity to talk to the writers about their work. It would mean a bit of reading, but we'll pay you an honorarium and take care of all transportation, lodging, and food. It's very pretty up here."

"So I've heard. I did something like that a few summers ago on Shelter Island." Claire wound the phone cord around her little finger as she talked. Ralph watched the cord through one opened eye, contemplating an attack, but was evidently too lazy to launch one. "How much reading would be involved?"

"Well, we've asked everyone to submit the first three chapters of a novel, or a couple of short stories. There will be a literary agent up here, too, so the two of you can kind of take turns talking to people individually . . . and then we thought we might hold a group class as well one evening."

Claire looked at the crumpled bag of unread manuscripts on the floor. "How long would this be for?"

"Well, you could come just for the weekend—or for the whole week, if you want."

Claire took a deep breath and held it for a moment. "All right, I'll do it. Thanks for thinking of me."

"My pleasure. It'll be good to see you again. I'll mail you the details and the manuscripts within the next couple of days."

Claire hung up and looked out the window at the brownstones across the street. The thought of reading yet more manuscripts was depressing. Even the work submitted to her by agents was often not very good—and the writers in Woodstock would more likely than not be unrepresented, unpublished, unpolished . . . and very needy. On the other hand, there was country life to look forward to . . . trees, crickets, the smell of honeysuckle at night. She had grown up in the country, and still longed for its rhythms, so seductive and peaceful.

"Well, old boy, looks like you're going to be left alone for a few days," she said to Ralph, who was circling the bed, waiting for her to lie down again. "Maybe I'll ask Liza if I can bring you; what do you think about that?"

In response, the cat jumped up on the windowsill and looked out. Claire sat on the bed and stared at the phone. Her fingers ached to dial her boyfriend Wally Jackson's home number, but he had just left that afternoon for San Francisco to visit his mother for her birthday. She decided to wait until he arrived in California and call him there.

Claire wandered into the kitchen and defrosted a container of clams she and Wally had brought back from

Cutchogue, Long Island. She made herself linguini in clam sauce and settled in front of a *Seinfeld* repeat to eat. It was the episode where Kramer is dating the Low Talker and Jerry gets conned into wearing the Pirate Shirt on the Jay Leno show.

"Well," Claire murmured, scratching Ralph's ears as he sniffed at her bowl of linguini, "at least there's always *Seinfeld.*"

A few days later Claire was barreling up the Palisades Parkway around sunset in her old brown Mercedes. Driving into the coming night, the road stretching out in front of her like a black river, she had an urge to go faster and faster, to put the road under her, as she watched the white lines sliding by, slipping under the wheels of her speeding car. As her heavy old car hurtled through the thick summer air, she felt the city falling away behind her, saw the looming grey hulks of the Hudson Highlands in front of her, and the tension drained from her shoulders like water through a sieve.

"By the time I get to Woodstock," Claire hummed softly.

Woodstock. She was leaving the city for a whole week. Ralph roamed the backseat restlessly, meowing anxiously from time to time. But by the time they were approaching Route 6, he had calmed down and lay quietly on the front passenger-seat floor. The sky was almost entirely dark now, sinking from deep midnight blue to black. Claire put in a tape, opened the sunroof, and let the mysterious opening bars of the Mozart Requiem float up and out into the dusky summer air.

She remembered the trips her family took when she was a child, driving at night through these same hills, her mother at the wheel. Claire would sit next to her brother in the backseat, looking out the window at the road spinning by beneath the car. Wrapped safely in the cocoon of her family's love, pressing her nose to the glass of the window, she would watch the pavement whiz by in strips of grey and black. Her father and her brother invariably fell asleep, and Claire would lean forward to talk to her mother. She loved these times, having her mother all to herself, just the two of them awake on a dark highway of dreamers.

The surrounding hills of the Hudson Highlands loomed over her as she turned west onto Route 6. The car's ancient diesel engine chugged slowly up the steep inclines of the narrow mountain road. A few cars passed her, and then she was alone, with just the hills for company. Claire let herself sink deeply into the sensation of solitude, savoring it; her pulse quickened with each breath of the humid air. Enveloped by the hills and by Mozart's magnificent music, she found herself wishing that she would never reach her destination. She wanted to drive all through the night, suspended in time, somewhere between leaving and arriving, wrapped in a cocoon of her own reality, like a space traveler moving at the speed of light. This was freedom, utter and complete: cut off from her past, hurtling toward an uncertain future, Claire experienced a release that was as close to pure joy as anything she had ever felt. She opened the car window and let the music swell out into the night.

Claire thought of Meredith, and of Wally, and of all the people in her life who meant something to her, but she did not want any of them to be there with her: this moment was about the deliciousness of solitude. Claire thought it must be this feeling that propelled explorers across hostile continents and frozen seas; this pushing forward into space, gloriously alone.

The Kingston exit finally came, though, and soon she was turning left onto Route 212, toward downtown Woodstock. Claire knew she was in Woodstock when she saw a pet store advertising Environment/Pet-Friendly Flea Collars and Organic Dog Food. She rounded the corner on 212 where it became Tinker Street—an appropriate name for Woodstock's main street, she thought.

She found the turn onto the Glasco Turnpike, then headed up the mountain toward Ravenscroft. A soft rain had begun to fall, and the old car climbed slowly, its headlights reflected off the shiny black surface of the road. By the time she pulled into the driveway, it was raining harder, and she had to tuck Ralph under her windbreaker and make a run for the house, sloshing through puddles.

Ravenscroft was a sprawling woodframe house perched on the side of Guardian Mountain. A flagstone path led from the dirt parking lot up to the front porch, a rambling vine-covered affair with rustic wooden railings. Liza was sitting on the porch, a candle burning on the table beside her. When she saw Claire she rose and came down the steps to greet her.

"You made it. Welcome to Ravenscroft! Is that Ralph? Poor kitty—he looks so miserable. How old is he now?"

"Too old to enjoy getting his feet wet," Claire said, putting him down once she was under the porch roof. Released, Ralph twitched his tail irritably, shook his feet one by one, then jumped up onto the musty daybed that served as a porch couch.

"Stupid of me not to bring an umbrella," Claire remarked.

"We've got plenty here," said Liza. "I'm glad you've got a car, though; we do have a shortage of those. Only two other residents own cars—Jack Mulligan and Billy Trimble." Liza was big and comfortable and wore her honey-colored hair short, lopped off around the ears. She was dressed in blue overalls and sandals over bulky socks. She looked utterly Woodstock. "Here, let me help you with your luggage."

"Oh, that can wait," Claire said. "Let me just look around for a minute first. This is wonderful!"

"Come on inside and I'll give you the tour." Liza opened the creaky screen door to the porch.

"What year was this built?" Claire asked as she followed Liza through the spacious living room with its stone fireplace.

"Turn of the century—1901, to be exact."

Claire breathed deeply, inhaling the familiar damp wood smell of her childhood on Lake Erie. A baby grand piano stood in the far corner of the room, and next to it was a bronze statue of Diana, bow and arrow in her hand.

"That's Sherry's addition to the house," Liza remarked with a laugh. "She found it at a garage sale. Her favorite

Greek goddess; just between you and me, I think she identifies with Diana."

Something in Liza's tone made Claire assume that Sherry was her lover. She didn't say anything, though, and they continued through the living room into the dining room, a cavernous wood-paneled room with half a dozen well-worn wooden tables scattered around it.

Liza led her into a small alcove off the rear of the dining room, where there was a pay phone attached to an answering machine. "This is the house phone for the residents. You can give people this number to call, and the answering machine will pick up. If you take a message for someone else, just slip it in their mailbox; the mailboxes are by the front staircase. I have my own phone at the cabin, though, so if you want to use that to call out, you're certainly welcome."

"Thank you." Seeing the phone made Claire want to call Wally. She had spoken with him the evening before, but had a sudden sharp longing to hear his voice.

"And there's the laundry room," Liza continued, pointing to a short hallway off the alcove that contained a washer and dryer. "I have detergent if you need some."

"Thanks."

"No televisions are allowed at Ravenscroft. You can have a radio in your room, but only if you keep the volume low enough so that it doesn't disturb the other residents. A couple of the painters have radios in their studios, I think, and Sherry and I have one in the cabin if you ever need a news fix or anything."

Claire nodded. "Thanks." She loved the idea of a week without television or even her beloved National Public Radio—with just the sounds of the surrounding woods to keep her company.

"Some of the residents are already asleep; most of the painters go to bed early and get up early to catch the daylight," said Liza as she led Claire through the dining room toward the kitchen. "But several of the writers are night owls; a couple of them work most of the night."

The kitchen was also huge, institution-sized, with a big

center island, two stoves, and a double sink. There were two walk-in pantries, one for pots and china; the other held five full-sized refrigerators.

"Everyone shares a refrigerator with one other person, and you each get your own shelf in the pantry for dry food," Liza said. "You can share Camille's refrigerator."

On one of the refrigerators someone had pasted a cartoon from *The New Yorker.* Two men in khakis and pith helmets stood in an African base camp, and one was saying, "Those drums all night, so insistent, repetitive, monotonous! It must be something by Philip Glass." Claire read it and laughed.

"Whose refrigerator is this?"

"Oh, the cartoon? Billy Trimble put that there. He shares the fridge with Gary Robinson."

At that moment an extraordinary-looking person entered the kitchen. He was enormous; he seemed to be built on the same scale as the house—everything about him was oversized. He was at least six and a half feet tall, and Claire estimated that his massive frame carried a good three hundred pounds. His great head was topped by a tall black ten-gallon hat, the kind movie villains wear, and long black hair fell down his back, halfway to his waist. He wore blue jeans, a black cowboy shirt under a fringed leather vest, and cowboy boots. His entire outfit was more evocative of the Wild West than of the Catskills.

"Hello," he said to Claire in a deep but curiously soft voice.

"Oh, this is Two Joe," said Liza, emerging from the pantry. "Two Joe, this is Claire Rawlings."

Two Joe enveloped Claire's hand in his; it was like shaking hands with a giant. His skin was as dry and leathery as alligator hide, and Claire could feel the power in his grasp.

"Pleased to meet you," he said. "You are Liza's editor friend?"

"Uh, yes, I am."

"Two Joe is one of the painters," said Liza. "He's full-blooded Cherokee."

"Really?"

"Yes. They call me Two Joe because of my size. And I have recently lost a hundred and fifty pounds."

Claire didn't actually want to picture Two Joe prior to his weight loss, so she just nodded. "Well, that's impressive."

"Liza didn't mention that you were a good-looking redhead."

Claire blushed and laughed. "Well . . ."

Liza laughed too. "Two Joe is such a flirt. He's only been here a week, and already he has all the women here eating out of his hand. Don't you?"

Two Joe just shrugged, but the right corner of his mouth twitched upward. Liza swatted his shoulder lightly. "Do you know what he told me when he first arrived? That if he'd known Southern women were so beautiful—"

"I would have moved to Georgia years ago," Two Joe declared solemnly, but the corner of his mouth still twitched upward.

"Well, I don't mind a little flirting, especially with a handsome Native American," Claire said with uncharacteristic boldness. After the long drive, she felt light-headed and a little loopy.

Liza laughed. "She's got you at your own game, Two Joe."

Two Joe grinned widely. "Who said anything about a game?"

"Would you mind keeping it down a little? It's late," said a voice behind Claire.

Claire turned to see a tall, angular black man standing in the hallway outside the kitchen. He wore old-fashioned round spectacles, and though he looked young, his thin-lipped face had a grave air, suggesting someone older—a college professor perhaps.

"Oh, I'm sorry, Gary," Liza apologized. "Sound really carries in this old house," she added, looking at Claire.

Claire turned to look at Two Joe, whose face was stolid and expressionless. It was clear that he did not like Gary.

"Gary, this is my friend Claire Rawlings, who just arrived from New York," Liza added quickly. "Claire, this is

Gary Robinson. He's a painter, and he teaches art at City College in New York."

"Pleased to meet you," Claire said.

"How do you do?" Gary responded formally. He did not offer his hand as Two Joe had, but made a stiff little bow. He paused as if he was about to say something else, but evidently changed his mind and turned to leave.

"If you'll excuse me, I'm going to try to get some sleep," he said, and left as soundlessly as he had come. After he was gone, there was a brief silence, then Liza spoke.

"He's not really as cold as he seems," she said apologetically.

Two Joe snorted softly in response. It was so like Liza to act as peacemaker; she had done the same thing when she and Claire worked together at Waverly. Liza hated it when people fought. Claire wondered what was between Gary and Two Joe, but this wasn't the time for gossip; she would get Liza alone later and find out. A wave of fatigue swept through her body. She tried to stifle a yawn, but Liza noticed it.

"You're tired, aren't you?" she asked sympathetically.

"I guess so. I just got caught up in the excitement of being here."

"Well, it's late. I guess we're all tired—except for Two Joe, who likes to burn the midnight oil."

Two Joe nodded.

"Two Joe likes to paint at night," he said. Claire wondered if that was really the way he talked, or if he was laying on the Native American shtick for her benefit.

"Well, Liza likes to sleep at night," Liza said, yawning. "Can I help you with your luggage?"

"Oh, I'll get it. I left it in the car. If I could just borrow your umbrella—"

Two Joe stepped forward. "Two Joe will get your luggage."

"Oh, that's very kind, but I can—"

"No, no; Two Joe will take care of you."

Claire looked at Liza, who shrugged.

"Well, thank you; that's very kind of you. It's nice to

find that chivalry is still alive in some parts of the world," Claire added as he left the kitchen, the ancient floorboards creaking under his weight.

"Being a full-time feminist can be so tiring, don't you think?" Liza said, smiling.

Claire laughed. "It's just too late at night to stand on principle."

"Let me show you to your room," said Liza when Two Joe arrived with the luggage. He insisted on carrying it upstairs, and Claire followed behind, down a long hallway covered with a thin, rust-colored carpet. Liza stopped at the last door on the left.

"I call this the Edwardian Room," she said, producing a key from her pocket. Claire was a little surprised that the rooms had locks. It made sense, she supposed; even artists and writers can be thieves.

The room was small but cozy, with a thick oak dresser and matching rocking chair. There was a single window overlooking the front drive, the curtains were white lace, and the floor was covered with a green and white hooked rug. A poster of a Turner painting hung on one wall, the murky yellow colors warm and fuzzy in the glow of the bedside lamp.

"It's quiet in this corner of the house," Liza said, fluffing the pillows on the bed. "The only room you're directly over is the dining room, and people don't even use it that much. Mostly we eat on the porch. There's a back staircase which leads down to the first floor, but again, people tend to use the main stairs more often. I think you'll find it pretty peaceful here."

"This will be great—thanks," said Claire as Ralph slunk into the room, making the half-purr, half-meow sound that was his way of announcing his presence.

"Hi, Ralph; are you settling in?" said Liza.

"Thanks so much for letting me bring him," said Claire.

"It is good to have your spirit guide with you," Joe remarked, heaving Claire's suitcase onto the bed. Claire knew it was heavier than it looked; she never went anywhere without her hand weights.

"Oh, is Ralph your spirit guide?" Liza asked.

"Everyone has a spirit guide," Two Joe said seriously, and again Claire thought he was laying the Native American thing on a bit thick.

"Well, I'll leave you to unpack," said Liza. "Feel free to use any bathroom, but the closest one is just down the hall to the left. They're all showers except for the one downstairs, where there's an actual bathtub."

"Where is your room?" Claire asked.

"Oh, Sherry and I are renting a little cabin next door; you can see it through your window, actually."

Claire peered through the window and saw the lights blazing in the windows of a cozy little bungalow sitting up the hill just a few hundred yards from Ravenscroft.

"They offered me a room in Ravenscroft, but Sherry and I wanted some privacy, and the cabins are very cheap. If you ever need anything, just come knock on our door."

"Thanks so much—and thank you for carrying my luggage, Two Joe."

Two Joe nodded solemnly and withdrew.

"Good night," said Liza, closing the door behind her. "Sleep well."

"Oh, don't worry—I will."

Claire decided to postpone her unpacking until the next day. She put on her flannel pajamas and soon was snuggling underneath a down comforter. It was much cooler up here than in town; Liza had warned her to be prepared for cold nights on Guardian Mountain. Ralph roamed the room for a while, sniffing into corners, then jumped up on the bed and settled near Claire's face, breathing his thin little cat's breath on her chin. She inhaled the odor of Purina Tuna Dinner.

"Very nice, Ralph," she murmured, turning over. Ralph responded by licking himself.

Claire lay for a long time listening to the rain outside. It murmured suggestively, softly, closing them inside the house, dripping from the window casements, sliding down the windowpanes, beckoning. The wind whipped and whistled in the eaves, rustling the curtains and nestling against the side of the house, whining and tapping like a dog begging to come inside. Lying in the soft warm bed, it was hard for Claire to resist the pull of sleep, the tug of the subconscious on her weary body. But there was something so delicious, so luxurious about lying there that she fought to remain conscious.

Then a memory surfaced from her subconscious, swimming its way up through layers of forgetfulness: the feel of Robert's hands closing around her throat. Panic seized her and she sat up in bed, sweating. Nine months had passed since he tried to kill her, but the memory of his hands on her neck had not faded.

Robert. How could a man with so much outward grace be so essentially rotten, like a house with a fresh coat of paint that is crumbling inside, decayed at its core. There had been the smell of decay about Robert, in retrospect, Claire thought; if only she had sensed it at the time. But she was blind to essential aspects of him, and that blindness had almost killed her. All along, she thought, he had used her—used to her get closer to Blanche DuBois—and then when Claire threatened, quite unwittingly, to close in on his secret, he had tried to kill her. If it weren't for Wally and Meredith, no doubt he would have succeeded. Their last-minute rescue of her was both dramatic and miraculous, and if Claire shared her mother's faith in God, she would have called it a miracle.

Claire snuggled back under the quilt, comforted by the idea of Wally and Meredith, unknown to her a year ago, now both so much a part of her life. There were so many imponderables, she thought; no wonder people grasped at the idea of a higher power to help them explain life's great questions. But Robert . . . Robert would always remain for her one of those questions. She could never answer why or how she could have come close to loving a man who had tried—and very nearly succeeded—in killing her.

She listened to the wind whistling in the eaves, curling around the side of the building, wrapping itself around the old house like a blanket. Finally she surrendered to the pull of fatigue, and sank into a deep and dreamless sleep.

Chapter 2

Claire awoke to the smell of coffee and the sound of sparrows squabbling outside her window. She sat up and brushed the cat hairs from her chin, then looked around the room for Ralph. He was seated on the window sill, watching the sparrows patiently. He glanced back at Claire when she rose and began to dress, then returned to his vigil.

Claire felt as though she had slept for days, and had trouble shaking the sleep from her body. She walked groggily through the long hall and down the creaking front staircase. The kitchen was empty, but Liza had left a note neatly taped to the coffee maker.

Good morning! Had to go to town on Guild business— help yourself to coffee. Back by noon—L.

Claire looked at the clock over the sink; it was already after ten. She rubbed her eyes and poured herself a cup of coffee, which she carried out to the porch. The cicadas were just beginning to drone their long descending scale, heralding the end of summer, as she settled into one of the canvas director's chairs scattered about the porch. On the other end of the porch was a picnic table with benches. No wonder no one used the dining room, Claire thought as she sipped her coffee. This porch was the most perfect spot imaginable, its dry old sun-bleached wood posts covered by winding honeysuckle vines, the sweet smell mingling with the musty odor of loam and peat moss from the garden. She took another sip of coffee, closed her eyes, and heaved a deep sigh of contentment.

Just then the screen door creaked, and Claire turned to see a short, dark, elegantly dressed woman enter the porch.

"Good morning. You must be Claire Rawlings."

"Yes. Good morning."

"I'm Camille Sardou."

Her voice was striking—low and husky, with a touch of the Continent about it—and it lent her an air of glamour that her looks alone might not have. Her eyes were too prominent, and her grey-stained teeth advertised the reason for that throaty voice—as did the box of Sobraine Black Russians poking out from her shirt pocket.

"Mind if I join you?"

"Please do."

She sat on the musty old bed that served as a couch, pulling her feet up underneath her, neat as a cat. *Chic,* Claire thought. *Her movements, her voice—everything about her is chic.* It was true; though she was dressed in jeans and a loose, flowing black shirt, the jeans were pressed and the shirt had the sheen of real silk. Large silver-and-turquoise earrings dangled from her ears, and even at this hour of day, Claire noticed, Camille wore lipstick.

"Everyone's very excited about your being here," Camille remarked, taking the cigarettes from her pocket and putting them on the coffee table. "Oh, don't worry," she added. "I'm not going to smoke one right now. Smoking is forbidden anywhere inside the house, actually, so I have to head off toward the woods if I want to indulge in my habit." She laughed, showing her darkened teeth. "Camelot Road is full of my cigarette stubs."

"Camelot Road?"

Camille pointed to the dirt road leading past Ravenscroft and into the woods. "It's not marked, but this is Camelot Road. If you walk it all the way to the end, it comes out on Rock Hill Road. They told me that you used to be able to drive it, but there's been a lot of erosion; the bridge has been out for years, so only a four-wheel-drive could make it now. It's a nice walk, though. I've done it several times."

"Good. I'm always looking for a place to jog."

Camille sighed. "Ah, a healthy person. I suppose there'll be a time when I'm one of those people, but for now . . . well, unfortunately I associated smoking with writing early in life, and I find it hard to separate them."

"I understand; I used to smoke myself."

Camille looked at Claire and laughed, a deep, velvety chortle. "Don't worry; I'm not going to talk about my writing. I'm sure some of the other writers here will have no such compunctions. They'll want to squeeze you dry, so to speak." She laughed again, a short little puff of sound, and again Claire caught a glance of discolored grey teeth through red lips. Claire had read the first three chapters of Camille's book, which was an interesting account of life in Paris during World War II. It was rather well written, with few of the usual mistakes in grammar, punctuation, and syntax that Claire usually encountered in first-time authors.

"I used to be an editor myself," Camille continued, "so I know how writers can be—believe me."

"Oh? Where did you work?"

"In Paris, and later in London."

"I didn't think you were American."

"Actually, I'm French, but I was educated in England. How's that for a schizophrenic cultural identity?" Camille smiled, and when she did, her face looked pretty, even beautiful. She had a quality Claire had seen before in French women: her grace and style gave an impression of glamour and beauty that went beyond mere physical appearance. She was at ease with herself, and thought herself attractive, so others did, too.

Just then the faint sound of a solo flute floated up from the direction of the woods. Claire thought she recognized it as Bach, the notes cool and sweet in the warm morning air.

"Who's playing the flute?" she said.

"Oh, that's Gary Robinson. He likes to practice in the woods sometimes."

"It's nice. He's good," said Claire, settling back in her chair to listen.

"Yes, Gary's talented at a lot of things," Camille answered, and there was something in her voice Claire couldn't read, a subtext she didn't quite get.

"I understand Liza's planning a little *soirée* tonight to welcome you; it's also a sort of end-of-season party," said Camille. "I just arrived last week, but some of the residents have been here all summer."

"Oh? I thought you were all here all summer long."

"No, you can come for just a month at a time. I'm here only for August, and I think a couple of the painters just arrived this month, too. I taught summer term this year and my classes only just ended last week."

"Oh, do you teach literature?"

"Yes, I'm an associate professor of comparative literature at Barnard."

"How nice."

Camille shrugged and was about to say something when the screen door squeaked and clanged shut. Claire turned to see a short, stocky man with a plump, blunt face partially obscured by a thick beard. The beard made his features look even rounder; he reminded her of one of Santa's elves.

"Good morning," Camille said pleasantly, but he just nodded distractedly. "This is Claire Rawlings. Claire, this is Terry Nordstrom, another of the writers."

"Hello," said Claire.

Terry Nordstrom looked as if he were pushing his way through a thick fog in order to comprehend this information. He stared at Claire for a moment and then spoke.

"How do you do." His voice was light and thin, a full octave higher than Camille's, but there was a tightness, a strain in it. His whole body seemed to vibrate from suppressed tension; even standing still, he gave the impression of movement, like an Impressionist painting. There was another pause, then he shook himself as a dog might shake water from its fur. "I'm sorry, I didn't expect to see anyone out here, and I'm a little distracted right now. I'm in the middle of a difficult problem, and I came out here to clear my head."

"Please don't let us disturb you," Claire began, but he shook his head.

"No, no—it's all right; what I probably need is to get away from it. Is there more coffee?" he added, seeing Claire's mug.

"There was half a pot a little while ago," said Claire.

"If you'll excuse me, I'm going to get some." He turned and went back into the house, the screen door slapping shut behind him.

"Writers." Camille sighed, with a longing look at her cigarettes.

"Oh, he doesn't seem so bad, just a little distracted."

"He's not. He just has the usual short man's chip on his shoulder—you know, thinks he has to prove himself all the time, just because he's little. It's too bad, really, that the way someone looks can have such an impact on their personality."

"I know what you mean. I think it's particularly true in America, don't you?" said Claire. It amused her that she wanted to show Camille that she, too, had traveled and knew something of the world.

"Well, of course Americans are obsessed with appearance, with cookie-cutter notions of beauty, but the French have their own image problems. And to make it worse for Terry," Camille said, lowering her voice, "he's in love with the Swedish meatball."

"What?"

"Dorian Gray, a.k.a. Maya Sorenson. She's the resident beauty. Every arts colony has one, you know."

As if on cue, the screen door opened and a tall, slender woman with shoulder-length ash-blond hair appeared on the doorstep.

"Why, Dorian, we were just talking about you," said Camille.

"Really? Vhat a coincidence."

She *was* tall and blond and willowy, and certainly pretty enough, though Claire would not have called her beautiful. Still, she moved with a shy grace, like a young colt. And although Claire would have put her well on the far side of forty, she had an ageless quality about her.

"This is Claire Rawlings, the editor Liza brought up from the city," said Camille. "Claire, this is Maya Sorenson."

"Pleased to meet you."

"How do yoo doo?" Maya shook Claire's hand with a firm grasp. Her hand was thin and cool, like her voice, with its rolling Scandinavian cadence.

"Why do they call you Dorian Gray?" Claire asked.

Maya smiled. "Oh, that was my *nom de plume* when I wrote briefly for a London tabloid." Claire noticed that her French accent was perfect.

"And we're all convinced she has a picture somewhere in her attic," Camille added.

"Won't you join us?" said Claire.

"Oh, no thank yoo; I am in the meddle of a chapter, and I am—how do you say—on a bun."

"On a roll," Camille corrected without smiling.

"Yes. These English idiots are so difficult for me," Maya said, turning to Claire.

"I've met my share of English idiots, too," she replied, and Camille laughed.

"What—did I say something wrong?"

"You meant idioms, not idiots," Camille said gently.

"Oh, yes, that's right."

The door opened again and Terry stood there with two cups of coffee.

"Coffee, anyone?"

"We've already got some," said Camille. "Maya, why don't you have it?"

"Thank yoo very much," she replied, taking the mug.

"That's how you can tell we're writers, by the way," said Terry.

"What do you mean?" said Claire.

"Oh, the painters all drink ginseng or echinacea or some weird unpronounceable herb," said Camille. "They wouldn't be caught dead caffeinating themselves."

"That's right; they're all lacto-flacto-embryo vegetarians; they live on sprouts and tahini sauce," Terry agreed.

"Whereas you're all—"

"Dissipated," said Terry. "It's part of our self-image. Camille here even smokes, for God's sake."

Camille laughed. "I'm like the resident drug dealer."

"You should see us all late at night, bumming cigarettes from her," Terry said. "I think you should start charging us."

Camille shrugged. "It's my penance for having them around to tempt you." She smiled at Claire. "Listen to me! You can take the girl out of the Church, but you can't take the Church out of the girl."

"You were raised Catholic?"

Camille rolled her eyes. "Oh, does it show?" she said, smiling. There was something about her smile—a kind of invitation to intimacy—that Claire found intriguing, even a little startling.

Terry perched on the edge of the sofa, next to Camille, his compact little body coiled tight as a spring. Sitting down, he looked even more restless, as if he were longing to burst into action.

"Maya and I were both raised Lutheran," he said, "and that can be just as bad—right, Maya?"

Maya folded her long body into one of the director's chairs.

"Vell, I suppose it depends upon how yoo look at it."

"I think it's ironic that Marx called religion 'the opiate of the masses,' " Terry continued. "I think it's more the oppressor of the masses."

"Yes, mass *can* be oppressive," Camille remarked with a smile. Claire felt she was trying to lighten the tone.

But Terry was not to be deterred; determined as a terrier, he pushed on.

"I mean, Barbara Tuchman once said that all wars are religious wars—and I think she was right. Look at Bosnia, for example. I was talking to Tahir about it the other day—"

"Who's Tahir?" said Claire.

"Oh, he's a very talented Muslim writer, from Bosnia," said Camille. "He won a literature prize just before he came here; he's written about the war over there."

"Anyway, we were talking about the difference between religious groups in Bosnia," Terry continued, "and how difficult it was for them to coexist, all because of religion."

"Vell, it's not that sample," Maya said, sipping her coffee languidly. "After all, there are profound cultural and ethnic differences which transcend religion." She smiled at Claire. "I spent some time there as a journalist," she added almost apologetically.

"Yes, but look at the Jews and the Palestinians," Terry said, his voice bristling with impatience. "They're both Semitic, they share customs like not eating pork, and yet they've been killing one another for centuries!"

"Do you know a book came out not long ago claiming that war is more or less hardwired into our brains, and that there will always be wars?" said Camille.

Maya sighed and let her head drop back, so that the sun peeking under the eaves glinted off her blond hair. "That's a depressing thought."

"Yes, I remember that book," said Claire. "A friend of mine was the editor. I kept meaning to read it."

"Now I've saved you the trouble," said Camille, laughing, which set off a coughing fit. The rest of them sat there uncomfortably while she coughed the deep, hacking cough of a heavy smoker.

After she stopped, there was a pause and then Maya said, "Yoo know yoo really should think about quitting, Camille. I know it's none of my business, but—"

Camille dismissed her with a wave of her hand. "I know, I know, Maya; as soon as I finish this book, I'm going to try hypnosis." She looked at Claire and shrugged. "It worked for my mother."

Maya stood up and stretched. "Vell, I have to go make my journal entry."

"You keep a journal?" said Claire.

"It was a habit I got into when I was working as a journalist. I always kept notes so I wouldn't forget anything. Now I use it to jot down things that interest me. It's also a good way to limber up, I think."

"Yes, I think you're right," Claire agreed.

"Do any of your authors keep journals?" Camille asked Claire.

"Some of them; it varies."

"I'll see yoo later," said Maya, gliding gracefully into the house. Terry looked after her, hunger in his eyes; when she was gone, it was as if all the air had gone out of his body. Claire rose from the couch.

"Well, this morning is my chance to see the town, so if you'll excuse me, I'm going to drive down and have a look. Does anybody want anything?"

Terry shook his head. Camille lifted her pack of cigarettes sheepishly. "I could use another pack of these. I thought I had another one but I can't seem to find them. You can get them at the gourmet food store on Tinker Street."

"Sobraines are expensive," said Claire.

"Exactly. I'm hoping that will make me smoke less."

"And does it?" said Terry.

Camille shook her head. "I don't know. Maybe."

Claire went back into the kitchen and put some food out for Ralph, who was nowhere to be seen, then she threw a sweater around her shoulders and went out to her car. It was much cooler here on the side of the mountain than in New York, and even with the sun climbing higher in the sky, there was a chill in the air. Next to her were parked the two cars Liza had mentioned earlier: a sprawling old yellow Chevy and a late-model white Toyota Corolla.

Driving down the mountain and into Woodstock, Claire wondered if the town would live up to its image. She was amused to see the number of people, men and women, wearing sandals—and yes, tie-dyed clothing. Looking at a couple dressed in matching batiked smocks, Claire felt a sudden burning nostalgia for the sixties, a decade she had never really felt in tune with at the time, being both too young and too conservative by nature to participate fully. Now, however, as she thought of all that had happened since—and what was perhaps to come—the sixties appeared as sweet and innocent as downtown Woodstock, gleaming in the late-summer sun. The low, crooked buildings nestled into the hillside, their secrets tucked away under ancient rotting roofs, fascinated Claire as she drove slowly down Tinker Street. The street, like the town, did not have a straight line in it. It swooped and dipped and turned as it made its way past shops and restaurants and the only hotel in downtown Woodstock, the Twin Gables, a turn-of-the-century farmhouse with white clapboards and green shutters. Claire drove to the end of town, where Route 212 headed out toward Bearsville, then turned around and went back. She parked in a lot behind some shops and walked back to Tinker Street to have a closer look.

What had happened to Greenwich Village was happening to Woodstock, only more slowly: once the haven of artists, dropouts, and bohemians, it now was in danger of being taken over by the people who inevitably followed them, like pilot fish on a whale, living on the detritus of their host. The makers of tie-dye and pottery and poetry were being replaced by the people who sold those things. Creation had given way to marketing, and process had become a product. Woodstock personified a paradox of the sixties: with its uneasy coexistence of ideology and commercialism, it was able to preserve its image—at the cost of losing the essence that image represented.

But Claire had a weakness for charm, and these crooked little buildings were seductive way before they housed Cynthia's House of Candles or Jake's Organic Foods Emporium. She walked past the stores catering to tourists, selling everything from Woodstock T-shirts to blueberry chutney, but beyond all of that—and inside all of that—Claire sensed something real and sincere and vital about this little town, with its Poetry Readings Every Friday and its carefully burnished image. Perhaps there *were* people living here whose feet remained planted firmly in the long-gone idealism of the sixties, and that was something worth preserving. Self-conscious innocence collided with unapologetic material-ism, and the prices for Birkenstock sandals were even higher than in New York. But as she wandered the streets, Claire sensed an earnestness in the local people who roamed the streets and ran the bookstores, a kind of hardy, defensive determination to preserve a lifestyle in danger of being swallowed up by its very popularity, like a serpent eating its own tail.

Claire stepped into a shop called the Village Peddler. It was modeled after an old-fashioned general store and car-ried a wide assortment of goods, from shoe polish to fish-ing tackle. She walked down the aisles browsing, not really looking for anything in particular. She needed to buy food for the week, but she had passed a Grand Union on her way into town and planned to go there for most of her sta-ples. Still, she liked stores like this one; even though the prices weren't always good, sometimes you could find in-teresting sauces. Claire loved sauces, and had a collection of half-finished bottles slowly growing mold in her re-frigerator. She picked up a jar of jalapeño sauce and was reading the label when she heard voices at the counter.

"Hello, I'd like to buy a hunting knife."

"Anything in particular?"

"Can I look at what you have?" The cultivated voice sounded familiar, but Claire couldn't place it. She peeked over the top of the row of Ronzoni spaghetti sauces and saw Gary Robinson, the moody black painter she had met the night before. Quickly she ducked down behind the aisle, feeling silly but not wanting to meet him here. She crept along the rows of canned goods to the back of the store and stopped behind a tall display of potato chips on sale.

"This is a nice one," she heard Gary say.

"Oh, that's our best one. I've got one of those myself."

"How much is it?"

Claire didn't hear the reply, because a mother and her daughter entered the store at that moment, and the child noisily dragged her mother over to the rack of toys next to Claire.

Claire picked up a bag of potato chips and pretended to study the list of ingredients.

"Can I have this?" said the little girl, a stocky child of about six with curly brown hair. She clutched a baby doll wrapped in plastic. The doll's shiny blond hair was matted inside the clear plastic wrapper, which pressed tightly against her rosy lips and stubby little nose. Claire suddenly had an irrational fear that the doll was going to suffocate inside her plastic package.

"No toys today," said the mother, who was young but tired looking, with circles under her dark eyes. Claire took this opportunity to peek over at the front counter again, but Gary was gone. She went around to the front door and peered out into the street just in time to see him climb into a white Toyota Corolla. Claire stood there for a moment wondering if he had gotten what he came for, and she tried to imagine what a painter would want with a hunting knife.

Chapter 3

"Would you like some tea?" said Liza.

Liza was always making tea; Claire remembered that from their days together at Waverly. Liza kept a hot pot in her office, and owned a dazzling assortment of black and green teas. Now, as she stood in front of Claire in the living room of her cabin, Claire thought that her broad hands looked as if they would be equally at home making tea or splitting wood. Liza had on jeans and a long red flannel shirt, and today she wore little round spectacles similar to the ones Claire had seen on Gary.

"Thank you," said Claire, "that would be nice."

"How about Irish Breakfast? That's my favorite right now."

"Sounds great."

"Have a seat; I'll just be a minute. The cats will keep you company."

"What are their names?"

"The one without a tail is Nubs and the black-and-white one is Velcro. He actually belongs to Marcel the handyman, but he's sort of adopted us. Actually, I think he's outside right now; he's not as friendly as Nubs, who's a real 'people cat.' "

Liza went into the kitchen and Claire sank down on the comfortable, tatty sofa, which was covered by a yellow wool blanket, to protect it from the cats, she supposed. The moment she touched the cushion, Nubs jumped onto her lap, purring violently.

"Where's Sherry?" Claire called out to the kitchen.

Liza appeared at the doorway with a plate of chocolate chip cookies, which she set on the coffee table. "She's over at her studio painting." Seeing the cat on Claire's lap, she laughed. "That one has no shame," she said, returning to the kitchen.

Claire laughed too. "I can see that." She ran her hand over the cat's short, thick fur, and Nubs arched his back, digging his claws into her thigh.

"Ow, Nubs," she said softly so that Liza couldn't hear. From the kitchen came the soothing clatter of dishes and tea things, and Claire thought how much Meredith would like it here in this cozy little cabin, with tea and cookies and cats to play with.

That afternoon Claire was scheduled to give the first of her talks to the assembled group of writers. Liza thought that it would be good for Claire to meet everybody en masse before she began meeting with them individually; it would also give her a little more time to read manuscripts.

"Do you have any questions about this afternoon?" Liza asked, pouring the tea from an ancient-looking blue willow teapot. "I thought it would be good for you to talk about the business of publishing. Most of these people have aspirations, even if they don't necessarily have the talent."

"That's fine; I think it's a good idea to start with that."

Liza sipped her tea, and as she did her eyeglasses steamed up. For just a moment Claire was reminded of Mr. Moto; Liza's round face framed by short hair and opaque spectacles could have belonged to the famous detective.

"I guess I should fill you in on the various 'situations' within the Ravenscroft community," Liza said, removing her glasses and wiping off the steam. "It's not necessary, but—well, if you know what's going on, it could help you deal with people." She smiled. "Besides, I'm a shameless gossip."

Claire laughed. "Well, at least you're honest about it."

Liza shrugged. "Why not? Self-deception serves no purpose." She leaned forward. "You met some people at breakfast, you said?"

"Yes. Camille and Terry—and Maya, a.k.a. Dorian Gray."

When she said Maya's name, Claire thought she saw Liza's face darken momentarily.

"Okay," Liza said. "Terry's in love with Maya, which isn't a secret to anyone except Terry; Camille had an affair with Billy last summer, but now rumor has it that Maya and Billy are an item."

"Who's Billy?"

"Billy Trimble, one of the painters. You haven't met him yet. He's a strange one—good-looking, but strange. He and Maya make a good couple, actually; they look like the product of eugenics, and they both play their cards pretty close to the chest."

"I see. So I suppose Camille isn't too crazy about Maya, if she stole her man."

Liza ran her finger along the edge of the teacup. "It's hard to say. I like Camille—she's classy, you know—and if she's hurt, she's hiding it pretty well."

"What about Gary? Is he involved with anyone?"

Liza looked at Claire curiously. "Why do you ask?"

"Just wondering. He seems to be such a loner."

"Typical painter. They're not very verbal, whereas the writers . . . well, they talk a lot, you know. Gary's okay—a little moody, as you saw, but he's actually pretty thoughtful; he bought Sherry and me each some earrings that he found at a house sale. That's another thing about Woodstock, by the way; if you have time, there's usually house sales on weekends, and you can pick up some great stuff."

"I'll keep that in mind."

"What else . . . let me see. Oh, *yes*—have you met our resident Nazi yet?"

"What?"

"Jack Mulligan, one of the writers. Well, he may not exactly be a Nazi, but he believes the Holocaust never happened."

"Oh my God." Claire set her teacup down on the table so loudly that it frightened Nubs, and he sprang from her lap. "I mean, I knew there were people like that, but I never *met* one of them."

"I know. You should have seen us all the night we found out. We were sitting around dinner, and the topic got onto the war somehow—Sherry's Jewish, by the way—and Jack just sits there for the longest time and then he comes out with this statement about there being no actual proof about the Holocaust, and we all just stared at him. And you know Tahir, the Bosnian writer—he's a survivor of the camps over there, and he just went pale . . . well, none of us knew how to react. We tried arguing with him; Gary and Camille really stuck with it—but it was just too depressing after a while, and so finally somebody changed the subject. It was ugly, it really was."

Claire shook her head. "How did someone like that end up *here*?"

"The Guild committee doesn't investigate people's political beliefs before accepting them; admission was based on their work as an artist."

Claire nodded. "Of course. It's just that—well . . ."

"I know; I'm always shocked when 'artistic' people don't share my political beliefs. But you know, Ezra Pound was an anti-Semite, and so was T. S. Eliot, and Hemingway was a pig—and I could go on and on."

Claire took a sip of tea, sharp and hot on her throat. "I know; I know talent and virtue have no direct correlation. It's just that . . . I mean, how could anyone presumably intelligent be so *wrong* and not know it?"

Liza shook her head. "It's a mystery to me. He *is* intelligent, by the way; that's what's so shocking about it. He's well read, and has an impressive breadth of knowledge; I've heard him quote the Bible, Jung, Goethe—you name it, he seems to have read it. That's what I can't get over."

"Is he just a raging anti-Semite?"

"Well, that's what no one seems to know. The odd thing is that his best friend back in New York is apparently Jewish, so God knows what they talk about . . ."

Just then the door opened and a young woman came bouncing into the room. She was short and dark, with smooth, well-toned skin and flat, shiny brown hair cut the same length all around, like a medieval monk. She wore yellow shorts that showed off her well-muscled legs, and a paint-splattered blue sweatshirt.

"Break time!" she said cheerfully. "Ah, good—tea! Hello," she continued in the same breath, addressing Claire. "I'm Sherry Bernstein. No relation to Leonard."

"Pleased to meet you. I'm—"

"Claire Rawlings, editor extraordinaire, cat owner, tea drinker—and, I presume, owner of an ancient diesel Mercedes, color chocolate brown, with just a splash of *eau de pigeon*."

Claire laughed. "Ancient is right. I was afraid it might not make it up some of these hills; it complained bitterly all the way."

Sherry poured herself some tea and plopped down on the couch, one leg tucked under her. She did everything vigorously; even pouring tea, she crackled with energy. Claire couldn't help noticing Liza's obvious admiration for her; she noticed, too, that Liza was at least ten years older, and hoped that Sherry wouldn't break her heart someday.

"Oh, hello, Nubs," Sherry said as the cat jumped up on her lap. She stroked him with one paint-splattered hand while balancing a teacup on her knee with the other. Claire noticed that her nails were jagged and short—bitten, she thought—and the skin on her fingers was red and irritated. "Please don't let me interrupt your conversation, unless of course you were talking about me," she said with a lopsided smile that was as charming as it was self-conscious. *She knows Liza's crazy about her,* Claire thought, *and she's playing on it.*

"I was just filling Claire in on the various residents," Liza said.

"Ah." Sherry nodded, taking a chocolate-covered cookie from the plate. "Of course. Personality profiles—the low-down, and all that." She turned to Claire. "You'll find it's quite a neurotic little group, though not as bad as some I've seen. Last year we had a woman who brayed at night, like a donkey. For the first week I thought there was a farm nearby, and then I found out it was Melissa."

"You've been here before?" said Claire.

"Oh, yes—that's how we met." Sherry leaned over and squeezed Liza's knee. Though her smile was warm and her gesture was relaxed, there was something not quite right about it, Claire thought it was a little too studied, done for effect. It was as if she were being too sincere, like an actress trying too hard to convince the audience of her emotion. Claire wondered who the audience was—Liza or herself?

"We were both residents at Ravenscroft last year," said Liza, "and then they asked me if I'd like to come run the place this year. Of course I leaped at the chance. There's really not that much to do, apart from the occasional Guild meeting. I make sure the garbage is emptied, troubleshoot any problems with the house, things like that. I'm supposed to go down and collect the mail, but the residents usually beat me to it every morning; they're like vultures waiting for the mailman to arrive. There's even a handyman who comes 'round to check on the water heaters and plumbing and things like that."

Sherry smiled her crooked smile. "Marcel, the Resident Stud. He's French-Canadian, and built like a moose." She sighed. "Sometimes I wish I were hetero . . . I'd show him a thing or two about plumbing."

Liza threw a couch pillow at her. "Oh, stop it—you'll embarrass Claire! I apologize for my partner here," she said, laughing. "Sometimes she says things just to get a reaction out of me."

Claire wanted to say that she knew exactly what Liza meant, but instead she looked out the big picture window and saw the late-morning sun, filtered through the tree leaves, dappling the ground with its lacy patterns. She stretched and yawned.

"Well, I'd better get ready for my talk this afternoon."

"Would you like to stay for lunch?" said Liza.

"Oh, thanks, but I bought lots of food in town, and I'd better study my notes while I eat. Maybe another time. The meeting's at two o'clock, you said?"

"Right. We'll meet in the library; it's cozier than the living room, and we can close the doors and not be disturbed by any painters wandering through the house. You know where it is—that room right off the living room, the side with the fireplace."

Claire nodded. "Yes, I took a look in there this morning to see what kind of books you had. It's an interesting collection, everything from Dostoevsky to Danielle Steel."

"Most of the books in there were left by residents over the years, or so I'm told," said Liza. "It's kind of like a swap library; you take a book, you leave a book."

"Well, nice meeting you," Claire said to Sherry, rising from the sofa.

"And you," Sherry replied quickly. She sprang up from the couch and seized Claire's hand, shaking it vigorously. Though her hand was small, the paint-stained fingers were surprisingly strong.

"See you in a few hours," said Liza.

Walking back to Ravenscroft, Claire saw a cat that she figured was Velcro. It was black and white, and as soon as it saw her, it slunk into the bushes, peering out at her from behind an azalea. Claire wondered how Ralph was getting along. She had left him eating happily in the kitchen, but she had no idea how he would react to other cats, having been an apartment cat all his life.

She entered Ravenscroft through the dining room, and as she passed the telephone alcove she felt a strong urge to check her messages. When she dialed her number the machine picked up after two rings, meaning there were messages. The first one was from Willard Hughes, her most profitable—and most annoying—author.

"Hi." Willard never identified himself on the phone. "I

know you're away, but I'm just wondering when we'll be seeing that advance money . . . I know my agent called last week but, well—it's about time, don't you think?"

Claire sighed. Willard . . . she had tried to palm him off on other editors, but no one could deal with him, and since his mysteries inevitably made the best-seller lists, he was important to Ardor House.

Claire's heart beat a little faster when she heard the next message. "Hi . . . San Francisco is foggy and beautiful and misty . . . what can I say? Uh, I miss you terribly, dreadfully; I miss your lopsided smile, your laugh, your body . . . and then I wonder if you miss me. It's good to see Mom, but I can't wait to come back to you . . . well, I guess that's all. I know I left you the number here . . . if you do call, just remember the time change; Mom's always in bed by nine-thirty sharp. Sleep well tonight; you'll be in my thoughts and dreams."

Claire hung up slowly. She loved the sound of Wally's voice: his dry, wary irony—and the world-weariness underneath it—pushed every button in her body. This message was unusually effusive for him, and Claire wondered if it was easier for him to say things to an answering machine. She liked his reticence, his carefulness about other people.

Claire went into the kitchen, fixed a tuna sandwich, and took it up to her room. As she climbed the staircase she heard the *tap-tap-tapping* of a manual typewriter coming from one of the second-floor rooms. A wave of longing washed over her; caught up in the bygone sounds of a million offices, banks, and newsrooms, she stopped to listen. Suddenly she was transported to her college days and the clicking of typewriter keys in dorm rooms, echoing through the halls on Sunday afternoons as students struggled with Monday-morning deadlines. She stood for a moment, caught up in the sharp sweetness of nostalgia, when the sound stopped and the door to the room opened and Camille emerged.

"Oh—hello!" she said, blinking as if the light in the hall were too bright.

"Hello," said Claire. "I was just listening to your type-writer."

"Oh, I hope it doesn't bother you. Some of the others have complained about the sound."

"No, no, I love it, actually; it's so—"

"Reminiscent? *Recherche du temps perdu?*"

Claire laughed. "Yes, I guess so . . . I was thinking back to my school days."

Camille nodded, her prominent eyes wide. "I know what you mean. People think I'm crazy for not entering the computer age, but I think if you're going to be a writer, you have to embrace your idiosyncrasies." She lowered her voice and leaned toward Claire. "Actually, I do have a computer back at home, but I always do my first drafts on the old Royal. Don't tell anyone. I'm cultivating my image as an eccentric."

Claire laughed. "Your secret is safe with me."

Camille fished a pack of Sobraines out of her breast pocket. "Thanks for getting these for me."

"Sure."

"Well, it's time for a smoke break. See you later; two o'clock, isn't it?"

"Right; see you then."

Camille turned and glided down the stairs, and Claire continued on to her room.

Claire ate her sandwich while reading Terry Nordstrom's manuscript. His writing was angry—clumsy and overly emotional, though not without a certain sense of poetry, particularly in his descriptions of the story's stark land-scape. It was the tale a working-class boy in the North-west who becomes infatuated with a svelte and elegant girl from a rich family. "*The Great Gatsby* goes Dutch," Claire muttered as she wiped a piece of tuna fish off the manu-script. Just then she heard footsteps out in the hall, and low voices in the corridor just outside her room—a man and a woman talking softly, as lovers do. She wasn't sure who the man was, but there was no mistaking Maya's Swedish lilt.

"Vhat makes yoo think I'll do it?" Maya said, and then the man said something Claire couldn't understand.

"Oh, fine—that's easy for yoo to say, but vhat about me?"

The man said something that ended with the words "only if you want to."

They both laughed softly. There was a long pause, then Maya sighed.

"I have to get back to work."

There was another pause, and then Claire heard the sighs and murmurs that accompany passionate kissing. She stared at the ceiling and thought of Wally, of those long afternoons at his apartment after they first met . . . Ralph chose that moment to jump up on the desk, scattering her papers. "Oh, for Christ's sake," Claire said, pushing him away.

The sounds in the hallway stopped abruptly and Claire realized that Maya and her companion probably thought she was talking to them. This struck her as very funny, and she had to put her hand over her mouth to keep from laughing. But the couple in the hall evidently took her remark seriously, because two sets of footsteps headed in opposite directions. One went down the hall and the other descended the back staircase that led to the dining room. Claire listened for a moment, then returned her attention to the manuscript in front of her.

She glanced at her watch and saw that it was almost two. Wiping the remnants of tuna fish from her mouth with a napkin, she gathered up her lecture notes and headed downstairs. Most of the writers were already gathered in the library when she arrived. Liza presided over them, seated primly in a straight-backed chair by the window.

"Hi," Claire said to Camille, who waved from the other side of the room, where she was seated on a stack of pillows. She smiled at Maya and Terry, who were sitting side by side on a sturdy-looking black horsehair sofa.

Liza rose from her chair by the window. "I think most of you have met Claire Rawlings?" she said, and everyone nodded.

"Where's Tahir?" said Terry, his little body bursting with nervous energy.

"Right here," said a voice behind Claire.

She turned and saw the darkest, most deep-set eyes she had ever seen. They were so startling and luminous that she had to turn away to keep from staring.

"I'm not late, am I?" he said, looking around the room for a place to sit.

"No; why don't you sit here, Tahir?" said Liza, indicating a tattered grey armchair next to her.

"Thank you," he said politely, then turned to Claire and offered his hand. "I'm Tahir Hasonovic," he said in a soft, smoky baritone. His accent was smooth, with only a gentle twist of the vowels to suggest he was a foreigner.

"Pleased to meet you," said Claire, shaking his hand, which was as smooth as his voice. It was impossible not to notice the clean jawline and the thick black hair surrounding his head like a dark halo. Though he was clean-shaven, his beard was so dark that already a shadow was gathering around his well-formed chin. His cheekbones were sharp as knives, jutting like ridges from his thin face. His lips were full, the one sensuous feature in an otherwise ascetic face. He was, Claire decided, an extraordinarily handsome man. There was something wounded behind those burning eyes, a trait she always responded to in a man.

He sat down next to Liza, folding his lean body into the tattered overstuffed armchair. As he did, the thought occurred to Claire that he was not used to such comfort; the softness of the chair seemed alien to him. Claire sat in a straight-backed chair near the door.

"Vhere's Jack?" said Maya.

Everyone in the room seemed to stiffen. Terry snorted, and Camille muttered something Claire couldn't make out. But the most pronounced effect was upon Tahir. His thin body became rigid, and his large dark eyes narrowed. He said nothing, but it was clear to Claire that there was bad blood between him and Jack Mulligan. Liza stood up quickly, ignoring Maya's remark.

"Well, shall we begin? Though I know most of you have met Claire, I'd just like to say a few words about her before we begin."

Liza proceeded to give a brief outline of Claire's career. She mentioned a few of the writers Claire had edited at Ardor House, being careful to include the "stars" she had worked with. Claire shifted in her chair and looked at the shining faces turned toward her friend. She knew that the chances of any of the people in this room having such an illustrious career—or any writing career at all—were slim. However, it was not her job to tell them that, she told herself.

"Okay, Claire, would you like to add anything?" Liza said when she was finished.

"Not really; I think you've pretty well covered it. Until I heard you talk about me, I had no idea I was so successful."

Everyone laughed, and the tension in the room softened a little. Claire glanced at Terry, whose short fingers were wrapped around his pencil, his thick neck rigid. His laugh was more like a bark, short and brusque. Next to him, Maya smiled dreamily, as if oblivious of his devotion to her.

"Well, I thought that we would begin by having Claire talk about the business aspect of publishing. Claire?"

"Thank you, Liza. I know it's usual to ask for questions afterward, but before I start talking, I'd like to know if any of you have questions that I might be able to answer."

Camille raised her hand. "Is it true that genre fiction sells better than 'literary' fiction?"

"I'm afraid so. So-called genre fiction has a built-in market, because there is a guaranteed audience for mystery, science fiction, and the like—"

"So I'd be better off bumping somebody off than telling them off?" said Terry, looking around to see the reaction to his joke. Several of the people in the room smiled politely; it was clear that Terry made many of them uncomfortable.

"Yes, mysteries do tend to sell well," Claire said carefully, "but—"

"If you write it, they will come?" said Terry, grinning.

A couple of the others sighed. *Poor Terry,* Claire thought. He was so needy, so edgy. "I was going to say that just because you write one, it doesn't necessarily mean you can sell it," she answered.

"There are no guarantees in life," Tahir observed.

"I know that," said Terry, bristling.

"I think it would be a mistake to write something just because you think it will sell," said Claire. "You should write about what interests you, not what you think will interest others."

"Follow your bliss?" said Maya languidly.

Camille snorted and rolled her eyes.

"Personally, I find murder very interesting," said a silky baritone behind Claire. She turned to see a stocky, white-haired man with a beard to match. With his pink skin and jovial expression, he looked like the perfect Sears Santa Claus, right down to his rosy lips and upturned nose.

"Come in, Jack," said Liza. "Claire, this is Jack Mulligan."

At that moment Claire realized that she was looking at Ravenscroft's resident Nazi.

Chapter 4

Jack Mulligan sat on the only available chair, which was next to Claire, so that she couldn't look at him without turning sideways. It seemed to her that the others avoided looking at Jack, except for Terry, who stared at him for a few moments before looking away.

"Well," said Claire a little too brightly, "why don't we have our first reading ... Tahir? I believe you've got an excerpt from one of your stories."

Tahir nodded shyly and shuffled through a stack of papers. "I'm going to read from 'Azu's War.'"

"All right."

All eyes in the room turned to Tahir; though he did not have the complexion of a blusher, Claire could feel he was nervous. He cleared his throat and read in a soft, hoarse voice:

"'What I remember most, what is impossible to forget, is the howling of my dog, Azu. He was a one-eyed, yellow mutt (we think he lost the eye in a fight before he came to us). The day the soldiers came for my father, Azu sat on the porch and howled. He bayed all day long and into the night. A little after midnight he suddenly stopped howling, and at that moment we knew my father was dead.

Azu crawled under the house, where he stayed for three days. My sister finally coaxed him out with a bowl of hot oatmeal. I think he felt he had to stay alive to protect the rest of us. He ultimately failed, though, because eventually the soldiers came for all of us, leaving Azu homeless. I often think about him and wonder if he found another family among the rubble of what was once our city.' "

After Tahir finished reading there was a heavy silence in the room. Finally, Claire broke it.

"Any reactions?"

"Well, clearly it's very powerful," Camille said slowly. "What I particularly like is the device he uses of showing the situation through the actions of a dog."

"Yes, what about that?" said Claire. "Anyone else—yes, Liza?"

"It works because it reveals the horrors of war at an angle, rather than straight on," said Liza.

"Right," said Camille, "like when filmmakers shoot a scene showing people's shadows, rather than the people themselves."

"Do you think it's . . . sentimental?" Claire asked.

"Nooo," said Jack after a pause.

"Anyone else?" Claire looked at Terry and Maya on the couch. Maya's face was red and her body was rigid. Terry had laid a hand on her shoulder and was attempting to whisper something to her, but she wasn't listening. Claire wondered if he had done or said something to upset her, but just then Maya got up from the couch.

"I'm sorry," she said, her voice shaky. "Weel you excuse me, please? I'm not feeling so well."

"Of course," Claire replied.

Maya stumbled a little on her way to the door, and Liza rose to follow her out.

"I'll be right back," she said.

Everyone sat looking puzzled until Liza returned. "She's just feeling a little ill . . . she'll be okay."

"Maybe she ate some bad granola," Jack Mulligan said under his breath. No one laughed, and Terry looked as though he wanted to kill him.

Claire finished the class as best she could. She talked more about what editors look for in a manuscript, answered a few more questions, and then it was four o'clock. As the others filed out of the room, Liza came over and put her arm around Claire's shoulders.

"That was great. Thanks."

"Oh, it was fun. They're a smart group."

"I'm glad you think so. I'll see you later. I promised Sherry a back rub."

Claire went back up to her room to put away her notes. As she walked down the hall she heard voices coming from a room across from hers.

"I think you're overreacting."

"Well, you can say that, but you'd have to experience life from my perspective, and that's impossible."

Claire didn't recognize the first voice, but she was fairly certain the other one belonged to Gary Robinson. The door to the room suddenly opened and she found herself face-to-face with a tall, sandy-haired man. He looked distracted, and when he saw her he frowned.

"Hi, I'm Claire Rawlings," she managed to say, wondering if he knew she had overheard his conversation.

"Ah, yes—the *editor*." There was a hint of a sneer in his tone, as if the word was a euphemism for something not quite admirable. "I'm Billy Trimble." He offered no hand to shake. There was an uncomfortable pause, and then he said, "How do you like Ravenscroft?"

"Oh, it's very nice."

"I think it's positively Victorian," he said enigmatically.

"I suppose it is," Claire agreed, trying to figure out if that was a criticism or not.

"That's your car out in the lot, I suppose?" he asked after a moment.

"Yes, the Mercedes. Liza said not many of the people who come here bring cars . . . one of the others is yours, I think?"

Billy's eyelids drooped. "The Toyota," he said with a sigh, as if it were a hardship to explain. Claire thought maybe she had insulted him by not coming to the conclusion herself; the Toyota was clearly much nicer—and more expensive—than the ratty old Chevy, which she now knew must belong to Jack Mulligan. She recalled seeing Gary get into a white Toyota, and concluded he must have borrowed Billy's car. She looked around the room for Gary, but he was nowhere to be seen.

They stood there awkwardly for a moment, then Billy Trimble cleared his throat. "Well, nice to meet you. Please pardon me, but my studio calls. I must paint while the light is still good."

"Yes, yes, of course," Claire replied, glad to see him go.

Later that afternoon, however, she came upon a scene that made her think again about Billy Trimble. On her way to Liza's cabin, Claire caught a glimpse of two people out behind the house. They were so still that at first she didn't see them, but when she turned, she saw it was Billy and Maya, their bodies locked in an embrace, a latticework of dappled sunlight falling softly on their shoulders. With their sandy hair and long, lean bodies, they could have been brother and sister, Claire thought, but there was nothing brotherly about the way Billy stroked Maya's cheek as he bent down to kiss her. It was a sweet sight, these two handsome creatures enjoying a kiss in the late-summer sunlight, and Claire sighed. She wished Wally were there; the thought of kissing him in that same sunlight made her heart beat faster.

She looked again at Billy and Maya. Who would have thought Billy capable of such tenderness? she wondered as his fingers lightly grazed Maya's blond hair. People have their contradictions, no doubt about it, Claire thought as she headed across the lawn toward Liza's cabin.

That night Liza threw a little party to welcome Claire.

"I've invited one of the Guild ladies, Evelyn Gardner," Liza said as she stood at the kitchen counter chopping vegetables. The big kitchen was empty except for Liza and Claire, the hum of the refrigerators in the pantry blending with the sound of crickets as dusk settled outside the screen door. "If I don't, I'll never hear the end of it," she added.

"Is she the one who hired you?"

"There's actually a committee, though Evelyn is the one I interviewed with," Liza replied, dumping a pile of carrots into a wooden bowl. "She's the one whose job it is to oversee Ravenscroft. She's . . . well, she's all right, I guess, but . . . Evelyn is what my mother used to refer to as a 'pistol.' " Liza finished chopping a pile of celery and swept the pieces into the bowl next to the carrots. "That ought to hold the little bastards for a while, as the man said."

Claire laughed. "I remember that one—my brother and I had it on a record of radio bloopers."

"Yeah, that was a famous one. I guess it was some well-known kids' show."

"My brother and I loved that one because he said a bad word on the air. Actually, we didn't even know what it meant; we just knew it was bad."

Liza laughed. "Yeah, right. In my family no one swore either, so it was a real thrill to hear a grown-up say a bad word."

Claire popped a piece of carrot into her mouth. "We were so easily amused then."

Liza opened the cupboard and took out a large bottle of red wine. "Here's some amusement for grown-ups. Let's have a pre-party glass of wine. Want some?"

"Sure, why not?"

Liza took two goblets down from the shelf. "Here's to Art with a capital *A*, which rhymes with fey," she said, handing a glass to Claire. "To Art; *l'chaim!*"

Claire raised her glass. *"L'chaim!"*

Sherry entered the kitchen. "Get a load of this—two goyim talking like a couple of Yiddishe mamas! Oo—hootch!" she said, seeing the wine bottle. "Please, sir, can I have some?"

"Only if you've been very, very good," Liza replied, holding the bottle above her head so that Sherry couldn't reach it. "Have you?"

"Oh, I can be if you'll just give me a chance. I promise I'll be *very* good!"

Liza laughed and handed Sherry the bottle. Claire

laughed, too, but felt a little uneasy. She was always uncomfortable eavesdropping on other people's relationships,
which was one reason she was an editor rather than a writer;
writers have to eavesdrop as part of their job. She thought
about the couple she had overheard arguing earlier, and almost said something about it to Liza, but decided against
it.

The first guest to arrive at the party was the "Guild lady,"
Evelyn Gardner, who was tall and handsome, with a long-
jawed face and thick, grey-streaked black hair that she
swept up into a bun at the nape of her neck. Her black
linen pantsuit was simple but expensive, and Claire had no
doubt the diamond brooch on her collar was real. Everything about her bespoke money.

"I am absolutely *starving!*" she announced as she descended upon the kitchen, where Liza was putting the fin-
ishing touches on a rack of miniature soufflés.

"*So* nice to meet you," she said when Liza introduced
her to Claire. "I *do* think it's *so* nice that Liza is giving
the folks here such a special treat! Mind you, I had to fi-
nagle a few extra *funds* your way," she said, lowering her
voice to a conspiratorial whisper—"but it was *worth* it, I'm
sure! Oh, can I have just a teeny-weeny piece of that
cheese?" She eyed a block of white Cheddar sitting on the
counter.

"Help yourself," said Liza mildly, but when Evelyn
turned away she looked at Claire and rolled her eyes.

"Well, I'm *sure* you're every bit as good as Liza says
you are," Evelyn continued, her mouth full of cheese.

"Well, I don't know about that—" Claire began, but Evelyn interrupted with a wave of her manicured hand.

"No need for modesty around here," she said gaily, "not
with all these artistic egos galloping around."

"Would you like a glass of wine, Evelyn?" Liza offered,
coming to Claire's rescue.

"I thought you'd *never* ask!"

After pouring Evelyn a generous glass of Merlot, Liza

handed her the bowl of crudités. "I wonder if you'd mind taking those out to the living room for me?"

"Not at all; glad to be of service!" Evelyn seized the bowl and strode vigorously out of the room.

"Good Lord," was all Claire could say when she had left.

"Yes, well . . ." Liza shrugged. "I guess we should take the rest of this out there," she said, looking at the plates of hors d'oeuvres scattered about the kitchen.

"Let me give you a hand."

"Thanks."

She picked up the soufflés and handed Claire the plate of cheese.

"Come on; it's time to face the music."

The Merlot was smooth and went down easy, and by the time the rest of the guests arrived, Claire was feeling no pain, as Wally would say. The living room looked nice: Liza had found some old-fashioned candleabras and placed them around—on the mantelpiece, on the sideboard—and their warm glow made the big room look cozier, the burnished wood of the ceiling beams rich and dark in the soft light.

Claire stood for a while with Liza as people wandered in, then she felt a heavy arm wrap around her shoulders. She turned to see Two Joe, decked out in a black silk shirt and tight black jeans, his thick dark hair pulled into a single braid hanging down his broad back.

"Hello," she said, wondering if it was obvious to him that she was feeling loopy. Two Joe pointed to Billy Trimble, who had just entered the room.

"See him? I call him Crooked Arrow."

"Oh? Why is that?"

But before Two Joe could answer, Liza appeared with a tray of hors d'oeuvres. "Would you care for some spinach soufflé?"

Maybe it was the wine, or the country air, but Claire suddenly felt very hungry. She took two of the tiny hot puffs from the plate.

"Thank you." She popped a pastry into her mouth, and

savored the warm rush of flavors as they mingled on her tongue. She ate the second one quickly and turned to Two Joe. "I'm going to get some more hors d'oeuvres; can I get you some?"

Two Joe shook his magnificent head. He reminded Claire of a landlocked leviathan. "Two Joe will eat later," he said.

Claire made her way over to the long table of food and began piling a plate full of raw vegetables. She really wanted more soufflé, but she decided to fill up on vegetables first.

"Enjoying yourself?"

She turned to see Gary Robinson, dressed very nattily in a grey Harris-tweed jacket and a maroon silk tie over a black shirt.

"Oh, yes, it's so nice of Liza to throw this party . . ." Claire stood there awkwardly, a celery stick teetering dangerously on the edge of her plate.

"Have you met Billy Trimble?" said Gary. Billy stood a few paces away, leaning against the wall, a drink in his hand, looking idly across the press of bodies in the room. An old-fashioned boating jacket hung loosely on his lean, rangy body. The jacket was blue with a yellow yachting insignia on the right breast pocket. With his classic profile and sandy hair, he looked as if he would be at home on a yacht.

"Uh, yes—briefly, in the hall."

Billy's eyes met hers and Claire smiled.

"I enjoyed that cartoon you put up in the kitchen," she said.

Billy looked at her as though she had just uttered a sentence in Urdu. He blinked, his eyelids heavy. "It's a well-stocked kitchen," he said, his hooded eyes already restless. Claire turned to Gary for help, but he had already struck up a conversation with Evelyn Gardner, who was gesturing dramatically, her voice rising and falling as she related some anecdote.

Claire stood holding her plate of vegetables, wanting to move away but unable to think of an excuse. She had the impression that Billy found the cartoon remark somehow embarrassing, that it had been the wrong thing to say.

"It's a wonderful house, isn't it?" she said a little desperately, suddenly uncomfortably aware of the sound of her own voice.

Billy cocked his head back and studied the curtain rods. "I can't imagine what it's like up here in the winter," he said, swinging his head slowly from side to side.

"Oh, I'll bet it gets really cold and snows all the time," Claire said too eagerly, a dip of panic in her stomach.

Billy stopped his head oscillations and sighed heavily.

Claire's left palm began to itch. She felt as though Billy was launching a series of conversational boats that she kept missing.

After a few more minutes with Billy Trimble, Claire concluded that he came at conversation from an oblique angle: no matter what you said to him, his reply invariably bore only a vague relationship to your remark, so that you weren't sure he had heard you correctly. But the most disconcerting thing about him was his eyes, which wandered about the room as if searching for someone more scintillating to talk to. Standing there, Claire had the feeling that she didn't have his full attention; it was as if he were a sailboat tacking madly at angles to avoid sailing into the conversational wind. His lazy, laconic way of talking reinforced the feeling that you were an insufficient source of stimulation.

Suddenly she saw her escape: Maya Sorenson glided into view across the room, and Claire decided to make a run for it.

"Oh, there's Maya!" she chirped. "Will you excuse me? I have to talk to her about something."

Billy nodded in his heavy-lidded way, dismissing her, and Claire fled. She pushed her way through the crowd and touched Maya's arm.

"Oh, hello, Klar," said Maya, a bright smile on her elegant face. She had evidently had a few drinks, and her accent had thickened as a result. "Have you met Rogare

Gardeener?" she said, turning to a short man standing next to her.

"Oh, you must be Evelyn's husband," said Claire.

"Yes; nice to meet you," he replied, offering his hand. Roger Gardner was pink and balding, with a high squeaky voice and skin as smooth as a eunuch's.

"Ve war just talking about yoo," Maya continued gaily, "weren't we, Rogare?"

Roger Gardner nodded emphatically. "Yes; Maya was just saying how helpful your talk was today. I was telling her that I don't know how you writers do it—keeping all those characters straight. And all those words; it would drive me crazy!"

"That's why you're a banker, seely," Maya said, tapping him playfully on the shoulder. Claire wondered if there was something between them.

"Well, I just think it's incredible, that's all."

"And vhat about yoo bankers—all those *numbers* all day long! Now, *that* would drive *me* crazy!"

Roger shrugged and studied his perfectly manicured fingernails. "You get used to it. At least numbers are predictable, unlike people."

Maya threw her head back and emitted a high tinkling laugh. Claire glanced over at Evelyn Gardner to see if she was watching, but Evelyn had cornered Gary Robinson and was heavily involved in acting out some incident, her arms flailing; Claire could make out her words even from across the room.

"And *then* you wouldn't believe what he said!" Evelyn bellowed dramatically.

Roger must have noticed Claire looking at his wife, because he laughed softly. "I see Evelyn is giving another one of her performances."

"Is she—was she an actress?" Claire said.

Roger shook his smooth pink head. "Once, long ago, she briefly tried a career on the stage, but like so many before her, she abandoned it in frustration." He looked over at his wife's gesticulations. "She claims she was too tall, but between you and me, I think she probably wasn't very good."

"Even if she *was* good, it's awfully hard to make a living at it," Maya said graciously.

"That's true," Claire agreed.

"I'm sure it is," said Roger. "Now she participates in the artistic life vicariously, as it were, through the Guild."

"Well, without a Guild there would be no Ravenscroft," said Claire. "The world needs people like her."

"And the world needs people like me," Roger said quietly, "but all the same I suspect there's a would-be actress lurking in the heart of every Guild lady, and a would-be novelist inside every banker."

"Really?" said Maya, her eyes dewy. "Yoo really think so?"

Roger shrugged. "I don't know . . . I *suspect* it's true that those of us in the 'mundane' professions envy the life of an artist."

Maya shook her head. "Really? There's nothing so glamorous about it. Every profession is tedious in one way or another. Even journalism—"

Roger swiveled his upper body toward her, the candlelight shining off his bald head. "You're a journalist?"

"Vell, I'm trying to branch out into fiction writing; that's why I'm here."

"Actually, you're here to drive us all wild."

Claire turned to see Jack Mulligan standing behind her, a drink in his hand.

"Hello, Jack," said Maya.

"Hi, I'm Roger Gardner," Roger said, offering his hand, which Jack shook heartily. It was only then that Claire noticed the index and third fingers of Jack's right hand were missing.

"Tell me, Mr. Gardner," he began.

"Call me Roger, please."

"Roger, then—tell me, have you ever seen such Nordic perfection?"

"I'm not sure what you mean."

"Such a classic profile, like a Norse goddess—"

"Stop it, Jack, it's embarrassing," said Maya, her color deepening in the dim light.

"Oh, come on, now; don't tell me no one's ever told you you were beautiful before!"

"Really, Jack—I'm sure Klar and Rogare don't want to hear about it."

Jack turned to Claire, his ruddy face flushed. "You're aristocratic looking yourself," he said, looking her over. "I'll bet you have some Viking blood in you, with that auburn hair," he continued, flicking a strand of hair from Claire's shoulder. He turned to Roger. "Roger. I'm sure you appreciate a fine-looking woman; otherwise, you wouldn't be standing with two of them."

A rush of crimson crept up Roger's neck, turning his already pink face a darker shade of red. "Well, I . . . I suppose no man is immune to female beauty—"

"Except faggots?"

Claire stared at Jack, momentarily unable to believe she had heard him correctly. Across the room, she saw Gary Robinson's head turn toward them.

"Jack, that's not a nice word," Maya said softly.

"Sorry; what word would you prefer I use? *Homo*sexual? Nancy boy? Gay?"

"Look, Jack—" Maya began, but Jack shook his head.

"Do me a favor; don't lecture me right now," he said. "I know I'm not 'politically correct,' but I just don't understand how a man could not appreciate a woman's beauty—"

"Well, I don't exactly *understand* it either," said Roger gently, "but that doesn't mean that—"

Jack laughed a big, hearty laugh, and it occurred to Claire that maybe he was just putting them on, testing them. He clapped Roger on the back. "Don't worry, Roger, your secret is safe with me."

Claire wondered what he meant by that, but just then Liza appeared with a tray of food.

"Hors d'oeuvres?"

"Don't mind if I do," said Jack, popping a tiny, hot soufflé into his mouth. Smiling broadly, he swallowed it in a single gulp, and Claire was reminded of the cat that ate the canary.

Chapter 5

The party went on until after midnight. The artists disappeared first, creeping off to bed one by one as the evening wore on. Finally, the writers began to retire, until only four of them remained. Claire sat on the couch next to Liza, with Sherry sitting on the rug at Liza's feet, while Camille sprawled out in the tattered grey armchair. Evelyn and Roger had just left, and with their departure Liza heaved a sigh and flopped onto the couch.

"God, I thought she'd *never* leave!"

"What's with that husband of hers?" said Sherry, leaning back so that her head rested on a couch cushion.

"Who knows?" Liza ran her fingers through Sherry's silky black hair. "Looks like a banker, though, doesn't he?"

"Does he have money?" Camille asked.

Liza shook her head. "I don't know . . . I think *she* might, actually."

Sherry closed her eyes and yawned. "I wonder what the deal is there? I mean, do they have *sex,* and if so, who's in charge?"

"There's no use trying to define the dynamics of other people's relationships," said Camille. She held an unlit cigarette in her mouth, and it made her speech sound slurred.

"I mean, there's an essential inscrutability about couples—even to themselves, I think."

"Oh, I'm not sure I agree with that," asked Liza. "After all, isn't that what you're trying to do as a writer, figure people out?"

Camille sighed. "Maybe. I think you try, but I'm not sure you ever really succeed. I mean, I don't think I ever quite figured out things between me and my ex-husband."

"I didn't know you were married," said Claire.

"Oh, yes—to an Englishman. That's why I lived in London for so long."

Suddenly reminded of Robert, Claire shuddered. Even now it was hard to believe that she could have been so deceived by him for almost three months. In retrospect, of course, the signs were all there, except that at the time she was blind to them until it was almost too late.

"But isn't half the fun *trying* to figure people out?" said Sherry.

Liza stretched herself and yawned. "Half the fun for me would be being in bed right now."

"So why don't you go?" said Sherry.

"Because the postmortem is the best part of the party," Camille said, laughing her smoky laugh. Claire held her breath, waiting for a coughing fit, but thankfully one did not arrive.

"That makes it sound so *morbid*," Sherry said, shivering. "*Postmortem* . . . like someone died or something."

Camille shrugged. "it's just a term."

"Well, *I'm* going to die if I don't go to bed soon," said Liza, rising from the couch. "Come on, pumpkin, let's go."

"Good night," Camille called from her armchair.

"Good night. 'Night, Claire."

"Thanks for a wonderful party," Claire said, hugging Liza, whose hair smelled of peppermint shampoo.

"Oh, glad to do it. I needed to throw a little bash anyway, and your arrival was as good an excuse as any."

When Sherry and Liza were gone, there was a silence, and Claire could hear the floorboards of the old house creaking and groaning underneath footsteps upstairs.

"Are you okay?" Camille asked after a few moments.

"Sure—why?"

Camille shrugged. "I don't know. I just had a sense a few minutes ago that there was something bothering you . . . I'm not sure exactly why."

Claire stared at the cold, empty grate in the fireplace. Maybe she would talk about Robert; maybe she would tell Camille the whole thing sometime, but not now—not yet. It was still too fresh, too raw to be related to someone she hardly knew. Still, she didn't want to lie about it to Camille; of all the people at Ravenscroft, Claire felt the most drawn to her.

"It's a long story," she said slowly, then she laughed. "But then, what isn't?"

Later, in bed, Claire lay there thinking of Robert, of waking up with his hands around her neck, her breath being choked out of her body. She could still feel the tightness in her throat, the roughness of his hands against her skin, the awful suffocating feeling that was like the fulfillment of so many nightmares. She had always had an unreasonable fear of being trapped—and that was exactly what it had been like, waking with that terrible feeling that his face was the last thing she would ever see and his voice the last sound she would ever hear.

Put out the light, then put out the light.

She lay there a long time staring into the darkness, trying to turn her mind to Wally, the touch and smell of him, the gentleness of his hands upon her body, but all she could think of was Robert. Finally she sat up in bed, thinking maybe a bath would help. When she was a child and couldn't sleep, her mother would give her a hot bath and that usually did the trick. Liza had pointed out Ravenscroft's only bathtub earlier in the day, located in a little bathroom attached to the side of the house, along the wooden catwalk leading out to the artists' studios.

Claire crept downstairs and out the side door. As she left the house she saw someone walking along the catwalk toward the house. As the light on the side of the house fell on her blond hair, Claire recognized Maya Sorenson. She was dressed in a bathrobe and carried a plastic soap dish and shampoo.

"Hello, Klar," she said softly as they approached each other. "Having a bath?"

"I think so," Claire answered.

"You should; I just had one, it's lovely," Maya said, and stepped into the house, leaving Claire alone on the catwalk. Claire opened the first door on her right and saw that it was indeed a large, old-fashioned bathroom, complete with a shower stall in one corner and a lion's-paw bathtub along the opposite wall. The entire room—the scrubbed hard-wood floor and heavy, old-fashioned sink, the wonderful bathtub—reminded her of her childhood years at Millmorr Farm, and she felt the sweet stab of nostalgia. Each of the three bathrooms at Millmorr Farm had a lion's-paw tub, and Claire and her brother loved them. Hanging her towel on the rack, she turned on the taps. The bare wooden floor was cold under her feet, and she stood upon the pink cotton throw rug to undress. The tub filled quickly; at Millmorr Farm, she remembered, the tubs took forever to fill, and bath time had to be planned in advance.

Claire stepped into the steaming water and let the vapors envelop her, sinking gratefully into the depths of smooth white porcelain. She closed her eyes and leaned her head on the rim of the tub, feeling her limbs surrender to the pull of hot water. She remembered her first bath with Wally, how shy he was, and how she had to coax him into letting go and enjoying himself. He had hidden so much away, storing his hopes along with his pain, that getting to know him was like walking down a long hall of locked doors, trying to find the key to each one. It was as if he were afraid enjoyment itself would bring disaster, that if he kept his feelings tightly under control, nothing bad would happen—at least nothing as bad as the death of his wife.

"I *know* it's magical thinking," he said one day while they were having dinner at The Parlour, Claire's favorite local restaurant since Patzo's had closed.

"I mean, intellectually I *know* it wasn't my fault, that it wasn't the result of anything I said or thought or felt, and ye ..." He shook his head, his basset-hound eyes drooping sadly. "Emotionally, it's a whole different story. There's th need to control what happens to me, to head off any other horrible things ... I know this sounds stupid and corny, but I feel as though we were *too happy,* and so we had to be taught a lesson."

Claire remembered how her stomach tightened as she felt a stab of jealousy at these words. *We were too happy.* She sensed an implicit challenge in his words: could *she* make him that happy? But then again, why was the onus on her? Wasn't it just as much his responsibility? And why should happiness be a challenge, a competition? Wally's first wife was dead, and that was the bleak fact of it: she could never compete with a dead woman.

But now, lying in the hot water, she felt her limbs drain of tension and even her memories of Robert began to lose their terror.

That night Claire dreamed deeply. To her ears, used to the whoosh of traffic, the sound of crickets was deafening at first. However, she quickly sank into the rhythms of the woods, no less insistent than those of the city, but with a different kind of mystery: the stillness that was no stillness at all, but the quiet presence of nature, as indifferent to her presence as a glacier. After life in New York, where everything *mattered,* where you were constantly being assessed and judged and interpreted, Claire found this indifference, this impartiality, oddly comforting.

She woke early the next day, refreshed and full of a sense of anticipation. She made a pot of coffee and took a cup out to the porch. There was no sign of any of the other residents.

Sitting on the porch listening to the thrumming of bees in the bushes, Claire felt happiness creeping up her spine like a vine. It was like a splash of cold water in her face: she realized how little time she had made in her life for this kind of happiness, how her life had sunk into a series of routines and tasks to be accomplished—that for her, doing had taken over being.

Now, away from phones and desks and appointment books, she saw that her life had become a tyranny of accomplishment. Perhaps it was an illusion, but living here on the side of the mountain, everything seemed so simple, so uncomplicated. Living with nature all around—not the version of nature that the city supplies, but the real thing— Claire could sit and watch the trees turn with perfect contentment. Suddenly there was nothing at stake, and instead of feeling adrift and purposeless, Claire felt herself slipping seamlessly into the calm regularity of life at Ravenscroft. Nothing here had an agenda; the trees, the vines—even the busy moths that fluttered their dun brown wings in the evening, scattering the glow of lamplight— seemed to have no goal other than to exist.

As she sat on the porch listening to the long cascades of cicadas, she was lulled into a remembrance of her childhood in the big house on the lake. It was all so familiar, so like a return—these sounds *were* her madeleine, her Proustian "memory trigger," and she wondered if the rhythms of the country had been imprinted upon her in childhood, hardwired forever into her brain.

I'm happy, Claire realized.

Happiness, she thought, *is like romantic love: life without it seems normal and natural enough, but when one is suddenly granted the extreme pleasure of being in love, the world is transformed and every moment infused with an almost unbearable sweetness.*

With Wally gone and Meredith away at camp, her summer until now had been a series of days barely dragged through, and nights of lachrymose longing. Now the wind in the trees stirred up feelings of wonder and expectation, and the cool days shivered with possibilities.

Ralph sauntered around the corner and disappeared into the bushes. Even he looked more relaxed, she thought, and even a little thinner; up here there was so much to occupy him that maybe food had lost some of its luster.

Later that morning, Claire had a private conference scheduled with Terry Nordstrom to talk about his manuscript. She had been wondering how to tell him that *The*

Great Gatsby had already been written, but he saved her the trouble. He plopped onto the horsehair sofa in the library with the same vigor with which he did everything, and stared moodily at the ground.

"It all sucks," he said angrily. "I'll have to scrap this book and start over."

"What do you mean?" said Claire.

Terry heaved a great sigh and shook his head. "Nobody's gonna want to read about the life of a working-class grunt like me."

"Oh, no, that's not true at all. Just think about—"

"Oh, yeah, I know; tell me about all the masterpieces which have been written about trailer trash—"

"Well, I wouldn't use—"

"Wouldn't use that term? What would you prefer—white trash, lowlife?" Terry took the couch cushion in his arms and hugged it as though he wanted to crush it.

Claire took a deep breath and held it. There was a pause and then she said, "Why are you so angry?" As soon as the words came out of her mouth, she regretted them.

Terry stared at her. "What?"

Claire took another deep breath. She was in it now; it was too late to turn back. "You're so *angry* . . . what are you so angry at?"

To her surprise, he laughed. "You really take the cake, you really do. You're just like the rest of them here. You people are so *pampered*! You have no *idea* what it's like to actually have to *work* for a living, to sweat in a stupid diner kitchen seven days a week just so your family can afford to buy shoes!"

There was a silence. Claire couldn't think of anything to say. Terry sounded exactly like her father, going on and on about his hard times growing up. She had no doubt he had suffered, but he had wielded his misery like a weapon, using it against Claire and her brother, beating them into a guilty silence.

"Oh, never *mind*!" Terry said suddenly, rising from the couch and throwing the pillow violently to the floor. "I don't know why I bother," he muttered, and stalked out of the room. Claire sat there in silence for a few minutes, then got up and went to look for Liza.

She found her in the little garden behind the house, pulling weeds. Seeing Liza bent over the ground, her face shrouded in a big floppy straw hat, Claire suddenly was reminded of her friend Amelia Moore, Robert's second victim. Amelia had not been as lucky as Claire; Robert had gotten to her before they got to him. Claire could still remember the moment she heard of Amelia's death, the cold chill she felt in the pit of her stomach as she listened to Amelia's terrified voice on her answering machine. *I'm scared, Claire—I need to talk to you.* Those were the last words Claire ever heard her friend utter, because within hours of that call, dear, sweet Amelia was dead, murdered by the man whose bed Claire had shared. Claire had not forgiven herself for this, her inability to see Robert for what he really was.

"Hi, Claire."

Liza's voice awoke her from her reverie.

"Oh, hi. I didn't mean to interrupt your work."

Liza straightened up and wiped the sweat off her face. "I was ready to pack it in anyway. Come on, let's go have some iced tea."

Claire laughed. "Do you ever drink anything else except tea?"

Liza smiled. "Bourbon. And wine, of course . . . in fact, I had a little too much of it last night. I'm trying to sweat it out now. Come on, let's go inside."

Over a glass of mint tea in Liza's cabin, Claire recounted Terry's fit of moodiness. When she had finished, Liza shook her head.

"Poor Terry. He's so gone over Maya, and he's convinced that she prefers Billy Trimble because he comes from money and privilege. Terry thinks the whole world judges him as inferior because he's working class. He doesn't just have a chip on his shoulder; he has a whole lumberyard."

"Well, I just feel bad because I'm afraid I said the wrong thing."

Liza took a swallow of tea, her breath frosting over the cold glass. "I wouldn't worry about it. Terry probably needs a therapist more than he needs a writing instructor anyway."

"Well, I didn't mean to insult him. Maybe I should apologize."

"I suspect he'll be knocking on your door by the end of the day, apologizing to you."

"Really? You think so?"

Liza nodded, sucking on the slice of lemon in her tea. "That's the usual pattern. We've all had our 'Terry run-in,' and he always apologizes later."

"Well, thanks . . . I feel better now."

As Claire passed the garden on the way back to Ravenscroft, she thought again of Amelia, of her cheerful face and sweet nature.

> *Put out the light, then put out the light.*
> *Being done, there is no pause.*

Claire had two manuscripts to read that afternoon, so before dinner she decided to drive down to a spot by the river Liza had told her about. Liza's directions were perfect, and soon Claire was sitting on the banks of the Hudson as it flowed majestically by, lazy as the day.

Looking at the even, serene ripples beneath her, Claire thought about the seasons of her childhood, inseparably linked to the rhythms of Lake Erie. With its variety of moods, the lake had a personality, and the locals often spoke of it as if it were alive.

Lake looks angry this morning; better stay away from it.

Water's calm today; must be in a good mood.

Now, sitting on the banks of the Hudson, Claire understood why water was a metaphor for life: mysterious, always in motion, teeming beneath the surface. The sun glinted upon the ripples, sending a flash of sparkles to her half-closed eyes . . . she didn't even feel her eyelids closing, and wasn't aware that she had nodded off until she was suddenly awakened by the flap of a fish jumping. She opened her eyes just as it slapped back into the river, leaving behind only a splash of white water.

The wind gathered in the trees, sending a shudder across the surface of the water. Claire shivered and pulled her sweater closer around her shoulders. It was getting late; the sun had sunk low into the sky and it wouldn't be long before it disappeared behind the highest mountain peak. If Claire had any regrets, she could not remember them now; if she had any sorrows, they had vanished into the shimmering sunlight that sparkled and leaped from ripple to ripple. If any fears gnawed at her, they sank into the soft sand of the riverbank, pulled under by the smooth, insistent, never-ending current, watched over by the gods that haunted and blessed these shores.

Out over the water, a crow croaked hoarsely. Claire strained her eyes to see it, but it was invisible to her. A black butterfly with yellow-tipped wings careened into view, did a crazy figure eight, following its own twisted flight path, and fluttered away as suddenly as it had come. Every time Claire saw a butterfly she couldn't help thinking of Carl Jung's story of the butterfly beating its wings against the window, asking to be let in, bringing with it the divine hand of Fate, of—what did Jung call it?—"synchronicity." Because of this, she always thought of butterflies as messengers from the world beyond our knowledge; she wondered what this one portended.

The river doesn't give up its secrets. The words suddenly popped into her head. Still, the buzz of blue flies and the whine of mosquitoes was calming to her mind, as tranquil as a lullaby.

The wind rattling through the rushes, the languid lapping of the water—all was stillness and peace. The longer she sat upon the bank, the more Claire began to feel she was a part of this landscape, this teeming river life. She thought about Two Joe. As a child, she had a fascination with Indians, with their ability to live close to nature—within nature, as it were—in a way that modern man can only imagine. Claire admired stories of Indian trackers so skillful that they could creep silently upon their prey, not breaking so much as a stick under their softly creeping moccasins.

"Hello, Redbird."

Claire turned to see Two Joe standing over her, his bulky body blocking out the sun's orb. He wore blue dungarees over a red flannel shirt.

"Forgive me for disturbing your silence."

"Oh, that's all right; the sun's almost down anyway."

Two Joe picked up a twig, snapped it, and sniffed at the broken end. "It's been a dry summer here."

Claire nodded. She wasn't sure if he was showing off—or if he could really tell that much from a broken twig.

"What did you call me just then?" she said.

Two Joe smiled. "Redbird. That would be your Indian name, because of your hair."

"Do you always give people Indian names?"

Two Joe shrugged. "Sometimes, if I like them . . . and sometimes because I don't like them."

"What is it you call Billy Trimble?"

"Crooked Arrow."

"Any particular reason for that?"

Two Joe shrugged and threw a stone at the river. It skipped and hopped across the water, barely touching the surface as it slipped into the air again. Claire watched it as she counted the number of skips: seven, eight, nine. When she was a child on Lake Erie, five skips was considered very good.

"Who else here have you given an Indian name?"

Two Joe squatted down beside her. "That little one, the angry one from Wyoming—"

"Terry?"

"I call him Bantam Rooster."

Claire laughed. "That's good. Who else?"

"The tall, thin blond one—"

"Maya?"

"Yes. I call her White Willow."

"That's nice; it's pretty."

"Redbird is pretty, too."

Claire couldn't tell if he was talking about the name or

her, so she said nothing. Two Joe was definitely a flirt, and Claire liked him because he made her feel attractive; there was nothing obnoxious or threatening in his compliments.

Two Joe threw his twig in the river and watched it float downstream. "You came here because you needed some time to listen to your heart speak."

Claire looked at his dark, lined face with its big blunt features and black eyebrows. His skin was the color of aged mahogany. She suspected he was laying this Native American thing on a little thick for her benefit, but she was drawn in nonetheless.

"It's very peaceful here," she said.

Two Joe nodded and looked out at the lazily flowing water. "My people have a saying: the river never gives up her secrets."

Claire stared at him. "That's so strange. I just—I mean, I was just thinking of those words when you came up."

Two Joe shrugged again. "That's not unusual. I come from a long line of medicine men." He pointed to a colorful circular pendant with a cross in the middle hanging around his neck. "This is my medicine wheel; it helps ward off evil spirits. Anyone can make them, but if a medicine man makes one, it's more powerful. Some of us are what your people would call psychic."

"Wow—really? Is that why you're a medicine man?"

"Hard to say. Could be the talent grows with time, and is passed on to the next generation. I believe everyone has the capability, but most people never develop theirs."

"Can you see into the future?" Claire said eagerly, half-believing, half-skeptical.

"Sometimes. I'll tell you one thing, though, since you ask: something will happen involving water while you are here."

Claire felt a shiver go up her spine. "What? What's going to happen?"

Two Joe shook his massive head. "I don't know; all I know is I had a dream last night, and whatever it is, it isn't good."

"But that's all you know?"

Two Joe stood up and brushed the dirt off his dungarees. "I can't say any more. I may be wrong. I hope I am."

Claire stood up, too, stretching her cramped legs. Her left foot had fallen asleep, and she shook it to rid it of the pins and needles. "What happened in your dream?"

"My spirit guides came to me—the bear and the wolf—and they gave me a warning involving water."

"So will it happen to you?"

Two Joe shrugged. "Perhaps . . . perhaps not. It will be somebody here, though—and within this phase of the moon."

The wind had picked up, sending little sprays of water over the once-smooth surface of the river. The ripples had turned into shivers, and Claire felt goosebumps forming on her skin, the tiny bumps prickling under her wool sweater.

Before thy hour be ripe.

Chapter 6

"We missed you at the party, Marcel."
Claire was sitting with Liza and Sherry on the front porch eating pasta primavera. Marcel had come by to check on the first-floor water heater, because there was no hot water in the east wing of the house.

"I'm sorry. I was planning to come by, but then my dog got sick and I had to stay with her." Marcel leaned against the porch railing, one of his long legs resting on the top step.

"Is she okay now?" asked Sherry, her mouth full of pasta.

"Oh, yeah, I guess she got into somethin' she shouldn't've."

Marcel was big and friendly and bland as a golden retriever. He wore a green-checked flannel shirt, blue jeans, and tan work boots.

"Wait until you meet the Ravenscroft resident stud," Liza had said to Claire when Marcel called to say he was coming over. Marcel was tall, with a hard, rangy body, big dark eyes, and a thick flop of dark hair, but Claire found him as sexless as a puppy. Liza said he was French-Canadian, though not much of it showed in his accent.

"Oh, this is Claire Rawlings," said Liza. "Claire, this is

Marcel LeMarc, our all-around handyman and lifesaver. He's the one who *really* runs Ravenscroft—or who keeps it running, at any rate."

"Pleased to meet you," said Claire.

Marcel reached out a big red hand, the knuckles bulging and raw. Claire shook it; it was knotty and hard as pine.

Sherry gave him a flirtatious smile. "Would you like some pasta?"

"Oh, no, thanks; I'll eat when I get back home. I gotta go check up on Ellie—that's my dog," he added for Claire's benefit.

"See you later," said Liza. "Thanks for coming by."

"No problem. You got hot water now. All I had to do was flip the switch on the heater; it was off for some reason."

"That's strange. I didn't even know there was a switch."

Marcel shrugged. "Well, maybe someone turned it off and forgot to turn it back on."

"I don't know who would do that."

"Never mind; it's back on now, anyways. Nice meeting you," he said to Claire, and she thought that if he had a hat, he would have tipped it. He got into his truck and drove away, leaving a trail of dust behind him that rose and settled in a thin grey layer on the vines that twined up around the porch railings.

"Pretty cute, huh?" said Sherry, winking and nudging Claire.

"Yeah, he's cute," Claire replied, thinking that golden retrievers were cute, too.

More interesting, she thought, was Tahir Hasanovic: short and dark and intense, with the burning eyes of a character out of Dostoevsky. Claire had recently reread *Crime and Punishment,* and she couldn't help thinking Tahir would make a perfect Raskolnikov.

After dinner she went upstairs to finish the reading she had started that afternoon. As she walked past Camille's room, Claire heard the *tap-tap-tap* of the typewriter. Camille was evidently hard at work, putting in some extra hours before bed.

When Claire came downstairs an hour later, she found Tahir and Maya talking in front of the fireplace. The night was unusually cold for late August, and a fire was blazing in the grate. The long grey couch was empty, but still Maya and Tahir chose to stand. They were talking in low voices, facing the fireplace, their backs to the rest of the room. Claire made herself a cup of decaf and brought it out to the living room. She sat on the empty sofa, its ancient springs groaning under her weight. Watching Tahir and Maya, she decided that they made an odd pair: long, willowy Maya with her Nordic features and pale eyes, a full half foot taller than Tahir, who was short and dark and hairy. *Elves and hobbits,* Claire thought, remembering the different creatures that populated *Lord of the Rings.* Meredith was reading it at camp, and after her last letter, Claire couldn't resist taking a peak at her own dog-eared copy, sitting for so many years on her shelf after making the move from her parents' house to New York. It was squeezed in next to *Modern German Poetry,* which Claire also couldn't bear to give away, even though her German was as rusty as the creaking spring of the old grey sofa.

Claire couldn't help overhearing parts of the conversation between Maya and Tahir.

"Why is it strange?" Tahir was saying.

Maya shook her head but did not reply.

"Why can't you tell me why you're upset?" he said, pressing his point. Maya swept back a chunk of her blond hair with her hand. It looked to Claire as if this was a conversation she didn't want to have, but he was insistent.

"I just don't understand what the problem is," he said, and again Claire was struck by the intensity of the man: with his deep-set dark eyes and thick black hair, she decided he really was very attractive, and more than a little sad. She didn't know why Maya didn't seem to want to talk to him, but since she hadn't come in on the conversation from the beginning, it was hard to figure out.

Claire looked around the living room. A few people had gathered at the far end of the room over by the piano. Gary Robinson, lean and dark, dressed in an elegant green

Harris-tweed jacket, was leaning against the piano talking
to Billy Trimble. With his wire-rim glasses perched on his
long, thin nose, Gary looked the part of the stern and stu-
dious college professor. Claire suddenly realized something:
Gary rarely smiled. Right now his brows were knitted in
concentration, one hand in his pocket, the other resting on
the statue of Diana.

Claire's attention was suddenly caught by the sound of
tense, raised voices—not really loud, but loud enough to
stand out from the low hum of conversation in the room.
She looked around and saw that the voices were coming
from the library. The door was partially open, and from
where she sat she could hear quite clearly what was being
said. The first voice was Liza's, and the other was Sherry's.

"Look, all I'm asking is that you be honest with me,"
Liza was saying.

"But there's nothing to *tell*!" Sherry replied, her voice
high and whiny.

"Shh! The others might hear you!"

"I don't care; let them! I'm tired of the way you treat
me, as though I'm a bad child!" Sherry said.

"Well, sometimes you *act* like one!"

"Look, there's nothing I can say if you insist on being
jealous all the time!"

"All I want to know is: Did you come onto her or not?"

"Why don't you ask your spies; they'll tell you!"

"What are you talking about?" Liza sounded genuinely
confused.

"Oh, don't act so innocent; I know you're keeping an
eye on me!"

Claire looked at the other people in the room to see if
they were listening, but everyone seemed too involved in
their own conversations. She was the closest one to the library, and not wanting to eavesdrop on her friend, she got
up to get more coffee from the kitchen. As she did, the library door opened and Sherry emerged, red-faced. She
glanced at Claire but then averted her eyes and walked
quickly through the room and out the front door. A moment later Liza emerged, hands in her pockets, a sheepish

expression on her face. Claire headed for the kitchen, where she lingered for several minutes. She refilled Ralph's water bowl, tidied up the counters, and put away some dishes from the rack. When she returned to the living room, she saw with relief that Liza was gone. Maya and Tahir were gone, too; only Billy and Gary remained, locked in conversation at the far end of the room.

They were talking in low voices, but Claire had excellent hearing and was able to make out what they were saying. She pretended to tidy up the living room, collecting stray coffee cups, while she listened to their words.

"You can tell me these things," Gary was saying. "There's no reason to keep secrets from me."

Billy's handsome face darkened. A lock of his sandy hair fell over one side of his forehead. "Look, I never promised you anything." His usual sleepy ironic tone of voice was gone, and there was an intensity to his voice.

"I'm not saying you did," Gary replied. "I'm just pointing out that if you are in love with her, maybe I have a right to know."

Billy shook his head, more in confusion than denial, Claire thought. "Look," he said slowly, "I don't know the answer to that."

He did look miserable, Claire thought. She could only assume they were talking about Maya. At that moment Gary glanced over at her, and not wanting to arouse suspicion, Claire decided it was time for her to make an exit.

She looked at her watch; it was past eleven. Normally, she was a night owl, but here in Woodstock she felt sleepy by ten o'clock. She finished her coffee, rinsed out the cup, and went upstairs.

Ralph was lying on the bed, and when he saw her he did his stretch-and-yawn routine, then rolled over onto his back, feet in the air.

"You look very silly, do you know that?" she said, scratching his stomach.

A rumble came from his throat that was halfway between a meow and a growl. Claire changed into her pajamas and slipped under the covers, the sheets cold and clean on her skin. She lay in bed reading for a while, until the rest of the house grew still and silent. Then she got up to brush her teeth, and remembered she had left her tooth-brush in the downstairs bathroom where she had taken her bath the night before.

"Damn," she said, reaching for her robe. Slipping on a pair of sandals, Claire padded down the hall. The house was quiet, and she tiptoed down the stairs and through the east wing, toward the door. Pushing it open gently, she crept out onto the wooden catwalk that led to the artists' studios. The clicking of crickets mingled with soft twit-tering, cooing, and rustling, the night sounds of creatures who shared this mountain with the people who lived here. Claire stood for a moment in the cool evening air, en-veloped by the nocturnal murmurings. Shivering, she stepped forward into the night.

On the right she saw the door to the bathroom. To her surprise, it was ajar. Seeping out through the thin crack, falling across the catwalk, was a horizontal bar of yellow light. The tip of it crossed Claire's feet as she stood there, neatly dissecting her toes where they protruded from her sandals. She took a step toward the door and knocked on it. There was no answer. She took another step and gently pushed the door open. A wave of steam brushed across her face, carrying with it the scent of apricot soap. Someone had taken a bath recently. Thinking they might still be there and hadn't heard her knock, Claire called out softly.

"Hello—anybody there?"

The only response was a dimming of the sounds of the night creatures, as if they, too, were awaiting a response. Claire pushed the door all the way open and stepped into the room.

At first her mind told her that the person lying in the tub simply had not heard her enter. From the back, she rec-ognized Maya Sorenson's blond hair. Maya lay on her back in the tub, her head resting on the porcelain edge, her legs stretched out in front of her. A knot forming in her stom-ach, Claire approached the tub, waiting for some sign of life from the still white form.

"Maya?" she called out softly, taking a step farther into the room. It was only when she saw the wide-open, staring eyes that she realized Maya was dead.

Her blond hair radiating out from her head, floating gently like yellow water weeds in a pond, Maya Sorenson lay on her back in the water. Beautiful even in death, not a mark on her perfect pale skin, she lay there like the doomed Ophelia, drowned by her passion for a madman. Still, Claire could not believe what she was seeing, and she stood waiting for Maya to breathe, move, to speak. But the only movement in the room was a tiny ripple across the surface of the bathwater caused by the breeze through the open door.

Claire's knees began to tremble and buckle.

I must sit down, she thought, but before she could move, the light from the single overhead bulb began spinning crazily. Then her vision went dark around the edges, and blackness enveloped her like a shroud.

Chapter 7

"Can you hear me?"
    Stay here; stay here in the dark where no one can see you.
    "Are you all right?"
    It's so cool and quiet here . . . why would you want to leave?
    "Redbird, open your eyes!"
    Finally, reluctantly, Claire obeyed. The darkness gradually gave way to a dim brown color, and she saw Two Joe standing over her.
    "Are you injured?" His face was grave, concerned.
    "No, I—I was just—shocked, I guess." For the first time in her life, Claire realized, she had fainted. Why, though? She couldn't remember what had caused her to faint. Struggling to sit up, she felt Two Joe's huge hands pressing into her shoulders, forcing her to remain where she was.
    "Not so fast; slowly, take it easy. Just breathe, nice and deep. Go on; just breathe for a minute."
    She took a deep breath. The smell of apricot soap stung her eyes, and then she remembered.
    "Maya's dead!" she cried out suddenly, looking desperately at Two Joe, waiting for him to contradict her.

Two Joe's expression did not change. "Yes," he said simply, "she is dead." His eyes softened, and his voice was kind. "Poor Redbird," he said. "You have never seen death before, have you?"

Claire shook her head, suddenly feeling nauseous.

"Come outside." Two Joe lifted her gently by the shoulders. "I will help you. We must get help."

Slowly, feebly, as if she were a hundred years old, Claire got to her feet. Leaning on Two Joe, she walked unsteadily back out into the night. She avoided looking at the tub with its horrible sight, averting her eyes until she was outside. Once outdoors, she felt better. The cool air made her shiver, but she no longer felt nauseous.

"What—what should we do?" she said.

"We must call the police," Two Joe replied, and together they went back into the main house.

"That's right," she said, feeling as though a fog had descended over her brain. "The police—we have to call them." She felt comforted by the idea. The police would come, and they would know what to do.

"Do you want to lie on the couch?" Two Joe said when they reached the living room, but Claire shook her head.

"No, I'm all right." The truth was that she was terrified of being alone, even for a moment. Two Joe studied her for a moment, then he nodded.

"Come; we will call them together."

Together they walked through the dining room to the pay phone, nestled in its cranny next to the laundry room. Claire stood next to Two Joe and watched him dial, grateful for his calm, his size, his reassuring hand on hers while they both waited for the police to pick up . . . and then the words, when they came, sounded so bald, so bleak:

"Tell the sheriff there's been an accident."

After he hung up, Claire put a hand on his muscular arm. She could feel the heat through his flannel shirt. Two Joe was a furnace, she thought; he must have the metabolism of a bear.

"What were you doing downstairs?" she said. "I mean, you just—"

"Just happened to be there when you fainted?" Two Joe finished for her. He shook his massive head. "I could not sleep, and I was on my way to the woods to consult my spirit guides."

"Consult them? About what?"

Two Joe crossed his arms over his broad chest. "Remember I told you I come from a line of medicine men?"

"Yes."

"And I told you that I sensed something bad would happen, something involving water?"

"That's right; you did." Two Joe's prediction by the banks of the Hudson didn't look so silly now. If anything, she thought, it was a little spooky.

"Well, I wanted to consult my spirit guides to find out more. But I was too late," he said, shaking his head sadly. "But come; we must wake up the others."

The police arrived so quickly that Claire and Two Joe had just barely finished waking up the other residents, knocking softly on doors one by one, breaking the news as gently as possible. Some took it better than others. Billy and Camille were surprisingly calm, while remote Gary, as well as Tahir—who had already seen so much killing— were both very upset. When they told Terry, he kept repeating over and over, "No, that can't be, it can't be."

When the police arrived, the residents were gathered in solemn little groups in the living room. Someone had made coffee, and people were standing around sipping from their mugs or just clutching them, as if trying to absorb their warmth. Terry sat in the corner sobbing quietly; others talked in low, hushed tones or just stood staring at the floor in disbelief. A thick rain had begun to fall outside, and Claire could hear the heavy drops splashing from the eaves.

Claire had overcome her initial shock and was now one of the more competent people in the room, so when she saw the flashing lights outside, she went to the door. Two patrol cars and an ambulance sat in the driveway. As she stood on the porch, a plain black sedan pulled up next to one of the patrol cars. A tall man in a trench coat got out of the black sedan.

Claire went down the steps to greet him.

"Hello, I'm Detective Hansom."

Detective Hansom was so much the opposite of his name that Claire found herself staring at him. He was tall and bony, with big hands jutting out from the sleeves of his raincoat like unpruned tree limbs. His enormous head was set upon a neck that looked too long and thin to support it, and his face was dominated by a heavy, overhanging forehead and thick dark eyebrows that met in the center, forming a single line of black moss above dark, deep-set eyes, which were his most attractive feature. He resembled not a man so much as a geological formation, hulking and craggy as granite, like something hewn out of the earth millennia ago. In the blunt glare of the porch light, his heavy brow and massive head reminded Claire of Frankenstein's monster.

In spite of his forbidding appearance, Claire liked him immediately. His voice was as gentle as his body was ungainly, with a surprisingly light timbre for such a large man.

"Are you the one who discovered the body?"

"Yes."

"I hope you won't mind answering a few questions," he said, sounding genuinely apologetic.

"Not at all," Claire replied. "Would you like to come inside? Everyone else has gathered in the living room."

Detective Hansom cocked his head, reminding Claire of a large bird dog.

"First I want to see the body." He turned and called over his shoulder. "Sergeant Rollins."

A short, pink-faced young man appeared at this elbow. He was clean-shaven and also clad in a trench coat. A red wool scarf was wrapped tightly around his throat.

"Yes, sir."

"I want you to start taking statements from people."

"Yes, sir."

Detective Hansom turned to Claire. "You said everyone is in the living room?"

"Yes."

He shook his head and sighed as he walked across the porch. "Things like this just don't happen around here. Any chance it was an accident, you think?"

"I doubt it," Claire replied, thinking of Maya's open, staring eyes. She ushered him into the living room, and as they entered, everyone immediately became quiet.

"Good evening; I'm Detective Hansom," he said. "I'm going in to take a look at the body; meanwhile Sergeant Rollins here will be taking statements from everybody. Normally, we would ask you to come down to the station, but since there are so many of you and the weather is bad, we're going to do it here. If we can just have your cooperation, we'll try to do this as quickly as possible. I will ask that you all remain in this area until we have finished. Sergeant Rollins?" he said, turning to the pink-faced young man, who sneezed in reply.

"Sorry, sir; it's this damn head cold," he said sheepishly. "All right, folks," he continued, his tone suddenly authoritative, "if you will just line up, I'll speak to you one by one." He turned to Claire. "Is there a room we can use? How about this room here?" he said, indicating the library.

"Uh . . ." Claire looked around for Liza, thinking that she should really be in charge. She hadn't seen Liza yet; Sherry had answered the door at their cabin, and Claire had hurried back to Ravenscroft before she could tell Liza in person. Since Liza wasn't anywhere to be seen, Claire turned to the sergeant. "I guess that'll be fine."

As Claire led Detective Hansom through the living room and toward the library, Two Joe appeared at her side.

"Are you all right, Redbird?" he said, laying a hand gently on her shoulder.

"Yes, much better, thank you. Thank you for all your help."

As they walked down the hallway, Detective Hansom turned to Claire, his voice low. "What were you thanking him for?"

Claire explained how she had found the body, and as she did, she felt her face reddening. She worried that her account was casting a suspicious light on Two Joe's role in Maya's death. She looked anxiously at Detective Hansom to see his reaction, but his big face was inscrutable, dull as a tree stump.

"Can you show me how you found the body?" he said gently.

"Yes—out this way," Claire replied, leading him down the hall toward the side door. She pushed the door open slowly and stepped out onto the catwalk. Rain poured down from the eaves into the puddles already forming on the lawn.

When they reached the bathroom, the faint odor of apricots was still in the air. Claire's legs began to tremble. She took a deep breath.

Detective Hansom looked at her. "That's all right," he said in a sympathetic voice. "Why don't you go back inside? I can handle it from here on in."

Claire turned to find herself face-to-face with two uniformed policemen and two paramedics in white. "Excuse me," she said, stepping out of their way.

When she arrived back in the living room, she saw Liza talking to Sergeant Rollins. He said something to her and she shook her head in response, then they both went into the library. *The first of the suspects to be interviewed.* As the phrase popped into her head, Claire realized that she herself was probably a suspect.

There was a knock on the front door, and since she was standing nearest to it, Claire went to open it, expecting to see another policeman.

Just then a clap of thunder sounded nearby, rattling the windowpanes, and Claire jumped, her heart pounding. At that moment her hand found the doorknob, and she opened the door. There, soaking wet, illuminated by a flash of lightning, pale as an apparition in the white light, stood Meredith Lawrence.

"I just couldn't stand it anymore," she said. "I *had* to escape! What's going on here?" she said, looking around the room. "What's happened?"

"There's been a—a death," Claire answered, not saying

what she was really thinking: *Murder. There's been a murder.*

Just then, as if in answer to her thoughts, Jack Mulligan's voice broke through the soft murmurings of the other people in the room.

"How do they know it's murder and not an accident?"

"Or even suicide," added Billy Trimble. He stood by the fire, one arm on the mantel, a cup of coffee in his other hand. He wore a white shirt and khaki slacks, and his sandy hair was neatly combed.

Meredith looked at them and back at Claire. "Murder?" she said, her blue eyes huge. "There's been a murder?"

"I don't know," Claire replied a little sharply. "Someone's died, that's all I know."

"You discovered the body, didn't you?" said Jack Mulligan, taking a few steps toward her. His presence was large, intrusive, and Claire had an impulse to back away.

"Yes," she said brusquely, not wanting to talk about it to him of all people.

"Well . . . ?" he said, staring at her as if she had the answer to the question now consuming everyone in the room.

Claire felt that everyone was looking at her, expecting something, but she had nothing to give them. She felt numb. She turned to Meredith, who stood dripping onto the carpet, a soggy knapsack at her feet.

"Let's get you into some dry clothes," she said, and taking the girl's hand, went upstairs.

The clothes in Meredith's knapsack were all damp, so Claire gave her one of her own flannel shirts, a pair of sweatpants, and some wool socks. Dressed in Claire's clothes, Meredith looked even thinner than Claire remembered. The clothes hung on her body, and strands of damp hair clung to her neck. When wet, her hair looked dark auburn instead of its actual color—bright orange. Claire thought that with her hair color muted like this, Meredith looked less alarming. She pulled a fluffy white towel off the rack and tossed it to the girl.

"Here, you'd better dry your hair."

"I could use some tea," Meredith said, rubbing her head vigorously with the towel.

They went down to the kitchen, where they were greeted by the smell of freshly brewing coffee. Sherry and Gary stood at the entrance to the pantry, deep in conversation.

"I'm not going to implicate him," Gary was saying as Claire and Meredith entered the room. He looked up and saw them, and with a curt little nod, left the kitchen.

"Oh, Claire, you poor thing," Sherry said. "Are you all right?"

"Yes, thank you; I'm okay," Claire replied. "Meredith, this is Sherry Bernstein."

"No relation to Leonard," said Sherry with a smile, offering her hand. Claire thought her fingernails looked even worse than before—bitten down to the quick, the cuticles red and torn.

"Meredith Lawrence," said Meredith, shaking Sherry's hand solemnly.

Sherry turned the coffeemaker onto "brew." "Are you Claire's niece?"

"I'm Claire's ward," said Meredith, hopping up onto the kitchen counter. "Who was that guy who just left?"

"Oh, that was Gary Robinson, one of the painters."

"And who was he talking about implicating just now?"

"Meredith," Claire warned.

"Well . . . it's hardly a secret," said Sherry. "Gary was worried about saying anything to the police about Billy's relationship with Maya."

Meredith looked at Claire. "Which one is Billy?"

"The tall one with the sandy hair."

"Oh. He and Maya were an item, then?" said Meredith.

"Well . . . in a way," Sherry replied. "I mean, Gary says that they sometimes took baths together."

"Oh, I see . . . that would look pretty suspicious, I guess," Meredith said thoughtfully. She sat on the counter swinging her legs back and forth while Claire put on water for tea. Just then Ralph emerged from the pantry, licking his whiskers.

"Hello, Ralph!" Meredith cried, and the cat froze, a panicked look on his face. Before Meredith could jump off the counter and pounce, he bolted from the room, his claws sliding on the smooth linoleum.

"Claire didn't tell us she had a ward," said Sherry, pouring some milk into a small blue china pitcher.

"Well, it's not official yet," said Meredith. "Do you have any cookies? I'm starving."

"If you're hungry, you should eat something other than cookies," said Claire, filling the teapot with Earl Grey, Meredith's favorite.

"But that's what I *want*."

"Whining will get you nowhere," Claire said firmly. "I'll make you a sandwich, and if you eat it, you can have some cookies."

"Okay." Meredith's moods came and went as quickly as a summer thunderstorm.

They took their tea and sandwiches into the living room and sat on the sofa, which was unoccupied. Everyone else was still huddled in little groups in the corners of the room. Tahir and Billy had made a fire, and the low hushed conversations were interspersed with the crackling of dry wood. Meredith and Claire sat on the couch in front of the fire.

"So how did you get here?" said Claire, blowing on her tea to cool it off.

Meredith took a huge gulp of hot tea and made a face. "I hitchhiked."

"Oh God, Meredith!"

Meredith shrugged. "I needed to get here, didn't I? I found a nice couple who were driving to Phoenicia and they dropped me off."

"Does your father know where you are?"

"No. I left a note at camp saying I'd gone to visit friends. They won't notice I'm gone until tomorrow morning," she added through a mouthful of cheese-and-tomato sandwich.

"You're going to have to call your father first thing in the morning."

Meredith sighed and bit off a chunk of a Mint Milano. "All right. I just couldn't stand it there anymore; you don't know what it was *like*. It was awful!"

"All right, never mind; you're here now. We'll have to ask your father what to do next."

"Okay, okay—but let's talk about the murder." Meredith tucked her thin knees up under her. "Tell me everything you know about the victim."

"I only knew her a couple of days . . . she was very pretty, a journalist, Swedish."

"With an accent and everything?"

"Yes, she had an accent."

"Pretty, huh?"

"Yes."

"Hmm . . . could be a jealous lover. Who was she sleeping with?"

"Meredith!"

Several people were looking at them now.

"Oh, come on, Claire; what's the big deal? We're talking about *murder* here, for God's sake!" Meredith leaned in closer to Claire. "It *was* murder, wasn't it?" she said hopefully.

Claire sighed. "Unless she had a stroke or a heart attack or something, I think it's unlikely that it was an accident."

"Well, the coroner's report will answer that," said Meredith. She took a gulp of tea and waved her hand in front of her mouth. "Ow, that's hot!"

"Don't drink it so quickly," said Claire, sipping her tea, which tasted like vinegar. She remembered that after Amelia's death, it was days before food tasted like anything other than sawdust.

Camille walked over to them and perched on the arm of the sofa. "Hello, I'm Camille."

Meredith looked up, her mouth full. "Meredif Rawrence," she said, swallowing.

"Pleased to meet you. Claire, this is so awful," Camille said, lowering her voice. "I understand you found the body?"

"Yes. I went down to get my toothbrush . . ." Claire paused, the image of Maya's still, white body burned into her brain. She wondered how long it would take for the image to fade.

"Who could have done such a thing?" Camille said, shaking her head. Her beautifully manicured hands fingered a box of Sobraines. "I'm dying for one of these," she said ruefully.

Claire noticed the pack was unopened. "Is that the pack I got you yesterday?"

Camille looked down at the box in her hands. "Uh, no, actually, I lost that one somehow. Liza got these for me today. It's strange; I don't often lose things . . . I wonder where it could have gone." She shrugged. "Maybe someone really needed a smoke and was afraid to ask for one."

Meredith was listening carefully, her mouth stopped in mid-chew. "Do you always smoke the same brand?" she said.

"When I can afford it."

"Does anyone else here smoke?"

"Plenty of people, but I'm the only one who buys them regularly."

Meredith said nothing, nodding slowly as she sipped her tea.

Slowly, Detective Hansom and Sergeant Rollins questioned each of the residents at Ravenscroft. Detective Hansom set up in one of the unoccupied first-floor bedrooms while Sergeant Rollins continued to interview in the library.

When Claire was summoned by the detective, Meredith jumped up from the couch.

"Oh, can I watch? Please, can I?" She hopped up and down, looking up at Claire, hands clasped in front of her thin chest. Detective Hansom looked at her, his face heavy with fatigue.

"Who are you?"

"Meredith Lawrence, at your service," she said, thrusting out a thin hand. Detective Hansom shook it thoughtfully, then looked at Claire and raised an eyebrow. Claire was about to explain, but Meredith beat her to it.

"I arrived after the murder, so I can't be a suspect," she

said cheerfully. "Besides, you might be able to use my help."

"Oh? Are you a detective?" said Detective Hansom without a hint of a smile.

"Oh, yes; I've already solved several burglaries, as well as one murder," Meredith replied breezily.

"Really?"

"Oh, yes—just ask Claire." Meredith was rocking back and forth on her heels. Detective Hansom turned to Claire.

"It's—it's really a long story," she began, but Meredith stopped rocking and touched the detective on the sleeve of his jacket.

"It's kind of painful for her to talk about," she said in a low voice. "See, what happened was—"

"I'm sure it's a very interesting story, but we have a crime of our own to solve right now," the detective interrupted.

"You mean you've already ruled out suicide?" said Gary Robinson, walking over to them.

"I'd have to say it's very unlikely," Hansom replied. "Most often in a case like this someone would cut their wrists and bleed to death if they really wanted to kill themselves."

"Besides, why would Maya want to kill herself?" said Camille softly. "She was beautiful, talented—"

"Any signs of sexual assault?" said Meredith.

"Meredith!" Claire said.

"That's for the coroner to decide," answered Detective Hansom, turning to Claire. "Ms. Rawlings . . . ? Would you come with me please?"

"Wait here," she said to Meredith. "If you need anything, just ask Camille or Sherry."

Claire followed the detective into the spare bedroom. He sat at the desk in the corner and she sank into an armchair next to the bed. She felt comforted by his gentle voice and shy manner, which, oddly, reminded her of Wally. Neither of them was anything like detectives she had seen on television or in movies—intimidating men with brash, assertive manners, or sneaky and crafty like Columbo. Detective Hansom seemed genuinely concerned as he gently probed Claire's memory of her discovery.

"Did you hear or see anything unusual before you found Ms.—er, Sorenson, anything remarkable at all?"

Claire tired to remember. As she sat there, shaky from fatigue and emotion, it all seemed to have taken place in another time period. She felt that her body was not her own, and the room, so solid and real just yesterday, now seemed as artificial as a movie set, made of plywood and canvas.

"Think about right before you discovered the body," Detective Hansom said softly. "Was there anything unusual or out of the ordinary that you noticed?"

"I did see that Maya's bedroom door appeared to be ajar as I passed it in the hallway . . . I remember thinking that was odd at the time."

"Yes . . . her door was open when we found it. Is it unusual for residents to leave their doors unlocked, do you think?"

"Well . . . I guess it would depend on the person."

"Is there anything else you can think of—anything at all—out of the ordinary?"

Claire strained to think of those moments right before she entered the bathroom . . . they seemed so distant now, so remote. She had the feeling that there *was* something, but she couldn't remember what . . . it hadn't seemed unusual at the time, but now the feeling of a memory gnawed at her, irritating because she had lost the memory itself.

Finally she said, "I'm sorry, I can't think of anything."

"That's all right," Detective Hansom said gently. He leaned forward, interlocking the fingers of his big hands, the knuckles like knots on a tree trunk. "Do you know of any reason Ms. Sorenson might have wanted to kill herself?"

Claire shook her head. "I just arrived here two days ago. I barely knew her."

He nodded. "I see. Is there any reason at all you can think of why someone would want to murder Ms. Sorenson?"

Murder. Claire's stomach tightened at the sound of the word. "No . . . not that I would know of. I mean, Terry Nordstrom had a crush on her, but that's hardly a motive for murder, is it?"

She looked at him for reassurance, but his big face was blunt, unreadable. He shook his massive head. "In my experience, almost anything can be a motive for murder."

Claire nodded slowly, her stomach sinking. Had she just made Terry the main suspect?

"Do you know if it was Ms. Sorenson's habit to take a bath every night?" Detective Hansom said, scratching his elbow. The library was cool—the house had no central heating—and he still wore his battered trench coat, the belt hanging loosely at his side.

"As a matter of fact, I saw her returning from the bathroom at about the same time the night before," Claire said. "But I don't know if she took one every night."

The detective nodded and made a little note in his notebook. "Just one more thing." He rubbed his eyes wearily in a gesture that reminded her of Wally. "Did you touch the crime scene at all?"

"No—why?"

"Not even to mop up any water from the floor?"

"No, of course not. I know better than to do something like that," Claire said sharply, suddenly irritated at this big, gawky man with his weary, patient voice.

Detective Hansom sighed, and Claire realized at that moment that he probably dealt with a lot of uncooperative witnesses in his job. She felt bad about snapping at him.

"I believe you," he said quietly. "You may have noticed, then, that there was no water spilled on the floor."

Claire looked out the library window at the rain falling steadily in soft sheets from the porch roof. It hadn't struck her at the time, but now that he mentioned it, there *had* been no water on the floor.

"Yes," she said slowly, "you're right; the floor was dry. I wonder what that—" she said, but Detective Hansom unfolded his long body from the chair and handed her a business card. "Well, thank you, Ms. Rawlings. If anything comes to you, just give me a call."

Two more hours passed, and then at last the questioning was over. Some people went back to their rooms after they were finished, but many of them stayed in the living room, unwilling to be alone, craving the nearness of others. After Detective Hansom left, some of them stayed staring at the dying fire, empty coffee cups still clutched in their hands, too tired or numb to move, all the conversation wrung out of them.

Liza offered to give Meredith a room of her own, but Meredith begged to be allowed to sleep on a mattress on the floor of Claire's room. Even though the rooms all had locks with dead bolts, Claire, too, wanted Meredith in with her; she would be safer. Claire was exhausted, and thought of the small bottle of codeine pills she had upstairs, left over from tooth surgery. She had been saving them for a time such as this, when sleep would not easily come on its own, but was desperately needed.

Meredith fell asleep almost immediately, and with the girl's raspy adenoidal breathing in the dark beside her, Claire felt somehow comforted.

Meanwhile, the storm continued to pound the house furiously, as though nature's rage paralleled that of man. As the wind rattled and shook the windows, Claire thought about coming to terms with loss. Ultimately the journey of life is one in which everything is lost, she thought—sometimes suddenly, like tonight. More often, though, it is a gradual ebbing away, like the steady drip of water upon rock, a slow carving at the surface until nothing remains. Claire's love of the people in her life was tempered by this knowledge, so that even in the joy there was always a sadness, for everything had a last time, an end; infinity might exist for physicists and theologians, she thought, but it was not a reality that could be touched or experienced.

"Since by man came death." The words appeared in her mind like a dark script ... death as a bookend to life, a coming as well as a going. Suddenly Claire remembered what it was she was trying so hard to recall when she was

talking to Detective Hansom, and realized why it had been
so hard to remember. She hadn't seen anything or even
heard anything, but as she stood out on the catwalk leading to the bathroom, she had caught a faint but unmistakable aroma of expensive tobacco. In fact—she was certain
of it now—it was the scent of a Sobraine Black Russian.

Chapter 8

Meredith entered the porch balancing a cup of tea on a plate packed with cookies. "Do you know what happens when you fall into a black hole?" she said, a spray of cookie crumbs drifting onto the floorboards.

"No, what?"

Meredith sat carefully on the musty daybed, setting the plate down beside her. She leaned toward Claire, her freckled nose wrinkled, blue eyes intense. *"You fall into another universe."*

"Oh really? How do they know that?"

Meredith snorted and rolled her eyes. "They don't *know* that; it's theoretical physics. They can't really *know* anything for sure. They just *think* that's what happens."

"Oh, I see. What do they think happens in this other universe?"

Meredith tucked her legs under her and set the plate of cookies on her knee. It was after ten, but she and Claire were alone on the porch, the only ones yet awake. No one had gone to bed before four A.M. In spite of the codeine, Claire had lain awake replaying the image of Maya's lifeless body over and over. Meredith had no trouble sleeping, though, and snored loudly most of the night.

The rain had stopped and a feeble sun was trying to push away the dull grey clouds lingering in the storm's aftermath. The vines and bushes surrounding the porch were still dripping wet, and pools of muddy water gathered on the usually dusty surface of Camelot Road.

"See, the whole thing about quantum mechanics is that you can't predict what will happen, so that *anything* might happen!" Meredith said, breaking a cookie in half.

"Anything like what?"

"Well, there's not just one possible sequence of events for a given time line, but a *number* of possible events. So, for example, even though there was a murder yesterday, in another time line there would be no murder."

"But we can only experience one reality—the one we know."

Meredith shrugged. "So far. But that's where black holes come in. What if it were possible to fall through a black hole and visit another universe? Maybe there's a universe in which we're all the same but our lives turn out different."

"But then we wouldn't be the same."

Meredith popped a cookie into her mouth. "Yeah . . . I guess you're right. Hell, I might never have been born."

Claire wanted to say something about the swear word, but she didn't have the energy; besides, was it really her job? Her relationship with Meredith was ambiguous, yet she knew the girl desperately needed more structure in her life. While Meredith loved her father, she was also disdainful of him for being weak and ineffectual. She utterly loathed her stepmother, and since her mother's death, that left Claire as the only adult in Meredith's life she respected. Sort of like a kindly aunt, except that in an odd way, though unrelated, Claire was more than an aunt.

"Well, I know one thing about the murderer, that's for sure."

Meredith's voice brought Claire out of her reverie. The girl sat, cookie crumbs clinging to her lips like tiny sentinels, her blue eyes translucent in the morning sun filtering through the canopy of leaves surrounding the porch.

Claire blinked. "What do you know?"

"Well, think about it for a minute. He or she was in a hurry; this was not a carefully planned murder."

"Why not?"

Meredith looked at Claire, her voice heavy with disdain. "Oh, come *on*—drowning someone in a bathtub within earshot of fifteen people. It's hardly a well-thought-out crime! Anyone could have heard, could have come upon them and seen it happen."

Claire shuddered. *Like me, for instance.*

"So this was someone who wanted her gone in a hurry— and was willing to risk discovery; so the stakes must have been pretty high."

"Exactly."

Meredith popped a Bordeaux cookie into her mouth. "You said the little guy was in love with her?"

"That's what Camille told me."

"Hmm . . . interesting. What's his name again?"

"Terry. Terry Nordstrom."

"But she was sleeping with the tall guy—what's his name, the WASPy one?"

"Billy Trimble."

Meredith stood up and went over to lean on the front railing. She shook her head. "Same old story; they always go for the tall ones. No wonder that little guy looks so angry . . . but I wonder if he was angry enough to kill?"

Meredith ate another cookie, chewing thoughtfully as she and Claire watched a pair of blue jays squabbling on the front lawn. The birds cackled and screeched at one another, beating their wings rapidly, a flurry of blue. Claire looked at Meredith: a peaceful look had come over her face. It was clear that she enjoyed this whole investigative process.

"Meredith."

"Yes?" Her voice was dreamy, relaxed.

"You have to call your father and tell him where you are."

Meredith sighed and kicked at a twig. It skittered across

the floorboards and fell into the dark thicket of vines surrounding the porch.

"You know everyone will be worried about you. I could
make the call, but I'd rather you made it."

Meredith shook herself like a dog and flung her body
onto the daybed. "He'll make me go back to Auschwitz-
on-Hudson."

"You really shouldn't joke about a thing like that, you
know."

Meredith lifted her head and gave Claire a withering
look. "Really? What about *Hogan's Heroes*?"

Claire had to admit Meredith had her there. *God,* she
thought, *how do parents do it? How do you pick your bat-
tles, and do you let things go?*

"Look," she said, "if you don't go call your father, I
will."

"All right, all *right*." Meredith dragged herself off the
bed as if the blood in her veins had suddenly been replaced
with lead. "Where's the phone?"

"There's a pay phone in a little alcove off the dining
room." Meredith lumbered off, the screen door clanging
behind her.

Claire sat in the stillness of the morning, listening to
the low buzz of insects all around her. It was a strange dynamic the two of them had, she thought, all the stranger
for its mutual dependency. Claire knew Meredith needed
her, but she realized she needed Meredith just as much.
She had never particularly missed the presence of a child
in her life; watching harassed and exhausted parents lug-
ging their children around the city, she had breathed more
than one sigh of relief, all the while feeling a nagging guilt
that she herself had not procreated. Her life was so simple, uncomplicated by the pulls and demands of children.

However, Meredith's abrupt entry into her life—falling
like a meteor from the sky—had changed everything. Suddenly there was a sense of unexplored emotional territory.
It was threatening to Claire's carefully constructed equilibrium—and yet seemed like an invitation to adventure.
Meredith reminded her of an earlier self: looking at her,

Claire remembered a time in her life when, like Meredith, she was hungry with longing for life, for experience: she wondered if age had closed her in, withered her ambitions and desires, flattened her capacity for experience.

She wanted to absorb Meredith's passion, her zest for knowledge, her impatience. Claire thought she had become too patient with age, too accepting of life's dullness. Like Robinson Crusoe, she was beginning to view civilization as a deadening influence.

Ralph came slinking around the side of the house, belly low to the ground, though Claire couldn't see what he was stalking. He moved through the tall grass as though each blade were made of glass and might break if he put his paw down too hard. Watching him, Claire marveled at the power of instinct: this behavior was hardwired into his genetic code, and was common to centuries of cats before him—and centuries of cats to come. Claire wondered what was hardwired into humans . . . a need to kill, perhaps? Was it possible that somewhere in our DNA structure there was a gene for murder?

"Claire, you'd better come hear this." Meredith was at the door, her voice thick with excitement.

"Hear what?"

"I'll show you."

She followed Meredith through the house into the little alcove that housed the pay phone and answering machine that served all the residents at Ravenscroft. The light was blinking once, indicating there was a message on the tape. Meredith looked at Claire, paused dramatically, then hit the play button. The machine whirred and spun into sound.

". . . this is a message for Maya Sorenson . . . it's Jeff Miller returning your call. I spoke with Ed and he does remember you from the London beat. So if you want to talk to me about the story you mentioned, give me a call back at the *Times* or use my beeper number: 917-787-5544. Thanks."

Meredith hit "stop" and looked at Claire.

"Is that a *clue* or not?" Meredith cried triumphantly.

"Well . . ." Claire began.

"Is what a clue?" said a male voice.

Claire turned to see Jack Mulligan standing behind them; she had not heard him come up.

Before Claire could answer, Meredith snatched the tape from the machine. "That's for the police to decide," she said, and dropped the tape into the pocket of her jeans.

Jack Mulligan shrugged and walked toward the kitchen.

"Let's call Detective Hansom!" Meredith said, grabbing the phone eagerly, but Claire put her hand on the receiver.

"All right, but first you will call your father."

"But this is so much more important!"

"Not to your family. Call him—*now!*"

Meredith sighed and dialed. "He's probably out somewhere with my evil stepmother, the Wicked Witch of Greenwich," she muttered as she waited for someone to pick up.

"Hi, Dad? It's me. No, I'm okay. I'm with Claire. What do you mean . . . I left a *note,* for Christ's sake!" Meredith rolled her eyes. "I'm *not* swearing, Dad, it's just that—I *can't* go back to that place, Dad—I absolutely *cannot!*" There was a pause. "Yes, she's here. I guess." She put her hand over the receiver and looked at Claire. "Do you want to talk to my father?"

"Sure." As she took the receiver from Meredith, Claire felt her palms sweating. Ted Lawrence always made her a little nervous. "Mr. Lawrence? It's Claire Rawlings."

"Ted, please. I'm sorry Meredith has imposed herself on you once again." His voice was the same as she remembered: smooth, cultivated, impeccable, the ultimate Connecticut WASP.

"Oh, it's—it's no imposition, really; it's just that . . ."

"What?"

Claire wanted to say "There's been a murder," but that sounded so dramatic. What she did say, however, sounded ridiculous. "Well, we've had an—accident here."

"What kind of accident?"

"Someone's been killed. But the rest of us are fine," she added hastily.

"I'm so sorry."

"Thank you, but . . . well, I think it's all under control now."

"When should I come get Meredith?"

"Oh, I—whenever's good for you, really."

"Is he talking about coming here?" Meredith said, lunging for the receiver.

"Yes," Claire answered, holding it above her head.

"Tell him not to come—*please, oh please!*" The girl looked so miserable that Claire began to relent.

"Uh . . . Ted?"

"Yes?"

"Is it possible that Meredith could stay just a day or two?"

There was a long pause on the other end and Claire heard a woman's voice in the background—Jean Lawrence, Meredith's stepmother, no doubt. Claire could hear her saying something that sounded like "peace and quiet," and then Ted Lawrence came back on the phone.

"Uh, Claire?"

"Yes?"

"That would be all right with us if it's all right with you, as long as she's not in the way."

"It's fine; she's not in the way at all."

"All right, then, if you promise. We'll call you in a couple of days and arrange to come get her."

"That's fine."

"May I speak to her?"

"Sure." She turned to Meredith, who was jumping up and down singing "Hallelujah" softly under her breath. "Your father wants to talk to you."

Meredith took the receiver. "Oh, thank you, thank you, *thank you,* and I promise, promise, *promise* I'll be good and I won't get in anyone's way and it's *really* beautiful here—much prettier than summer camp—oh, wait'll you see it; you'll just *love* it here and I'm going to help solve the—" She stopped abruptly. "No, she *said* she didn't mind. Why would she lie? Not every one feels the same way about me as the Wicked Witch does, you know; incredible as it may seem to you, some people actually *like* me . . .

well, she *is* a witch, at least to me. Oh, come on, Dad, she hates me and you know it! Yeah, she's still here. Okay." Meredith turned and handed the receiver to Claire. "He wants to talk to you."

Claire took the receiver. "Yes, Mr. Lawrence?"

"Are you sure Meredith won't be in the way?"

Claire wanted to voice her concerns about Meredith's safety in the aftermath of the murder, but it wasn't even clear yet whether it *was* murder, so she said nothing. "It will be a pleasure to have her here," she said firmly, a little angry at the way Meredith's father treated the child. She knew he loved his daughter, but he was puzzled by her, didn't understand her, and had a pathological fear of imposing himself on other people.

"All right," he said dubiously. "Thank you. If you'll give me the number up there, I'll talk to you in a couple of days."

Claire gave him the number on the pay phone. After she hung up, Meredith began doing cartwheels across the dining-room floor.

"I'm free—free at *last!*" she bellowed, doing a bad imitation of Martin Luther King. "Thank you, Claire; thank you so much for delivering me from purgatory! Oh!" she said suddenly. "We still haven't called Detective Hansom!"

By the time Detective Hansom arrived at Ravenscroft, most of the other residents were up. Some of them did not look pleased to see him, no doubt expecting further questioning, but Camille approached him with a cup of steaming coffee.

"Good morning, Inspector," she said with a broad smile. Claire noticed that even at this hour she wore lipstick.

"Detective," Hansom corrected her quietly. "Thank you," he said, taking the coffee. He looked a little disheveled this morning—and with a sudden stab of longing Claire thought of Wally and his rumpled appearance.

"Here's the tape, Detective," Meredith said, pressing it into his hand. "I think you'll find it interesting."

"I'm sure I will," he replied. "Was there anything else?"

"I have some theories, if you'd like to hear them. For example, I feel fairly certain—"

"Not right now, Meredith," Claire said quickly. "I'm sure Detective Hansom is a very busy man."

"Perhaps another time?" the detective said kindly.

Meredith shrugged. "All right; but by then it may be too late."

"How are you all holding up?" he asked Claire, lowering his voice.

"Pretty well, I guess . . . I mean, everyone's pretty shaken by this."

He nodded, his big head tottering on its ridiculously thin neck. "Of course. We have forensics going over everything, and I hope to have a lead soon."

"So it *was* murder?" said Meredith.

The detective nodded slowly. "I'm afraid so. The actual cause of death was drowning, but there was evidence of ligature marks on her neck; so although she inhaled water, she was definitely strangled."

"Any fingerprints?" Meredith asked.

Detective Hansom shook his head. "The murderer may have worn gloves—or the prints may have been washed away in the bathtub. That reminds me," he said, locking his long gnarled fingers together as if in prayer. "We're going to ask the residents to participate in a voluntary fingerprinting; we lifted quite a few sets of prints from the porcelain in the bathroom. The presence of your prints in the room is, of course, no evidence of guilt; we assume you all may have used the bathroom at one time or another. It's really for the purpose of what we call 'elimination prints'; we're looking for any fingerprints *not* belonging to one of the residents."

"Did they find any signs of sexual assault?" said Meredith.

The detective put his coffee cup on the fireplace mantel. "Not so far. We're still awaiting analysis of—"

"Of her vaginal fluid?" said Meredith.

Claire reached over and pinched Meredith's arm.

"Ow! What?" she said, rubbing her arm.

"Meredith, I think you should let the detective do his job and stop bothering him."

Meredith glared at Claire. "May I remind you that you wouldn't be *alive* right now if it weren't for me?"

Detective Hansom looked at Claire, surprise sitting on his big craggy face like sap on a gnarled tree trunk. "Is that true?"

"Yes," Claire said softly. "Yes, it is."

"I *told* you I have experience in solving crimes!" Meredith trumpeted as Camille came back into the living room with a cup of coffee.

"Well, I can believe it," said Camille, perching on the edge of the couch. She took a sip of coffee, leaving a thin red layer of lipstick on the rim of the mug. "I'd love to hear the story sometime."

"So would I," said Detective Hansom, and Claire had the feeling he really meant it.

"You're probably getting some good clues from Maya's journal," said Camille.

Inspector Hansom looked at her, his face blank as glass. "What journal?"

"Maya kept a journal; wasn't it with her things?" said Camille.

"Are you *sure*?"

"Absolutely. She used to talk about it—remember, Claire?"

Claire nodded. "Yes; she mentioned it once when we were sitting on the porch."

"The murderer stole her journal!" Meredith's voice trembled with excitement. "Probably while she was in the bath; her bedroom door was left open, after all. Then he—or she—went downstairs and murdered her."

Detective Hansom stood up. "Well, I'm going to check with Officer Connors to see if he knows anything about it. Then I'm going back to the station and go through her things carefully."

"Would you like some more coffee before you go?" Camille said in a silky voice.

"Uh, no thanks; that was very good," he said, handing her the empty cup.

"Glad you liked it." Camille held his eyes just a little longer than necessary. *She's flirting with him,* thought Claire. Maybe she genuinely liked him; his awkwardness was appealing in its own way . . . but Claire couldn't help thinking there might be another motive. *God, I'm starting to think like Meredith.*

But Meredith was following her own train of thought. "Who's Officer Connors?" she said, following Hansom into the hall that led to the bathroom.

"He's the man we posted to watch the crime scene overnight."

"Ooo, was he here all night?"

"Yes."

"Can I come while you talk to him?"

"I don't see why not. There's nothing much to see."

With a triumphant glance back at Claire, Meredith followed the detective down the hall. A moment later Claire heard the screen door open and close.

Camille sank down on the couch and laughed softly. "She's something else, isn't she?"

"Yeah, she is," Claire replied, suddenly exhausted. Fatigue was beginning to replace the adrenaline in her body, and her eyelids felt as if they had weights attached to them. She sat next to Camille and rubbed her forehead, a gesture she always associated with her father, who, when he was tired, used to rub his head until his thin grey hair spiked out in all directions, like the crown on the Statue of Liberty.

"You look worn out," said Camille. "Did you sleep at all?"

"Not much."

"Well, I think we're in good hands with Detective Hansom. *Je le trouve très sympatique . . .*" Camille added.

"Yes," Claire agreed. "He is very nice."

Camille laughed. "I always do that."

"Do what?"

"Say things in French when they're a little . . . embarrassing. So you speak French?"

"Yes," said Claire. "A little—not like you."

"So you like our detective?"

The voice came from behind them, and Claire turned to see Jack Mulligan leaning against the double sliding doors that led to the dining room. They had been pulled partially closed by Detective Hansom the night before.

"Good morning, Jack," Claire said, wondering how long he had been standing there.

"Good morning," Mulligan replied, sauntering toward them. Claire sensed something threatening in his presence, but thought maybe she was just reacting to what she had heard about him.

"Well, I've always said there was no accounting for taste," he continued, settling himself in one of the overstuffed armchairs on either side of the couch. "I used to try to figure out what women liked, but I've stopped trying. Some things just defy logic."

"Oh, it's really very simple," Camille replied sweetly. "If you want to know what women go for, think of the opposite of what you are."

For a split second his face remained expressionless, but then his mouth softened and he laughed. "*Touché*. Well parried. I didn't mean to imply that women are the only ones who are illogical, of course. Men have their share of it— some men, anyway."

"But not you?" said Claire.

"Oh, I have my moments . . . I have my moments."

Jack looked around the room, and in spite of her dislike of the man, Claire noticed that he had a handsome profile—straight nose, high forehead, and a strong chin under the white beard. "Are we the only ones up?" he said, running a hand through his thick white hair. Once again Claire noticed the missing fingers, and was burning to ask how he lost them.

"No, you are not." This time they all turned, and saw Two Joe standing on the porch, speaking to them through the screen door. He opened the door and entered the house.

He wore his broad-brimmed black leather hat and was sweating heavily.

"Hello, Two Joe," said Camille as he settled his bulky body into the other armchair.

"Good morning," he answered, removing his hat and wiping the sweat off his broad forehead with a blue kerchief.

"You look like you've just been for a walk," said Claire.

"I have," he answered, offering no further information. Claire thought he looked preoccupied. Maybe she would talk to him later, alone, but not with Jack here.

Camille looked down the hall. "I wonder what's keeping them so long?" she said, but just then they heard Meredith's voice from down the hall.

"See, the fact that there's no evidence of forced entry suggests three possibilities: 1) Maya knew her killer, and let him in; 2) she left the bathroom door unlocked for some reason; and 3) he was waiting for her in that little shower stall." Meredith entered the living room and stood looking at the little group gathered around the fireplace. "Hello, everyone," she said, smiling. She was in her element. Detective Hansom stood in the doorway behind her.

"Well, Inspector, how's it going?" Jack Mulligan asked cheerfully. *He's not a bit upset at this tragedy,* thought Claire. *In fact, he's enjoying it.*

"Detective, not Inspector," Hansom answered wearily. "Do you think I might have some more of that coffee?" he said to Camille.

"Of course!" she said brightly, jumping up from the couch.

"Could you bring me some cookies?" said Meredith.

"Meredith," Claire suggested, "instead of asking people to wait on you, why don't you go get some for everyone?"

"Oh, all *right.*" Meredith sighed, and followed Camille into the kitchen. Detective Hansom sat heavily on the red leather hassock just in front of the hearth. A little puff of ashes rose and settled again on the stones. The hearth was cold now, but Claire remembered how the fire had burned late into the night, the embers glowing like red eyes in the dark.

"So, Detective, how's it going?" Jack repeated.

Hansom looked at him. "It's early yet," he said. "I can't really—"

"Discuss it with the suspects?"

Hansom sighed. "I didn't say that, sir."

"But we *are* all potential suspects? You don't really believe it was an outsider, do you?"

"Not this time." Two Joe's voice, low and soft, seemed to come from deep inside him. They all turned to look at him, but just then Camille and Meredith returned from the kitchen. Meredith carried a dinner plate full of cookies.

"Here," she said, plopping it down on the coffee table, "help yourselves."

After another cup of coffee Detective Hansom left, accompanied as far as his car by both Camille and Meredith.

"I hope the tape is a useful clue," Meredith said as they stepped out onto the porch.

"So do I," said the detective, his face grim. "This killer deserves to be caught, and I intend to catch him."

Shortly after Detective Hansom left, another uniformed officer arrived to relieve Officer Connors, who had guarded the crime scene all night. By that time most of the residents were awake. They wandered around the house looking dazed, talking quietly to each other. A few people tried to work, but mostly they sat on the porch clutching cups of cold coffee, faces haggard and pale from lack of sleep. Liza had put Claire's seminars on hold until further notice.

Meredith lurked around the crime scene all morning. No one was allowed near it, but she sniffed around the catwalk and the woods that surrounded the artists' studios at the end of the catwalk.

Liza and Claire were sitting on the living-room couch talking when Evelyn Gardner came swooping in through the front door, her face set in a tragic mask.

"I came as *soon* as I heard!" she bellowed. "This is *so* upsetting; nothing like this has ever happened here!"

Claire noticed that she wasn't too upset to wear makeup

and jewelry. She wore an expensive black silk pantsuit; her lashes glistened with mascara, her wide mouth was outlined in red, and her hair was elaborately coiffed, not a strand out of place. Evelyn would have been perfectly at home on the Upper East Side of Manhattan, but in Woodstock she looked out of place. The only other woman at Ravenscroft Claire had seen wearing lipstick was Camille; even glamorous Maya had only dabbed her blond lashes with a little mascara.

"You poor *thing*," Evelyn said, throwing herself down next to Liza. "It must have been terrible!"

"It was worse for Claire," Liza replied. "She found the body."

"You *did*? Oh, good Lord, that must have been absolutely traumatic!"

Claire didn't want to play into Evelyn's little drama, so she just shrugged. Claire knew her type: some people just thrived on a crisis, no matter what kind.

"I already called Maya's family," said Liza. "They're shipping the body out to Minnesota."

Evelyn shuddered. "Ugh. That's where she's from—Minnesota?"

"Yes. We're going to have a little memorial service here for her tonight if you'd like to come."

"I wouldn't *miss* it," said Evelyn. Then she said in a low voice, "Do they—do they think she . . . ?"

"She was murdered," Liza replied.

Claire thought Liza emphasized the word *murder* to shock Evelyn, but Evelyn did not look shocked.

"Well, I'm just so *sorry* you had to come up here for *this*!" Evelyn said to Claire. There was a pause, then she got up, brushing the cat hairs from her clothes. Claire noticed with satisfaction that Ralph's white hair really showed up on black silk. "Well," Evelyn said, walking briskly toward the front door, "if there's anything I can do, please call me! Meanwhile, I'll inform the Guild at our weekly meeting."

"I'll come to the meeting if you like," Liza offered, escorting her to the door.

"All right; you can tell them exactly what happened."

"As best I can," said Liza. "No one knows what really happened."

Except the murderer, thought Claire.

"Well, *il existe toujours la mort dans la vie,*" said Evelyn in a deep, dramatic voice. "Death exists even in the middle of life." She laid a hand on Liza's shoulder, then turned and went down the steps to her car. Claire and Liza watched her drive off in her jazzy little red Chevy.

"Well," said Liza, "at least *that's* over." She paused, squinting into the midday sun, which was winning its battle with the clouds, shining bravely through the trees, causing a thin mist to rise from the soggy earth. "Is it just me, or does Evelyn seem to regard life as one big *performance*?"

Claire shook her head. "It's not you."

Just then Meredith came striding around the corner of the house carrying something. "Look what I found by the crime scene!" she crowed triumphantly, holding up a crushed cigarette butt. Claire bent over to examine the stub, and immediately recognized the elegant gold filter of a Sobraine Black Russian.

Chapter 9

The next day Claire helped Liza in the garden all morning, weeding around the pink impatiens and coleus that grew in the shady areas around the outbuildings in back of Ravenscroft.

"It's therapeutic, gardening—or at least that's what I tell myself," Liza said, wiping the sweat off her face, which was beginning to freckle in the late-morning sun.

"I think it is." Claire carefully pulled a fat worm clinging to the roots of some weeds and deposited him on a clod of overturned dirt. He wriggled down into the dark soil gratefully, his shiny pink body twisting and writhing in the cool earth.

"It's a way of negating death, planting something," said Liza, panting from the heat as she pulled a clump of weeds from the ground. "And since I'm never going to have children, this is as close as I'll get to procreation, I guess . . ."

Claire looked at Liza. Her big friendly face was covered with a thin layer of grime and sweat. "Do you feel bad about that?" she said, surprised at herself for asking something so intimate.

Liza straightened up and removed her leather gardening gloves. "It's too damn hot for these. No, I don't feel bad . . .

though Sherry and I do talk about adoption." She paused and cocked her head to one side. "What's it like—do you mind if I ask? I mean, Meredith—I know she's not—you know . . . but you seem very close, almost as though she *was,* you know what I mean?"

Claire laughed softly. "Yes, I know what you mean. I've thought about it a lot, about whether there was some way to—formalize our relationship, but after all, she does live with her father and stepmother."

"By the way, where is she?"

"When I left her she was on the porch reading a book on physics. She reads all the time."

Liza paused, and a thin little smile crept onto her face. "She's . . . different, isn't she?"

Claire laughed. "Oh, yes, and she'd be the first one to admit it. She's proud of it. She has no time for most of her peers; she calls them 'alien beings.' "

"Well, bless her. I just hope she makes it into adulthood without too much trauma."

"Now, *that* would insult her. She thinks she's already there."

Liza laughed, and the sound echoed hollowly off the out-buildings and disappeared into the woods surrounding the property. Just then Ralph emerged from behind the toolshed, his belly skimming the long grass, a predatory look in his eyes: he was hunting. Claire pointed to him.

"Look. Even Ralph has turned into a different animal up here. In town all he thinks about is food; but now look at him."

"He's still thinking about food, only this time it's still moving."

Claire laughed. "Yeah, I guess you're right. It's just that—well, life suddenly seems so . . . *unsafe,* I guess."

Liza squinted at her. The sun had climbed up over the tree line and was shining brightly in a cloudless sky. "When did it ever feel safe?"

"Oh, in childhood, I guess . . . for a while."

"Really? You had a nice childhood."

"Yeah. Yeah, I guess I did . . ."

"I had a strange visit last night," said Liza, pulling at a stubborn weed with long roots.

"Oh?"

"Yeah . . . it was odd."

"What? What was strange?" said Meredith, appearing suddenly around the side of the house. "What—are you afraid it's unsuitable for my young ears?" she said, seeing Liza's hesitation.

"Meredith, Liza and I are talking," said Claire.

Meredith threw herself down on the grass. "God, you sound just like my *father*," she said with as much disgust as she could muster. She lay on her stomach kicking at the ground with her bare toes.

"Grown-ups have a tendency to all sound alike," said Liza. "We're boring that way."

Meredith rolled over onto her elbow and looked at Liza. "You should have kids. You'd be a good parent."

Feeling a little jealous, Claire said, "Meredith, why don't you go in and make some tea for us all and we'll come in and join you in a few minutes?"

Meredith got up and brushed herself off. "Okay. But don't think I don't see your technique; you're distracting me so you guys can talk."

"Curses, foiled again!" said Liza.

"Meredith—" Claire began, but Meredith was already heading toward the house.

"I'm going, I'm going," she said.

"And put some shoes on," Claire called after her.

They heard the screen door bang shut and Liza laughed softly. "You might as well be her mother," she said. "She's playing you as if you were."

What about me? thought Claire. *How am I playing it?* "So what was your visit?" she said to Liza.

"Well, it was Evelyn Gardner."

"Evelyn? What did she want?"

Liza stood up and brushed the dirt from her overalls. "At first it was hard to tell; she was pretty upset."

"Upset?"

"It seems she discovered some photographs in the glove compartment of Roger's car."

"What kind of photos?"

Liza ran her hand across her forehead, where little beads of sweat had gathered under her blond bangs. "Kiddie porn."

Claire swallowed hard. "Oh, God."

"Yeah, I know; it is pretty upsetting. I don't blame Evelyn for needing to talk to someone; I just don't know why it had to be me. I mean, doesn't she have any friends?"

"Well, maybe it's the kind of thing you can't talk about to friends."

Liza shrugged and scratched her shoulder. "Maybe."

"What's she going to do about it?"

"I guess she'll have to confront him about it. Either that or go to the police."

"Wow. That's the first clue she had about it?"

"Apparently. I mean, I didn't ask about the details of their personal life. Frankly, I didn't want to know."

"I don't blame you."

"Well, I don't envy her, that's for sure." Liza bent down and picked up her gardening tools. "Come on," she said, "let's go have some lunch."

Meals at Ravenscroft were a hodgepodge of various kinds of cuisine: brown rice and broccoli were ubiquitous, and there was a conspicuous absence of animal protein. From what Claire could see, about half the people at the house were vegetarians, and almost no one ate red meat. (Liza called it "Arts Colony Chic.") While Claire thought the emphasis on vegetables was good, after days of looking at plates of vegetarian stir-fry, she longed for a big juicy steak.

The major exception to this spartan aesthetic was Terry Nordstrom, who deliberately flaunted his Middle American tastes before this collection of "effete artistes," as he called them. And so as people chomped their kale and scallions and Chinese cabbage, the kitchen would fill with the aroma of Terry's London broil and pork ribs, clogging the air with the odor of grilled flesh; even upstairs in the hallway you could smell the thick aroma of carnivorous cooking.

If the other residents were irritated by this—and Claire

was pretty sure Terry hoped they were—they said nothing. When she and Liza entered the kitchen, the only person at the counter was Gary Robinson. He wore a black sweatshirt, which looked at though it had been ironed, over crisply pristine khakis. His shoes—he wore penny loafers without socks—were shiny and unspoiled, and even his hands were immaculately manicured. Most of the painters at Ravenscroft had chafed, paint-stained hands with torn nails, red from chemicals and dotted with a myriad of cuts from matting knives.

Liza must have been thinking the same thing Claire was, because she said, "Gary, why do you always look like you stepped out of the pages of *GQ*?"

Gary put down the paring knife he was using to cut into a grapefruit and went to the sink to rinse his hands. "Just because I'm a painter doesn't mean I have to advertise the fact by looking like a slob."

"But your hands," said Liza, taking off her sun hat and wiping her forehead. "How do you manage to keep them so—*clean*?"

Gary shrugged. "I use gloves when I paint."

"It doesn't affect your technique?" Claire said.

Gary looked at her, his eyes steady behind his wire-rim glasses. "I have them custom-made; they're a very thin cotton blend."

"By the way," said Liza, rummaging through the cupboard under the sink, "has anyone seen the kitchen gloves? I can't find them."

"The big yellow ones?" said Claire.

"Yeah. They disappeared a couple of days ago."

"No," Claire replied. "I didn't really use them."

Liza stood up and wiped a thin line of sweat from her upper lip. "I just can't understand where they might have gone."

"Maybe they were borrowed by one of the painters," Claire suggested.

"Or by the murderer," Meredith said, sauntering into the kitchen with a miserable-looking Ralph tucked under her arm. "Just the thing if you're going to strangle someone without leaving fingerprints."

Gary looked at Meredith. An unreadable expression crossed his usually impassive face; it might have been alarm, or perhaps distaste. He picked up his grapefruit and left the kitchen. If Meredith noticed his reaction, she paid no attention to it. She disappeared into the pantry and emerged with a box of Mint Milanos.

"Brain food," she said, and ducked out of the kitchen just as Tahir Hasonovic entered it from the back door. In contrast to Gary, Tahir always looked a little disheveled, as though he had things on his mind other than neatness. His black hair sprang out from his head in thick ringlets, and his beard was so dark that even by this hour he looked unshaven. His clothes were dingy in the way that clothes get when they have been washed too often, and he wore scuffed running shoes that had once been white a very long time ago.

"Hello," he said, smiling shyly. Liza walked up to him and put her hand on his shoulder.

"Hi, Tahir," she said. "How are you holding up?" She was a perfect choice for this job, Claire thought. With her easy manner and warm Southern accent, she was someone you wanted to confide in. After Maya's death she remained steady as a rock, and gave the impression that she was there for the residents who needed her.

"I'm doing okay," Tahir answered, though Claire thought he looked tired—haunted, she would have said, with circles under his big dark eyes. She supposed that anyone who had lived through what he had might look that way. She could only imagine what those dark eyes had seen.

"Well, we've just got to do our best to stay in there," said Liza. "In fact" she continued, looking at Claire, "I was thinking we might resume classes and meetings with you today. I think it might be good for all of us to try to move on."

"Okay," said Claire, "that's a good idea."

"What do you think, Tahir?"

Tahir looked down at his hands. "I think that would be good," he said softly. "It's not good to dwell too much on these things . . . there is so much sadness in life, but we must try to rise above it."

"Rise above what?"

Claire turned to see Jack Mulligan standing at the kitchen door. He wore a broad-brimmed green leather hat and a khaki hunting jacket. *Safari Nazi,* thought Claire, but she said nothing.

"We were just talking about resuming classes," Liza replied brusquely, and with one stroke neatly halved a honeydew melon.

"Capital idea." Jack removed his hat and put it on the counter. "I was beginning to get bored staring at my computer."

Liza didn't reply, but walked into the back pantry where the refrigerators were kept. Her dislike of Jack was so strong that Claire could almost see her twitching with the discomfort of being near him. Even Tahir retreated to the other side of the kitchen, busying himself over one of the two stoves. Claire herself felt a certain nervousness in Jack's presence, though she didn't always trust her intuition about people anymore—not after Robert. Robert, whose hands were so sure and firm on a piano keyboard, on her body, around her neck. *Being done, there is no pause.*

"What's going on in here?" Meredith stood in the doorway, a book under her arm, her kinky orange hair shooting out in all directions, as though on an escape attempt from her head.

"I don't believe we've been formally introduced," Jack said gallantly, offering his hand. "I'm Jack Mulligan." Meredith looked at him through narrowed eyes and took his hand.

"Meredith Lawrence."

"Ah, yes; you're the child genius."

Meredith's eyes widened and she blushed. "I'm thirteen years old, hardly a child," she answered briskly, but Claire could tell she was pleased.

"I believe Mozart had already composed several symphonies by the time he was your age," Jack remarked.

"I don't write music, I solve crimes," Meredith replied crisply.

"Do you? Well, that's just capital. The world needs more people like you."

"I haven't ruled you out as a suspect," Meredith said. "And the avuncular act won't work on me; I'm from Connecticut."

Jack laughed, a big full-bellied sound, the laugh of a man who was pleased with himself, who slept well at night. "Well, well, I'm glad to hear it. I thought Connecticut only produced golf matrons and bankers."

Meredith screwed her face up. "Very funny."

"Well, back to work," Jack said cheerfully, putting his hat back on. "I have miles to go before I sleep."

"You do look a little like Robert Frost," said Meredith.

Jack looked at Claire and smiled. "She *is* smart," he said, then tipped his hat and left the kitchen.

Tahir turned around from the stove and Claire could see that he was trembling.

"Are you all right?" she said.

"Yes," he replied in a low voice. "I just—I just cannot stand that man. Every time I am around him, I feel like killing him."

"Why?" said Meredith.

Liza came back into the kitchen carrying a yellow ceramic bowl. "Because Jack Mulligan is a Nazi," she said, placing the bowl on the counter.

"*What?*" said Meredith. "How can—what do you mean?"

Liza poured the broth into a saucepan and put it on the other stove. "Jack Mulligan believes that the Holocaust never happened."

Meredith looked at Claire. "Is that true?"

"That's what everybody says. I have yet to discuss it with him."

"A man like Jack Mulligan has no idea what it is to suffer," Tahir said, his voice shaking, "no idea at all. I would like him to spend a day just once as I have spent it. In the Bosnian camps he would not last a month. He—he . . . I'm sorry," he said, his voice thick. "I cannot talk about it; it is too soon."

He took his plate and left the kitchen the way he had come, through the back door leading to the garden and the back studios. Meredith turned to Liza. "He was in the Bosnian camps?"

Liza nodded. "He survived, but several members of his family died."

Meredith shook her head. "Wow."

"All right, how about some nice chicken soup, just like Mama used to make?" Liza held up a steaming pot of broth.

"Smells great," said Claire.

The memorial service that evening was simple but moving. Liza collected every candleholder she could find in the house and made a little altar over the fireplace. Claire and Camille spent the afternoon picking wildflowers, which grew abundantly around the house. They filled Ravenscroft's many vases with bouquets of Queen Anne's lace, honeysuckle, Indian paintbrush, black-eyed Susan, and wild daisies. Maya's possessions had been confiscated by the police, but Sherry had taken photos of everyone at Ravenscroft. She and Liza made a display of pictures: Maya at breakfast; Maya and Sherry returning from a walk in the woods; Maya and Terry on the front porch, smiling in the sunshine that spilled over the eaves onto their faces.

Even though she had barely known Maya, the pictures filled Claire with a heavy sadness; to think that someone so alive as the woman in these photos now lay dead in a cold metal drawer somewhere was deeply disturbing. Photographs in general made Claire uneasy; to her they always represented times gone by, frozen moments lost forever. She thought again of the jokes about Maya as Dorian Gray, with her "picture in the attic" . . . in the end, her youthfulness had not saved her.

Now, as she sat among the little huddle of people in the living room, she felt comforted by the presence of others. She thought not for the first time that funerals are not so much to honor the dead as they are to comfort the living. There is a reassurance in a coming together of people, even such an odd group as this one. Everyone had been invited to say a few words, and Tahir Hasonovic was speaking now.

"She was a gentle soul," he said softly, his sad eyes drooping, "and she had a sweetness which was more than just her physical beauty."

Terry Nordstrom sat by himself sobbing quietly. Claire felt sorry for him. He might be angry, and he might be annoying, but in sorrow he was just a sad little man. There was something about the basic emotions that equalizes everyone: a man suffering is in some essential way like every other man who has ever suffered.

Claire looked around the room. Liza and Sherry sat together holding hands. Sherry's eyes were red and swollen and her upper lip trembled as Tahir spoke.

"She had a way of making us all feel . . . well, happy. That's the only way I can express it."

Two Joe sat on a straight-backed chair, rigid and silent as a stone, his big hands clasped on his lap. He wore his medicine wheel on its leather string, and several strands of brightly colored beads hung from his neck. Next to him was Camille, chic in a black silk kimono and black tights. Gary Robinson and Billy Trimble sat across from them. Gary stared down at the floor, a petulant look on his face, but Billy's eyes wandered as ever around the room, settling on nothing in particular, searching for God knew what. Jack Mulligan sat slightly apart from the rest of them, a kind of half smirk on his face.

Evelyn and Roger Gardner shared the couch with Marcel. On the handyman's big friendly face the emotion of sadness sat so awkwardly that Claire had an impulse to pet him as one might pet a big dog. Evelyn had changed her outfit: she wore an elegant black dress with black stockings, the only splash of color a heavy green jade necklace. Roger looked self-conscious and miserable, his perfectly smooth pink hands clasped around his knees. It was hard for Claire not to stare at him; she imagined him poring over the pictures of naked children he kept stuffed in his glove compartment.

Next to Claire, Meredith squirmed and fidgeted, her body racked with restless kinetic energy.

"Is it almost finished?" she whispered, and Claire shook her head.

"Be patient, Meredith; it won't be long."

Two Joe rose and gave a brief Native American blessing. To Claire's surprise, when he finished, Camille crossed herself. Claire felt Meredith's elbow digging into her ribs.

"Did you see that? Camille crossed herself."

"Lower your voice," Claire whispered.

"I thought she was a lapsed Catholic."

Claire shrugged. "Maybe old habits die hard."

Liza got up to say a few words, then they all adjourned for some wine and hors d'oeuvres left over from the party two nights before. As Claire stood sipping Merlot, she couldn't believe that she had only been at Ravenscroft for three days. Already it seemed like a lifetime since she chugged into the driveway in a pounding rainstorm.

That night Claire lay in bed, the air heavy with Meredith's thick breathing. She stared into the darkness and thought about parallel universes. Maybe Stephen Hawking was right, and this was not the only possible history. Maybe by some act of will she could transport herself to another history in which no one died a violent death at someone else's hands, where no one in this house of sleepers was a murderer.

The next day was bright and sunny, and the Ravenscroft residents looked a little dazed, as if maybe they had just dreamed everything after all. But the yellow police tape labeled "Crime Scene" still cordoned off the downstairs bathroom, and all day policemen came and went, their patrol cars stirring up waves of dust on the dirt road outside the house.

Meredith had been trying all morning to get Detective Hansom on the phone, to ask about the phone message she had discovered.

"He may not tell you anything, Meredith," Claire said, but the girl wasn't deterred. She kept calling the station house until finally Billy Trimble came down to use the phone and she was forced to relinquish it.

Now she was seated at the piano in the dining room, playing the C-major prelude from Bach's *Well-Tempered Clavier.* Claire recognized it because she had played it as a child. Claire noted with satisfaction that Meredith didn't play particularly well. She did play with conviction, however, and when she got a passage right, she phrased it in such a way that you felt compelled to listen.

Claire stood at the kitchen counter making egg salad sandwiches. Meredith loved egg salad sandwiches. She once confessed to Claire that her mother had made them for her when she was ill, and that they were for her a kind of "madeleine experience." Claire was afraid to ask if the girl had actually read Proust—she doubted it; even Meredith had her limits—but she was flattered that Meredith had shared that memory with her, and so she made egg salad whenever possible.

Ralph sauntered into the kitchen, perched himself neatly at Claire's feet, and complained about the general state of things.

"What?" said Claire, mixing mayonnaise in with the eggs. You could never put too much mayonnaise in anything as far as Meredith was concerned. "You already had breakfast. You want some egg salad?"

Ralph responded by rolling over onto his back and licking his stomach.

"Oh, that's charming," said Claire, slicing a loaf of whole wheat bread. She had never seen so many natural-food stores and restaurants as in Woodstock; she had bought this bread at the Whole Grain Baker, a little store tucked away in a corner of Tinker Street.

Marcel appeared at the kitchen door. He wore a green-and-blue-checked flannel shirt, jeans, and work boots. Claire wondered if he owned anything but flannel shirts; he had even worn one to the memorial service.

"Hi, Marcel."

"Hi, there," he said, bending over to scratch Ralph's stomach. The cat let his head fall back and wriggled his body in response.

"He likes you," said Claire, "and he doesn't like everyone."

"Really?" said Marcel. "I guess cats are like that. My dog Ellie likes everyone. Long as they pay attention to her, she likes 'em."

"How is she, by the way?"

"Oh, she's fine. I think she just ate somethin' that disagreed with her. She's okay now, though." He stood up and went to the sink to wash his hands. "I gotta be careful; cat hairs make my eyes water if I don't wash my hands."

"Actually, it's the dander, not the hair, that people are allergic to." Meredith stood in the doorway on one leg, the other one folded behind her, like an egret. "Leg's asleep," she said in response to Claire's look. "Always happens when I play the piano."

"Maybe you're sittin' funny," said Marcel. "Is that egg salad?"

"Yes," said Claire, spooning it onto the bread. "Would you like some?"

"I love egg salad," he answered wistfully. "But thanks . . . I just came to talk to Liza. Is she around?"

"She drove to town to buy coffee." Meredith was now pounding her thigh with her fist. "Ow, ow, ow."

"Why don't you have a sandwich and wait for her?" Claire said. "There's plenty."

Marcel looked at the egg salad longingly. "Well . . . all right, if you're sure there's enough."

"Eggs are cheap," said Meredith, "like talk."

"What?" said Marcel.

"Talk. You know—talk is cheap."

"Oh, yeah, right. I've heard that."

They took their sandwiches out to the porch, sitting at the long picnic table, its wood scratched and scarred from years of use. Claire had made Earl Grey iced tea—Meredith's favorite—and she poured them all tall frosty glasses with plenty of ice. Meredith loaded a plate full of dill pickles to go with the sandwiches. Meredith loved dill pickles.

"This is great," said Marcel, his mouth full of egg salad. "How d'you make it?"

"It's real simple," said Claire. "Just some mayonnaise, a little garlic salt, and eggs. It's my mother's recipe."

"Mmm," said Marcel. "Give her my compliments."

"She's dead," said Meredith abruptly.

"Oh, I'm sorry," he mumbled, looking embarrassed.

"Claire and I are both orphans," Meredith said, taking a large bite of pickle.

"Really?"

"Meredith, your father is still alive," said Claire.

Meredith shrugged. "So? He's been possessed by the Wicked Witch; I might as well be an orphan."

"He's possessed by a witch?" said Marcel.

"Meredith calls her stepmother the Wicked—"

"The Wicked Witch of Greenwich," Meredith interrupted.

"That's cute," said Marcel. "That's funny."

"You wouldn't feel that way if you had to live with her," said Meredith. "Oh, guess what?" she added, the words partially obscured by a mouthful of egg salad.

"Meredith, swallow *before* you talk," said Claire.

"But how come Marcel—" Meredith began, but Claire glared at her. "Oh, all *right,*" she said, swallowing with elaborate exaggeration. "What I was going to say was that Camille told me that Maya took a bath every night before bed."

"Really? Did anyone else know that?"

Meredith shrugged. "Maybe. Camille knew because she and Maya talked about it once; see, a lot of people take showers in the morning but Maya said that in Sweden people liked baths at night to help them sleep because it was so cold."

"Oh, that reminds me—you had any more trouble with the water heater?" said Marcel.

"I don't think so," said Claire. She turned to Meredith. "Does Detective Hansom know what Camille told you?"

"Camille says she was too upset to remember what she said that night." Meredith flicked a tiny piece of eggshell into the thicket of greenery surrounding the porch. This was followed by a flurry of wings and some agitated twittering, and then the inhabitants of the bushes settled down again. "But if Hansom would answer his phone messages, *I'd* tell him."

"You've been calling the police station?" said Marcel. "How come?"

"Because it's clear that they need a little *help*," she replied, getting up from the table. "May I please be excused?"

"Sure," said Claire.

"I'm going to go see if Billy's done with the phone yet," Meredith said, taking her plate inside.

Marcel stood up and patted his flat stomach. "Well, that was great—but I gotta get back to work."

"I'll tell Liza you were looking for her," said Claire.

"Oh, thanks. It's nothing important. I'll call back later."

"Okay."

"Thanks for the sandwiches."

"Anytime."

As she watched Marcel climb into his truck, Claire noticed there was something in the way he moved that reminded her of Robert . . . hard, muscular Robert, whose body was as beautiful as his soul was evil.

"Hello, Redbird."

The screen door slammed behind her and Claire turned to see Two Joe standing on the porch.

"Hi."

He sat down on the bench beside her. "I made you a medicine wheel," he said, pulling from his pocket a woven pendant like the one hanging around his neck. Only the colors were different: his was mostly red and yellow, while this one was made up of blues and greens.

"It's beautiful; thank you," she said, examining it. It was very light, and twirled in the breeze on its leather string when she held it up to look at it.

"Wear it for protection," said Two Joe, "even at night. Take it off only to bathe."

He slipped it around her neck. As he did, his fingers grazed her neck, and she felt her flesh shiver in response. It weighed barely an ounce, and yet once it was around her neck, she felt as if she had put on another garment.

"That's good," he said, stepping back to look. "That will be powerful medicine for you." There was something in the way he looked at her that made the blood rise to her face.

It wasn't exactly sexual . . . or was it? Whatever it was, it had an effect . . . and she supposed he knew that.

"What's it made of besides twine?" she said.

"Bent cactus needles. You wet them and bend them—if you know how."

"Where do you find cactus needles around here?"

"They are from my home in Arizona. I carry them with me wherever I go. You never know when someone may need a medicine wheel."

Meredith came out from the house, letting the screen door slam behind her. "Hiya, Two Joe."

"Hello."

"Cool!" she said, seeing the pendant around Claire's neck. "Can I see it?"

She bent over to look, the sun spilling onto her thin, pale arms with their light dusting of blond freckles. "Cool. Did you make it?" she said to Two Joe.

He nodded. "I did. Redbird needs protection."

"Redbird?"

"That's her Indian name."

"Oooo, can I have one—can I have an Indian name?"

Two Joe thought for a moment. "I will call you Lightning Flash."

"Cool! I like that—Lightning Flash! That is *way* cool. Now, if camp had stuff like that, I wouldn't have left. Lightning Flash," she repeated softly. "I want people to call me that. Remind me to tell my father that my Indian name is Lightning Flash, will you, Redbird?"

"Okay," said Claire, laughing. "And now Redbird has things to do, if Lightning Flash doesn't mind washing the lunch dishes."

"Tell me more stuff about being an Indian," said Meredith to Two Joe as they went inside.

"I can see this is going to be the beginning of a beautiful friendship," Claire murmured to herself as the screen door closed behind them.

Chapter 10

L iza wanted to talk to Claire about possibly resuming classes, so she and Meredith were invited over for tea later that day.

Claire and Meredith started across the broad lawn to Liza's cabin, past the row of artists' studios behind Ravenscroft. Gary Robinson was seated on the steps in front of his studio, a pile of wood shavings at his feet. As they got closer, Claire could see that in his right hand he held a small mahogany figurine. In his left hand was a hunting knife. He whittled with a sure, confident movement, the knife digging easily into the soft wood.

"What's that?" said Meredith.

Gary answered without looking up and without pausing in his carving. "It's a Nigerian fertility god."

"Mmm," said Meredith. "That explain the size of its—"

"Come on, Meredith." Claire grabbed her by the wrist. "Liza's waiting for us."

"Nice god you got there," Meredith called over her shoulder. Gary didn't reply.

As Meredith and Claire walked across the lawn they could hear angry voices coming from the cabin.

"It's not good enough!" Claire heard Liza say.

"Oh, fine, Little Miss Perfect!" Sherry answered. "You never had a crush on anyone, I suppose?"

"I just want to know if it's true or not!" Liza said.

Claire cleared her throat loudly as they approached the cabin. The voices ceased abruptly. Claire waited a moment, then knocked on the front door. There was a pause, then Liza came to the door.

"Hi," Claire said, wondering why she hadn't just turned around and gone back when she heard them arguing.

"Hi," Liza replied, opening the door. A moment later Sherry emerged from the bedroom, a backpack slung across her shoulder.

"I'm going out," she said brusquely, with a nod to Meredith and Claire. Claire winced as the screen door whacked against the doorframe behind her as Sherry left.

Awkwardness hung in the air like smoke. Liza stood in the middle of the living room, her big hands hanging at her sides, looking miserable and lost. She wore her gardening overalls and a red kerchief was wound around her forehead. Claire had an impulse to hug her.

"We could come back later—" she began, but Liza shook her head again.

"No, I'm sorry if you heard any of that, but—well, girls will be girls," she said with a forced little laugh.

"We can talk later—really," Claire said, but Liza shook her head.

"No, we really shouldn't put this off anymore. I think it would take everyone's mind off things a little if we started the seminars again, don't you?"

Meredith, busily engaged in looking for the cat under the couch, straightened up and wiped the dust off her hands. "Absolutely," she said. "Nothing like a little learning to take the mind off other things. That's why they keep kids in school so much of the time, you know; it's so they won't think about sex."

"Oh, is that it?" said Liza. "I always wondered."

"Oh, sure," Meredith replied breezily. "Otherwise they'd be f—"

"Meredith!" said Claire.

"Fornicating like pagans," Meredith finished. This time it was Claire who rolled her eyes. Liza just laughed. "Well, they would," Meredith said. "God knows they're not *teaching* us anything worthwhile—at least not in East Haddom, Connecticut."

"That's too bad," said Liza. "Meredith, would you mind making us some tea while we talk? I think there's a bag of Lemon Crunch cookies in the kitchen."

"Sure!" Meredith sprang off toward the kitchen.

"Well done," said Claire. "You have a way with her."

Liza smiled. "I'm glad I have a way with *someone* . . ." She sighed and shook her head. "Sorry," she said. "Self-pity is so unbecoming, isn't it?" She sat down on the couch and unlaced her dirt-spattered gardening shoes. "So do you agree that we should start meeting again for classes?"

"Sure," said Claire. "I mean, that's what I'm here for. Especially if you think it'll help people feel better."

Liza tugged at a muddy shoelace. "Why not? It couldn't hurt. People don't have to come if they don't want to."

Meredith appeared at the door holding a tea tray. *"Voilà,"* she said, though it was apparent from the cookie crumbs around her mouth that she had a head start on the Lemon Crunch cookies. "Oh, I had to sample them to see if they were safe," she said in response to Claire's look. "You never know who might be trying to poison you."

That night Liza made lasagna for everyone. Usually the residents fended for themselves at meals, but Liza was taking her job as "house mother" seriously. "This will be good for morale, I think," she said to Claire that afternoon. "Everyone likes to be cooked for."

The smell of baking cheese simmering in tomato sauce permeated the house, drifting up through the hallways, making Claire salivate, taking her mind off her work. She was trying to read a manuscript, but the prose was not exactly gripping, and her mind kept wandering. Finally, dinnertime arrived, and she gladly put aside her work and went downstairs to help Liza. Two Joe and Meredith were already in the kitchen helping her when she arrived.

"This one is vegetarian," Liza said as she pulled the steaming casserole dish out of the oven, "and this one has meat."

"I'll have some of the one with *meat*," said Meredith, spooning a huge helping onto her plate.

Two Joe shook his head. "I think your eyes are greedier than your stomach."

"Lightning Flash can eat anything," Meredith said, helping herself to salad. "Did you know my Indian name is Lightning Flash?" she said to Sherry, who had just walked in.

Sherry smiled. "Oh, really? What's mine, I wonder . . . Stump of Tree? Chipmunk Cheeks?" Sherry was barely five feet tall, and though she joked about her size, Claire could sense that she was sensitive about it.

"How about Half-a-Glass?" said Camille, putting some wineglasses on a tray. "If he's Two Joe, and you're Sherry, then you can be—"

"Half-a-Glass. I like it," said Sherry. "What do you think, Two Joe?"

Two Joe shrugged. "If you like, it's good."

"But is the glass half-empty or half-full?" said Liza, touching Sherry lightly on the shoulder.

"Oh, the NEA would love this; it's so politically correct. I can just hear the grant papers being shuffled now." Jack Mulligan stood in the hall, hands in his pockets, wearing his usual uniform: khaki pants, green army shirt, and hunting vest. He always looked as though he were about to go on a military maneuver.

"Okay, everybody, come and get it!" Liza yelled, ignoring him. One by one the rest of the residents appeared, a few of them paint-splattered, some looking as though they had just awakened from naps. Everyone still looked exhausted from the events of the last couple of days. Some people were returning to work, but the stress and lack of sleep showed on their faces.

The sun was setting as they gathered on the porch, sitting on the wooden benches on either side of the picnic table. It was a tight squeeze with all of them there, and Meredith jumped up from the table.

"I'll sit over here," she said, pulling one of the canvas directors' chairs up to the coffee table on the other side of the porch.

"I'll join you," Camille offered, taking her plate over and sitting on the daybed. She pulled her legs up under her, neat as a cat.

"Where's Billy?" Sherry looked at Gary, who shrugged.

"I don't know; I haven't seen him."

"Am I my brother's keeper?" muttered Jack.

"What?" said Terry.

"Nothing," said Jack. "Would you please pass the salt?"

Gary handed him the saltshaker. Claire looked over at Tahir, who sat quietly at the far end of the table. She thought he looked particularly tired, with deep circles under his eyes. She couldn't help thinking again what beautiful eyes they were, with their long dark lashes. As usual Tahir was quiet and retiring, a little island of stillness in the midst of the more talkative types like Jack and Terry. Terry was subdued, too, though; ever since Maya's death he had been walking around like a lost soul, forlorn and lonely.

"That's bad for your arteries," said Meredith as Jack poured salt onto his food.

He shrugged. "If one thing doesn't get you, something else will. It's all the same to me."

"That's kind of nihilistic," said Gary.

"No, it's just realistic. We're all going to die, but at least I will have *lived*."

Just then Billy appeared at the screen door with a plate in his hand. "Sorry I'm late. I was in the middle of a painting and I had trouble finding a place to stop."

Claire thought that it was unusual for Billy to be apologetic, but everyone else just nodded. Gary moved over and made a space for Billy to sit between him and Sherry. Billy's usually immaculately groomed hair was mussed, and he looked distracted.

"This is great lasagna," said Camille from the other side of the porch.

"Yes, it is excellent," Two Joe added solemnly.

Just then there was the sound of the phone ringing inside the house.

"I'll get it!" cried Meredith, leaping up from her chair and almost stepping on Ralph, who had chosen that moment to saunter across the porch. He crouched, ears flattened, as she charged past him, the screen door slamming loudly behind her.

"Take it easy," Claire called after her.

Jack Mulligan shook his head. "I don't know how you do it. You're to be congratulated for your patience with her."

"Oh, she's fine," said Sherry, helping herself to more wine. "I've seen much worse kids than her. She's just a little hyperactive."

"I understand she's an orphan," Tahir said quietly from his end of the table.

"Well, her mother died quite tragically not long ago," said Claire, "but she has a father and a stepmother."

"I know what this is like, to lose your mother," said Tahir softly.

"The Grim Reaper comes to all sooner or later," Jack said.

"Yes, but there's a big difference between sooner and later," said Gary, "especially when it's your mother."

"Or anyone you love," added Terry. His face still looked swollen from crying.

Meredith appeared at the door. "It's for you," she said to Camille. "It's a man with a French accent."

Claire saw the color creep up Camille's neck as Meredith said this. But whatever Camille's feelings were, she did not betray them in her voice—which immediately made Claire wonder what she was hiding.

"Thanks," she said simply, and went into the house.

Meredith sat back down and picked at her salad, but Claire could tell she was more interested in Ralph, who sat invitingly just a few feet away. He had his eye on her, though, ready to spring to freedom at any moment.

"Fine people, the French," said Jack, and when no one

responded, he added, "unless any of you have reason to disagree with that."

Tahir looked as if he were about to reply, but just then there was the sound of tires crunching on stones and Evelyn Gardner's natty little red sports car pulled up in front of the house. The sun was sending its last feeble rays of light through the trees as she climbed out of the car, shielding her face from the glare.

"Hello, everyone!" she called out cheerfully. "I'm sorry if I picked a bad time to come. I just wanted to see how you all were doing after—well . . . *you know.*" She closed the car door and took a few steps up the porch. "Mmm—that smells *delicious,*" she said, eyeing the lasagna greedily.

"Have some," said Sherry. "There's plenty more."

"Oh, no, I *couldn't,*" Evelyn replied unconvincingly.

"Go ahead," said Liza, "there's lots."

"Well, if you *insist,* I don't see how I can resist. It looks so *good!*" she said, disappearing inside.

Sherry rolled her eyes. "Her timing is impeccable—as usual."

"Oh, she's a freeloader, is she?" said Jack.

"Shh," Liza whispered. "Let's not talk about it now."

Gary smiled. "She's a woman of existential hungers. I understand that," he added, with a glance at Billy.

Evelyn reappeared at the door with a plate piled high with food. "I'll sit over here," she said, pulling one of the director's chairs up to the coffee table, next to Meredith. "So, how *is* everyone doing?"

"We're okay," said Sherry.

"Considering that someone in this house is a murderer," Meredith said calmly.

"Meredith!" Claire said sharply.

"Well, nobody really has an alibi," Meredith added sulkily.

"That doesn't mean—" Claire began, but Jack interrupted her.

"Oh, she's probably right, you know," he said, looking around the table to judge the impact of his remark. Terry was staring fiercely at his plate, Tahir was biting his lower lip, and several of the others looked distinctly uncomfortable.

But Billy Trimble laughed softly. "The only real question, then, is who is more prone to violence—painters or writers?"

The screen door opened and Camille came back onto the porch. "Definitely writers," she said, pouring herself some wine. "They're much more violent than painters. Painters only mutilate themselves, like Van Gogh." Claire thought that Camille's cheeks were redder, and her eyes brighter than before, though it was hard to tell in the dim evening twilight.

"It *could* have been a stranger," Liza said tentatively, but Jack shook his head.

"I think we all know down deep that's not likely. Most murders are committed by people who know the victim."

"You're right," said Meredith breezily. "I personally think it's most likely someone who knew her—especially if forensics hasn't shown any sign of sexual assault. Whoever stole her journal—"

Terry Nordstrom rose abruptly, sending his chair flying behind him. "I don't need to listen to any more of this!" he said, his voice tight with rage, his whole body trembling. He strode from the porch, heading down the steps, past Evelyn's car and toward the woods.

"Terry, it'll be dark soon! Where are you going?" Liza called after him. He didn't answer, but continued along Camelot Road until it entered the woods.

There was silence on the porch as they all listened to his footsteps becoming fainter, disappearing into the trees, swallowed up by the sounds of the forest. Then Sherry spoke.

"Wow, I guess he really loved her."

"Someone stole Maya's journal?" said Jack Mulligan.

Meredith shrugged. "Yep. And I think whoever stole her journal is probably the murderer."

No one said anything. At that moment the sun dipped behind the side of the mountain, sending a chill across the little group on the porch. The murmurings of nighttime forest creatures, just beginning to stir, filtered through the canopy of leaves surrounding the porch, enveloping everyone in the sounds of the woods at night.

That night Claire decided to call Wally; she needed to hear his voice. She waited until everyone else was in bed. She wanted him all to herself; she didn't want Jack Mulligan or anyone else overhearing her or making sardonic remarks over breakfast. Just as she had guarded her passions carefully when she was a child, now she felt the impulse to protect her feelings for Wally from this ersatz family of strangers. And so with Meredith snoring softly in the dark beside her, she got out of bed and crept downstairs through the darkened house. A pale shaft of moonlight fell across the statue of Diana in the living room. Her polished shoulders glimmered in the dim light, her bow and arrow cocked, aiming at unseen prey. It was past midnight as Claire tiptoed into the dining room, still and silent as a graveyard. Moonlight spilled through the windows and across the vacant chairs, bone white in the pale light, stiff and expectant as tombstones. The smell of damp wood combined with the faint odor of mildew seeping from the floorboards. Claire stepped into the phone alcove, her palms sweating as she picked up the receiver.

She dialed his mother's number, glad for the three-hour time difference; in San Francisco, it was only just after nine o'clock.

"Hello?" a woman's voice answered.

"Mrs. Jackson? This is Claire Rawlings."

"Oh, hello, Claire. Wally's just in the other room. I'll get him."

Claire had never spoken to Wally's mother before, but she recognized the same New England reserve, a touch of wariness in the voice. Claire forced her breathing, which was shallow, deeper into her lungs. She felt a buzzing sensation in her head—whether it was tension or excitement or the lateness of the hour she didn't know—but all her senses felt sharpened. Even the backs of the dining-room

chairs looked sharp, their white edges clearly outlined
against the blackness all around them. She stood listening
to the old house creak and groan around her. The wooden
floor was cold underneath her bare feet, and she was sorry
she hadn't thought to put on a pair of socks. Nights were
so much cooler up here than in the city, and she hadn't yet
gotten used to the change.

"Hello?"

Claire's heart quickened at the sound of Wally's voice.

"Oh," she said. "Oh, Wally," and then she could not stop
the flow of tears that pushed their way from behind her
eyes.

"What is it, Claire, what's wrong?" he said, and she
hated hearing the alarm in his voice. Still she couldn't stop
the tears, which slipped down her cheeks and into her
mouth. Feeling foolish, she wiped her face with her sleeve;
she had no tissue with her.

"Oh God, I didn't want this to happen," she said, then
it all came out: Maya's death, Meredith's arrival, the whole
series of events at Ravenscroft.

"Oh, darling, I'm so sorry," he said when she had finished. "I'll come right away. I can get a flight tomorrow."

"No! No, please; stay with your mother as long as you
planned. I'd feel awful if you left now. Really, Detective
Hansom is handling it, and there's policemen here every
day."

"I would come to be with you, not to help on the case,"
he said, sounding hurt.

"Oh, I know," she said quickly, "but—well, I've got
Meredith."

There was a pause and then they both laughed.

"Well," he said, "it's all right, then; as long as Meredith's in charge of things, there's nothing to worry about."

"She did save my life, you know."

"And she won't let you—or anyone—forget it. Besides,
I thought I had a little something to do with that."

"Of *course* you did, but you know what I mean."

"I know. I can't—well, it's hard for me to think that I

almost lost you, when I had just found you. You—I mean, are you still having dreams about it?"

"Sometimes. But since I've been up here, I only dream about you."

"Liar."

"I wish it were true, but unfortunately you can't control your dreams."

"Let me come back—"

"No, please, it's only—what, three more days? Spend them with your mother; she needs you as much as I do."

There was a pause and he sighed into the receiver. She imagined him in his rumpled corduroy jacket—worn partly to please his mother, who liked to preserve "some of the civilities," as she called them—his curly grey hair disheveled from lying on the couch reading, his heavy-lidded eyes red with fatigue because of the time change. She thought of his hands, long and fine as a painter's, and the thought of him filled her body with heat, with juice, like a tree with its sap flowing.

"All right," he said. "I—I just can't . . . *please* promise me you'll be careful."

"I promise. And anyway, whoever it is, they're not after me. I never even met these people before; how could one of them want to kill me?"

Standing in the pale moonlight, the house surrounding her with its womblike embrace, holding its own secrets within its ancient walls, Claire had no way of knowing how wrong she was.

Chapter 11

Claire slept late the next day. By the time she awoke, Meredith was already up and out, her mattress neatly made and pushed under Claire's bed. There was an empty bedroom next to Claire's, but Meredith continued to sleep on the floor of Claire's room. Claire was glad to have her there, to hear the girl's raspy breathing in the dark beside her; it made her feel they were both safer. She wandered downstairs and made fresh coffee; the coffee in the pot from earlier in the morning was already old. There was a note on the counter in Meredith's sprawling script:

Gone to town with Liza. Back soon—M.

Claire sat on the porch sipping her coffee, listening to the brittle rattle of cicadas heralding the end of summer. She watched the treetops sway in the light morning breeze. The sound of Gary's flute wafted up onto the porch, held aloft by the same breeze. The tune was sad and plaintive, a slow Celtic melody rolling and turning upon itself like water over stones. Claire sat listening for quite a while, until the melody stopped abruptly in the middle of a phrase, as though a switch had suddenly been turned off. She listened for it to begin again, but when it didn't, she got up and went inside, washed out her coffee cup, and put some food out for Ralph. Feeling restless, she went upstairs and tidied up her dresser. As always, there was an unread pile of manuscripts beckoning from her book bag in the corner of the room, but she couldn't read just now. Ever since the murder she had been fighting back the old feelings of claustrophobia: she just had to get away from this house, this room, even for just a while.

There were no classes scheduled until after lunch, so Claire decided to go for a run. She left a note on the dresser for Meredith: *Gone jogging—back soon.* She hesitated; she had an impulse to add *Love, Claire,* but knowing how Meredith hated displays of sentiment, just signed it *C.* Claire put on her running shoes as Ralph watched her from the windowsill. No one was on the porch when she went back out to do her stretching before taking off at a brisk pace down Camelot Road. It was a bright, crisp day, the kind of day in which summer gives way reluctantly to fall, holding on tenaciously in spite of a creeping chill in the air. The road dipped down into a little gully, twisted around a bend, and soon she was surrounded by deep woods on either side.

Liza had told her that there was a turnoff to the hiking trail up Guardian Mountain, and Claire saw the sign indicating the spot about a quarter of a mile down the path. She kept going straight, though, remembering that Camille had said that Camelot Road came out the other side onto Rock Hill Road. As she ran, her feet pounding a steady rhythm on the hard-baked dirt, Claire thought about Meredith. Now that she was in Claire's life, her going would leave a gap that could not easily be filled. Once Claire had asked her aunt Jane whether she loved all her children equally.

Her aunt had paused and said, "Love equally? Yes, I suppose so. But I think a parent always feels closer to some than others . . . it's a great source of guilt, I think, but . . . well, you feel—how can I say it?—more *simpatico* with certain children. Why this is I don't know, but I've never known a parent who didn't feel that way. It's as though you just *understand* some children better than others."

Claire could not explain why, but she felt she understood Meredith. They were so different, and yet it was as though Meredith were her flip side, her unexpressed self, her doppelgänger. It was as though Meredith had always been a part of her, a part of herself that she had denied for a long time but that now had come to assert itself and claim her attention.

"Time to go back into therapy," she muttered as she jumped over a tree branch that had fallen over the path. Up ahead was a mountain stream, a shallow little brook bubbling and shimmering in the light falling through the trees. Claire wiped the sweat from her forehead as she approached it. As she got closer something dark lying on the bank caught her eye. As first she thought it was another log, swept downstream by the storm a few nights ago. But when she was just a few paces away, she stopped dead where she was, her veins filling with horror. At this distance there was no mistaking what it was: there, tossed casually against the bank as if it were a sack of worn-out clothes, was a body.

For the second time in her life, Claire fainted.

When she came to, the first thing she was aware of were the sounds of the forest all around her. She lay with her eyes closed for several moments, listening to the chirping and rustling, the twirping and cooing and humming of all the unseen creatures of the woods.

It was only after she opened her eyes that Claire remembered why she was lying on the ground. Shaking, she sat up and got slowly to her feet. She had an impulse to run away as fast as she could. Instead, she took a deep breath and took a couple of steps toward the still form lying facedown in the shallow stream. The only movement was the slow trickle of water over the smooth round stones of the riverbed. From where she stood Claire could see quite clearly that even with his face in the water, she was looking at Terry Nordstrom. A thin red swirl of blood ran from his neck into the shallow water of the brook. A Walkman lay on a rock where it had fallen, black and shiny as a turtle's shell.

Suddenly Claire's stomach began to convulse. She dropped to her knees, racked by the intensity of the waves; it wasn't exactly nausea, but like nausea, it was an utterly involuntary reaction she was powerless to control. After a couple of minutes the feeling passed. She remained on her knees for a while longer, stones and twigs digging into her skin, until she was sure it was over, then she got to her feet again. She brushed the dirt from her legs, took a deep breath, and started back toward the house.

"Wait a minute, Redbird."

At first Claire thought she had imagined the voice, but then she turned and saw Two Joe standing at the edge of the path on the other side of the stream.

"H-how did you get here?" she stammered, suddenly feeling breathless again. Two Joe took a step toward her, and she instinctively backed away.

"The same as you. I walked." He looked at the body lying between them and shook his head. "This is an evil thing," he said somberly. "There is much badness about."

Claire glanced back at the path behind her, stretching off into the forest. Above her the sun glinted through the leaves, splashing the ground with yellow. Fear began to seep through her intestines like ice water. *This could be my last view of the sun,* she thought. Even if she took off at a run, she was sure he could easily catch her, and they were deep enough in the woods that no one would hear her screams.

If Two Joe was aware of what she was thinking, he didn't show it. He carefully picked his way down the bank and leaned over the body. He sank down on his haunches and looked at it for what seemed to Claire like a long time. But as she stood there watching him her fear begin to evaporate. Why would a murderer act like this? She felt the tension draining from her body. She noticed that Two Joe was careful not to touch anything.

Finally, he straightened up and brushed off his jeans.

He stepped across the stream, straddling it easily in one stride, and came to stand beside her.

"This murderer was very clever, and covered his tracks well," he said.

"How do you mean?"

"Look here." He pointed to the ground. "He has covered his tracks by brushing the ground with tree branches—here."

Claire looked at the ground and saw where the dirt had been raked over, eliminating all signs of footprints around the body. "But what about the path itself?" She looked behind her. Two sets of footprints led to the spot where they stood; one was hers, and the other, she assumed, was Terry's.

"Whoever did this disappeared back into the woods," said Two Joe. "He—or she—couldn't risk going along the path, because the recent storm wiped it clean of all other tracks. Also, the ground is so soft that the imprint of a shoe is perfectly captured."

Claire looked at Terry's lifeless body, stretched out so casually in the muddy water. "Could a woman possibly have done this?"

Two Joe shook his head slowly. "You'd be surprised what a woman can do; he's not a big man, you know." She thought she detected a slight satisfaction in his voice, the sense of superiority tall men always feel around shorter ones. Two Joe pointed to the Walkman and scowled, the corners of his mouth pulled down in disgust. "The woods is no place for one of those things. He might still be alive if he had not worn it. Whoever killed him caught him unawares."

Claire looked at Two Joe towering over her and tried to imagine anyone catching *him* unaware. She looked again at the two sets of prints on the dirt path, hers and Terry's, and felt again the icy little thread of fear in her stomach.

"Then how—did you get here?"

Two Joe shrugged. "Through the woods. I don't need paths to find my way," he said disdainfully. "And besides, the best mushrooms don't grow along the path," he added, holding up a handful of fat white mushrooms. "Come, we'll go to the police together," he said gently, laying a huge hand on Claire's shoulder. She nodded, but she was not entirely relieved of her suspicions. The fact that she was attracted to Two Joe did not reassure her; it only reminded her of Robert. If she could misjudge him, then she could not entirely trust her instincts about men.

Several hours later Claire was seated on the front porch looking out through the trees at the deepening dusk. The ambulance was just pulling away from the house, its lights revolving slowly, throwing her into a kind of trance state. All around there was hurried movement; everyone was rushing about, talking, bringing trays of coffee back and forth from the kitchen to the small army of policemen who now patrolled the house and grounds, searching rapidly, almost desperately, as the light faded from the late August sky. But in the midst of all of this activity, Claire felt calm, almost as though she were on tranquilizers. She had refused Camille's offer of Valium earlier, and now some chemical in her brain had kicked in, deadening her feelings, and she sat silently on the porch, shrouded in her stillness, placid as a Buddha.

Detective Hansom stood on the bottom step, talking with Liza, looking more tired than ever. His big dark eyes drooped even lower, the circles under them deeper and more pronounced. He was clearly upset by this new turn of events, and his jaw was set in anger as he pulled himself through the task of interviewing everyone again. If people had been shocked by Maya's death, they were stunned by Terry's. This time there was no denying the brutal fact: Terry had been murdered, his neck slashed by a sharp object—something like a hunting knife, the coroner said. The time of death was approximately 12:30 P.M., about half an hour before Claire found him. Once again, Claire wondered how close she had come to actually witnessing a murder.

Finally, Claire went up to her room to lie down. She lay on the bed staring at the ceiling while Meredith sat beside her eating cookies. The more upset everyone else got, the calmer Meredith became. She reminded Claire of a border collie, those black-and-white dogs that herded sheep, creeping close to the ground, every muscle in their body intent on their task, their eyes projecting pure intelligence and purpose. Now, with two murders to solve, Meredith was all purpose; her thin body glimmered with determination.

"The key lies in what Terry and Maya have in *common;* what common thread *unites* them?" she said, swinging her legs back and forth under the bed. "It's odd that you found *both* bodies . . . it's almost as though the murderer *wanted* you to find them."

"But he—or she—couldn't know that I'd be going to that bathroom in the middle of the night—or jogging along that path at the time."

"Who else uses that path?"

"Plenty of people."

"Like who?"

"Well, I've seen Liza and Sherry go for walks along it . . . and Camille goes into the woods to smoke sometimes. And Two Joe."

"Yes, that's another curious thing," Meredith mused. "Two Joe's involvement both times. What did he do, sneak up on you?"

Claire shook her head. "No, I fainted. But, now that you mention it, did you notice how Jack Mulligan never seems to enter a room—but then you turn around and he's just there?"

"Kind of like Judith Anderson in *Rebecca*?" said Meredith.

"Judith Anderson?"

"Yeah. Hitchcock never filmed her entering a room; Joan Fontaine would look up and she'd be there."

Claire looked at Meredith and shook her head. Half the time she didn't know whether to admire the girl or be irritated by her. "Where did you get *that*?" she said, fighting back an impulse to laugh.

"Don't tell me you haven't read Truffaut's book on

Hitchcock!" Meredith said. A tiny piece of lemon cookie clung tenaciously to the corner of her mouth.

The piece of the cookie was the last straw. Laughter erupted from Claire's body like lava from a volcano.

"Ha-a-aha-a-a!" she exploded, her body shaking with heaving gasps of hysterical laughter. She collapsed back onto the bed, rolling from side to side as the laughs tore through her. She surrendered to the rhythmic, convulsive waves pumping her diaphragm, tears coursing down her cheeks. As she lay on her bed tossing and cackling like a madwoman, she remembered scenes of hysterical giggling with her cousins as a child, laughter so deep that it tore into the center of her body, like the contractions of child-birth.

Claire was aware of Meredith standing over her, a distasteful expression on her face, but she didn't care. This felt good, like something she had to do. She didn't care either if any of the other residents heard her; if they thought she had lost her mind, fine.

Finally, the convulsions subsided and Claire lay limply on the bed, stomach aching, drained.

"Well, I'm glad you got *that* out of your system," Meredith said tartly, and she sounded so much like Claire's mother that it set her off again.

"Haa-a-a!" The sound exploded from her as though set off by a tiny detonator inside her, and again she began rolling and clutching her sore stomach.

Meredith sighed heavily and sat down in the armchair. She picked at the arm of the chair, studied her nails, and leaned her head back against the headrest to wait it out. When the second wave subsided, Claire wiped her eyes, sat up, and looked at Meredith.

"I still don't see what's so funny," Meredith said impatiently, pulling one thin white leg up underneath her. The baggy brown cotton shorts she wore made her legs look even thinner.

"Nothing . . . there's nothing funny about any of this," said Claire. "I just needed a release. Haven't you ever gotten hysterical?"

"Nope."

"Well," Claire said slowly, "maybe that's one of your problems. Maybe you need to let go, loosen up a little, you know?"

Meredith regarded her icily. "I don't see why. Sherlock Holmes was right: emotions just get in the way."

"Well, look what happened to him."

"What?"

"He became a cocaine addict."

Meredith snorted and was about to reply when someone in the hallway outside sneezed loudly. Claire and Meredith looked at each other, but before they could say anything, there was a knock on the door.

"Yes?" said Claire.

"It's Sergeant Rollins. Uh, we're ready to see you now." His voice was thick with phlegm.

Claire opened the door. Sergeant Rollins stood in the hall, a handkerchief pressed to his nose.

"Looks like you've still got that cold," Claire said.

He nodded. "Yeah. I haven't been able to take any time off, what with—well, it's been busy down at the station."

Meredith poked her head out of the door. "Which one of us does the detective want to see?"

"Uh, either one."

Claire noticed that the sergeant was only an inch or two taller than Meredith. Claire herself was a good three inches taller than he was. He looked overheated in his tight blue uniform and solid, thickly soled shoes; his smooth pink face was shiny with perspiration.

"Aren't you doing any of the interviews?" said Meredith.

"Uh, no; the detective wants to do them all himself this time. I've been present for most of them, though," he added, tucking his handkerchief into his hip pocket.

"All right; I'll go," said Meredith. Sergeant Rollins blinked. His eyes were watery, and he looked as if he were about to sneeze again. But the moment passed and he turned and escorted Meredith down the hall. As Claire watched them go she suddenly felt exhausted. She went back inside the room, closed the door, lay down on the bed, and stared at the ceiling. A centipede was carefully making its way across the white painted plaster.

"Where are you headed?" she asked softly.

The centipede paused, swiveled its tiny head from side to side as if testing the air, then continued on its way. Claire picked up Meredith's book from the bedside table: *Black Holes and Baby Universes,* by Stephen Hawking. The author looked out from the cover of the book, smiling broadly. His smile was lopsided and awkward, his eyes bleary; if you didn't know he suffered from a debilitating muscle disease, you would think his publisher had done a lousy job on publicity photos. There was something jaunty in the angle of his head, however, and Claire found the picture touching. He knew anyone reading the book would probably know of his condition—and yet there he was, grinning crookedly at his public. Claire opened the book to Chapter Eight, "Einstein's Dream":

> *In the early years of the twentieth century, two new theories completely changed the way we think about space and time, and about reality itself...*

Space and time, and reality itself...

Claire turned the page and came to this sentence: *Space-time is not flat, but is curved by the energy and matter in it.*

Space-time is not flat, but curved...

Claire closed her eyes, and saw the earth surrounded by space-time, which looked like a three-dimensional asteroid belt, encircling the planet like a big grey blanket. Space and time, and reality itself...

"Well, *that* was a waste of time!"

Claire opened her eyes to see Meredith entering the room, slamming the door behind her. "What?" she said, her eyes heavy with sleep, her mouth brimming with undrooled saliva.

Meredith flung herself into the oak armchair. "Well, he

didn't *begin* to ask the right questions, for God's sake! I mean, how he can call that an *investigation* I don't know!"

"Meredith, you didn't . . . you wouldn't *say* that to him, would you?"

Meredith looked at Claire as though she were a small, dirty rodent. "Of *course* not!" she said, her voice dripping with disdain.

"You know, Meredith," Claire said icily, "all the other people in the world besides you are not idiots."

Meredith threw her hands up in an odd combination of surrender and dismay. "But he didn't even ask half the right *questions*!"

"Well, maybe he's looking at things from a different angle than you are. Did you think of that?"

Meredith slumped down in her chair and picked at a scab on her arm. "Maybe . . . I guess."

There were so many unanswered questions, Claire thought, so many . . . the little ones might someday find an answer, but they inevitably led to bigger, more important questions, and those, she thought, probably had no answer . . . Terry wasn't the most popular resident at Ravenscroft, but Claire couldn't imagine anyone wanting him dead.

Clearly, however, someone did.

Chapter 12

By the time Detective Hansom got around to interviewing Claire, it was after the dinner hour. No one really had the heart to eat, but after much prodding, the detective did accept Liza's offer of leftover lasagna for Sergeant Rollins and himself. When Claire entered the library, which he had again set up as a makeshift interrogation room, Detective Hansom stood and motioned her to a chair.

"Hello, Ms. Rawlings. If you'd just take a seat I'll be right with you," he said, and went out into the hall to speak to Sergeant Rollins.

Claire sat on a straight-backed chair with a cane seat and looked around the room. A tape recorder sat on the table next to a half-finished plate of lasagna; piles of papers lay scattered about the floor. She had an impulse to look at them, but instead she went over to the bookshelves and studied the book titles: *Anatomy of a Murder, In Cold Blood, Fatal Vision*. The books seemed to be arranged loosely by genre, and she was looking at the crime section.

"Sorry about that, Ms. Rawlings; if you're ready, we'll begin."

Detective Hansom stood at the door, a mug of coffee

in his hand. Something about the slope of his shoulders reminded her of Wally, and her stomach tightened.

"Please call me Claire."

"All right, Claire. Why don't you start by just telling me everything you can remember, starting with your entry onto the jogging path. Do you mind if I tape this?"

Claire shook her head. She told him everything she could remember, and when she had finished, Detective Hansom took something out of a bag at his feet.

"Do you recognize these?"

It was a pair of round wire-rim spectacles, similar to the ones Liza wore.

"Uh, not exactly. Where did you find them?"

"In the woods not far from the body. Do you have any idea of how they might have gotten there?"

Claire shook her head. "A couple of people here wear glasses similar to these. You might ask if anyone is missing a pair."

"Yes, we're going to do that," Detective Hansom said a little impatiently, then continued in a kinder voice. "Did you see or hear anything else that was unusual?"

"Not really . . ." Claire began, but then she remembered hearing Gary's flute while she was sitting on the porch with her coffee. "Well, there was—I mean, it's not unusual, but—"

"What? What is it?" Detective Hansom leaned forward, his big gangly body suddenly tense.

"Well, just before I went out, I heard Gary playing his flute in the woods, as he does sometimes—"

"Yes?" The detective's voice was tight.

"Well, it—stopped."

"It stopped?"

"Yes; I mean it stopped sort of suddenly, in the middle of a phrase."

"And did it resume again?"

"No . . . no, it didn't."

"And then what happened?"

"Well, after a while I got up and went inside."

"And you didn't hear it again?"

"No . . . no, I didn't."

"Thank you." The detective rose from his chair and opened the door for her. She entered the living room to find the rest of the residents all gathered there. Two police officers stood on either side of the front door. Sergeant Rollins was talking to Liza, and when Detective Hansom entered the room behind Claire, the sergeant walked briskly over to him.

"All here and accounted for, sir."

"Thank you, Sergeant," the detective said, his voice hoarse with fatigue. "All right, everybody, if I could have your attention now, please," he continued loudly, clearing his throat. Everyone stopped what they were doing and looked at him. Claire looked at Meredith, who sat next to Camille on the couch: she was biting her lower lip, her eyes bright.

"I'm going to ask that nobody leave the premises for at least twenty-four hours," said Hansom. "I'm going to have a police officer posted here around the clock. If you need something from town, please ask one of my men to arrange it for you. You will notice we've placed a yellow crime-scene tape over the entry to the woods on Camelot Road. We ask that you all please stay out of the woods."

Meredith's hand shot up.

"Yes?"

"Are we all suspects?"

Detective Hansom's face went blank, and Claire could hear air escaping from his lungs. "At this time we have no official suspects—"

"But—" Meredith protested.

"That's all, folks," he said firmly. "If you remember anything that you forgot to tell me, anything at all, please call me at the station. In the meantime, Sergeant Rollins here will be in charge if you have any questions." He nodded toward Sergeant Rollins, who sneezed.

He headed for the door, but Camille intercepted him. "Excuse me, Detective, I wonder if I might have a quick word with you."

He looked down at her, his grave dark eyes all but disappearing under his thick eyebrows, the lines in his basset-hound face deep as the crevices of a river valley. He was hard to read; Claire couldn't tell if he responded to Camille's evident interest in him—or even if he was aware of it. They went out onto the porch together, standing under the single lightbulb, silhouetted in the mad flittings of minuscule white insects swarming around the light, zigzagging in crazy flight paths like tiny fighter pilots. Hansom was a head taller than Camille, and as he stood over her, the curve of his thin neck catching the light, weight shifted onto one leg, he reminded Claire of a large, ungainly water fowl—a crane, perhaps, or a heron. She couldn't hear what they were saying, but finally he nodded and headed out toward his car. Camille watched after him, and when she came back into the house, her cheeks were glowing.

Jack Mulligan walked over to her, and Claire expected him to say something sarcastic, but to her surprise he reached out his arms and hugged her.

"I could use some wine," said Sherry, heading toward the kitchen. "Anyone else like to join me?"

"I'll come with you," said Tahir, following her.

There was a pause and then Gary got up abruptly and started for the stairs.

"Gary?" said Billy, and Gary stopped and looked at him, but then continued up the steps. Billy looked around the room, then got up quickly and followed him.

"What was that all about, I wonder?" said Jack Mulligan, with a glance at the policeman who stood guard inside the front door. The policeman's face was impassive, though, stolid and bland as grass. Another policeman stood outside on the porch. Claire was glad for their presence, and wondered if everyone in the house felt the way she did—or if there was someone who would like very much to see them go away.

That night Meredith and Claire lay in bed watching the pattern of headlights from the occasional car out on the road make its way across the ceiling. It was very late, but neither of them was asleep.

"Claire," said Meredith, her voice small in the darkness.

"Yes, Meredith?"

"Do you believe in God? I mean, do you think that there's anything after death?"

Claire exhaled heavily. "I don't know, Meredith; sometimes I think there is, but . . . well, other times I really don't. I don't know what to think."

Meredith propped herself up on one elbow. "Is this *it*?" she whispered into the darkness. "Are we just a compilation of—of cells and atoms?"

Claire rubbed her forehead and pushed back the thoughts of sleep that were crowding her. "I don't know, Meredith."

"I mean, what about altruism and love and all that stuff? What about *consciousness*, for Christ's sake?"

Claire turned her head to look out the window, where a thin pink dawn was just beginning to flower in the eastern sky. "You're asking the questions that men have asked for centuries . . . I don't think anyone really has the answer."

"And if there *is* something else, then it can't just be in us; it has to be in everything . . . no wonder the Church wanted to ban the teaching of evolution; it's the biggest evidence against us having souls. I mean, who can imagine a cockroach having a soul?"

"Franz Kafka, for one," Claire said.

"Very funny."

There was a pause and Claire could hear the wind outside whipping the tree branches until they rattled against the windowpanes.

"Do you believe in evil?" Meredith whispered.

"You mean do I believe it exists?"

"Yeah. Do you?"

Claire took a deep breath and let it out slowly. "I don't know, Meredith . . ."

"Like a force in the universe, you know? Maybe it's the equivalent of antimatter . . . if good is matter, then evil is like antimatter."

Claire watched a thin slice of pale yellow light break through the gap in the curtains and creep across the opposite wall.

"I mean, was Robert evil?"

"What he did was wrong—" Claire began slowly.

"Good Lord, he tried to *kill* you! If that's not evil, what is?"

The strip of sunlight widened, shining on the metal knobs of the dresser drawers, turning the brass into gold.

"The devil is an angel, too," said Claire.

"Where did you get that?" Meredith's voice was wary, as it always was when she felt challenged.

"From one of your books."

"Which one?"

"Miguel Unamuno."

Meredith sighed. "Figures. I should've known; it sounds like him. He's a mystic; you can never trust a mystic." Her voice was sleepy now, and Claire could sense she was sliding into sleep. Pretty soon she was snoring gently, her head thrown back on the pillow as the early-morning sun made its way across the room, falling on her hair, a blaze of orange on the white sheets.

Claire lay awake in bed trying to remember the feel of Wally's hands on her body, the touch of his hands upon her breasts, his mouth, soft and moist as a peach, upon her nipples. She imagined him there in the darkness beside her, enveloped by the sweetness of his breath, his chest rising and falling with the calm, steady rhythm of a ship rolling gently on the waves. She always felt safe when he was there, but now as she lay between the cold white sheets of her narrow bed, the memory receded from her into the darkness. She thought of the other sleepers who lay all around her, each alone with his own thoughts, trying to sleep as she was—and knowing what she knew: that someone among them was, in all probability, a murderer.

Chapter 13

No one was prepared for the swarm of newspaper and television reporters that descended upon Ravenscroft like locusts. After Maya's death a few journalists had come and gone, covering the story with a few camera shots and some more or less random questions to the residents, who were still in a state of shock. But now the air was suddenly thick with them, scurrying about with their cameras and tape recorders, leaving gum wrappers and cigarette butts behind them everywhere. Camelot Road had turned into a parking lot for vans, which were crammed along the deep ditch that ran along side the road, satellite dishes perched on their roofs like metal nests for some giant predatory birds.

Cables twisted and coiled across the lawn like thick black snakes, tripping residents who tried to make their way through the tangle of media people camped out along Camelot Road.

"Damn media vultures," Jack remarked, looking out the window at the flurry of TV reporters in brightly colored jackets, their perfectly sprayed prime-time hair gathering another coat of fine white dust every time a car rattled along the dirt road.

"You don't like reporters?" Meredith said, pouncing eagerly on his words.

Jack snorted. "Didn't like 'em when I was a cop, don't like 'em now. All they do is distort and interfere. Look at that," he said as a policeman picked his way through the tangle of cables and cameras. "Damn bunch of jackals, make their living off other people's misfortunes."

He turned and strode into the kitchen, where Camille was brewing another fresh pot of coffee. Claire thought that Camille had seized this task of coffeemaking as a way of keeping her fear at bay; it was something to do, something to focus on. The smell of freshly ground beans drifted through the house day and night now as one team of policemen replaced another.

"Maya was a journalist," Meredith said thoughtfully, sinking down onto the window seat.

"But Jack liked her—or at least he gave that impression," said Claire.

"Hmm," said Meredith. "He did, did he?"

Claire rubbed her forehead. A small pinpoint of pain had begun to form over her right eye. What game was Jack Mulligan playing, she wondered, what game were any of them playing, for that matter? She was beginning to have second thoughts about whom she could trust; perhaps her instincts about human nature had utterly deserted her. She looked out over the jungle of reporters and camera people. The sun glinting off the satellite dishes suddenly seemed too bright, the reds on the reporters' jackets too red; the blaze of light and activity made her dizzy.

Claire knew the signs by now: a migraine was on its way. "I'm going upstairs to lie down," she said to Meredith.

Meredith looked up at her, her head cocked to one side. "You okay?"

Claire nodded. "I've got a headache coming on. I just need a little peace and quiet."

She didn't want to say the word *migraine* because it tended to upset people. Her migraines weren't that bad, really, and didn't last very long. But as the stiffness in her neck increased she was glad she was headed for her nice dark, quiet bedroom. She opened the door and stood for a moment in the gentle breeze blowing in from the open window, then lay on the bed and pulled the spread around her legs.

Claire gazed out of the window at the worn white trail of a jet high in the sky. Once just a thin line, it was now crumbling, dissipated, and resembled a long white spinal column of clouds, its ribs slowly fading in the wind as she watched. A narrow line of pain formed just over her right eye, thin and jagged as the white jet trail up in the sky.

She lay there on the bed, her eyes slit open like a cat's, the room dissolving into half-seen images. She thought about the nature of things seen out of the corner of one's eye, when you are almost asleep, but not quite, the world around you resembling a dream . . . the tunnel vision in a dream state is like this falling-asleep consciousness . . . like the tunnel vision in a migraine. She closed her eyes and let the room dissolve into darkness, giving herself over to sleep.

Terry's memorial service was held that night, and was much like Maya's, except that it was a little shorter. Not many of the residents had warmed up to Terry; his anger had held them at arm's length, but now that he was dead, everyone seemed very sad. There was another feeling in the air, one Claire was all too familiar with: fear. Even Jack Mulligan seemed more edgy than usual, rubbing his hands together as he sat and listened to Camille talking about Terry. She had probably been closest to him, even acting at times as a confidante. Only Evelyn and Roger Gardner were not at Terry's service.

Early the next morning Claire called Detective Hansom to ask permission to leave for the day so she could go into town for the weekly editorial meeting at Ardor House. He sounded weary and defeated on the phone, and she felt almost guilty for asking if she could leave, as though she were abandoning him. But she didn't want to miss the meeting; they were scheduled to discuss Willard Hughes's next book; there were several things she wanted to talk about with her editor in chief, Peter Schwartz. Every time she used the phone at Ravenscroft, she felt the lack of privacy. It was so public, standing there in the little alcove just off the dining room; Claire listened to the sound of her voice echoing through the big, empty room and felt everyone in the house could hear her.

Rather than go back immediately, she decided to spend the night in the city and return the next day. That way she could pick up her mail, check her apartment, and sleep in her own bed for one night.

"Oh, please let me go—please, please, *please!*" Meredith begged when Claire announced her plans.

"Isn't it time you went back to Connecticut?" Claire tossed her toothbrush and dental floss into a small bag. "I can drop you off on the way."

"But I *love* the city!" Meredith protested, throwing herself on the bed, kicking at the bedspread with one sneaker.

"Take off your shoes if you're going to lie on the bed," said Claire.

"Oh, *jeez.*" Meredith rolled up to a sitting position, brushing her hair out of her face. "Why can't I come?" She kicked at the braided throw rug with her heel.

"How are you going to solve the murder if you're in New York?" Claire said, stuffing a manuscript into her bag. She hoped to catch up on some reading, having done practically none since her arrival at Ravenscroft.

"How can I do it in Connecticut?"

"Look," said Claire, zipping up her bag. "I'm worried that it's not safe for you here, and I'd feel better if you were at your father's."

Meredith made a face. "It's not safe for me *there*. My stepmother's a coke addict."

"I thought she was over that."

"You never get *over* being an addict; you're just in recovery. *Duh.*"

Claire sighed. "Okay, look; if your dad agrees, you can come to town with me, but—"

"Oh, thank you, thank you, *thank* you!" Meredith leaped up and threw her arms around Claire's neck.

In the end they decided to take the bus rather than make the long drive both ways. Claire could get started on her reading—and as Meredith pointed out, she often fell asleep on buses.

Sure enough, the bus had not been on the highway for five minutes when Meredith fell asleep, her head lolled over to one side, breathing heavily. Claire leaned back against the plush headrest and stared out the window, watching the countryside of upstate New York sweep by. The tree leaves were the deep, lush green of late summer, poised on the cusp of ripeness before turning the corner toward decay. Claire thought of her own body, of the little signs of aging that greeted her every day. *Mirror mirror on the wall.* She was glad for Wally in her life, for the ability to revel in the pleasures of the flesh before they, too, fell away like tree leaves.

Pulling herself away from these thoughts, she opened the manuscript in the bag at her feet: *Death by Foul Means,* Willard Hughes's latest book. She had promised Peter Schwartz that she would finish it by the end of the week. In addition to being Ardor House's best-selling author, Willard was also its most impatient. As soon as one of his manuscripts appeared on Claire's desk, her phone would ring; it would be Willard asking for her opinion. To his credit, he took her suggestions for rewrites seriously; unlike some successful writers, Willard was interested in the quality of the finished product and not just the royalty checks.

When the bus arrived, Claire sent Meredith up to her apartment in a cab while she went straight from Port Authority to the office, since the meeting was already in progress. Willard's book didn't take up much time. Afterward, there was some venting about certain authors or their agents, always a popular activity.

"And then he didn't even *listen* to what I said but *demanded* the rewrites by Friday!"

"It's not like his book is going be a big moneymaker."

"It's as though she thinks she's the only writer we *have.*"

"She doesn't realize I have other things to do than be on the phone with her goddamn agent all day."

Heads were nodded in agreement, coffee was sipped in righteous indignation, and bagels were chewed in sympathetic solidarity.

"They just don't understand the kind of pressure we're under."

Nobody ever understands, Claire thought. *Nobody ever understands anybody else fully and completely, the way they want to be understood. We all keep looking, but that kind of understanding doesn't exist.*

After the meeting Claire stuck her head in Peter's office. Peter Schwartz was seated at his desk working, head bent, the green light from his Tiffany desk lamp falling on his thinning grey hair.

"Hi. Got a minute?"

Peter looked up from his desk. Some obscure law of physics kept the reading glasses perched on his short nose from sliding off. They always looked as if they were about to fall, but never did.

"Hello there. Have a seat," he replied, half rising from his chair as Claire entered. Peter Schwartz affected the manners and speech of a perfectly well-bred upper-class Englishman; he was, in fact, a perfectly well-bred upper-class New York Jew, and had never quite eradicated the flattened vowels of the Upper West Side from his accent, which was a curious combination of the West End and West End Avenue.

Claire sat on the soft couch opposite his desk. Peter's office, with its deeply cushioned sofa, thick Persian rugs, and Tiffany lamps, was a relaxing place. English hunting prints adorned the walls, and a portrait of the queen mother occupied a place of honor behind his desk.

"Tea?" said Peter, plugging in a small electric kettle. Peter's love of all things English extended to his unwavering devotion to afternoon tea; at precisely four o'clock you could find him brewing tea in his office, no matter who was with him. Claire was certain that if the CEO of

Ardor himself were to be sitting in Peter's office, he would be offered tea at exactly four o'clock.

"How are you holding up?" he asked sympathetically, settling his round little body back into his leather armchair, an exact duplicate of a London club chair, down to the royal crest on the armrests.

"I'm okay, thanks."

"Are you frightened?"

"Well, maybe a little, but whoever it is, I don't think they're after me."

Peter shrugged, and what there was of his neck disappeared. Everything about Peter was stubby: with his plump, fleshy hands, short little legs, and round torso, he resembled a cartoon character, a Jewish Elmer Fudd. In spite of his appearance, though, he evidently exuded something, because women went for him. Claire thought it was because he made them feel safe; it wasn't just that he was courtly, but that he was protective in some fundamental way.

"Oh, by the way, remember that neo-Nazi you told me about up there?"

"Jack Mulligan?"

"Yes." Peter pulled a book out of his briefcase and handed it to her. "I came across this on my shelf at home, and I thought it might interest you."

Claire looked at the book: *The Holocaust: Fact or Fiction?* On the cover was a blurred photograph of Dachau, over which was superimposed a swastika.

"It's one of those 'revisionist' texts that these people write . . . I'll bet your friend Mr. Mulligan has read it, if he's one of them."

Claire turned the book over to the back cover and gasped. There, posed before a backdrop of a rocky coastline, wearing the same khaki hunting vest Claire had seen him in, his white hair dashingly windswept, was Jack Mulligan.

"Oh my God."

"What? What is it?" said Peter.

"It's him—it's Jack," she replied, handing back the book.

"*Really?* But this book is by Klaus Heiligen—or so it says here."

"Well, one of those names is an alias."

"Hmm . . . I wonder which one," Peter said, studying the picture on the back of the jacket.

"Hard to say. His accent is American, as far as I can tell."

"And he's calling himself Mulligan . . . he looks Irish enough, I guess."

"Well, there were plenty of Celts in northern Germany, so it's hard to tell from his face. He could be either German or Irish—"

"Or both?" Peter added.

"Can I have this?" Claire said.

"Sure, go ahead, take it."

Just then the phone rang. "I'm expecting a call from the Big Guy," Peter said as he picked up the receiver. Peter called the president of Ardor House the Big Guy, which was odd since he was actually a tiny, birdlike man, thin and dry as a cornhusk.

"Peter Schwartz speaking." Peter put his hand over the mouthpiece. "I'm sorry, I'm going to have to take this," he whispered to Claire. "Yes, I'm here. I just had someone in my office . . . no, no; this is as good a time as any," he said, waving to Claire was she left the office. Claire admired Peter's ability to maintain his equilibrium. Things were not good at Ardor lately—things were not good anywhere in publishing these days—but Peter seemed to float above it all, buoyed up by his cheerful self-confidence and endless cups of tea.

Claire called Meredith to check on her; she caught her in the middle of a movie on AMC.

"Okay," said Claire. "I'll be back soon, go back to your movie."

When he heard they were staying the night in town, Peter suggested they meet for dinner after work.

"I have a meeting which shouldn't go late, if you want to meet me down there around seven," he said.

"That's fine," said Claire. "Can I bring Meredith?"

"Of course—she's always stimulating."

As she was leaving the building around six-thirty, a sudden summer shower shook loose from the sky, catching people unaware, drenching them as they scurried down the steps to the subway. Soon Claire was standing in a crowded subway car on the Broadway line, pressed in among the other waterlogged passengers.

The air on the train was close and damp and smelled thickly of wet clothes and hair. Claire was reminded of the smell of the puppies in the toolshed when she was a child—the warm, musty aroma of wet fur, little mouths still damp with their mother's milk. That was a good smell, and yet, standing among her fellow passengers, their bodies so close to her, she was uncomfortable, holding back the claustrophobia that always threatened to close in. The other passengers stood there passively, mute and lumpy as sheep in their wet clothes.

Claire was reminded of a scene in *War and Peace* in which Prince Andrei sees a group of soldiers bathing in a pond. Watching the press of naked bodies tumbling over each other in the muddy water, he is overcome by revulsion, by a kind of existential despair. Oppressed by the sight of this mass of humanity, Andrei turns away, unsettled. This passage had always stuck in Claire's mind because she understood it so perfectly: there *was* something oppressive in the crush of bodies, whether in a muddy pond in nineteenth-century Russia or a Manhattan subway train. And so she stood there stolidly with her fellow travelers, silent amid the clattering of wheels as the train hurtled onward through its underground tunnels.

Peter's current favorite restaurant was a little Vietnamese place on the Bowery. Peter was an aficionado of ethnic cuisine, especially Asian food, and methodically visited as many restaurants as he could before choosing favorites; finding a good restaurant was one of his passions. Avantgarde theatre was another, and the weirder the production, the more Peter liked it. He had seen everything Richard Foreman ever produced; to Peter, understanding a piece of theatre was not necessary in order to enjoy it. (In fact, Claire thought intelligibility actually interfered with his pleasure.)

Claire had accompanied him in the past on some of these excursions. She had seen people jumping around in leotards to sound effects of whale noises, a production in which the only word spoken was "fish"; she had sat watching a man crawl out of a garbage bag for a solid half hour, and she had seen an avant-garde opera in which the main character was a robot named Sam. Finally, Claire decided that her tastes were more plebeian, and though she admired Peter's sense of adventure, she eventually stopped accompanying him on his theatrical forays.

Peter's taste in restaurants, however, was a different matter. Claire had to admit that he knew a good restaurant, and she always looked forward to his latest find. Ever restless, he never settled on one place for very long; after a few months he would move on, always searching for the perfect meal. People would come into the office and say things like, "Oh, I tried that restaurant you told me about; it was great!" Peter would roll his eyes and then Claire knew what was coming:

"Oh, I never go *there* anymore. I've found a much *better* place."

For Peter, there was always a better place somewhere, just waiting to be discovered, just around the next corner, through the next alley, some unassuming little hideaway that only he would find and appreciate—and then as soon as too many people knew about it, he would be gone, slipping away into the night, off again on his never-ending quest for culinary perfection. Peter's love of a restaurant was connected to it being *his* place, *his* discovery. As soon as it was everybody's place, he lost interest; the thrill of conquest was gone. Peter pursued restaurants with the same passion and restless possessiveness of a Don Juan pursuing women. The appearance of a favorable review in the press sounded the death knell of a restaurant as far as he was concerned.

"Oh, the *Times* has found out about it!" he would groan, tossing the paper onto his desk, and Claire knew he would never go to that restaurant again.

The *Times* had not yet discovered Pho Pun, though, and

so as Claire and Meredith sat waiting for Peter she ordered a cup of Vietnamese coffee. Physically, Pho Pun was a strange place: long and narrow, more like a hallway than a restaurant space, it was festooned year-round with Christmas decorations. Cheerful Vietnamese Muzak poured soothingly from speakers in the back of the room, bland and banal. The pink tablecloths, shiny black chairs, and gold tinsel hanging from the ceiling gave the place an eerie cheer, a kind of surrealistic coziness. Tiny white holiday lights dangled from the tinsel, blinking on and off, reflecting endlessly in the long mirrors covering the walls on both sides of the room. The effect was a hall of mirrors, with the customers sitting along each side, their images endlessly duplicated in ever-receding waves, like an Escher painting.

"Wow," said Meredith. "It looks like Christmas in here!"

The staff was entirely Vietnamese, and so were most of the patrons. Peter always said this was a good sign: he thought an ethic restaurant frequented by its own countrymen must be doing something right. This would not hold in Claire's neighborhood, where most of the restaurants were likely to be a sea of white faces, but down here in Chinatown it was not unusual to be the only Caucasian in a given establishment.

While Claire drank her coffee Meredith ordered a mango soda.

The waiter was a cheerful, stocky older man with thick white hair and a square face. Claire loved Vietnamese coffee: thick and strong and black as mud, it seeped slowly through the little metal filter into the cup below, mixing with the condensed milk lying in wait at the bottom of the cup. The resulting drink was a mix of strong sensations: the dark, rich coffee combined with the thick sweetness of the milk was almost unbearably flavorful, and made American coffee seem thin and pale.

Claire took a sip and closed her eyes, enjoying the rush of flavors. She opened her eyes to see Peter breezing into the restaurant, coat askew, shirttails flying.

"*So* sorry I'm late," he said, collapsing into a chair opposite her. "The meeting went late, and I tried to call you but you had already left."

"That's all right," said Claire.

"This place is cool," said Meredith.

"Isn't it?" Peter answered, energetically seizing the menu. He scanned it, eyes narrowed, put it down firmly on the table as if he were afraid it would jump up again, and signaled for the waiter. Peter did everything vigorously, decisively; he treated inanimate objects as though they were recalcitrant employees who needed to know who was boss. As a boss, however, he was the soul of gentleness, supportive and kind—a major reason Claire had remained at Ardor House as long as she had.

After they had ordered, Peter leaned forward, resting his short arms on the table. "So, what do you make of our Nazi friend's *nom de plume?*"

Claire shook her head. "I don't know what to make of it."

"Can you trust Liza?" said Meredith. "Maybe you should tell her."

Claire shook her head. "Well, if I can't trust Liza, then I don't know who I can trust. I don't know; maybe I shouldn't have left . . . it's just that I was feeling so—"

"Claustraphobic?" Peter suggested.

Claire sighed. "Yeah. The old fears, you know, rising up."

Peter nodded. "The whole Robert incident."

Claire laughed, but the sound was stiff and dry and died in her throat. "It sounds like a miniseries: *The Robert Incident.*"

Peter shook his head. "I'm not sure you're over that yet. I mean, I don't know if you ever really get over something like that, but I think maybe you should take it easy, you know?"

"That was part of the point of going up to Woodstock—to take it easy."

"And look how that worked out. Ah, here's our food," he said as the waiter arrived with steaming platters of shrimp and pork dumplings, noodles in chili and lemon grass, and skewers of grilled chicken in peanut sauce. Peter had ordered several bottles of Vietnamese beer, and as their food arrived he poured a glass for himself and Claire.

"Bloody good place, this," Peter said, and tucked into his food vigorously.

As they ate they discussed Willard Hughes's new book, a political thriller involving international terrorists.

"I don't know," Peter said, heaping delicate white rice noodles onto Claire's plate, "I think Willard should stick to mysteries."

"But you have to admit thrillers sell," Meredith remarked, pulling a piece of chicken off its thin wooden skewer.

"Sure they do, but so do Willard's mysteries. I'm just worried that Willard . . . well, politically, I suspect he's somewhat to the right of Pat Buchanan. I'm not publishing anything I find offensively right-wing. Simon and Schuster can do it if they want, but I swear to God I'll block it—"

"Simon and Schuster broke their contract, remember?" Claire pointed out.

Peter nodded. "They were fools to consider a book like that in the first place. It didn't do them any good in the long run."

"So you don't believe any publicity is good publicity," Meredith remarked.

Peter shook his head and poured them both some more beer. "No, I don't. And I think any publishing house has the right to turn down any book, the First Amendment notwithstanding."

Claire took a sip of beer. "Well, I've just started it, so I'll let you know. Willard's mysteries are fairly innocuous, after all."

They decided to stroll uptown after dinner, "to walk off some of this food," as Peter said, though Claire just wanted to look around. She loved downtown Manhattan, and got there rarely enough that when she was there she wanted to explore a little. The Upper West Side was lovely—quiet and almost bucolic—but downtown held its own unique

pleasures, mysterious lives squirreled away behind store-
fronts and warehouses; here, squeezed between darkened
stoops and alleyways, was the real history of New York,
the original city, already hundreds of years old when the
Upper West Side was still farmland.

Now, having been away for a few days, Claire was surprised at how glad she was to be back again; after the
bizarre events at Ravenscroft, the city felt strangely *safe*.
Here, it seemed, nothing could happen without someone
seeing it, whereas at Ravenscroft, sitting on the side of a
mountain, when you were alone, you were really *alone*.
Now, wandering through the narrow streets of lower Manhattan, Claire felt strangely protected, wrapped in a cocoon
of buildings, surrounded by the comforting buzz of the
lives humming within them.

And so they tramped up the Bowery through Chinatown,
past the tearooms and noodle houses, curiosity shops selling everything from glazed pottery to ground tiger bones
and shark fins. They moved through the ceaseless press of
bodies that fills the narrow twisting streets every Friday
and Saturday night, turning Chinatown into a swarming
carnival of sights and sounds. They stepped over fetid piles
of garbage, the smell mingling with the aroma of freshly
roasted duck and brewed green tea swirling from every
other doorway. Families hurried along, small children in
tow, wearing the flat cotton slippers favored by many of
the Chinese in the summer. The families were in turn followed by sinister-looking roving groups of teenagers, no
doubt some of them members of tongs, as Chinatown gangs
were called. Here, then, in all its contradictions and glory,
was a microcosm of New York itself: gangsters coexisting
with families, locals and tourists, garbage and Peking duck,
all packed together in less than two square miles.

"It's so odd, isn't it?" said Peter as they picked their
way through the crowded streets, stepping over the dis-
carded crates and cardboard boxes that merchants had
tossed onto the curb. "When I was in college we were at
war with Vietnam, and now we sit eating in a Vietnamese

restaurant, being served by some of the same people our soldiers were shooting at twenty-five years ago."

"I know," said Claire. "I think about that, too."

They continued on through Little Italy, past pastry shops and *ristorantes,* cappuccino bars and clam houses, and into SoHo, with its art galleries and French bistros, filled with young, black-clad patrons, their silky hair as smooth as the skin on their unlined faces under the track lighting. Here, young couples strolled arm in arm, their fashionable footwear striking the pavement crisply, ringing against the flagstones with the unmistakable sound of success and optimism.

They walked up Second Avenue and into the Eastern European enclave of the East Village, past Polish butcher shops and Ukrainian-owned bakeries, past the Pakistani-owned Indian restaurants of Sixth Street, past the Veselka with its flamboyant wall murals and hand-lettered sign advertising six kinds of homemade soups daily. So many people, so many lives, Claire thought, stacked atop each other in concrete hives on this rock jutting out of the sea.

When they reached the northern edge of the East Village at Fourteenth Street, Peter stopped at the bus stop.

"I think I'll hop on the M15 uptown," he said. Peter lived on the Upper East Side. "Oh, look—there it is," he added as the bulky blue-and-white bus bore down upon them, brakes squealing, metal against metal. "You taking a cab?"

"Sure," said Claire, Meredith loved riding in Taxicabs.

"Okay," said Peter. "Good night." He kissed Claire on the cheek and flung an arm out at the passing traffic. Immediately a taxi screeched to a halt in front of them. Peter hopped onto the bus as Claire and Meredith climbed into the cab, waving to them as they sped off into the night.

"Hey, look at that guy!" Meredith said as their cab stopped at the intersection of Broadway and Seventy-second Street. The man was leaning up against the building housing Gray's Papaya, home of the fifty-cent hot dog. He was dressed in a blanket tied at the waist with a thin little rope, frayed and dark with dirt. What caught Claire's attention, though, was that he was laughing—a deep, toothless laugh, his mouth opened in a parody of mirth. His red, puffy face, with its big bare-gummed grin, was grotesque, reminding Claire of a nineteenth-century Daumier caricature. There was something timeless about this man; he seemed to have always existed—and like the grotesques of Daumier, his vices and follies appeared to be imprinted on his face. Gluttony, sloth, intemperance: all were written upon the slack, broadly open mouth, the rheumy bloodshot eyes, the ruddy cheeks, red from sun, wind, and alcohol, and the bulbous nose, with its maze of tiny broken capillaries, creeping like crimson spiderwebs across his cheeks. Here was a face with a million other identical faces before it, ancestors stretched out across the centuries in a direct line. Some things are passed down from one generation to the next, in ways other than heredity, Claire thought; some things are as cyclical as the seasons, an ever-renewing cycle of birth and death. There will always be men like him on streets around the world, she thought, and no amount of social programs or welfare will eradicate their ranks entirely. A quote from Goethe sprang into her head: *Du must Hammer oder Anvil sein.* "You must either be the hammer or the anvil."

The light changed and the cab jerked away from the intersection.

"He was *weird,*" Meredith said, looking out the back window at the man. "You know who else is weird?"

"Who?"

"Jack. What's *with* him, anyway?"

Claire could imagine Jack's face as the face of a drunk; a few years of dissipation, living on the street, and he would look like the man's brother. But it was more than that: there was a slyness about him, a roguish rudeness, that reminded her of the homeless man.

"Funny you should ask." Claire told Meredith about the book Peter discovered, and Jack's other identity.

"Wow," Meredith said when she finished. "That's really weird. What are you going to do about it?"

"I don't know . . . I need to talk to Liza first. She's the

director of the program, and I don't want to put her in a difficult position."

"Do you think she knows?"

"I doubt it. She would have said something."

"But we should tell Detective Hansom."

"Yes," Claire replied. "He should know about it."

As the cab turned onto West End Avenue, Claire looked at the bulky brownstones of the Upper West Side, feeling a sudden, unexpected rush of affection for mankind: for their earnest, heartfelt search for comfort on this cold ball of minerals hurtling relentlessly through space, traveling inexorably away from the center of a frozen universe.

Back at her apartment, Claire threw down the pile of mail on the table by the front door and checked her answering machine while Meredith roamed the kitchen looking for cookies. The light was blinking once, indicating one message, but when Claire played it back she heard only a dial tone; whoever called had hung up without leaving a message. She considered calling Liza to see if everything was all right, but it was after eleven and Liza was an early riser.

She wandered into the kitchen, where Meredith was rummaging through the cupboards.

Meredith held up a box of Fig Newtons. "This is all I could find," she said, disappointment in her voice.

"Haven't you had enough to eat tonight?"

Meredith shrugged. "There's always room for cookies."

Later, the girl lay in her bed reading as Claire tidied up the room around her. Meredith put her book down, rubbed her eyes, and yawned. "You know, I was thinking about Billy Trimble, and something just popped into my head."

"Oh?" Claire pulled a sock out of the shoe it was stuffed into. Meredith's ability to create havoc in a room in a matter of minutes was astonishing. She scattered her possessions around as though she were sowing a field: her shirt was tossed over the back of a chair, her shoes were left in the middle of the floor. Her knapsack lay open in a crumpled heap on the foot of the bed, its contents spilling out of it like fruit from an overturned basket. Claire had tried to change the girl's untidy habits, but she didn't spend enough time with her to have a lasting effect. Meredith tried, she really did, but tonight they were both tired and Claire didn't want to make an issue out of it.

"What popped into your head?" Claire said, sitting on the edge of the bed.

Meredith raised herself onto one elbow. "Well, it's just that he was the only one at Maya's funeral service who didn't cry."

"Really?" said Claire. "You mean even Jack cried?"

"Well, yeah. His eyes were wet, anyway. I was watching everyone, you know," she added, lying down on her back again.

"Hmm," said Claire. "Interesting. I wonder if it means anything. Of course, some people are just more private, and they do their grieving alone."

Meredith shrugged. "I guess. Anyway, just thought I'd mention it."

"Okay, well, now it's time for bed. Claire kissed her on the forehead. "We're catching an early bus tomorrow."

"Okay," said Meredith, snuggling down under the covers. *She must be tired,* Claire thought, *to not argue at all about going to bed.* She turned off the bedside lamp and tiptoed out of the room. A single shaft of moonlight fell on Meredith's wiry hair, copper-colored in the pale blue light.

Claire took a bath and crawled into bed. Next to her bed was *Forgotten News,* by Jack Finney, a book she had deliberately left behind when she left for Woodstock, afraid that she would read it instead of all the manuscripts she ought to read. Now, however, it lay on the table beside her bed, and she couldn't resist picking it up.

The first half of the book was about the murder of a Dr. Harvey Burdell in 1857 in his residence at 31 Bond Street; he was knifed to death in his own study late one night in January. Now, a hundred and forty years later, Jack Finney had meticulously reconstructed the extraordinary series of events leading to his murder, a murder probably orchestrated by a woman who claimed to be his wife. Claire's appetite for nonfiction was enormous, and she often sat up in bed reading until well after midnight. Finally, when she heard the chimes of Riverside Church strike twelve, she put the book down and rolled over on her side to look out the window.

The apartment seemed empty without Ralph lurking about; she half expected him to leap up on her stomach as she lay on the bed. She looked at the clock on the bedside table: 12:03. She translated that into California time: three hours earlier. Wally's mother's number was on the pad on her bedside table. Claire ran her fingers over the phone, feeling the square little Touch-Tone buttons. After her trek through downtown Manhattan, with its echoes of old New York, the wonder of it all hit her: a movement of the wrist, a light pressure of her fingers upon a plastic console, and she would be connected to Wally in a room somewhere on the opposite coast on the other side of a vast, dark continent.

Savoring the moment, excitement spiraling slowly upward through her stomach, she dialed the number. His mother answered.

"Hello, Mrs. Jackson. It's Claire Rawlings."

"Oh, hello, dear. I'm so sorry—you just missed him. He's gone out to meet an old friend for a drink."

"Male or female?" Claire wanted to say, but instead she said, "Oh, that's all right. I was just back in New York and thought I'd call."

"Oh, are you done with your seminars?"

"Oh, no—not yet." Claire wondered what Wally had told his mother, whether or not she knew about the murders. From the cheerful sound of her voice, it appeared as though she didn't. "I have to go back tomorrow," Claire said. "I just came into town for a meeting."

"Well, I'll be sure to tell him you called."

"Thank you." Claire's brain whirred as she tried to think of something else to say.

"Well, Wally will be glad to hear you called," said his mother. "Shall I have him call you when he gets in?"

"Uh, no, I guess not . . . I'm going to bed." Already she

could feel the pull of exhaustion on her body, her eyes heavy with fatigue.

"All right. Good night, then," said Ina Jackson.

"Good-bye—and thank you."

After she hung up, Claire felt dissatisfied and unfulfilled.

Even after she turned off the light, she lay there thinking about Dr. Burdell, lying in his bed at 31 Bond Street, afraid for his own life, waiting for death to come at the hands of a woman who lived under his own roof, staring into the darkness of his bedroom, the only light in the room coming from the gas lamps outside, as he listened to the sound of her footsteps upstairs. Like him, the residents at Ravenscroft lay in their beds at night, listening to the footsteps coming and going down the long hallway, wondering, always wondering, whether or not they belonged to a murderer.

Chapter 14

Claire awoke with the sound of Robert's voice hissing in her ear, her body frozen in terror. A grey dawn crept slowly up the buildings across the street, casting its pale light on their facades, their windows still dark, no movement behind them. Claire shivered under her thin cotton quilt, and then, throwing off the quilt, sat up and swung her legs out of bed, placing her feet firmly on the parquet floor.

"Time for coffee," she muttered, trying to erase the memory of Robert's voice from her ears with the sound of her own.

Ninety minutes later she and Meredith were sitting on the early-morning bus to Woodstock, watching the countryside speed by in reverse of their trip the previous day. As she watched the trees spin by she pondered the nature of time. What if you could turn back the clock and travel backward in time just as easily as you could through space?

The bus pulled into Woodstock ten minutes ahead of schedule. It was Saturday, and Tinker Street looked almost as crowded as the streets of downtown Manhattan had the previous night; on weekends, the crowds in Woodstock thickened, swelled by tourists from surrounding counties as well as the boroughs of New York City.

Liza was waiting as they climbed off the bus. Her friendly round face was sunburned; she looked as though she had spent a lot of the previous day in her garden. In her blue overalls and wooden-soled sandals, she looked as though she had always lived in Woodstock.

"Do you mind if we pick up a few things at the store?" she said as Claire heaved her bag into the trunk of the old Mercedes.

"Not at all," Claire replied, and they trudged up the hill toward the top of Tinker Street.

"I thought I'd get a couple of fruit pies for everyone tonight," Liza said as they stood in line at the Well-Bread Loaf. The bakery was crowded, and Meredith fidgeted as they waited their turn.

"I have to go to the bathroom," she complained.

"Why didn't you go on the bus?" said Claire.

Meredith made a face. "I *hate* those bathrooms; they smell *awful*!"

"All right." Claire sighed. "We'll be right back," she said to Liza, who nodded.

They found a restaurant just down the street, a cozy little Mexican place where the waiter let them use the bathroom. After Meredith was finished, Claire decided to go herself. She didn't take long, but when she emerged, Meredith was gone. Figuring she had returned to the bakery, Claire walked back up Tinker Street. Liza stood on the corner, a white cardboard cake box in one hand, a loaf of bread in the other.

"Where's Meredith?" she said as Claire approached her.

"I thought she'd come back to the bakery," Claire answered, a little arrow of fear forming in her stomach. Under normal circumstances this would be merely annoying, but these were not normal circumstances.

"Maybe she went back to the car," Liza suggested.

She and Liza walked back down Tinker Street to where the car sat in the municipal lot behind a cluster of shops, but Meredith was nowhere to be seen. They left the groceries in the car and went back out to the street.

There, standing on the corner, waiting to cross the street, was Meredith. She squinted into the sun, which reflected off her hair, smooth and shiny as a bright orange helmet. Standing there in the late-summer sunlight, she looked like a mirage.

"Meredith! What the hell are you doing?" Claire yelled. Meredith turned and saw them, her face blank with astonishment. Claire had seldom seen the girl caught so off guard, and was surprised at how vulnerable she looked. Meredith crossed the street to where they stood.

"Oh, hello," she said, trying to regain her composure.

"You scared us half to death! What do you mean by pulling something like this?" Claire scolded.

Meredith gazed at her with icy dignity, and her usual expression of amused scorn returned to her face. "I had an errand to perform."

"Then you should have *asked* me!"

Meredith rolled her eyes and let her whole body slump in exasperation. "I was afraid you'd say no."

"Where were you?" said Liza.

"At the library."

"The library?"

"I went on-line with the library computer and connected to the New York Public Library. Then I just looked up what I wanted and printed it out."

"Wow," said Liza. "They just let you do that?"

"I made it clear it was important."

"Woodstock must have a good library," said Liza, "if you can do all that."

"It's not bad," Meredith replied, "for a small town. Better than the one in West Hartford, anyway."

"So what did you find out?" said Claire.

"Check this out," Meredith said, handing the paper she was holding to Claire. The headline read TROUBLE BREWING IN THE BALKANS. The byline was Dorian Gray. Meredith pointed at it. "Look here. She talks about this little village in Bosnia; you think it might be Tahir's village?"

"There are a lot of villages in Bosnia," Claire answered. "I suppose it's possible, but I wouldn't think it's likely. But listen, Meredith: don't you ever go off again without permission, or—"

"What? You'll send me back to Connecticut?" Meredith said derisively.

"In a minute," Claire snapped. "Yes, I will."

This seemed to give the girl something to consider, because she was very quiet after that, sitting silently in the backseat of the car, her hands folded in her lap.

On the drive up to Ravenscroft, Claire noticed Liza seemed preoccupied about something. She stared out the window and sighed a lot, and when Claire spoke to her, it was a moment before Liza heard her. When she did answer, she seemed faraway, as if it were an effort for her to concentrate on what Claire was saying. This was so unlike her friend that Claire made up her mind to ask Liza what was going on.

When they pulled into the driveway to Ravenscroft's parking lot, Meredith leaped out of the backseat.

"I'll take the bags upstairs!" she said cheerfully, throwing her knapsack over her shoulder. There wasn't much to carry, only a light overnight case for Claire and Meredith's knapsack.

"Okay," Claire called after her. "I'll see you inside." As Meredith skipped up the steps to the house, Claire turned to Liza. "You want to talk?"

Liza hesitated and then sighed. "Is it that obvious?"

"Well, you're not very good at hiding your feelings, let's put it that way."

The uniformed policemen nodded to them from their patrol car as Liza and Claire passed them on the way to the house. A box of doughnuts sat between them on the front seat. The front porch was deserted and Liza settled herself in one of the director's chairs.

"What is it?" said Claire. "What's wrong?"

Liza's big friendly face crumpled. She looked deflated, like a balloon slowly losing air. "It's Sherry. We—we had a fight. We're kind of . . . on the rocks, I guess you might say."

"Oh, I'm so sorry," said Claire. She wondered if Liza knew that she had overheard them fighting a few nights ago.

Liza stared down at her hands, dirt encrusted under her fingernails. "Well, I suppose it's my fault, really. I accused her of being a flirt—and worse. I mean, she *is* a flirt, you know, but that's not the worst thing in the world."

"Right. Camille's a flirt," Claire pointed out.

Liza smiled sadly. "True. But I'm not in love with Camille. The thing is, Sherry's always assured me that the age difference between us doesn't matter to her, but I worry about it anyway."

"Just how much difference is there?"

"Sixteen years."

Claire shook her head. "Yeah, that's a lot. But if it really doesn't matter to her—"

"That's the thing. She says it doesn't, but then I get insecure when I think she's flirting with someone, and I get—well, possessive, I guess. That's what Sherry says, anyway."

"So what happens now?"

"Well, last night she slept in the big house—in Terry's old room, actually."

"Really?"

Liza smiled. "Yeah. I would have been scared to sleep in there . . . I'm not sure why. But you know Sherry; she's not afraid of anything." She made no attempt to disguise the admiration in her voice, and Liza felt sorry for her old friend.

Just then the screen door swung open and Two Joe strolled onto the porch.

"Speaking of flirts," Liza murmured under her breath, and Claire laughed.

"Hello, Two Joe," she said.

"So what if I'm a flirt?" he responded.

"You *heard* that?" Liza said.

He nodded. "In the deserts of the Southwest, I trained my ears to hear the wings of a hawk overhead." He shrugged. "It is a skill like any other, and can be developed."

Meredith came charging out of the house and down the porch steps toward the line of mailboxes across the road. "Anyone get the mail yet?" she sang out as she went.

"I don't know," Liza called after her as Two Joe took out a long hunting knife from a sheath around his belt and cut off a branch of the honeysuckle hanging over the porch.

"Hey," said Claire, "You have one of those, too?"

He shrugged. "Why not?"

"Does Detective Hansom know?" Liza asked.

"I don't know," he replied. "Should he?"

Just then Meredith came flying up the stairs. "Hey, look—a letter from Paris!" she cried, displaying the envelope.

"Who's it for?" said Liza.

"Camille," Meredith said. "It's okay; I'll give it to her."

"Just a second, let me see that," said Claire, taking the letter from her. There was no name on the return, only an address on Rue Léopold-Robert. She handed the letter back to Meredith.

"Hmm," Liza remarked. "The plot thickens?"

"Camille is a lady of mystery," Two Joe remarked.

"What's *her* Indian name?" Meredith asked.

Two Joe scratched his smooth chin. "Let's see . . . how about Veiled Iris?"

"Ooo, I like it! Veiled Iris," Meredith repeated.

"That captures her sense of mystery," said Liza. "You know, I'm not sure I want to know what my Indian name is," she added with a laugh.

"I like mine!" Meredith chirped. "Lightning Flash— that's a good one for me."

"Yes," Liza replied, still smiling, "it is."

Just then Sherry emerged from the house, and the temperature on the porch seemed to fall.

"Hi," she said in a pleasant enough voice, but she avoided Liza's eyes as she walked down the steps toward the road.

"Meredith already got the mail," Liza called after her.

Sherry stopped and turned around. "Oh. Anything for me?"

"Uh—nope," Meredith said, leafing through the pile.

"Okay, thanks," Sherry answered, and headed in the direction of her studio.

"Well, back to work, I guess," Two Joe said, and started off toward his studio.

"I wanna talk more about Indian names," Meredith declared, walking after him.

"Meredith, Two Joe has work to do," Claire said.

"It's all right," he answered. "Come talk to me while I work, Lightning Flash."

"But—" Claire began, but he stopped her.

"It's all right, I can concentrate. After all, my work isn't about words, it's about images."

"That's true," Liza pointed out. "Did you know Mozart's wife used to recite poetry to him while he composed?"

"Cool!" said Meredith, taking Two Joe's arm. "Come on, let's go!"

Liza watched them leave. "Someone's got a crush."

Claire shook her head. "You think? I don't think of Meredith as having sexual feelings."

Liza laughed. "Boy! Spoken like a parent; can you say 'denial'?"

"No, I mean it," Claire protested. "I really think sexuality isn't a part of who she is—not yet, anyway. Hey, listen, there's something I have to tell you," she added. She went on to tell Liza what she knew about Jack—the book in Peter's office, the whole thing. Liza agreed that they should tell Detective Hansom.

"It may be of no significance, but we can't take that chance," she said.

"Right," Claire agreed. "It's weird, though; it feels a little bit like tattling."

Liza shrugged. "Whatever. Listen, as far as Jack is concerned, I don't really care. He's so irritating."

"Well, that may be," said Claire, "but—"

She was interrupted by the screen door, which was suddenly flung open. Sherry stood in the doorway, her face flushed under her deep tan.

"Look," she said, her voice trembling. In her hand she held a small bound book with a blue-and-pink-flowered cover.

"What is it?" said Liza.

Sherry held up the book reverently, as though she were holding a sacred text. "It's Maya's diary."

Chapter 15

"Where on earth did you find it?" Liza asked.

"It was tucked away behind a little false cubbyhole in the closet. It's no wonder the cops didn't find it . . . the only reason I stumbled on it was that I tripped trying to find the closet light and fell forward—and I caught myself and the wall caved in."

"Wow, this house has more secrets than I thought," Liza said.

"I bet Terry cut the hole himself," Claire suggested.

Liza looked surprised. "Really? Why?"

Claire shook her head. "I don't know . . . I just got the feeling he was the kind of obsessive person who would do something like that."

Liza called Detective Hansom right away, but before he arrived, she and Claire had plenty of time to peruse the later entries, the ones written just before Maya's death. When Meredith heard they had found the diary, she came dashing in from Two Joe's studio.

"Cool!" she said, running up the porch steps. "Can I see?"

Though there was nothing conclusive, there was one intriguing entry written the day after Claire arrived. *What can I do? I know about him but who can I tell? Worse, I think he* knows *I know; I see it in his eyes,* the entry read.

"So that means the killer *was* a man!" Meredith observed after reading it over Claire's shoulder.

"Not necessarily," Claire corrected her. "This may not be about the person who killed her."

"Yeah, right—and I'm Madonna," Meredith scoffed, throwing herself on the musty daybed.

"It's true," Liza agreed. "We can't necessarily conclude Maya wrote this about her killer."

"But we know one thing for sure: Terry *did* steal her journal," Sherry pointed out.

"Yeah," said Meredith. "So the murderer guessed right when he—or she—killed Terry: he did have Maya's diary."

"But the murderer never got his hands on it . . . I wonder if he knew what was in it?" said Sherry.

"From the looks of it, nothing very conclusive," Claire pointed out. "Certainly nothing worth killing someone over."

Liza shook her head. "Whoever this is, one thing is for sure: they're pretty ruthless."

No one disagreed with that.

Detective Hansom arrived before long, and when he saw the journal, he shook his head. "I'll be damned . . . where did you say you found it?"

Sherry told him the whole story, and he listened carefully, asking a few pertinent questions along the way. Then, after a trip upstairs to inspect the closet, he slipped the diary carefully into a small plastic bag, tipped his hat, and turned to go.

"You going to dust it for fingerprints?" Meredith said.

He nodded. "Probably won't do much good, but it's standard procedure."

"Wait a minute," Claire said as he was halfway down the steps. "I have something to tell you."

"Yes?"

She proceeded to tell him about Jack Mulligan, the book with his photograph in it, the *nom de plume,* everything.

"Good Lord," he said when she finished. "We've run

an FBI check on everyone, but nothing came up for Mulligan. I'll have to try this alias—what did you say it was?"

"Klaus Heiligen. I've got the book upstairs, if you want to see it."

"Yes, of course; thanks."

She ran up to her room and returned with the book. "Here you go," she said, handing it to him.

"Thanks. Thanks a lot," he said, laying a big bony hand briefly on her shoulder.

"You're welcome," she said earnestly, but even so, she felt a little bit like a tattletale.

Later, she and Meredith sat on the porch with Two Joe watching the sun go down behind the trees. Meredith was going on and on about the workings of the criminal mind, but Claire just wanted to watch the sunset. Finally, she had had enough.

"Look, Meredith, do you mind if we just watch the sunset for a while?"

"Oh, that's right. I'm sorry, I forgot," Meredith said, looking sheepish.

"Forgot what?" said Two Joe.

Meredith sighed and picked at a bug bite on her knee. "Claire was nearly strangled to death by a man . . . well, he was her boyfriend at the time."

Two Joe looked at Claire. "Why didn't you tell me?"

Claire looked away. "It's not something I really enjoy thinking about."

Two Joe nodded slowly. "No. But it does explain things I see in you."

Claire looked back at him. "What do you mean?"

Two Joe fingered the long smooth braid hanging over his right shoulder. "Oh, a sadness, perhaps, a sense that I have of you as being wounded in some way. I believe we are all wounded in some way, but with you the feeling is stronger, nearer; it's hard to put into words."

He looked out over the hills of the Catskills, which rose and swelled all around, purple in the dying light, enshrouded in their ancient mystery. "These hills are very old," he said. "There must be many legends about this valley."

"Tell me an Indian legend," said Meredith, "please?"

Two Joe leaned back in his chair and locked his thick strong fingers behind his head. "My people have legends," he said slowly, "about spirits who can change their form at will."

Meredith leaned forward, her body tense with excitement. "You mean shape-shifters?" she said. "Are you talking about them?"

Two Joe leaned toward her. "Some people call them that. Some say they roam the hills at dusk, looking for a new form to inhabit. Some say they are the spirits of ancestors long past, left to watch over the living . . . others say they are neither human nor animal, but a creature somewhere in between, halfway between this world and the next."

Meredith sat quietly as he talked; Claire had never seen her so still except when she was sleeping. "Wow," she said. "That is *so* cool. Are they good or bad, these shape-shifters?"

Two Joe shrugged. "It depends. Some spirits are evil, and some are good. Some can be helpful . . . my grandfather was a great medicine man, and I have heard that he had the ability to change his form at certain times."

"Cool!" said Meredith. "What about you? Can you . . . ?"

"I inherited some of my grandfather's skill," said Two Joe, "but not that one, I'm afraid." He turned to Claire. "I am a medicine man, though, and I can help others to heal." He reached over and took her hand, and once again she was struck by how warm his skin was.

"Some wounds take a long time to heal," he said, "and some never seem to heal entirely. See that you attend to yours, Redbird; the healing process can be long, but it is there for those who seek it."

Meredith looked up at Two Joe with admiration. "Wow," she said. "You're so wise."

Two Joe laughed. "Wise? Sometimes I think I'm just a person who talks to hear my own voice." He got up and stretched his long torso. The size and solidity of his body were comforting to Claire; she found his presence reassuring.

"Well," he said, "back to work, which is really the best medicine of all." He looked at Meredith solemnly. "You will help me take care of her, Lightning Flash, won't you?"

"Don't worry, I will," Meredith said seriously. "You can count on me."

Two Joe nodded. "I know I can."

Later that afternoon Sherry was on the porch fussing with a bouquet of wildflowers, arranging them in a pewter pitcher, when Tahir came onto the porch, hands in his pockets. Claire was settled comfortably in the wicker armchair with a manuscript while Meredith hovered over a chessboard, studying possible moves.

Sherry looked up from her task when Tahir entered the porch. "Happy birthday a day early," she said cheerfully.

Tahir looked at her blankly. "What?"

"Isn't it your birthday tomorrow?" she replied, a sprig of Queen Anne's lace in her hand.

Tahir gazed at her sadly. "Oh. I stopped counting these things when . . . when I lost my family."

Sherry's brown face reddened. "Oh," she said. "Sorry to remind you."

Meredith looked up from her chessboard. "Seems to me that's even more reason to remember."

Tahir sighed. "It's hard to explain . . . excuse me," he said, and went back into the house.

Sherry shook her head. "Oops. Open mouth, insert foot."

Claire looked at her. "You couldn't know. How could you know?"

"I know," Sherry replied. "But I feel sorry for him. He's so thin and—well, haunted looking."

"I know what you mean," said Claire. "he looks like he needs someone to feed him up a little."

Meredith scratched her head. "Interesting," she said, "very interesting." Claire wasn't sure if she was talking about Tahir or the chess game.

Chapter 16

That night the residents decided to have a communal
dinner. Everyone was beginning to feel like a prisoner,
watched over night and day by the police, and Liza thought
a big dinner together would be good for morale. Liza made
a vegetarian stir-fry, Billy bought fresh sweet corn, Sherry
baked muffins, and even Jack got in on the action, prepar-
ing a tomato-and-basil salad with Bermuda onions. To
Claire's surprise, Gary contributed a plate of barbecued
pork chops.

"You're not one of the vegetarians?" Claire said as Gary
stood over the barbecue grill. Immaculate in khaki slacks
and a pressed blue-and-white-striped shirt, he looked as if
he had just stepped off a yacht.

Gary snorted softly. "Oh, please. Some people spend entirely too much time thinking about what they put in their
stomachs."

"That smells good," said Claire, inhaling the woody
aroma of the roasting meat.

Gary poked at the chops with a long, sharp fork. "An
old family recipe, straight from the Georgia plantation."

"Your family is Southern? You don't sound Southern."

Gary raised one thin eyebrow. "Honey," he drawled, "if

you's a *Negro* in this country, you's from the South at some point or other."

Claire wasn't sure how to react to this; was she supposed to laugh? She found it hard to relax around Gary; he was so formal, so professorial, and this ironic little impersonation was out of character.

She gave a dry little chuckle. "I see. Well, it certainly does smell good." She looked around for an excuse to leave. "I'd better go see if Liza needs any help in the kitchen," she said. "Do you need anything?"

Gary shook his elegant head. "No thank you."

The sun was just sinking over the mountains when the residents seated themselves around the picnic table on the porch, surrounded by steaming platters of food, four bottles of Merlot on the table in front of them, courtesy of Evelyn Gardner and the Woodstock Guild. The mood was oddly festive, as if everyone was tired of feeling bad; cheered by the food, people seemed more relaxed than Claire had seen them since she arrived. It all had the feeling of a wartime celebration. Worn-out from being suspicious of one another, the residents were making a special effort to get along.

Sooner or later, though, the conversation inevitably bent around toward crime. Sherry advanced the idea that you could tell some people were criminals just by looking at them.

"That's ridiculous," said Gary. "If that were true, then innocent people would never get wrongly convicted."

"Not *everybody,* just *some* criminals," said Sherry.

"What about the criminals in your books?" Jack said to Claire, spearing a pork chop and dropping it onto his plate.

"What do you mean?" said Claire, also taking a pork chop, which smelled irresistibly good.

"Well, aren't they . . . just like other people? I mean, you wouldn't necessarily recognize someone was a murderer just by looking at them?"

"Of course not," said Camille, daintily plucking a piece of arugula from her salad plate. She put it in her mouth, her red lips closing over it. Claire noticed Tahir staring at

Camille, a hungry look in his deep-set eyes. "I mean, if you *could,* they wouldn't be able to hide so well in the general population, right?"

"Isn't the point that they look like everyone else?" Liza observed.

"But they *are* different in some way, aren't they, whether you can see it or not?" said Sherry.

"Anyone at all is capable of murder," Tahir said softly, putting down his pork chop. "That's one thing I learned in the war. Your neighbors, people you thought were your friends . . . they can become killers overnight if the circumstances are right."

"But I can't believe just *anyone* would kill another person; there have to be some of us who would refuse no matter what the pressure," Billy said angrily. Claire saw Gary trying to catch his eye, but Billy did not return the look.

Two Joe stood up. "The mind is a dark place," he said, and went into the house.

Tahir shrugged. "All I know is what I saw."

"But what about free will?" said Sherry. "If we're all potential murderers, what's the point of anything?"

"Actually, even free will is a relative concept," said Meredith, her mouth full of salad.

"Swallow before you talk, Meredith," said Claire.

Meredith swallowed heavily, her face red. "What I mean is, we're all programmed to some extent by our circumstances, by genetics—"

"And genetically we're all killers," said Gary. "Everyone knows that. It's even built into our societal structures."

"What do you mean?" said Camille.

Gary spread his long hands with their beautifully manicured nails. "Well, what's war except legalized slaughter? I mean, we're training young people to go out and *kill strangers* and then we think it's horrible when a murderer is loose in Ulster County."

"But it's different," said Sherry.

"How? How is it different? We reward soldiers for doing

exactly the same thing. Isn't killing just killing on some level?"

Camille put down her salad fork. "But in one case people are killing because they're *told* to do it by—"

"By their superiors," Jack interjected, smiling. "Careful, now, you're skating on thin ice. This defense didn't work too well for the men at Nürnberg."

Sherry stared at him. "They committed atrocities against mankind," she said angrily, her voice sharp as flint.

"Oh, as opposed to the bombing of Dresden, which killed thousands of civilians and destroyed an ancient city— or Hiroshima? I suppose there were no crimes committed there," Jack replied.

"Japan declared war against *us*," said Sherry.

"And that makes it all right to sacrifice millions of innocent civilians? At least soldiers *know* they might die."

Sherry's face reddened under her deep tan. "Japan showed no sign of surrender, and the war might have gone on and on—"

"Oh, I see." Jack smiled. "So the good ol' USA was in the right then, too. And what about the Indians, look what we did to them. I guess that was understandable, too?"

Just then Two Joe appeared at the door, a mug of coffee in his hand. "What happened to my people was destined to happen. We were not strong enough, and the way of nature is the strong always overcome the weak."

"*That's* a depressing thought," said Liza.

Two Joe shrugged. "To the victor belong the spoils."

There was an uncomfortable silence as people stared at their plates and sipped their wine. Meredith poked at a june bug crawling up the table leg.

"Well," Camille said finally, "if we're all murderers, then why aren't we all killing each other all the time?"

Jack shrugged. "Because we don't need to. People will usually take the path of least resistance."

"In other words, there aren't more killings not because people are good, but because they're lazy," said Liza.

"Or scared. Most people know there's a better than fifty-fifty chance of getting caught."

"And these days with modern forensics the chances are even greater," said Meredith.

"The exception, of course," said Jack, "is serial killers. They're so driven that risk becomes secondary to them. And, of course, to them their crimes *seem* necessary, fulfilling as they do a deep need in their psyche."

Meredith looked at him. "How do you know so much about serial killers?"

Jack studied his napkin. "Because I was once a cop."

No one said anything for several moments. Meredith stared at Jack, a bit of hamburger caught on her lower lip. Claire could hear the busy twitterings of birds in the bushes nearby. A fly landed on the table, inspected the corn bread, then took off suddenly, buzzing off in a circular flight pattern.

Finally, Liza spoke. "Do you think we're dealing with a serial killer here?" she said softly.

Jack shook his head. "I don't think so. The victims are too different, and there's no sign of obsessive ritual. A serial killer is endlessly reenacting a psychological drama in his head, and there's an obsessively repetitive quality to serial crimes which doesn't fit this killer."

"Wow," Meredith said respectfully, "that's good. You know what you're talking about."

Jack brushed the crumbs from his hunting vest. "Well, that's enough shoptalk for one evening."

Claire thought she heard Two Joe snort softly at the other end of the table.

"Well," said Meredith, "I gave Detective Hansom some of Maya's old articles, just in case the answer to her murder lies somewhere in her past."

"But how would that link her to Terry?" said Sherry.

"I don't know, but some of them are pretty interesting," Meredith replied, reaching across the table for some bread. Claire was just about to reprimand her boardinghouse reach when Jack Mulligan's wineglass tipped over, spilling out onto the tablecloth, a quickly spreading red stain. Sherry sprang from her seat and soaked up the excess with her napkin.

Camille rose and headed for the kitchen. "I'll get a dish-cloth."

To Claire's surprise, Jack turned to Tahir Hasonovic. "Be careful, for Christ's sake!" he said.

Tahir looked at him, a bewildered expression on his face. "What do you mean?" he said softly.

"Oh, come on; you knocked it over," Jack replied angrily.

"All right, all right," said Liza. "Let's not fight about it, okay? There's no harm done."

Jack muttered something under his breath but sat down and resumed eating. Everyone else did the same, but an uncomfortable hush settled over them, broken only by the mournful howl of coyotes up on Guardian Mountain.

Later, sitting in front of the fire at her cabin with Meredith and Claire, Liza said, "So, Jack's an ex-cop. That explains a lot about his political views."

"Hey, careful," said Meredith from the sofa, where she lay with Nubs curled at her feet. "Claire's dating a cop, you know."

Liza and Sherry both looked at Claire, who felt herself blushing.

"Oh *really*?" said Sherry. "Dish, dish—what's he like?" She and Liza had apparently worked out their differences, though Liza had not spoken further to Claire about it.

"He's okay," said Meredith. "He's old but kinda sexy."

"You probably think everyone over twenty is old," said Liza.

"Naw, he's got grey hair and everything."

"I'll bet it's nice grey hair," Sherry said to Claire, "nice and thick. Is it?"

"Well, I like it," Claire replied, feeling both pleased and embarrassed.

"I'll bet it falls over one eye in a really sexy way," said Sherry. She was sitting on the rug at Liza's feet, while Liza sat in a low overstuffed armchair. A blue cotton Indian spread covered the chair; on it were stenciled multilimbed gods, sitting cross-legged, waving their many arms over their heads.

Liza casually ruffled Sherry's smooth black hair. "You're embarrassing Claire," she said.

"Oh, she loves it. You love it, don't you, Claire?" said Sherry.

"Well . . ." Claire replied.

"So what's it like dating a cop? Are they good in bed?"

"Sherry!" said Liza, flicking the top of Sherry's head with her open palm.

"Ow," said Sherry.

"That's no way to talk in front of Meredith."

"Don't worry; I've heard worse." Meredith rolled over onto her elbow. "Once I even walked in on my dad doing the nasty with the Wicked Witch herself. If *that* didn't warp my young mind, then I'm immune to damage."

Liza laughed. "Sometimes I wonder who's more of a child, you or Sherry."

"I am," said Sherry, grinning. "I'm a bad girl and I deserve to be spanked." Liza flipped a hand at her head again, but Sherry ducked.

"Well, I'm smart but I'm very immature," said Meredith.

Everyone laughed, startling Nubs, who leaped off the couch and stood in the center of the room, looking irritated, then walked slowly into the kitchen.

"Hey," said Meredith, "I thought you told me Tahir was supposed to be a Muslim."

"That's right," said Liza.

"Then how come he was eating pork chops?"

Liza shook her head. "Maybe he's not practicing anymore."

"After all, not all Jews are kosher," said Sherry. "I'm not, for example."

"It's so ironic, isn't it?" said Claire. "Arabs and Jews are both Semitic, they share some of the same dietary rules, and yet . . ."

"Go figure," Sherry said. "I've stopped trying. My parents are such Zionists, too. You know, the first question is always 'Is this good for Israel or bad for Israel?' "

"Hey," said Meredith, "what's with Billy and Gary? I saw them looking at each other during dinner."

Sherry smiled and leaned back on a camel-hair hassock that sat to one side of the woodstove.

"Gary and Billy? Didn't you know?"

"Know what?" said Meredith.

"Sherry . . ." Liza said, reaching for her, but Sherry laughed and shook her off.

"Oh, come *on;* it's no secret!"

"*What* isn't?" said Meredith.

"Gary and Billy were an item last summer—very hot and heavy and all that."

Claire tried to imagine cool and aloof Gary Robinson being hot and heavy with anyone, but she couldn't picture it.

"Anyway," Sherry continued, "what I understand from talking to Gary, Billy was the one who pursued him, and then when the summer ended, he suddenly went from hot to cold, leaving Gary all confused. They exchanged letters over the winter, but Gary's still not sure what happened."

"So Gary confides in you?" Meredith said.

"Mmm." Sherry nodded and reached for Nubs, who had just sauntered in from the kitchen. She scratched the top of his head; the cat flattened his ears and smiled, his purring gathering volume, rumbling like a little diesel engine. "Maybe it's because we're both 'minorities' or something— I don't know—but he's always seemed to be able to talk to me."

Claire nodded. "So he comes back here and finds Billy involved with this—"

"Shiksa goddess," said Sherry.

Claire thought Liza tensed at these words; she remembered the argument she overheard the night Maya was murdered, with Sherry accusing Liza of being jealous—and it occurred to her that Maya might have been the object of Sherry's affections as well.

". . . and no wonder he's pissed at Billy," Meredith was saying. "He doesn't know whether he's coming or going."

"But if Gary killed Maya, why would he then use his own knife to kill Terry? Gary's much smarter than that."

Meredith's eyes narrowed as she looked into the glowing coals of the potbellied stove. "Maybe there were two killers," she said slowly. "Maybe whoever killed Terry did it to protect Maya's killer."

The rest of them in the room looked at each other.

"Or to punish him," Claire added. Her implication was clear: Billy.

"But if Billy did kill Terry, thinking he had killed Maya, why would he use Gary's knife?" said Liza.

Meredith smiled enigmatically. "Why indeed?"

"That's a very good question," said Claire.

"One thing I know," said Meredith, "*this* killer will slip up sooner or later, and then we'll have him."

"Or her," said Sherry.

"Or her," Meredith repeated.

The flames from the stove reflected yellow on her face, turning her hair the color of burnished copper. A silence fell over the women in the room and Claire tried to imagine a woman slitting Terry's throat or wrapping her hands around Maya's white neck.

Chapter 17

The media frenzy that greeted Terry's death lasted two days, then the vans and cables and parade of TV reporters in pressed polyester and shellacked hair vanished as suddenly as they had come. When no arrests were forthcoming, they slid off into the night to cover local mayoral politicking; a fight between an Ulster County Republican incumbent and a Democratic challenger showed promising signs of getting ugly.

The police presence, however, remained. Claire still had not gotten used to the constant presence of patrol cars in front of Ravenscroft. It was startling to walk onto the porch and see the patrol cars parked out on Camelot Road. Detective Hansom had ordered a twenty-four-hour police presence (Meredith liked to call it "surveillance") at the house, and every eight hours one black-and-white patrol car would pull out from the dusty dirt of Camelot Road, only to be replaced by another identical one. The policemen who came and went were almost as much alike as their patrol cars. Young, with close-cropped hair and pink scrubbed faces, they looked chubby and soft in their uniforms, which always appeared to be one size too small. Watching them consume a steady supply of Dunkin' Donuts and coffee,

Claire wondered if joining the police force led to the same mandatory weight gain college freshmen traditionally experienced.

Sergeant Rollins, Detective Hansom's second in command, was no exception. Puffy-faced from his cold virus, he stumbled into the kitchen every morning to load his thermos with coffee; Camille insisted on making coffee for the officers whenever possible. "They're our protectors," she would say as she poured another steaming pot of black coffee into a thermos carafe and carried it down to where the policemen sat in their cars, the ubiquitous box of Dunkin' Donuts nestled between their chunky blue-clad thighs on the front seat.

Claire thought Camille just liked policemen. She could certainly relate to that; after all, Wally Jackson was a police detective. Claire had tried to imagine him in his previous life as a professor, but when she tried to picture him standing in front of eager college students, she always saw him in his rumpled trench coat.

This morning Sergeant Rollins stood in the kitchen doorway, his eyes streaming, sniffling loudly.

"Oh, you poor thing," Camille purred as she poured water into the coffeemaker. "What you need is some really nice herbal tea."

"Well, I don't—" the sergeant began, but Camille cut him off.

"Now, don't argue; caffeine just dehydrates you," she said, taking his thermos.

Sergeant Rollins looked to Claire for help, his eyes pleading. "I really—" he began, but the shrill whistle of the teakettle drowned him out.

"You'll like this," said Camille, pouring water into a pot filled with green flakes. They smelled like a combination of freshly mowed grass and mud.

"This has slippery elm in it," Camille said cheerfully, pressing the thermos into his hands. "Very good for the throat. Drink a cup of this every hour and you'll feel better in no time."

Sergeant Rollins opened his mouth as if he wanted to

speak, but Camille took him by the shoulders and turned him toward the door.

"No need to thank me," she said. "I'm glad to do it."

Sergeant Rollins gave one last desperate glance over his shoulder at Claire and walked out of the kitchen with the slow, heavy tread of a condemned man.

Meredith brushed past him into the kitchen, sniffed at the air, and wrinkled her nose. "Who farted?"

"Meredith, that's rude," said Claire.

"It's medicinal tea for Sergeant Rollins's cold," said Camille, cleaning out the teapot.

"Ugh," Meredith grunted. "Smells like elephant farts."

"All right, Meredith, that's enough," Claire said, ushering her out of the kitchen.

They went out to the porch, arriving just in time to see Sergeant Rollins pouring the contents of his thermos into the bushes. When he heard the screen door bang, he looked up furtively.

"Oh, it's you," he said, returning to his task.

Meredith leaned over the porch railing, her legs dangling. "That stuff's awful, isn't it? It smells like—"

"All right, Meredith," said Claire, "we've heard enough from you on the topic of what it smells like."

"You won't tell Camille, will you?" Sergeant Rollins said. "I don't want to hurt her feelings."

Meredith swung one leg over the railing and perched herself on top of it. "Don't worry, your secret's safe with me."

Claire had the feeling she had heard those words recently, and tried to think where. Then she remembered: Jack Mulligan had said the exact same thing to Roger Gardner at the party Liza gave for her. *Don't worry, your secret's safe with me.* At the time she remembered wondering what Jack was talking about. Now that she knew, she wondered how on earth Jack knew.

The screen door opened and Gary Robinson entered the porch.

"Hello, Gary," said Claire.

"Good morning," Gary said, his manner stiff and formal as usual.

"Claire tells me you own a hunting knife," Meredith said, affecting a casual air.

Gary looked at them, the sun reflecting off his wire-frame glasses, making them opaque, so Claire couldn't see his eyes. "You saw me whittling with it," he said simply. "But it disappeared."

"Oh? When?" said Meredith.

"A couple of days ago."

"Before—"

"Before Terry was killed," Gary finished for her in an irritated voice. "I told Detective Hansom all about that."

"Don't be so blasé about it," said Meredith. "If they find the knife is the murder weapon and your prints are on it, you're in trouble."

"Oh, for Christ's sake, that only happens in movies," said Gary, going down the stairs and out toward the artists' studios.

Sergeant Rollins drew a soppy grey handkerchief from his pocket and blew his nose loudly. "Uh, excuse me, sir, may I ask you where you are going?"

Gary turned and looked at the sergeant. His eyes fell on the handkerchief, which he gazed at with the same disdain one might regard a dog who has just tried to hump someone's leg.

"To my studio," he said curtly. "If you don't mind, I'm going to get some work done. This place is still an arts colony, and that's what I came up here for." He then continued on his way without looking back.

Sergeant Rollins looked after Gary. "Just trying to do my job, that's all . . . and these people treat me as if I'm accusing them of being the killer. That one," he said, shaking his head, "he hasn't got a chip on his shoulder, he's got a whole goddamn log. Oh, begging your pardon, ma'am," he said quickly, looking at Claire, who couldn't help smiling.

"Don't worry, Sergeant," said Meredith. "I heard worse

than that before I was old enough to have a golf handicap."

Sergeant Rollins's round face clouded over. "Before you . . . ?"

"It's a joke," Meredith said wearily. "I'm from Connecticut."

"Oh, I get it," he said, frowning. "A *golf* handicap; sure, sure."

The faint sound of the phone ringing came from inside the house, and Meredith lunged for the door. "I'll get it!"

A few moments later she emerged from the house, the screen door banging loudly behind her. "It's my father. He wants to know when to come get me," she said, her voice heavy with disgust. "He wants to talk to you."

Claire got up and went inside. She picked up the dangling receiver.

"Hi, this is Claire."

"Hello, Claire." Ted Lawrence's voice was tight, as tense as she'd ever heard him. "I was wondering when you'd like me to come for Meredith."

"Well, I—"

"As usual, she's not anxious to come home; but I suppose you know that."

Claire felt that it was more polite not to say anything, so she remained silent. Ted Lawrence continued.

"Well, I can understand how she feels . . . she and her stepmother don't get along very well, though whose fault it is I'm not sure."

Knowing Jean Lawrence, Claire was somewhat biased— she didn't see how anyone could live with that woman— but she also felt sorry for her. Meredith had probably been against her from the very beginning. She was, after all, in the unenviable position of not being Katherine Lawrence— and therefore not Meredith's mother.

"Look," said Ted Lawrence, the discomfort in his voice almost palpable, "what would you think about keeping her there for a few more days? Would that be a terrible imposition?"

"No, not at all. I'm enjoying having her around, and I think everyone else is, too."

"Good. Good, I'm glad." He paused, and Claire thought, *Uh-oh, here it comes.* She didn't want to hear any details of his troubles with his wife. The tension was increased by his upper-crust Connecticut dignity; it was kind of like knowing about Walter Cronkite's bathroom habits: you just didn't want to think about it.

To her surprise, though, he just sighed and said, "Thank you again. I'll send you a check for expenses, and please feel free to call me if there are any problems at all."

"All right." Claire was a little surprised he had not expressed concern over Meredith's safety; surely the girl told him about the second murder. She opened her mouth to say something, but he had already hung up.

When Claire returned to the porch, she saw that Meredith had somehow managed to capture Ralph. Pinned down on the daybed, he submitted to her caresses with a martyred air, ears flat against his head, eyes tragic. He looked up at Claire with the wronged innocence of a melodrama heroine, pleading for deliverance from this fate worse than death. Claire decided on distraction as the quickest route to liberation.

"How about some cookies?" she said. "There's a fresh box in the kitchen."

"Okay!" Meredith cried, jumping up and releasing her captive. Ralph fled immediately, leaping from the porch into the thicket of bushes that surrounded it. Claire was glad that age and experience gave her some advantages; bright as Meredith was, she was unaware of such manipulations—or so Claire hoped.

Claire sat down on one of the director's chairs and sighed.

"It's a constant job, isn't it?" said Camille, coming out onto the porch as Meredith rushed inside.

"What? Oh, yeah, I guess it is . . ." Claire looked around for Sergeant Rollins, but he had vanished.

Meredith emerged from the house with a box of assorted Pepperidge Farm cookies. "Well, what did the Ur-

WASP say?" she said, plopping down onto the daybed, her thin legs akimbo.

"Who's that?" said Camille.

"That's what Meredith calls her father," said Claire.

"Well, what did he say?" said Meredith, popping a Bordeaux cookie in her mouth.

"He said you can stay."

"*Yes!*" Meredith flung her arms into the air like a running back after scoring a touchdown.

"Hmm . . . I'm surprised he isn't concerned for her safety," said Camille.

Claire looked at Meredith. "You *did* tell him about the second murder, didn't you?"

Meredith rolled her eyes and sighed. "Why *should* I? What *difference* does it make?"

"You know perfectly well what difference it makes! Your father should know everything before he makes a decision like that. I'm going to go call him back."

"No, please no!" Meredith cried, tears springing to her eyes. "You can't call him back; he'll think you don't want me!" Her mood changed abruptly from casual to tragic.

"But he should know—"

"No, no—don't you *see*? He'll think you're trying to get out of it!"

Claire thought for a moment. Meredith was right; that was exactly how Ted Lawrence would interpret another call right now.

"What about you?" Camille said to Meredith. "Aren't you concerned about your safety?"

"No way," she answered breezily. "I can take care of myself."

"I believe you," said Camille, smiling.

"I still think we should call him back," said Claire, but her heart wasn't in it, and she knew Meredith sensed this.

"I'm safer here with policemen all over the place than I would be up in Hartford with the Wicked Witch."

"Speaking of the cops, have you seen Sergeant Rollins?" said Camille. "I made him some tea, but then he disappeared."

As if in response, at that moment Sergeant Rollins appeared, walking along Camelot Road, coming from the direction of the woods.

"Good morning, Sergeant; we were just wondering where you were," Camille called out.

Sergeant Rollins sneezed loudly. "Sorry," he said, fishing his soggy handkerchief from his pants pocket.

"What's going on out there at the scene of the crime?" Meredith said.

Sergeant Rollins blew his nose and stuffed the handkerchief back into his pocket. "Well, the boys are combing the woods for clues."

"Find anything?"

"If we did, we wouldn't be able to reveal it to you, I'm afraid."

Meredith snapped a twig off a tree branch in an attempt to look casual. "Sure . . . I understand how it is . . . you probably haven't found anything anyway. This killer's pretty clever."

"Not *that* clever," the sergeant replied, sounding a little peeved.

"Well, no offense, but you're only a country police department," Meredith said, studying her shoelaces. "You can hardly be a match for . . . well, you know."

Sergeant Rollins's already pink face reddened. *My God, she's playing him,* thought Claire.

"We've learned a few things about this killer," he said defensively.

"Oh?" said Meredith. "Like what?"

Claire exchanged a glance with Camille, who smiled and went into the house.

"Well, the killer's right-handed, for one thing."

"Yeah? How do you know that?"

Sergeant Rollins was about to answer, but just then a plain black sedan pulled into the driveway, scattering dust and gravel. The driver's side door opened and a tired-looking Detective Hansom climbed out. His broad, bony shoulders slumped, like a tree bent by too many storms.

Weight of the world on his shoulders, thought Claire. Why did she find that quality so appealing in a man?

The detective walked over to where they were gathered on the porch and rested one long leg upon the bottom step.

"Hello, sir," said Sergeant Rollins.

"Anything to report, Sergeant?"

"Nothing yet, sir; McGill and Evans are out there now."

Just then Camille emerged from the house carrying a tray of tea. "You're just in time for tea, Inspector."

"Detective," he corrected gently.

"Sorry—Detective," Camille replied, setting the tray down on the shaky beechwood coffee table. As she poured the tea Claire admired her slim fingers and immaculately manicured nails. The only jewelry decorating her elegant hands today was a simple silver band on the fourth finger of her right hand. She wore a chic little tan jacket over a crisp white shirt, and black linen pants. Even though she dressed more elegantly than the rest of the residents, Claire thought, Camille never looked overdressed.

Detective Hansom settled his bony frame uneasily in one of the canvas director's chairs. He looked as if he were to move too suddenly, the chair might topple.

"Tea, Sergeant?" Camille said. Rollins hesitated, looking at Detective Hansom, who nodded.

"Go ahead—might help that cold of yours."

"Thank you, sir," said Rollins, taking the cup Camille handed him. He sniffed at it, and then, apparently satisfied, leaned against the porch railing and sipped it greedily. Camille had evidently given up on the idea of herbal tea.

"What can we do for you, Detective?" said Meredith, trying unsuccessfully to conceal her excitement.

"What I was wondering," Hansom said as he stirred milk into his tea, "was if any of you knew whether Mr. Nordstrom was accustomed to smoking cigarettes."

"Why?" said Meredith, her thin body tense.

"If you would just answer the question, I'd appreciate it," Hansom replied.

"He used to bum them from me," said Camille, "but to my knowledge, he never bought any."

"And what brand do you smoke?"

"Sobraine Black Russians," Camille replied, taking the pack from her jacket pocket.

"Why?" said Meredith.

Detective Hansom laughed suddenly, a little explosion of mirth shaking his lanky frame. "You never stop, do you?"

"You scratch my back and I'll scratch yours," said Meredith, undeterred. "I might be able to dig up some information you'd find useful."

"All right, Meredith, that's enough," said Claire.

Detective Hansom leaned back in his chair, the canvas straining under the pressure. Claire looked over at Camille, who was busy looking at the detective, a little smile on her face.

"Well . . . I don't see how it could hurt to tell you this," he said. "An unopened box of Sobraine Black Russians was found among Mr. Nordstrom's things."

"So that's what happened to my cigarettes!" said Camille, setting her teacup down so hard the china rattled.

"What do you mean?" asked Sergeant Rollins from his perch on the porch railing.

"Well, I had a new box of Sobraines disappear right before . . . actually, it was right before Maya was killed," she said softly.

"Are you certain about that?" said Detective Hansom.

"Yes, I remember; I got you a pack while I was in town," said Claire.

"Right."

"And that's the pack you have now?" said Hansom.

"No," answered Camille. "That's the pack that disappeared. Liza got me these."

"Hmmm," said Meredith, swinging her legs back and forth under her chair, "the plot thickens."

Their little tea party was broken up by the appearance of Jack Mulligan, who drifted out onto the porch and sat down in one of the director's chairs. He wore his green army fatigues over thick-soled boots. He held an unlit pipe in his right hand, the three remaining fingers curling around the wooden bowl of the pipe.

"Hello, Detective," he said to Hansom. "What brings you to our humble little mountainside dwelling? Did someone else die?"

Detective Hansom ignored the question. "How did you lose your fingers, Mr. Mulligan?" he said evenly.

Jack Mulligan smiled broadly, his blue eyes almost swallowed in a thick web of crow's-feet. "It was in 'Nam. Serving my country and all that. A shell came along and took part of me with it."

The crow's-feet vanished along with his smile. " 'Course that's better than what happened to my buddy."

"What was that?" Meredith said softly, leaning forward in her chair to catch his words.

Jack Mulligan looked at her, the usual tone of bravado melted from his voice. "Caught one right in the chest. Wasn't much of him left."

His fingers closed around the pipe he held, and Claire sensed the strength in those hands, even with the missing fingers.

"At least he died quickly," he said with a little catch in his voice. Claire wondered whether it was put on or real; if this was an act, though, she had to hand it to Jack: he was an impressive actor. If it was a performance, it was subtle and convincing.

"You ever fight in a war, Detective?" he said, swiveling his head toward Hansom.

"No, I never did," Hansom replied. "Had asthma since I was a kid."

"Well, count yourself lucky . . . I'll never forget the things I saw over in 'Nam. Like to, but I never will. In all my years on the force, I never saw anything like it."

"You were a cop?" said Sergeant Rollins. He teetered on his perch on the porch railing, teacup precariously balanced on his knee.

"Twenty years. Took early retirement when my pension came due. I'd had enough; feet were shot, back was bad." He leaned back and stretched, and Claire saw the power in those broad shoulders. " 'Course I was just an ordinary beat cop—nothing fancy like a detective or anything. We wear out shoe leather before brain cells."

Just then Sergeant Rollins sneezed loudly, sending Ralph scurrying for the safety of the bushes.

"Gesundheit," Jack said amiably. "Well, back to work." He sighed, rising from his chair, the dry wood creaking under his weight. "Good luck with your investigation, Detective," he said, and sauntered back into the house. There was a moment of silence and then Camille spoke.

"I just don't like that man," she said through gritted teeth. Claire thought such candor was uncharacteristic of Camille, especially in front of Detective Hansom.

Meredith chewed a cookie thoughtfully. "He isn't everything that he seems."

Inspector Hansom unfolded his long body from his chair. "Thank you for the tea," he said to Camille, who smiled sweetly.

"Can I have a word with you?" Claire said as Hansom made his way down the porch steps.

"Certainly."

They went out to the side lawn, out of hearing distance of the others.

"Is what I told you about Jack useful in your investigation?" Claire asked.

He shook his shaggy head. "Could be. It's early to say. Thank you for telling me, though."

He put his large, knotty hand on her shoulder. "I know this has been hard for you," he said gently. "We're doing everything we can, you know."

She nodded. "I know."

The unspoken question hung like mist in the air between them: would it be enough?

Chapter 18

That night Claire decided to turn in early. She made herself a cup of hot cocoa and passed through the living room where Two Joe sat cross-legged in front of the fire playing cards with Meredith. Two Joe had brought his own cards from Arizona, a beautiful hand-painted deck with Native American motifs. The kings were various chiefs—Crazy Horse, Sitting Bull, and the like—and the jacks were buffalo, wolves, beaver, and other animals important to various tribes. Two Joe said his cousin had made it, and that there were only twelve such decks in existence.

"Wow, this is so cool," said Meredith, turning the cards over in the firelight as she lay on her stomach. Two Joe towered over her, his enormous thighs tucked neatly underneath him, his thick torso straight as a tree trunk. His straight black braid glistened in the glow of the fire, shiny as sealskin.

The rest of the residents had already retired, except for Camille, who lay on the couch reading.

"What are you reading?" Claire said as she passed by.

Camille held up the book. *"In Cold Blood."*

"Isn't that a little gruesome—I mean, with everything that's happened?"

Camille shrugged. "I guess. I found it in the library, and I've always wanted to read it. Now I can't put it down. He sure can write, that Truman Capote, don't you think?"

Claire nodded and took a sip of cocoa. "Oh, sure. He's wonderful. I just don't know if that's the book I'd choose to read right now."

"What shall we play?" said Meredith, handing the cards to Two Joe.

"I will teach you a Native American game," he replied.

Claire had never seen Meredith respond to anyone the way she responded to Two Joe; she clearly respected him and looked up to him—and was even a little in awe of him, Claire thought. There was no hint of the usual breezy superiority Meredith showed around other people. She went around the house trying to get everyone to call her by the Indian name he had given her.

"Well, Lightning Flash, just don't stay up too late," Claire said. "Remember you have a lot to do tomorrow."

"Detective Hansom needs your help," Two Joe said solemnly, dealing out the cards, his thick, lined fingers red like old mahogany.

"Well, I'm turning in." Claire started up the stairs. "Don't let her stay up too late, will you?" she said to Two Joe.

"Don't worry, Redbird, you can count on me."

Claire saw no sign of Ralph when she entered her room; no doubt he was out hunting, heeding the call of ancient instincts.

It was a wind-tossed night, and as Claire crawled into bed the old shutters were rattling for all they were worth, as though the hand of heaven itself were shaking them. The wind outside moaned and pitched, whistling through the eaves, making the old clapboards shudder. Claire lay awake listening to the wind as it swept and rolled through the trees outside. She watched it fling the branches back and forth, whipping them mercilessly, with the inexhaustible force of nature.

Force of nature.

Claire drifted off and awoke to see Meredith asleep on her mattress. She listened to the rising and falling breath of the girl beside her, so peaceful now, her demons locked up inside her dreams. Meredith was indeed a force of nature; when she was awake she could be as fierce as the wind that tore through the tree branches. Asleep, however, she looked like any other child: serene, innocent, almost sweet, her hands folded on her stomach as if in prayer. (Meredith would hate that image: she called herself "an avowed agnostic.")

If Meredith could pray for anything, Claire wondered, what would it be? The answer was clear and immediate: to have her mother back again. She looked out at the furiously swaying branches. Given that was impossible, she hoped Meredith would settle for the next best thing. Claire smiled. She didn't even mind being the next best thing . . . sometimes, she knew, that's all we have, and for the second time that day the thought came to her: *At least it's better than nothing at all.* She drifted off to sleep with the sound of the gale in her ears.

Claire awoke suddenly to see Meredith's face hovering over her in the half darkness. "What?" she said, alarmed. "What's wrong?"

"I've got it!" Meredith whispered fiercely. "I've finally figured it out!"

"Figured what out?"

"The *key;* it's all *there,* in quantum mechanics!"

Claire turned on the bedside lamp, shielding her eyes from the light with her hand. She propped herself up on one elbow. "What are you talking about?"

"Quantum mechanics states that it is impossible to *observe* an object without changing it; in other words, the *act of observation itself* influences the outcome of an event!"

Claire looked at the clock next to the bed. It was 2:25 A.M. "Is *that* what you woke me up to tell me?"

Meredith stood up and began pacing the room. The lamplight glinted off her hair, dark rust in the pale yellow light.

"It's been there all along; I can't believe I didn't *see* it!"

Claire sighed and sat up in the bed, propping herself up

with two pillows. When Meredith was in this mood there was nothing to do but listen.

"See, the murderer is being *watched* now—and that alters their behavior!"

"So? I don't see what you're getting at."

"Terry was murdered because he was observing the murderer!"

"You mean he knew who—"

"Or the murderer *thought* he knew—or was getting close."

Claire was wide awake now. "So Terry was killed before he could talk."

"Exactly. Now, the question is what led the murderer to believe that Terry was about to figure out his or her identity. I personally don't think Terry had put it all together yet—"

"Because if he had he would have gone to the police."

"Exactly. I do think he had some pieces of the puzzle, though."

"I wonder what that could be."

"So do I."

"Okay; can we save the rest of this until morning?"

Meredith shrugged. "I guess."

"Right. We'll talk about it tomorrow."

Meredith sat back on her bed and pulled the blanket up over her bony knees. Claire switched off the light, but she could see Meredith sitting hunched over in the dark, hugging her knees to her chest, moonlight falling on her thin shoulders, her restless mind working.

Claire fell into an uneasy sleep. She dreamed she was on a big white horse, galloping through fields and woods. Exhilarated, she could feel the motion of the horse under her, pounding the ground with its big hooves, through meadows and over streams, past houses and roads, across a landscape of faded yellow grasses and falling leaves. She wrapped her legs tightly around the horse as it surged forward, leaping over fallen tree limbs and soaring over fences, faster and faster, until it felt as though they had left the earth behind and were flying through space.

Claire had always been captivated by the power and grace of horses, and now she felt a part of that power, of the unapologetic beauty of nature itself. There was terror in that beauty, but Claire felt only wonder as she sailed over a dream landscape of impossible loveliness. Caught up as she was in this breathless rush forward, time had ceased to exist.

Space and time, and reality itself...

Claire awoke to the sound of a catfight. She sat up in bed and listened to the hissing and yowling, which sounded as though it were coming from just outside her window. She peered into the darkness at Meredith, lying on the floor beside her. In the moonlight shining through the window, Claire could see her, mouth open, sleeping heavily. The digital clock next to the bed read 4:16 A.M.

Claire threw off her covers and crept out of bed and down the back staircase. As she did, the sounds outside became louder. There was such a commotion of spitting and angry meowing that she was afraid the cats would kill each other. She pushed open the side door and stood on the slab of stone that served as a top step, the stone cold under her bare feet. There, in the flat pale light of the moon, she could see Ralph and Velcro facing off just a few yards away, in front of Liza's flower bed.

Their fur standing out in all directions, the cats' bodies arched and pulsed with aggression. Their movements resembled a strange dance as they circled one another tensely, sizing each other up. Claire knew better than to touch one of the cats; her left hand still bore the scars of meddling in such an encounter at the age of five. She looked around for something to protect herself and saw Liza's hoe leaning against the side of the house. She picked it up and advanced toward the cats, but just then she heard the door open behind her and turned to see Tahir Hasonovic standing on the steps. To her surprise, instead of pajamas he wore jeans and a windbreaker.

"Here, let me help you," he said quietly, taking the hoe. "I've done this before."

He walked calmly up to the cats, who by now had lost

some of their concentration on each other and were looking at this human who stood before them brandishing a
strange weapon. Tahir stood completely still for a moment,
then he suddenly let the hoe fall to the ground in the space
between the cats, while at the same moment he let out a
terrifying screech. The cats froze, panic in their eyes, then
bolted in opposite directions. Ralph took off toward the
woods while Velcro headed for the porch, reaching the
cover of bushes surrounding it in two leaps. Claire watched
them for a moment and then turned to Tahir, who stood
looking after them.

"That was good," she said.

He shrugged, picked up the hoe, and leaned it back up
against the side of the house. "Cats aren't so hard. Sepa-
rating fighting dogs is much harder." He paused. "Humans
are hardest of all," he said softly.

"It sounds as though you've done a lot of that."

He shrugged again and sighed. "Do you know," he said
slowly, "some things are just . . . difficult to talk about."

Claire suddenly realized that the grass under her feet
was wet with dew; she shivered and took a few steps back.
"I'm surprised no one else woke up," she said as they entered the deserted dining room.

"Some people are heavy sleepers."

"I guess so. And it was right under my window. The
next nearest room to me is quite a ways down the hall."

"That would be Camille's room?"

Neither of them mentioned the rooms, now empty, that
had belonged to Maya and Terry.

"That's right. You're over in the west wing, aren't you?"

"I was awake working. I like to work at night when
everyone else is asleep."

They were now standing in front of the kitchen. Claire
heard footsteps on the staircase and turned to see Camille
coming down the steps. She wore a long blue flannel night-
shirt, grey leggings, and thick wool socks.

"What was that awful sound?" she said.

"A catfight," Tahir replied softly.

Camille shivered. "It sounded as though someone were dying."

Tahir smiled shyly. "We prevented that from happening."

"Good for you," said Camille. "We really don't need a dead cat on top of everything else."

Tahir rubbed his forehead. "Well, I'm going to go turn in, if you don't mind."

"Good night," said Claire. "Thanks for saving Ralph's life. I'm afraid he's not much of a fighter."

Tahir smiled, but there was no mirth in his dark face. "Sometimes cats as well as people can surprise you."

He turned and padded quietly up the stairs, making hardly a sound even on the creaky old floorboards. After he had gone, Camille said, "I wonder what he meant by that."

"I was wondering the same thing," said Claire.

The next morning all that was left from the fight was a swirl of cat hair on the lawn. The hoe still stood against the side of the house, but there was no sign of the combatants. Claire was a little worried about Ralph, and wondered if he had actually been injured; neither cat had looked hurt, but in the moonlight it was hard to tell. All morning she waited for him to appear, until finally he showed up on the porch, hungry and a little scruffy from a night spent in the woods. The only sign of the big fight was a small cut on his right ear, which Claire dressed with Neosporin. Ralph immediately tried to rub it off, shaking his head back and forth and dabbing at the spot with his paw. He then ate an entire can of Liver 'n Onions and fell fast asleep on a porch chair.

Meredith was very upset at having missed the big event.

"Why didn't you *wake* me?" she said when Claire told her over breakfast.

"Well, I thought it was more important that you got your sleep. It was all over in a couple of minutes."

"But I could have *helped* you! I *hate* missing stuff," she added, picking at her scrambled eggs.

Claire sighed. She hoped Meredith wasn't going to punish her by not eating, a ploy she had tried once or twice before. Claire didn't want to reinforce the behavior, so she said nothing, but it worried her; she had seen young women with eating disorders and it was disturbing. And so she tried not to show the relief she felt when Meredith reached for another bagel, wondering if the girl knew how effective her manipulations really were.

Meredith sat happily chewing her bagel, though, swinging her legs under the bench in front of the picnic table on the porch. Sleepy yellow jackets hovered drunkenly over the jar of blackberry jam sitting on the red-and-white-checked tablecloth.

"It's funny how territorial animals are," Meredith said.

"Well, it's instinct-driven behavior," said Claire. "Even house cats retain those instincts. People are the same way."

"That's for sure . . . even when the behavior is no longer adaptive, as the scientists would say."

No longer adaptive . . . what about murder? Claire wondered. She watched the yellow jackets reeling sleepily around the blackberry jam, like tiny yellow moons caught in its gravitational pull.

"Do you know that according to Willard Hughes there are basically only three motives for murder?" Meredith said through a mouthful of bagel.

"Swallow before you talk," Claire said reflexively. "You've read *A Date with Death,* then?"

Meredith rolled her eyes. "Of course. You *gave* me a copy, remember?"

"Oh, right." Claire didn't remember. She was always giving people books; access to free books was one of the few perks of being an editor.

"The first one, of course," Meredith went on, "is passion—lust and revenge and all that stuff. I don't think that's what we're dealing with here, though," she said thoughtfully, wiping a bit of butter off the side of her mouth. "Neither of these was exactly well planned, but they . . . well, it's almost as if there was too much stealth involved to be the product of a crime of passion. Those kinds of crimes are usually messier, more reckless. Here there was not a lot of planning, I think, but a good deal of clearheadedness, what the experts call an 'organized killer.' I mean, they wiped up the water on the bathroom floor, for God's sake."

"I agree," said Claire, helping herself to some eight-grain bread and jam. Sherry had bought two loaves for dinner the night before, but there was so much other food no one had touched it. "Someone who takes the time to wipe up water on a bathroom floor is hardly in the throes of uncontrollable passion. On the other hand, maybe after a moment of reckless rage, the murderer collected himself and wiped up the water—or maybe he didn't even realize what he was doing. Someone's state of mind at times like that must be hazy at best, I would think."

"Good point." Meredith sounded a little surprised. She looked at Claire suspiciously, as if she thought Claire was just humoring her, then continued. "The second motive is self-protection . . . that's a little harder to prove, because you'd have to know what the murderer was protecting himself or herself from.

"And the third and probably most obvious is, of course, greed. Again, it's hard to see how killing Maya would lead to monetary gain . . . still, there's a lot we don't know."

"True."

Just then the screen door opened and Billy Trimble wandered onto the porch. Both before and after the murders, he had kept largely to himself, and Claire was a little surprised when he sat down on the musty daybed. His fingers were paint-stained and he wore paint-splattered white work pants.

"I understand there was a catfight last night," he said, not quite looking at them. Claire studied his profile—straight nose, square chin; it was a strong face. There was no doubt that he was a good-looking man, but she did not feel at all drawn to him. There was something icy at his core, something that all the good looks in the world could not melt.

"You slept through it, too?" Meredith brushed away a yellow jacket as she reached for the jam.

"Sound travels oddly in this house," he replied, oblique as always.

"I slept through it because Claire didn't wake me up," Meredith said in an accusing tone.

"If you can sleep through your own snoring, I guess you can sleep through anything," Claire replied cheerfully. Meredith rolled her eyes, which Claire ignored. "You're all the way at the other wing of the house, so I'm not surprised you didn't hear it," she said to Billy.

Billy let his head fall on the top of the mattress that made up the backing to the porch "couch" and sighed. "You know, this porch really needs a better couch. Maybe I should look for one at a yard sale—that is, if Inspector Clouseau would let us go into town."

"You can go, you just have to ask permission," said Meredith.

Billy shook his head wearily as if the idea were just too much trouble to contemplate.

"Did you hear anything unusual the night of Maya's murder?" Meredith said suddenly.

Billy stared at her as though she had asked the question in Swahili, then he laughed. "Has the inspector hired you as a part-time assistant?"

"Detective, not inspector. Did you hear anything?"

Billy scratched himself and looked out over the valley, where some wispy white clouds lingered over the treetops. At first it seemed as though he wasn't going to answer, then he ran a hand through his thick, paint-spattered hair and sighed.

"All I remember hearing that night was somebody going to the bathroom at some point. I was awakened by the sound of the commode flushing—the bathroom is right next to my bedroom—and then I heard the footsteps of someone going back to their room."

Meredith looked at him intently. "Do you have any idea of who that might be?"

Billy shrugged. "I can't really say. It could have been anyone whose room is in the east wing."

"Unless the west-wing bathroom was occupied at the time," said Claire.

"True," Meredith said. "That would mean it could have

been anyone except for Two Joe or Jack, whose rooms are on the first floor, and who would presumably use the first-floor bathroom."

"Unless that was occupied, too." Claire was beginning to enjoy this—and it kept Meredith occupied and less restless than usual.

"So the residents in the east wing besides you are Gary and Tahir, right?" said Meredith.

Billy rolled his head as though he had a crick in his neck. "That's it," he said laconically.

"And in the west wing . . ."

"Only Camille and you and I are left now," said Claire.

"Oh," said Meredith, "I guess you're right."

"Why don't you ask Tahir what he heard?" said Billy. "He often stays up at night working and his room is across the hall from mine."

"And Gary's room is right next to you, right?" said Meredith.

Billy didn't reply. Claire wasn't sure if he had heard the question or if he was deliberately ignoring it, but he stood up and stretched his lanky body. "I'm going back to work," he said. "See you later." He strolled back inside the house, leaving Meredith and Claire alone with the yellow jackets.

"Hmm . . . something's going on there," Claire said. "Did you see how he reddened when you mentioned Gary's name?"

"He did?" Meredith tossed the rest of her bagel into the bushes, where a flurry of sparrows descended upon it, twittering loudly.

"Oh, yeah . . . there's some Gary/Billy thing going on." Claire watched the birds pecking and spatting over the bagel, their short harsh chirps mingling with the drone of katydids in the surrounding woods. "He's a cold one, that Billy," she added, collecting the breakfast dishes.

"Mmm . . ." said Meredith. "Camille said that Billy and Maya were involved with each other?"

"That's right."

"I wonder . . ."

"What?"

"Well, promise me you won't get mad at me if I tell you?"

Claire smiled. She could remember using those exact words with her mother, and also remembered her mother's response: "How can I know until you tell me?"

She decided she wouldn't be so relentlessly logical with Meredith. "Okay," she said, "I promise."

Meredith leaned forward on her skinny elbows. "Well, I overheard part of a conversation between Gary and Billy last night after you went to bed. I was on my way upstairs, and heard them arguing." She looked at Claire apprehensively. "You're not angry, are you?"

Claire smiled and shook her head. "Under the circumstances, I'm just relieved you didn't tape record it."

"Well, Gary seemed angry about something, because he kept saying, 'I never should have come back, I should have known better.' "

"I wonder what he meant by that?"

Just then the screen door opened and Liza came out, an odd look on her face.

"Hi, Liza—what's wrong?" said Claire.

"Have you seen Marcel?" said Liza. Marcel had shown up at Ravenscroft with his dog Ellie about an hour ago.

"I think he went into town for some parts for the water heater. Why?"

"I—I think Ellie's found something."

"What is it?" said Meredith, following Liza and Claire back into the house.

Liza didn't answer, but led them through the kitchen and out the back door, across the back lawn to her little garden at the edge of the woods. There, between the garden and the woods, sat Marcel's golden retriever, Ellie. She looked up at them and grinned, her tongue lolling out the side of her mouth, which was covered with dirt.

"What's she got there?" Meredith pointed to the object Ellie held underneath her paws.

Claire leaned over and looked. There, its blade dull and encrusted with dirt, was a hunting knife.

"Call Detective Hansom," she said.

Chapter 19

Detective Hansom wasted little time bagging the knife and taking it down to the forensics lab. Gary and Billy had received permission from Sergeant Rollins to go into town to shop, so after ascertaining from Claire that the object in question was in all likelihood Gary's missing hunting knife, Hansom refused Camille's offer of a cup of coffee and pulled away in his black sedan, leaving a puff of white dust behind him.

Liza and Claire stood on the porch and watched his car disappear around the sharp turns of Camelot Road.

"Wow," said Liza. "Wait till we tell Marcel what his dog dug up."

"Well, it's not necessarily of any importance," said Meredith from where she lay sprawled out on the daybed, picking at a scab on her leg.

"Meredith, leave that alone," said Claire. "Why do you do that?"

Meredith shrugged and plucked a sprig of honeysuckle from the bush that hung over the porch railing. "I dunno." She pulled the stamen out of the honeysuckle.

"Do you think the knife is . . . ?" Liza said softly.

"The murder weapon?" Claire finished for her. "Could

be. I mean, why would anyone go to the trouble of bury-
ing it if it weren't? But there might not be any fingerprints
on it, so that still puts us close to square one. Unless . . ."

"Unless what?" said Meredith, sitting up.

"Unless someone was seen stealing the knife from Gary."

Just then Marcel's red truck pulled into the parking lot
and the handyman got out. Ellie came running from around
the side of the house to greet her master, throwing her big
lean body on his, licking his face. On her hind legs she
was nearly as tall as he was, and the two of them looked
well suited: big-boned and lanky, goofy and sweet, dog and
master.

"Hey there, girl, did you behave yourself while I was
gone?" said Marcel as Ellie followed him up the steps to
the porch, her feathery tail slapping against his legs.

"She may have unearthed a piece of evidence—liter-
ally," said Liza.

"What do you mean?" Marcel's big brown eyes were as
innocent as a child's.

"Wow," he said when they told him about the knife.
"Where'd you find that, girl?"

"From the look of it, she brought it in from the woods,"
said Liza. "We couldn't find any holes here on the property."

"Wow," he repeated, then smiled shyly. "I wonder if
there's any reward money or anything."

"I don't think so," Meredith replied disdainfully. "This
is a *murder* investigation, not a kidnapping."

"How do you think she found it?" said Claire.

"Well, she's a retriever." Marcel scratched the dog's ears.
"She's got a good nose for blood, and she's trained to follow a scent." He straightened his long back and shrugged.
"Digging is something she's always done; I tried to break
her of it, but I finally had to put a fence around my garden. Sometimes she just gets it into her head to dig; can't
say why exactly. Instinct, I suppose; you can't cure a dog
of that. Well," he said, "I gotta go finish with the water
heater so you all can have hot baths tonight."

He strode into the house, his work boots clomping loudly

on the wooden floor. *Hot baths* . . . Claire shuddered. She was sticking to showers at Ravenscroft from now on.

Meredith's latest sleuthing idea was to study the psyches of the resident writers by reading their work. She began with Jack Mulligan, whose writing, Claire had to admit, was rather good. He wrote mostly short stories—mythical, poetic stories of men and the sea—but his writing style owed more to the magic realism of Borges and Márquez than to Hemingway. Meredith lay on her stomach on Claire's bed, her nose close to the text (she was nearsighted but refused to wear her glasses), one finger in her mouth, chewing absently on her cuticles.

"Well, he's pretty good," she said, tossing the manuscript aside when she finished. "You'd never guess from his writing that he's a Nazi."

"Get any clues from his work?" Claire was fishing through her dresser for a sweater. A wind had whipped up from the west, the sky was overcast, and the temperature had dropped ten degrees since morning.

Meredith rolled over onto her back and stared at the ceiling, her thin arms behind her head. "Hard to say. Maybe, maybe not. He's real into the whole seagoing mystique, and there are resonances of German folk myths . . . other than that, there's not that much to go on."

"Well, keep me posted," said Claire. "I'm going downstairs to make lunch."

"Got any tuna fish?" said Meredith. "I'm in the mood for brain food."

Claire laughed. "What you really like is all the mayonnaise I put in it."

Meredith rolled her eyes and sighed. "Whatever."

When she returned to the room with sandwiches for Meredith, Claire found her with her nose buried in *A Piece of Earth*, Tahir Hasonovic's award-winning collection of short stories.

"Hey, this is really good," Meredith said when Claire entered the room. "This guy can really write."

"Yes, he's good, isn't he?" Claire set a plate of tunafish sandwiches on the dresser. Meredith liked them cut up in quarters; she liked what she called "dainty food," little hors d'oeuvres and such, bite-sized morsels she could pop in her mouth. She preferred the crusts cut off of sandwiches, but Claire refused to do that, insisting Meredith eat her crusts. Occasionally she found damp little piles of rolled-up crusts in the garbage, that Meredith had managed to throw away when she wasn't looking.

Meredith rose from the bed, stretched, and plucked a sandwich from the plate. "You know," she said, "it's interesting that Tahir writes about an alter ego who's tall, when he's so short." She sighed and took a bite of her sandwich. "Men hate being short, and women don't like being tall. It's too bad, really."

"I don't mind being tall," said Claire.

"Well, you're not all *that* tall," said Meredith. "What are you, about five-nine?"

"Five-eight."

Meredith snorted, blowing a little scrap of sandwich across the bed. "Oh, *please.* That's not *tall;* my *mother* was tall, but five eight is *not* tall!"

Claire smiled. Katherine Lawrence had been tall—close to six feet in her stocking feet. That, along with her dynamic personality, made her hard to ignore—or to forget. *Like mother, like daughter,* she thought as she watched Meredith chewing vigorously on her sandwich.

"Well," said Meredith, "next I guess I'll read Liza's work. Have you got anything of hers?"

"Uh, I think I have something." Claire fished through the stack of manuscripts on the floor. She pulled out a collection of short stories entitled *Southern Gothic.* "Here's something," she said. "Why don't you look at a couple of these?"

"Okay." Meredith bounced on the bed, a fresh sandwich clutched in her thin fingers.

"Meredith, why don't you calm down a little while you're eating?" Claire suggested.

"All right—whatever." Meredith stuffed the sandwich in her mouth and reached for the manuscript. Claire left the girl lying on her side, a sandwich in one hand, the manuscript spread out in front of her, and went downstairs to make some tea.

After Meredith finished with the writers, she moved on to the artists. Without telling them why, she obtained permission to tour each studio. "After all," she said over a bowl of Grape-Nuts that afternoon in Liza's cabin, "whoever heard of an artist who didn't want to show their work?"

Sherry stirred half-and-half into her coffee. "But what does a painting really tell you about the painter? It's even harder to decipher than a book . . . apparently Picasso was a real bastard."

"Well, at least as far as women were concerned," said Liza, taking a bite of an onion bagel. She and Sherry kept a supply of bagels in their freezer: Sherry was addicted to bagels and Starbucks coffee.

Sherry sighed. "Ah, yes, the separation of art and soul. That's a rich topic. Think of all the great writers—and painters—who were real shits."

"The correlation of one's work with one's personality is tenuous at best, I would think," said Liza.

"Ah, yes." Meredith wiped a dribble of milk off her chin. "But the work gives some indication of how the psyche functions. There are patterns which persist within people, things which remain more or less constant. I liked your work, by the way," she said to Liza. "It really *is* Southern gothic, but with a twist. I love the character of the mother in that one story . . . what's the title?"

" 'Perennials'?" said Liza.

"Right. Is that based on your own mother?"

"More or less. I've exaggerated a little, but not much."

Meredith nodded. "That whole thing about wearing white gloves whenever she goes out is great. I guess that's a real Southern thing, huh?"

Liza shrugged. "I guess. I think maybe it's more generational—and class, too. My mother was very into the old-Virginia-family thing, being upper class and all that."

Sherry smiled and ran her hand along Liza's neck. "And look how low you've sunk; you're shacked up with a Polish-Jew dyke. Your mother would roll over in her grave."

Claire was a little embarrassed by the intimacy of Sherry's gesture, and her eyes roved around the room. Sherry's paintings were all over the walls of Liza's cabin: bright, primary colors in cheerful designs, amusing paintings of cats, all of it fun and accessible if not particularly groundbreaking.

After breakfast, Claire accompanied Meredith from one studio to another, viewing finished and half-finished pieces. Two Joe's work consisted mostly of sculptured animals—clay, wood, and occasionally bronze. There was a raw unfinished power to his work, and he told Claire that it sold very well in the Southwest. He had a dealer in Sante Fe who regularly sold thousands of dollars' worth of his sculptures.

"She markets me as a 'Native American' artist," Two Joe said as Meredith ran her hand along the smooth flanks of a rearing bronze mustang.

"I like it," she said. "Your work is really good." She sighed. "I wish I could afford it."

"Thank you, Lightning Flash," Two Joe replied solemnly, but Claire could see the corners of his mouth twitching.

Next they visited Gary Robinson's studio. Gary wasn't there—he and Billy had taken Billy's car into town to run errands for Liza—but he had given them the key to both studios. Claire wondered why Gary had the key to Billy's studio.

As they roamed Gary's immaculate, tidy studio, sunlight filtering through an overhead skylight, Claire studied his use of form and style. Not surprisingly, she thought, his paintings were a series geometric designs, precise and mathematical and as rigidly structured as a Bach partita. To Gary, color was secondary, Claire could see; design was everything. There was beauty within the formality of his work, Claire thought, but it was cool and controlled, the effect carefully calculated, reflecting a deep desire for order and precision.

Billy's paintings, on the other hand, were wild and flowing, with swirling colors out of a psychedelic nightmare. They appeared to be an uncensored expression of his subconscious, an unleashing of pure id upon canvas. His work was raw and exhilarating; the brush strokes swelled with impatience and passion, with all the energy of a runaway train. Claire felt a little dizzy as she stood before one large sprawling painting of reds and ochers that pulsated in every direction, as though they wanted to escape from the confines of the canvas.

Claire looked at Meredith, who stood, chin in her hand, head cocked to one side, contemplating the painting. "The title on this one is interesting," she said finally. "*Marieke*. Sounds like someone's name . . . an old girlfriend, I wonder?"

"Well?" said Claire. "Any clues there, you think?"

Meredith sighed and shook her head. "I'll tell you one thing: I wouldn't have thought Billy had it in him."

"It *is* a little surprising, isn't it? They seem almost— well, out of character for him."

"Ah," said Meredith. "Characters exist only in plays. People are much more complex—or, as I always say, contradiction makes the man." She did a cartwheel across the floor, then brushed her hands off. "Shall we go have lunch? I'm starving."

Claire laughed. "You frighten me sometimes, you know that?"

Meredith shrugged. "I frighten myself. It's not easy being a genius, you know."

Claire laughed again. "No, I don't suppose it is."

A little before five Claire went to the kitchen to take inventory and realized she was out of just about everything. After getting permission from Sergeant Rollins to go into town, she went to find Liza, who was bent over her garden weeding tomato plants. It seemed to Claire that her friend was spending more and more time in the garden; perhaps it was her way of dealing with death, working to make things grow.

"I'm going into town, you want to come?" she said to Liza, who paused in her weeding, sweat dripping from her face.

"No thanks. I want to finish this."

Claire walked around to the front porch, enveloped in a haze of afternoon sun. Katydids chortled harshly in the bushes nearby. Meredith had fallen asleep on the couch, her book lying across her thin chest. Sherry sat in the old brown armchair reading.

"You want anything in town?" Claire said to Sherry, who yawned and stretched her muscular brown arms.

"No, I don't think so . . . oh, wait; how 'bout some cigarettes?"

"Cigarettes?" said Claire. "I didn't know you—"

Sherry shrugged. "I don't usually, but the stress is getting to me. Don't tell Liza, will you?" she added in a low voice.

"What brand do you want?"

"Sobraines."

"The same brand Camille uses."

"I know, I know. I bummed a couple off her and grew to like them." Sherry dug a crumpled five-dollar bill from her shorts. "C'mon, be a pal; what do you say?"

Claire took the money. "Okay, but you know how Liza feels about smoking."

"I know, I know; her dad died of lung cancer." Sherry rolled her eyes. "I've heard it all a million times. Don't you start lecturing me, too."

"Okay." Claire pointed to Meredith, who lay on her back snoring softly, her skinny limbs flung in every direction, all elbows and knees. "Keep an eye on her while I'm gone, will you?"

Sherry nodded. "Sure."

Claire stuffed the money in her knapsack and headed down to the dirt parking lot where her old Mercedes sat alone under a shedding maple tree. The driver's-side door creaked when Claire opened it; the car's rusty joints were full of the stiffness of old age, and it groaned and complained like an old woman.

She slid into the driver's seat, carefully avoiding the place where the upholstery was ripped, the springs underneath exposed. The interior smelled musty and damp from all the recent rain, and Claire opened the window to let in the cool mountain air as she turned onto Camelot Road. She thought about the artists and their work . . . she had half expected to see a portrait of Maya in one of the studios, aging like the portrait of Dorian Gray. Well, there was no such portrait, and even if there were, it wouldn't have saved Maya.

Claire hung her arm out of the window and felt the cool breeze on her skin. The speckling of sun through the tree leaves was hypnotic. The air was sweet, and once again she was reminded of her childhood summers on the lake. The thing she missed most living in the city was the smell of the air—the clear, sharp smell of the woods. In the city there were just too many people and cars and dogs and restaurants; even in Central Park there were too many competing smells. But up here, where trees outnumbered people by far, the air smelled as she remembered it from childhood. It was for her the smell of pure summer days stretching on into one another like perfect pearls strung on an endless necklace, from a time in her life before she realized that all summers must end.

As she rounded the turn toward Rock Hill Road, Claire's right foot felt for the brake pedal. At first she thought she had missed it entirely, because her foot hit the floor of the car. She glanced down and saw to her horror that she had indeed hit the pedal but that it hadn't caused the car to slow down. She groped for the parking brake and pulled hard, but there was no response. In an instant she realized the situation: she had no brakes at all. It was at that moment the thought came to her: *This is deliberate; someone is trying to kill me.*

As the big car rolled down the hill gathering speed, Claire knew she had to think quickly. She remembered the time the brakes had gone soft on the Volkswagen Beetle she had in college, and remembered driving to Chapel Hill downshifting whenever she had to slow the car.

But the Mercedes was a much heavier car—and it was not a manual transmission. She gripped the handle of the automatic transmission and shifted into the middle gear, the one meant for climbing hills. The old diesel groaned and heaved; she heard a grinding sound coming from the transmission, and the car jerked to a slower speed. Claire took a deep breath and pulled the lever into the only gear left—"low." Again the car jerked and slowed its pace, but it was still rumbling down the hill toward town. She thought about shutting off the engine, but that would leave her without steering. She was now less than a quarter of a mile away from the T-junction at Route 212.

Claire considered the options: turn the car off the road into a tree and brace for the impact, or continue down onto Route 212 and pray she wouldn't be broadsided by oncoming traffic. That seemed the less sensible alternative: Route 212 was a main road in this valley and there was not even a yield sign on it for the cars speeding by at sixty miles an hour on their way to Bearsville and beyond.

She thought about rolling out of the car like in the movies, but that was both dangerous and irresponsible: she didn't want to leave an out-of-control car, and she was probably safer staying in it. She looked around: there were fields to her left, but they were bordered by fences and by a deep ditch alongside the road. To her right was a shallower ditch and woods. Ahead, she could see the red-and-white stop sign at the bottom of the hill.

Taking a deep breath, Claire turned the car off the road and into the woods, toward a grove of white birches. As the car left the road and skimmed over the ditch, she wrapped her arms around her head and closed her eyes.

She heard the leaves and bushes rattling on the doors as the Mercedes crashed through the underbrush, and then the dull thud as its front end hit a tree. The jolt was stronger than she expected. In spite of her attempt to protect herself with her arms, she felt her forehead hit hard against the steering wheel. Her shoulder harness did its job, though, and the big car shielded her from the impact.

Claire opened her eyes and put her hand to her forehead. A large bump had already formed, and the skin was tender. Dazed, she opened the door and got out to assess the damage. She walked stiffly around to the front of the car. The hood was slightly dented, but the heavy old Mercedes had stubbornly resisted any extensive damage. Her mechanic's words rang in her ears: "Best car to be in during an accident—protect you well." Her mechanic was Russian and spoke in broken English and she suspected he had connections to Russian gangsters in Brighton, but she trusted his opinion when it came to cars.

Claire stood for a minute looking at her car. The ground was damp and wet leaves clung to her ankles. A solitary crow cawed in the distance, its harsh cry breaking the stillness. The silence was strange after all the commotion. Claire opened the back door and sat down on the backseat. Her head throbbed; she felt the bump and it seemed larger than before. Suddenly the contours of her own head were foreign. She leaned over the front seat and inspected her forehead. The bump was centered between her eyes, and ringed with red and purple.

She remained sitting for several minutes, trying to think what she should do next while the woods began to come alive once again: the animals frightened by the sound of her car crashing through the underbrush were now returning to inspect the odd creature that had so abruptly invaded their territory. The old car sat among falling leaves and dead twigs, steam slowly rising from its radiator, a beached leviathan, harmless as an old shoe.

The animals seemed to realize this: a pair of chipmunks scurried across the ground and perched on a dead log just a few feet away from where Claire sat, chattering loudly at her. A catbird sat in a tree branch just above her, nattering noisily, scolding her for disturbing its peace.

"All right," she muttered. "It's not my fault, you know."

Just then she heard the sound of a car coming up the hill. She got up and headed toward the road, and recognized Evelyn Gardner's natty little red sports car. The car jerked to a halt and the driver's-side door was flung open.

"Oh my God," Evelyn said, leaping from the car. She was elegantly overdressed as usual, in a grey linen jacket over a creamy silk dress, stockings, and black pumps. For some reason, seeing Evelyn so blithely, obliviously overdressed cheered Claire up. "What on earth happened to you?" Evelyn said, her heels clicking on the road as she rushed over.

Claire hesitated. "I lost control of the car and hit a tree." She looked at Evelyn to see her reaction, but all she could read in her face was concern.

"That's a nasty bump." Evelyn touched Claire's forehead gently. "Here, let me take you to a hospital." She opened the passenger-side door of her car and helped Claire in.

"I'd just like to go back to the house," Claire said, fumbling with her seat belt. She only just noticed that her hands were shaking, and she dropped the buckle as she tried to fasten it.

"Here, let me help you." Evelyn reached over the stick shift. As she did, Claire caught a whiff of perfume. She wasn't sure, but she thought it was "Obsession," familiar from magazine samples. Evelyn's long crimson fingernails were perfectly manicured, not a nick or a scratch on the smooth red surface. It occurred to Claire that these did not appear to be hands that would tamper with a brake cable, but . . . she didn't know whom she could trust anymore, or even if she could trust her own observations. When Evelyn asked how she lost control of the car, she mumbled something about the steering.

Evelyn seemed satisfied with this response. She put the car in gear and started up the hill. "Are you sure you don't want to go to a hospital?"

"No, I just want to go back to Ravenscroft."

"But you have a head injury; it could be a concussion or something."

Claire shrugged. "It's only a little bump."

"All right," Evelyn replied, putting the car in third gear. Claire looked in the rearview mirror and saw a grey suede coat lying across the car's tiny backseat. She didn't know much about fashion, but she could tell Evelyn's clothes were expensive.

"We can send Marcel back to get your car," said Evelyn. "Does it start?"

"I don't know," Claire replied. Her head was beginning to pound. She just wanted to take some aspirin and lie down.

They reached the house just as the police were changing shifts. One patrol car was pulling away as another took its place. "Here, let me help you," Evelyn said as Claire unbuckled her seat belt. She came around to the other side of the car and helped Claire climb out, holding her elbow while Claire pulled herself up out of the bucket seat. It was no easy task; the car was low to the ground and Claire felt her knees buckling underneath her.

"I'm okay, thanks," she said, walking unsteadily up the front path to the porch. She remembered the first night she had walked this path in a terrific thunderstorm . . . it seemed so long ago now.

There was no sign of anyone downstairs. As she and Evelyn walked toward the kitchen Claire could hear the *rat-a-tat-tat* of Camille's typewriter upstairs. The kitchen empty.

"Are you sure you're all right?" Evelyn said as they stood in the big empty kitchen, the late-afternoon light falling through the curtains onto the pots and pans hanging over the stove. Claire put her hand to her head. The bump was surprisingly hard, as though she had just grown an extra bone in her forehead.

"You should put ice on that," Evelyn said, pulling open one of the refrigerators and rummaging through the freezer. "Here." She pulled out an ice tray. "I'll just wrap some of this in a towel." She pulled a clean dish towel from the drawer and wrapped a few cubes in it, twisting the end tightly before handing it to Claire. "You wrap the ice in plastic to keep it from leaking, but I always think the wetness is soothing."

"Thank you," said Claire. "You did that very well."

"I used to be a nurse," Evelyn replied. "Just an LPN— licensed practical nurse—but I worked the trauma wards and got good at handling injuries. And head injuries shouldn't be treated lightly. Are you sure you don't want to get that X-rayed?"

Claire shook her head. "No, I'd really rather not. Thanks anyway."

Evelyn sighed, concern written on her large, handsome

face. "I'll call Marcel to go get your car, then." She pulled a cell phone out of her black Gucci bag.

"Actually, I'll take care of it," Claire said quickly.

"Oh, it's no trouble," Evelyn replied, her bright red nails poised over the phone.

"I—uh, have a mechanic I can call," Claire lied.

"Oh, all right." Evelyn shoved the phone back into her bag. She glanced up at the wall clock over the stove. "If you'll excuse me, I've got an appointment with Liza over at her place." Claire wasn't sure if her voice had taken on a cold edge or if she was just imagining it.

"Thanks so much for the ride," Claire said.

"Oh, it was no problem at all; I'm just glad it wasn't more serious. That's a steep road," she added, fishing around in her bag for something. "I'll check on you on my way out," she said, heading for the back door.

"Uh—don't tell Liza yet, will you?" Claire said suddenly.

Evelyn stopped and looked at her. "Why not?"

"I—I don't want her to worry. You know what a mother hen she can be," Claire said, wondering if Evelyn would buy this. "I'll tell her myself."

"All right." Evelyn's gold bracelets tinkled as she opened the door. "Be careful, though; don't sleep for at least six hours, and if you start to feel woozy or nauseous call a doctor right away."

"Okay, thanks," Claire said as the screen door creaked shut behind her. She watched Evelyn pick her way carefully across the lawn, her high heels sinking into the soft grass. Claire hadn't seen a pair of stockings since she arrived in Woodstock except on Evelyn, and she wondered how the woman could possibly be comfortable in her fancy clothes—and what drove her to dress as she did. There was something else, too: all during their conversation, Claire had the impression that Evelyn's mind was on something else; even with her acting talents she couldn't disguise this.

Claire left the kitchen and walked toward the laundry area, where the pay phone was located, in the back of the mostly unused dining room. As she entered the empty dining room she heard Camille's husky voice coming from around the corner; she was on the phone.

Camille's voice was low and intimate. *"Mais non . . . tu sais que je t'aime. Il n'existe plus de raison pour moi, mais pour toi, c'est différent . . . oui, c'est tout à fait différent."*

To her surprise, the words were mostly simple ones Claire remembered from her college French. She translated in her head: "No, you know I love you. There's no reason for me, but for you, it's different . . . yes, it's completely different."

Claire stood for moment deciding what to do. She could go to Liza's and make the call from there, but that would mean the news would get out before she was ready, before she had told Detective Hansom about it.

She heard Camille sigh. *"D'accord. Oui, d'accord. Au revoir, mon cher."* Claire heard her sigh again and hang up the receiver. A moment later she emerged from the phone room, her face red. Claire couldn't tell if she had been crying or if it was just red from emotion. When Camille saw Claire, she looked startled and, Claire thought, distinctly guilty.

"Hello. Back already?" she said.

Claire decided she couldn't hide the news forever. "I had a little accident," she said as calmly as possible.

"Oh, no," said Camille. "Your car—what happened? Are you all right?" Her eyes fell on the bump on Claire's forehead. "Oh God—your poor head!"

"I'm all right; I just have to make a call," Claire moved toward the phone.

"Are you sure you're okay?"

"Yes, I'm fine, really. I've got ice—see?" She showed Camille the impromptu ice pack Evelyn had made her. "I'll be done in a minute," she said, leaving Camille standing in the middle of the dining room. She had never seen Camille so flustered, she thought as she dialed the precinct's number. She didn't want to tell the young policemen sitting in their patrol car in front of Ravenscroft; she wanted to talk directly to Inspector Hansom. If the murderer was after her now, she wanted him to be the first to know.

Chapter 20

"What did she say?" Meredith was lazily poking a stick at a spider that was crossing the porch railing.

"Don't do that," said Claire, taking the stick from her. They were waiting for Detective Hansom; Claire hadn't mentioned the accident to anyone but Camille, who, after expressing her concern by making Claire some tea, disappeared into her room upstairs. Claire could hear the steady click of her typewriter coming from the open second-floor window.

Meredith sighed and threw herself on the daybed. "What did she *say*?" She was angry at Claire for not waking her up to go with her into town. When she heard about the brakes malfunctioning, she was furious. To Meredith, Claire thought, missing the car accident was like missing a trip to the zoo was for other children. Now, however, Meredith was focusing on Camille's mysterious phone conversation.

"It was something like 'I love you . . . there's no reason for me but for you it's different, completely different,'" said Claire.

"Hmm . . . interesting," Meredith remarked, perking up. "Very interesting, in fact. Camille has a boyfriend somewhere who speaks French—someone she doesn't want anyone to know about."

"How do you get that?"

"Well, she hasn't *told* anyone yet, has she?"

"Well, no, but—"

"Trust me, Claire; women *always* tell someone when they have a boyfriend."

Claire looked at the girl, her spiky orange hair disheveled from lying on the couch. At thirteen, she was as androgynous as a wood nymph. Claire couldn't imagine her kissing a boy; she seemed outside sexuality, a gender unto herself.

"Well, I'm going back to my physics." Meredith hopped to the door on one foot.

"What's wrong?"

"Foot's asleep."

"Oh."

Meredith disappeared inside the house, the door clanging loudly behind her. Claire sighed and took a sip of the tea Camille had made her. If Liza was dealing with her stress by gardening, Camille was coping by making tea and coffee for people constantly. The kettle always seemed to be boiling, its shrill whistle cutting through the air like a scream.

Claire wandered to the other side of the porch and watched the policemen sitting in their patrol car. One was laughing at something the other one had said, head thrown back, his mouth open wide. An image of Terry's face flashed before Claire: head thrown back, mouth open, the red gash around his neck darkening as the blood dried.

She turned away. How long would this last, she wondered, how long would laughing policemen continue to evoke images of death for her? She walked over to the picnic table, where Willard Hughes's latest manuscript lay open on the table: *Death by Foul Means*. Claire shook her head. She was beginning to wonder if there was any other kind of death. She picked up the manuscript and looked at it.

Claire knew that the ability to write was no guarantee

of virtue; Willard Hughes was proof enough of that. Irascible, insecure, and suspicious, Willard was someone you would avoid at a party. One look at his nervous tic—his right shoulder twitching uncontrollably toward his ear—and your impulse was to avoid him. Willard might be a disaster personally, but professionally he was the goose that laid the golden egg. His mysteries sold off the shelves as soon as they hit them, grossing more for Ardor House than the work of any other author.

Claire opened the manuscript and read a few lines. *Living in fear all the time, do you know what that does to you?*

Living in fear all the time ... for some reason she thought of Tahir Hasonovic and his haunted eyes. She could only imagine what his life had been like, moving from one place to another to escape people whose sole aim was to kill him.

The crunch of tires on gravel brought Claire out of her reverie. She looked up to see Detective Hansom's familiar black sedan, its windows rolled up tightly, swivel into the dirt parking lot below Camelot Road. He emerged from the car with a rickety hop, as though arthritis had already stiffened his joints. He wore a battered fedora and his usual dingy raincoat. When they saw him, both of the officers in the patrol car stepped out of their car and went over to talk to him. Claire watched them, heads bowed, one of the policemen poking at a stone at his feet. Hansom glanced up to where Claire stood on the porch, his dark eyes shaded under the fedora, and raised one hand as if in greeting. It wasn't exactly a wave; it was more like an acknowledgment of her presence.

A moment later he clapped a large, knotty hand on one of the policemen's back, then turned and trudged up the path to the house. The policemen followed obediently behind him single file. When they reached the porch, Detective Hansom removed his hat and nodded to Claire. She had an impulse to seize his hand and shake it, but she restrained herself.

"Thank you for coming, Detective."

"Not at all. Can my boys use the house facilities?"

"Of course. I think there's some coffee in the kitchen; please help yourselves," Claire said. The young patrolmen, looking a little uncomfortable, tipped their hats courteously and went into the house.

"Now," said Dectective Hansom, settling his long body into one of the director's chairs, "what is it you needed to see me about?"

Claire hadn't told him anything over the phone, and now she proceeded to tell the entire story carefully from the beginning, trying not to miss any details. When she finished, he sat for a moment pulling absently at his lower lip with two fingers.

"The car is still there?"

"Yes, I left it just where it was."

"And you haven't told anyone else about this incident?"

"Evelyn Gardner knows—but I lied and told her it was the steering."

Detective Hansom nodded slowly. "I see. We'll have it towed down to the station and I'll have it looked over."

Claire took a deep breath. "Am I crazy or do you think I'm right to be concerned?"

Detective Hansom cocked his big head to one side. "Under the circumstances, I think anything is possible. Meanwhile, your instinct to not tell anyone about this was good. If I were you, I would invent a story for the absence of your car. Say it's down in the shop being worked on or something—at least until we've had a chance to go over it. If you notice anyone behaving strangely or asking a lot of questions about it, you might make note of it."

Claire nodded. "All right."

Detective Hansom rubbed his forehead wearily, a gesture that reminded Claire of Wally. "This Gardner woman; do you think she can be trusted not to say anything?"

Claire shook her head. "I have no idea. She strikes me as the gossipy type. But I'll see what I can do."

"Good. Delay revealing anything for as long as you can. Oh, and you might keep a watch for anyone who seems surprised to see you alive."

Before Claire had time to react to this, the detective had risen from his chair and replaced the battered fedora on his oversized head. She wondered if he had trouble finding hats large enough for that enormous head of his, and whether he had to order them specially.

"I'll tell Sergeant Rollins what happened, and we'll assign someone to keep an eye on you around the clock."

"Is that necessary?"

He nodded. "To me it is. We can move you into town if you like."

Claire could hear voices coming from the kitchen—probably the policemen—and she was pretty sure she heard Camille's throaty, musical laughter. Then someone sneezed. "No, thanks," she said.

"Oh," he said, his hand on the screen door. "There's one more thing I should probably tell you."

Claire's stomach tightened. "What is it?"

"The forensics came back on the knife."

"Yes?"

"Based on a match of fibers and skin from Mr. Nordstrom's body, we have concluded that it is the murder weapon."

Claire nodded. "Oh. I see. Any prints on it?"

The detective shook his head. "If there were, they were wiped off." He cleared his throat. "I understand Mr. Robinson owns a similar knife, which he claims has been missing. Is that true?"

Which he claims . . .

"Is that true?" he repeated.

"What? Oh, yes, Gary does—did—own a hunting knife. I—I was in the store when he bought it." Claire swallowed raggedly.

"I see. Would you have any idea where Mr. Robinson is right now?"

Claire shook her head. "I haven't seen him all day. He might be in his studio—out behind the house."

Detective Hansom nodded. "Thank you; I know where the studios are." He opened the door and went into the house, his soft leather-soled shoes squeaking on the hardwood floor.

Claire stood for a moment watching an afternoon haze descend on the dusty driveway. The brittle sound of cicadas rose from the woods, deafening and mournful, the swan song of late summer. Detective Hansom's words swam in her ears: *Keep a watch for anyone who seems surprised to see you alive.* Another thought, even more disturbing, entered her head: if the knife was used to kill Terry, the chances were greater than ever that a resident was the murderer. Who else would bury the knife in the woods surrounding Ravenscroft?

"Hello, Redbird."

Claire looked up to see Two Joe standing on the porch steps. She hadn't heard him approach. She was always impressed by how quietly he walked; in spite of his size, Two Joe barely made a sound as he padded across the porch. Today he wore soft leather moccasins, but even in his thick cowboy boots he was amazingly silent when he walked.

"What is it?" he said softly. "What's happened?"

She looked at him, at the desert lines etched in his face. His medicine wheel hung as always on a leather string around his neck, bright against the sunburned skin of his chest. Her hand felt for the medicine wheel around her own throat, but it was gone.

"My—my medicine wheel," she stammered. "I seem to have lost it." She wondered if it had come off when her car collided with the tree.

Two Joe folded his arms, the muscles in his shoulders swelling as he did. Today he wore his flannel shirt rolled up to the elbows, and his forearms were strong and thick as tree limbs. "I can make you another one," he said. "Still, it is not a good thing to have lost it." He pointed to the bump on her forehead, which Claire had forgotten about. "That was no accident, am I right?"

Claire blushed. She wanted so much to tell him what had happened, but remembered her promise to Detective Hansom. She tried to think of what to say, but Two Joe smiled and shook his head.

"Never mind," he said. "I can see that you don't want to tell me. But I can tell you this: Evil spirits gather around you when you are unprotected."

Evil spirits. Claire shivered; it did feel as though evil spirits lurked about Ravenscroft; evil certainly, but more earthly than spiritual, unfortunately.

"I'm sorry," she said. "I feel terrible about losing it. I was wearing it all the time, just like you said."

Two Joe shrugged. "I doubt that it is your fault. Someone—or something—is trying to separate you from your protection. You must be careful. I will make another one right away."

He sat down on the battered lawn chair, which creaked under his weight. "I had another vision last night."

Claire sat across from him on the daybed, so close that their knees were almost touching. "A vision? What was it?"

Two Joe shook his enormous head slowly. "I am still trying to figure out what it means. I saw an eagle swooping down on a rabbit from high atop a mountain." He rubbed one thick thigh thoughtfully, rocking back and forth slightly. "In my vision, the eagle captured the rabbit—but the rabbit turned around and devoured the eagle."

"That's odd."

Two Joe nodded. "Yes, it is. I know there is a meaning there, but I cannot find it. I must go down to the water and meditate, ask my spirit guides for help." He sighed. "There are bad forces at work here." He indicated the house and grounds with a sweep of his arm. "I can feel them in the air, in the trees themselves. Evil is very tangible, once you get used to sensing its presence," he said, leaning in toward Claire, his black eyes shining with intensity. Slowly he reached up and touched the bump on her head.

Claire closed her eyes, enjoying the feel of his fingers upon her forehead. He let his hand linger a moment longer than necessary, but she didn't mind. She opened her eyes and sighed. "What's it all for, do you think?"

"What do you mean?"

"Oh, I don't know. The murders . . . wars . . . everything."

Two Joe smiled. "Ah. That's a big question."

Claire shook her head. "I just can't see how we're any improvement over animals, you know . . . to hunt and kill for food, to defend territory or mates is what animals do, but to hunt for bigger or better or more insidious ways to annihilate one another . . . I guess I'm feeling disgusted with our whole species right now."

As she spoke, Two Joe surprised her by closing his eyes. He remained like that without responding for some time, half a minute or more.

"You know, Redbird," he said slowly, "I have had to learn many bad things about men in my time walking this earth. I know all the stories of your ancestors and my ancestors—how we bled each other, how we took violence to bed with us every night and wept as we slept yet got up the next day to commit more crimes upon each other.

"I know that your ancestors won not because they were more virtuous or smarter, or even because they loved the land more than my people, but because in the end they were better at killing. They had harnessed the power of fire to help them with their killing; we had not. We pounded our crude warheads from the earth herself; they were sharp as our hands could make them, but your people had weapons quick as flame, and our poor earthbound weapons were no match for them."

He paused and inhaled deeply, letting the air out slowly before he spoke. "Our leaders knew this and still they kept fighting. They knew it would end in defeat, but they had no choice but to keep the faith strong in the hearts of their followers—because once you have lost hope, you have lost everything."

He sighed and picked up a twig from the ground and rolled it around in his thick brown fingers. "You see, Redbird, we have to keep hoping or we will die. So whatever you do, don't lose hope—hope that someday people will change, that the qualities which make us different from animals can perhaps someday make us better."

In the woods somewhere, a mourning dove called to its mate. The sound, low and hollow, clung to Claire's heart whenever she heard it. Two Joe took a step toward her and wrapped his strong arms around her shoulders, pulling her gently to him. He smelled of cedar and sandalwood. Gratefully, Claire let go of the knot in her chest and gave in to the sobs welling up from within her.

That evening, when everyone else was in bed, she crept downstairs to the pay phone and dialed Ina Jackson's number in San Francisco. Wally answered after two rings.

"I just wanted to hear your voice," she said, realizing that her own voice was trembling.

"Claire, what is it?" He sounded alarmed.

She bit her lip, furious with herself for letting her emotions spill over like this. "I—I think someone tried to kill me today."

There was a silence on the other end, and when he spoke, his voice was tight with fury. "That's it. I'm taking the first plane out there tomorrow."

"No, no; there's nothing you can do, really. The police are around here constantly—really."

"I'm coming, no matter what you say. This is ridiculous; they should have caught him by now!"

"Wally, it's not that easy. He—or she—has left very few clues—"

"But isn't it someone *in the house*?"

"Maybe. Or maybe it's Evelyn, or Roger—or even Marcel." Claire tried to imagine big, goofy Marcel strangling Maya, or cutting Terry's throat, but she couldn't. "It could even be someone no one has thought of yet, someone we don't even know."

Wally sighed heavily. "My God, Claire, why don't you just go back to New York? They can't keep you up there forever."

"No, I guess not . . . but I want to do everything to help them catch the killer."

"But that shouldn't include getting killed yourself." There was a pause, and then he said, "Do they suspect you?"

Claire swallowed. "I'm not sure . . . I don't *think* so."

She watched as a pale sliver of moonlight fell upon the windowsill, slicing across the floor of the alcove and trailing off into the dining room, a thin blue line of light falling jaggedly on the tables and chairs. "I've decided to send Meredith back to Connecticut."

"Good; it doesn't sound like it's very safe there now."

"I haven't told her yet."

"Well, she'll just have to live with your decision."

"That's easy for you to say. You don't have to tell her." She had left Meredith snoring loudly, lying on her side, her face obscured by a thick mass of orange hair. Claire planned to call Ted Lawrence first thing in the morning and ask him to come up and get Meredith. Any doubt in her mind as to the girl's safety was now removed: Ravenscroft was not a safe place to be right now, especially for Meredith, with her nosy ways and her constant bragging about "solving the crime." She didn't know if anyone else took the girl's boasting seriously, but she wasn't going to wait to find out.

"Well, I'll book the first flight I can tomorrow," Wally said.

"But your mother—"

"Don't argue. It's settled." Wally's voice took on an authoritative edge, and Claire could hear in it the college professor he once was—imperious, a little stuffy, used to having the last word.

"Look," she said slowly, "I'll go back to New York as soon as I get Meredith off to Connecticut. Why don't you at least wait until then. It's a long way up to Woodstock," she added. "It'll add at least half a day to your trip."

There was a pause on the other end and then she heard him sigh. "Okay," he said. "But don't do anything foolish before then; just sit tight and try to stay out of trouble."

Claire laughed. "Okay. But you're barking up the wrong tree. It's Meredith who needs that advice."

"Well, you tell her for me."

"Will do."

"I miss you."

"Me, too." There was a pause between them. Claire thought she heard a door open somewhere in the house, then the old floorboards above her creaked with the sound of footsteps. "I've got to go check on Meredith," she said. "She's upstairs asleep." Claire had left the bedroom door ajar, and she suddenly had a vision of Meredith sound asleep, unprotected, in the open bedroom.

"Be careful."

"I will."

Claire hung the phone up gently and crept quietly into the dining room. The same shaft of moonlight fell across the empty tables, and in the pale light the room looked even more deserted and ghostly than usual. She shivered and walked across the bare floorboards, cold and hard under her bare feet. As she ascended the stairs she heard a door close quietly upstairs. But all was quiet as she walked down the long hallway to her room. A narrow band of yellow light glowed softly from underneath Camille's door. As Claire approached the room she thought she heard whispering coming from inside, but then it stopped. She heard the creak of bedsprings, and then the yellow light went off, leaving the hallway in darkness except for the red exit sign at the end, over the back staircase.

Back in her room, Claire crawled under the covers and pulled her knees up to her chest. She listened as the house creaked and settled around her, then looked down at Meredith. Even asleep, the girl radiated the careless confidence of youth, the guileless egocentricity that is granted only to the young. In spite of her amazing intellect and her interest in crime, there was so much Meredith didn't *know*. There was a difference, Claire thought, between understanding and *knowing*. She wished Meredith many years of freedom from such knowledge.

Chapter **21**

"Well, I finally got through to that *Times* reporter," Meredith said at breakfast, slathering a thick layer of butter on her bagel. It was already after ten o'clock, but Liza, Sherry, and Camille were the only other residents on the porch.

"Meredith, do you think you need quite *that* much butter on your bagel?" said Claire.

"Yes," Meredith replied firmly. "In Connecticut, I am systematically deprived of animal fat. My stepmother believes in a low-fat diet; her eating habits resemble those of grazing animals, say, on the Serengeti Plain. A few tufts of wild grasses, dried fruits, and scattered tree leaves. Therefore, I try to make up for it when I am away from her evil influence by stuffing my young body with as much saturated fat as I can possibly stand."

Claire couldn't help smiling at this, and Camille laughed out loud.

"Oh, please," she said. "Don't let us prevent you from enjoying your butter." She punctuated this with a loud sneeze.

Sherry looked at her slyly. "I see someone has caught Sergeant Rollins's cold."

Camille stared at Sherry. "I have *a* cold; I don't know that it's necessarily his."

Meredith reached across the table for the peach jam. "So," she said, smearing a thick orange layer of jam on top of the butter, "it seems that Maya worked as a foreign correspondent for the *Times* in Europe a few years ago. This guy Jeff Miller knew her from that time period; he didn't know what she was calling him about, though. I suggested to Detective Hansom that he look at some more of Maya's old articles."

"How would that help, do you think?" said Camille.

Meredith shrugged. "It might not. But it might turn up a clue or two as to why someone would want to kill her."

"You mean you think it's someone from her past as a reporter?" said Sherry.

"Could be. Or it could be that Maya's call to this guy Miller had nothing to do with her death. Time will tell," she said mysteriously. "Time will—"

Just then Camille's coffee cup slipped from her hand and fell to the table, where it rolled over onto its side, the black liquid spilling out, staining the checkered tablecloth, spreading like a dark jagged shadow over the red and white material.

"Oh, sorry," she said, snatching the cup up again. "That was so clumsy of me. I guess I'm a little tired today," she said as she sponged up the coffee with her napkin. "I hope it won't stain the cloth."

"No harm done," said Liza. "I'll just pop it in the laundry with my things later."

"Cold water," said Sherry, scooping the cloth up from the table. "We need to put cold water on it. Coffee's a protein stain."

"Like blood," Meredith remarked.

At that moment Velcro appeared at the side of the porch, his eyes wide, head lowered in a stalking position. He sniffed the air—looking for his nemesis, Ralph, perhaps—and continued on his way, slinking silently into the bushes. Claire watched his black-and-white form glide quietly through the dusty azaleas, belly low to the ground. She hadn't seen much of Velcro since the night he and Ralph had their run-in. She was sorry the two cats hadn't made friends, but at least they seemed to be keeping away from each other.

Later, when they were alone, Meredith said to Claire, "I'm asking Jeff Miller to send me as many of Maya's articles as he can get his hands on."

Claire nodded. She could postpone no longer telling Meredith that she was sending her back to Connecticut. She had expected a scene when she told the girl the news, but she was not prepared for a full-blown tantrum.

"What, are you *crazy*?" was the first thing Meredith said when Claire told her that she had arranged to have her father pick her up the next day. When Claire made it clear that she was not going to back down, Meredith threw herself into such a fit that Claire feared for her sanity. She stood looking at Claire without speaking, her face getting redder and redder, while tears collected in her blue eyes. Her body began to tremble, and a loud sob erupted from her, a volcanic expression of grief that Claire thought was about more than just leaving Ravenscroft; still, it was frightening to see her in such a state.

"You *can't* do this to me," she wailed, "you *can't*!"

"Meredith," Claire said softly, "please calm down." They were standing in the kitchen and Claire didn't want to disturb the other residents. She imagined them running in from all directions, wondering if Meredith was the next murder victim.

"Noooooo!" Meredith moaned. "Please, please, please don't do this!"

"Look, Meredith, it's for your own safety," Claire began, but just then Sergeant Rollins appeared at the door, his normally ruddy face even redder than usual.

"Is everything all right?" he said meekly when he saw Meredith's tear-stained face.

"No, everything is *not* all right!" Meredith snapped, and ran from the room. Claire started to go after her, but changed her mind. Meredith would have to work this out on her own, she decided; she couldn't hold her hand through every disappointment. Claire knew that what she was doing was best for the girl, and yet she, too, felt disappointment over her decision.

Sergeant Rollins stood there awkwardly, looking after Meredith. The front screen door banged loudly, then all was quiet.

"She knows to stay away from the woods, doesn't she?" he said.

Claire nodded. "Yes." She had told Meredith that if she so much as set foot in the woods, Claire would confine her to the house. Suddenly worried that Meredith would go off to the woods to spite her, Claire tiptoed to the front door and looked out. Meredith sat on the porch steps, a stick in her hand, poking at the dusty flagstone path leading up to the house. Claire decided to leave her to her sulking for the time being. She returned to the kitchen, where Sergeant Rollins stood waiting for her.

"She's out on the porch," Claire said in response to his inquiring look.

"Good," he said. "Can't be too careful these days, I say." He sneezed loudly, sending a thin spray of saliva across the room. "Sorry," he muttered, fishing the perpetually damp handkerchief from his pocket and dabbing at his nose with it. "Can't seem to shake this damn cold," he said, pocketing the grisly handkerchief.

"Have you tried zinc and echinacea?"

They turned to see Billy Trimble standing in the doorway, hands in his pockets. He wore a white Brooks Brothers shirt, khakis, and Docksiders without socks. He always looked like a clothing ad out of *New England* magazine, Claire thought.

"Echi-what?" said Sergeant Rollins, sniffling.

"Echinacea. It's an herb, supposed to be good for the immune system."

Sergeant Rollins shook his head. "Nope. Never heard of it."

"You should be able to find it downtown; in this town, I'll bet they sell it everywhere."

Sergeant Rollins nodded dubiously. "Well, maybe I'll

give it a try . . . I'm not big on those herbal things. Tried some herbal tea once, thought it smelled like—" He paused and glanced at Claire. "Well, it was pretty bad, anyway."

Claire smiled. "It was. It was awful."

Sergeant Rollins shifted his body uncomfortably in his thick blue uniform. "Well, I just came in to see if everything was okay . . . see you later."

"Okay." Claire watched him back out of the room, bumping into the wall as he turned to enter the hallway.

When he was gone Billy turned to Claire, his usual vague manner replaced by a surprising directness. "Have you seen Gary?" he said.

"Not today. He's not in his studio?"

Billy shook his head. "I looked there first. He usually paints in the mornings . . ."

"No, I haven't seen him. If I do, I'll tell him you're looking for him."

Billy's eyes wandered about the kitchen as if searching for something. "I guess I'll get back to work," he murmured, his vague manner returning. He wandered out of the room without another word, hands in his pockets, looking very preoccupied.

Claire went out to the porch to see how Meredith was getting along, and found her sitting on the daybed, Ralph clutched in her arms, crying softly.

"You don't want to see me go, do you, Ralph?" she said as she stroked the cat. Ralph had a stoic expression on his face; he was not exactly enjoying this, but was making no dramatic escape attempts. A haze of short white cat hairs, gently airborne, floated around his head like a halo.

Claire opened the door slowly and stepped out onto the porch. As she expected, Meredith ignored her and continued to address the cat. "You'll miss me, won't you?" she said pathetically to Ralph. "You may be the only one, but you'll miss me."

Claire sat down on one of the director's chairs. "You know that's not true, Meredith."

Meredith continued to ignore her. "No one else will care

that I'm gone." She wiped at the tears that slid across her cheeks.

"Meredith," Claire said carefully, "I'm not sending you back because I don't want you here. I'm doing it because it isn't safe here anymore."

Meredith looked up at Claire; her upper lip was swollen from crying. "Then why are *you* staying?" she said in a small voice.

Claire shook her head. "I'd like to leave, too," she replied. "And by the end of the week, I will, whether the detective has his murderer or not."

"If I stayed, I could help him," Meredith said, wrapping her arms around Ralph's neck and holding him close to her.

"Be careful—not so tight," Claire warned. "Ralph doesn't like that."

"You're always telling me what to *do*!" Meredith snapped angrily. She released Ralph and jumped up off the couch. Ralph stood uncertainly on the floor, his tail twitching, confused by his sudden freedom.

"Meredith—" Claire began, but Meredith stomped off into the house. Claire sighed and leaned back in her chair. This time she would let Meredith go; let her brood for a while, get it out of her system. She sat for a few minutes watching the late-morning haze settle over the woods. Just as she was about to go back inside, she saw Detective Hansom's black sedan winding up the hill toward the house. She sat and watched as he pulled his lean body from the car. A wind had begun to pick up off the side of the mountain, and as Hansom approached the house, his black trench coat flapping about his legs like wings, Claire was suddenly reminded of the Grim Reaper.

Detective Hansom's face was indeed grim as he ascended the steps to where Claire stood. "We have the report back on your car," he said. He stood with one foot resting on the top step, holding his battered fedora in one bony hand.

"Yes?" she said.

Detective Hansom wiped a sleeve across his brow and squinted into the haze. "There's no easy way to say this.

It was sabotaged—the brakes cut clean through—so that the fluid just leaked out."

Claire felt the heat rise to her head. She was suddenly dizzy. "Are you sure?" she asked, trying to stay focused on his face.

He shook his head. "There's no doubt about it. I can show it to you, if you like."

Claire shook her head. "No, I believe you . . . it's just that . . ." The whole scene suddenly seemed unreal. Everything—the house, the woods, this gawky, gentle man who stood talking to her, one foot perched on the top step—felt unnatural. Patterns swirled before her eyes, and she had to blink to keep everything from dissolving in front of her; the edges of the world around her were fuzzy and blurred as a watercolor. "Well," she said finally, "what do we do now?"

"We think maybe you should return to New York," Detective Hansom said gently. "We have increased the police presence here, put more officers on duty, but I don't feel that will necessarily keep you safe."

Claire smiled thinly. "So I guess I'm not a suspect anymore?"

The detective looked down at his feet. "We don't really have any suspects, Ms. Rawlings," he said slowly. "That's one of the problems. To tell you the truth, we haven't even found any reliable leads."

Claire nodded. "I see."

"But if you mean are we satisfied that you're not the killer—well, it's possible, I suppose, but I never thought it was very likely in the first place."

"Oh? Why not?"

This time Detective Hansom smiled ever so briefly. "Oh, call it instinct, I guess."

Just then Claire heard a familiar, urgent pounding of feet descending the front staircase and turned just as the screen door was flung open.

"Ah, Detective Hansom," Meredith cried, her face still streaked with dried tears, "just the man I wanted to see!"

"Yes?" he replied politely.

"Come with me," she told him cheerfully, all traces of her former mood vanished. "I have something to show you."

They followed Meredith upstairs to Claire's room, where Claire's laptop computer sat on top of the desk. America Online was opened, the blue-and-white logo glowing dimly in the late-morning haze.

"Voilà!" said Meredith, clicking on the icon indicating there was an e-mail message. "That guy at the *Times* looked up some of Maya's old articles and came across one about Maya that I thought was of particular interest."

Claire stared at the headline on the screen. REPORTER GOES UNDERCOVER TO EXPOSE WORKINGS OF MBLA. She read on. "Maya Sorenson is a woman, but for a few months she pretended to be a man who liked boys—even going so far as becoming a member of the Man-Boy Love Association, a group that caters to the desires of pedophiles."

Claire looked at Meredith. "Oh my God," she said. "Roger Gardner."

Meredith poked an index finger in the air triumphantly. "Bingo," she said.

Chapter 22

By the time Detective Hansom left, it was early afternoon. Claire didn't like exposing Roger's story to him, but she had no choice, given Meredith's discovery. They had gone into the library to talk; the detective sat listening quietly, elbows on his knees, his square chin supported by his bony hands, his basset-hound eyes focused on Claire as she talked in a low voice, not wanting anyone to overhear them. Meredith sat next to her in a rattan chair, her bare legs swinging back and forth, shoulders hunched over, investigating a bug bite on her arm. When Claire finished, Detective Hansom nodded solemnly and rose from his chair without a word. There wasn't much to tell; she only knew what she had heard from Liza.

When they got to the front door Claire said, "Is it relevant, do you think?"

The detective shook his head. "Hard to say. I'll go talk to Ms. Gardner and see if there's anything she can add."

"Are you going to arrest him?" Meredith asked breathlessly.

Detective Hansom swiveled his large head to look at her. "There's no real evidence yet tying him to the crime. I mean, it's a shame that he's into—well, if it's true, it's too bad, but so far it shows no direct relationship to our case. I'll pass the information on to vice, and they'll make their own arrest, most likely."

Detective Hansom scratched his scalp. "Well, I always say you can find the heart of darkness in a small town just about as like as anywhere."

Shortly before dinnertime, as Liza and Claire stood in the kitchen chopping vegetables, Tahir staggered in the back door, his face flushed. His clothing was even more disarrayed than usual; his shirt collar was torn and there was dirt on his face. He was breathing heavily, and as he entered he clutched at the counter to steady himself.

"Tahir, what is it?" said Liza.

"Someone grabbed at me from behind. I had to tear myself away and run to escape."

"Did you get a look at them?" said Meredith.

Tahir shook his head. "No. I was scared and I ran." He took a washcloth and wiped the dirt from his face. "I tripped on a root or something and fell down. I was so afraid." Claire saw that he was trembling all over. "It was terrible," he said softly. "It brought back such awful memories."

"So you didn't see who it was at all?" said Meredith, unmoved by his emotional state. "Did you get a sense of whether it was a man or a woman?"

Tahir shook his head. "I just ran," he repeated. "I just pulled away and ran."

"What were you doing out in the woods in the first place?" said Meredith. "It's off-limits."

Tahir hung his head as though he were a student being upbraided by an angry teacher. "I had to walk and think a little," he replied softly.

Meredith shook her head. "Don't go down to the end of town without consulting me."

"What?" said Tahir.

"It's A. A. Milne," she explained. "The guy who wrote *Winnie-the-Pooh*," she said in answer to Tahir's blank look.

Tahir shook his head. *"Winnie-the-Pooh?"*

"It's a children's book," said Liza. "Most kids in America read it."

Tahir nodded slowly. *"Winnie-the-Pooh,"* he repeated, as if the sound of the words were a magic incantation that could release him from the fear that had them all in its thrall.

When they called Detective Hansom about Tahir's fright in the woods, he again cautioned them not to stray from the grounds, then sent two patrolmen out to the woods to look around. Tahir didn't have much more to tell him; Meredith suggested that Tahir's torn shirt be sent in for fingerprinting, but Hansom didn't hold out much hope that would provide any conclusive results.

After dinner Meredith washed the plates and went over to Liza's cabin for a game of checkers with Sherry while Claire scoured a few pots and pans. When Claire was done, she wandered out onto the porch. As she watched the sun sink lower over Guardian Mountain, she heard Ralph's plaintive cry coming from the woods. He sounded as if he were hurt or in trouble. Claire went out to where the patrol car was usually parked, but it was empty. The policemen were probably still in the woods, she concluded. Again she heard Ralph cry out—louder this time. He sounded terrified. Claire slipped out through the back door, taking the shortcut through the woods to the road below. She hurried along the path toward the sound, the deep woods alive all around her. Tiny unseen animals darted and scurried in the bushes; birds twittered and scolded each other, their voices rising above the constant low hum of insects.

Don't go down to the end of town without consulting me.

She quickened her pace, walking in time to the internal rhythm created by the words running in her head:

Don't—go—down—to—the—end—of—town—without—consulting—me.

"Ralph!" she called, but there was no reply. Suddenly she emerged from the woods onto a field of crops alongside the road. Rows of golden grain waved and bent under the gathering wind, their shaggy brown heads swaying on slender stalks. The sky, which had been clear all day, was beginning to blacken. The clouds that hung over the setting sun were heavy and swollen with rain. Claire stood there for a moment, wondering if anyone at the house would notice her absence. If she returned soaking wet, there would certainly be comments and then she would have to explain to Sergeant Rollins where she had gone.

"Ralph!" she called again. This time there was another meow in reply, a plaintive, sad sound, as though he were lost—or injured.

Following the sound, Claire came to the bend in the road where she had driven off the pavement and into the tree; there was a large white birch, its bark chipped off where the heavy car had plowed into its trunk. The imprint of tires could be seen through a thin layer of leaves that had fallen on the ground. Claire bent down and flicked a few leaves away from the place where she had climbed out of the car, looking for her medicine wheel. She poked around with her foot, peering closely at the ground, looking for a glint of bright color in between the fading brown-and-yellow leaves. She found nothing, though, and saw that dusk was slipping into twilight.

"Ralph!" she called again, but this time the woods were silent. She sighed and started back toward Ravenscroft.

As she approached the cutoff leading across the field to the shortcut through the woods, Claire hesitated. A few feeble rays from the dying sun shot up through the cloud cover and visibility on the road was good; she felt safe on the road. Though not heavily traveled, it was public, and the occasional car whisking by gave her a sense of security. The woods, though, were already growing dark, and the thought of traveling that dusky path alone made her shiver.

Don't go down to the end of town without consulting me.

She felt a few drops of rain on her shoulders; and as she stood there trying to decide which way to go, the drops increased. Putting her fears aside, Claire headed for the woods. The shortcut would save fifteen minutes of walking, and with the rain coming on, she needed to hurry. If she arrived at Ravenscroft soaking wet, there were bound to be questions, maybe even suspicions.

She loped across the field at a jog, the thin stalks of wheat rubbing against her bare legs, their fuzzy heads tickling her thighs. She hesitated once more when she saw the entrance to the path looming up before her, dark and uninviting.

At that moment the woods seemed to represent everything she feared: death, loss—and most of all, fear itself. *I have to,* she thought. *I have to go in there.* Somehow she had a feeling that by entering that dark forest, she would finally overcome the fear that had been haunting her ever since that night Robert tried to pry the life out of her body.

Claire took a deep breath and charged into the woods. The path was soft under her feet, and the woodland creatures were suddenly silent, the sound of her own breathing her only accompaniment as she pounded along the path. She could hear rain on the canopy of leaves above her, and a few drops made their way onto her face as she ran.

Don't—go—down—to—the—end—of—town . . .

Up ahead, an ancient oak tree loomed, gnarled and twisted, its branches curling like deformed arms over the path. Just beyond the tree, the path turned sharply to the right.

. . . without—consulting—me.

Claire quickened her pace, peering ahead for the break in the trees where the path ended. Just as she made the turn by the old oak tree, she caught her foot on an exposed root and fell forward hard. She put out her hands to catch herself and felt the ground rise up to meet her, dirt and pebbles grinding into her palms as she rolled onto her side to lessen the impact. She lay on her side, the air knocked out of her, trying to catch her breath, her palms smarting from the sharp stones. She lay gasping for air, her lungs feeling flattened by the impact. It was raining harder now, the drops falling more thickly through the trees.

Suddenly she heard a noise behind her. A scraping, a rustling of leaves, a rushing forward—a large animal perhaps, but she had no desire to find out. Panting, Claire heaved herself to her feet. She took a step but her twisted ankle gave way and she flopped onto her back, helpless as a beached flounder. The rushing sound grew closer, the branches of trees crackling as whatever it was approached through the darkened forest. The thought came to her; shape-shifters, those creatures who came out at twilight . . .

A scream welled up in her throat as she struggled to her feet once more. This time her ankle didn't buckle, and she limped forward as fast as she could without looking back. Up ahead she could see the break in the trees where the trail ended behind Ravenscroft. Claire hobbled along the ground in a kind of crooked canter, pumping with her arms, her skin slippery from the rain, which fell ever more insistently from the sky.

Don't go down to the end of town . . .

Don't go down . . .

. . . to the end of town . . .

She was breathing so heavily she could hear only the struggle of her own lungs, and couldn't tell whether she was still being pursued; only a few hundred yards ahead lay the end of the path.

without . . .

without consulting . . .

me . . .

Another noise behind her, closer this time, made Claire lunge toward the final few yards at a spring. She emerged onto the back lawn of Ravenscroft at a full run and dashed across the wet grass with the last bit of energy she had, toward the yellow light of the windows, toward other people, toward safety. A great clap of thunder sounded as she reached the back door and bounded up the stone steps.

The back door to the kitchen was open, and she almost broke through the wire mesh as she pushed the screen door open. She stood in the brightly lit kitchen, blinking, sweat and rain coursing down her neck. On the other side of the room, a bowl of ice cream in his hands, stood Billy Trimble. He stared at her, his handsome face blank as stone.

"What happened to you?"

Claire took a deep breath. "I . . . I just went for a run."

Billy looked at her jeans and white oxford shirt. "In those clothes?" he said dubiously.

Claire shrugged. "It was an impulse. It was getting dark, so I didn't want to take the time to change."

"What happened to your hands?"

Claire looked down at her palms, which were grazed and bleeding. "Oh—I fell down," she answered as casually as possible. "Tripped on a root."

Billy nodded and ate a spoonful of ice cream. "You should be more careful."

"Well, you're probably right." Claire edged toward the door to the dining room. "I guess I'd better go shower; see you later," she said, rounding the corner into the hallway. She didn't run into anyone on her way upstairs, and her hand trembled as she pulled the key from her pocket to unlock her bedroom door.

Don't go down to the end of town without consulting me.

Claire sat on her bed, her legs tingling from the effort, and wiped her face with a bath towel. The curtains fluttered in the breeze from the open window and another clap of thunder sent a quiver of adrenaline through her body. She thought about what Two Joe had said about shapeshifters, and tried to imagine the shape of the creature crashing through the underbrush behind her in the woods. She imagined a wolflike creature—something mythical, like a werewolf. She tried to imagine one of the Ravenscroft residents as a werewolf: Jack with his white beard and predatory smile, dark, hairy Tahir, with his deep eyes and haunted look . . . the thought of either Gary or Billy as a werewolf was laughable. She didn't know if she should mention the incident to Detective Hansom. She knew there were coyotes in these woods, and what if it was a deer— or a bear, even? She knew there were bears in these woods, and sunset was a likely time to see one. She hoped whatever it was had not gotten Ralph.

That night she dreamed Robert was chasing her through a dark forest, his eyes glowing yellow through the trees, his face the face of a werewolf, with thick long fangs and

shaggy brown fur instead of skin. In her dream she tried
to run, but her legs did not respond to the frantic message
from her brain. It was as though she were moving through
molasses instead of air; the atmosphere itself seemed to
hold her back as she tried vainly to increase her speed, her
lungs pulling harder on the thick air in an attempt to breathe,
while he gained ground on her. She could hear him snarling
and growling behind her, heard his body crashing through
the trees, felt his hot breath on her neck as she lurched forward in a fruitless attempt to free herself from his hand,
which fell, cold and heavy, on her shoulder . . .

She opened her eyes and saw Meredith lying asleep on
her mattress, orange hair framed a halo of light from the
lamp on the dresser. Claire had left the light on when they
went to bed, reluctant to be in total darkness. She turned
over and stared at the shadows on the ceiling. A thought
swam up unbidden from her subconscious, a thought she
did not like at all. Whoever cut the brake cable on her car
might have not been after her after all: the intended target
could very well have been Meredith Lawrence. Claire shivered and pulled the blankets closer. She was glad Meredith was leaving tomorrow.

Chapter **23**

Meredith was very quiet all the next morning. Her father was supposed to arrive sometime in the late afternoon to get her, and Claire sat on the bed watching as she piled her few belongings into her battered green knapsack.

"Well, it was nice while it lasted," Meredith said sadly. Her tactic had changed: instead of arguing with Claire about leaving, she was attempting to elicit sympathy by acting pathetic. She sighed heavily as she pulled the strings of her knapsack together. "What did my father say when you called him?" she said, heaving the bag into the corner by the dresser.

"Oh, he just said he understood my concern," Claire replied, flicking a stray thread from the bedspread.

"Did he seem disappointed?"

"No, he said he would be glad to see you," Claire lied. Ted Lawrence had actually sounded a little put out. It was inconvenient for him to come up to Woodstock just now, he complained, but in the end he agreed with Claire; it was time to get Meredith away from there.

"Just as long as he doesn't send me back to Camp Steroid," Meredith said. "Anything's better than that. Hey,

wha'chou got there?" she said, pointing to a slip of paper
Claire held in her hand.

"This? Oh, this is just a phone message someone took
that Wally called."

"Who took it?"

"Uh, Tahir, I think."

"Yeah? Let me see it."

Claire handed her the slip of paper. Meredith studied it
for a moment and then sighed. "Guess I'll take a shower,"
she said, tearing off her T-shirt and kicking her shorts into
the corner next to her knapsack. She wrapped a thick blue
towel around her lean white body, flat and undeveloped,
still the body of a child. "Indoor plumbing is the key to
civilization," she remarked, scooping up her plastic soap
container and going out into the hall. A few minutes later
she was back.

"Forget something?" said Claire.

"There's no hot water!" she declared irritably.

"Oh? That's odd. Are you sure you waited long enough?"

Meredith shrugged. "See for yourself."

Claire got up from the bed and went into the bathroom.
After three minutes of running the water, it was still stone
cold. She went downstairs and into the kitchen, where
Sherry was fixing herself a vegetable stir-fry. She wore her
painting smock over black rugby shorts.

"Hi," she said cheerfully when she saw Claire.

"Hi. Do you know Marcel's number?"

"Oh, getting desperate, are you? The isolation up here
can do that to you."

"Very funny. The hot-water heater's gone off again."

"Really? That's strange. Let me go take a look before
we bother Marcel." Sherry put down the kitchen knife she
was using to chop the broccoli and onions. Claire couldn't
help noticing how long and sharp the blade looked.

She followed Sherry down the hall to the water heater,
nestled in a little corner of the east-wing bathroom.

"Let's just see, shall we?" Sherry knelt to inspect the
heater. "Yup, there it is," she said after a moment, "and
it's switched off for some reason . . . There." She straight-

ened up. "I turned it back on. You should have hot water shortly."

"Why would someone do that?" Claire asked as she followed Sherry back down the hall.

"I dunno. No reason I can think of. Well, see ya." Sherry disappeared into the kitchen as Claire went back upstairs.

Later, after Meredith's shower, Claire agreed to join her in a game of chess. On the way downstairs, they heard voices coming from the porch.

"Why can't you admit the possibility of redemption?"

Claire recognized Camille's smoky voice, raised in anger. Her impulse was to avoid entering the fray, but Meredith swung open the porch door and marched out. To Claire's surprise, the person to whom Camille was speaking was Jack Mulligan.

He was leaning indolently over the porch railing, an unlit pipe in his mouth; he removed it and tapped it on the porch railing. "Redemption is a myth propagated by the Catholic Church," he announced.

Camille put down her coffee cup. "And sin? Is that a myth, too?"

Jack smiled and let a puff of air escape his nostrils. "Of course. Religion exists for two reasons only: people's refusal to accept the finality of death and the need of the reigning powers to control the populace. The Catholic Church is especially guilty of that." He replaced the pipe in his mouth. "Do you know that abortion is illegal in Ireland?"

Camille leaned forward, her coffee cup clutched tightly in her well-groomed hands. "I'm not defending the Catholic Church," she declared impatiently.

Jack continued as though he hadn't heard her. "In Ireland, teenage girls can be thrown in prison for becoming pregnant. Now you tell me the Church's definition of sin makes sense."

"I don't give a damn about the Catholic Church!" Camille answered angrily, the color rising to her face. "What I'm talking about is *sin* as a moral reality—"

"But the whole idea of sin is an invention of religion."

"That doesn't necessarily make it wrong."

"What I'm saying is that you can't talk about sin without bringing religion into it sooner or later," Jack said with conspicuous patience, as though explaining himself to a child.

"Oh, but that's where you're wrong! Both sin *and* redemption are possible outside any church—without the intervention of organized religion of any kind."

Jack shrugged his shoulders. "If you want to believe that, I can't stop you. All I'm saying is that the whole notion of sin and redemption is a religious construct. How can sin exist without the presence of a watchful God?"

"It can exist in the eyes of other people—or in the eyes of the sinner."

Jack shook his head. "Then it isn't sin."

"Oh? What is it, then?"

"Bad behavior."

"And redemption? What is that if there's no God?"

Jack opened his palms up as if he were making an offering. "Like I said before, it doesn't exist."

"So without religion there's no redemption?"

"You got it, sister."

Camille stood up and shook nonexistent coffee-cake crumbs from her lap. "I'm *not* your sister, fortunately for me. Frankly, I can't think of anything worse than that." She turned and stalked across the porch toward the front door. Her dramatic exit was somewhat hindered by Ralph, who lay directly in front of the door. She was forced to step awkwardly over him; he ignored her, eyes half-closed, tail flicking lazily. To Claire's great relief, he had appeared as soon as she got up that morning, apparently none the worse for wear.

Jack laughed softly. "It never fails. You can take the girl out of the church, but you can't take the church out of the girl."

Just then Marcel LeMarc's pickup truck pulled into the driveway, sending a thin white spray of dust behind its thick tires. He climbed out of the cab of the truck, his long legs stretching to the ground as he heaved himself down from the truck. Claire noticed that he was walking with a limp as he ambled up the path to the house.

"Came to fix the water heater," he said as he climbed the porch steps. "Seems there's a faulty valve."

"What happened to you?" said Jack, indicating Marcel's left leg, which he was favoring.

"Oh, this?" Marcel said. "Ellie ran off again last night and I went looking for her and tripped and fell over a root, kinda twisted my leg a bit. I had a flashlight, but . . . well, it was dark last night."

Jack nodded and looked at Claire. "Yes, it was." Claire wondered if he meant anything by the look. Had he been out in the woods last night, too? she wondered. Or maybe it was Marcel's dog she heard crashing through the bushes after her.

"Did you find her?" said Jack.

Marcel brushed a fallen leaf from his shoulder. "Well," he said, ignoring Jack, "I'd best get to work before someone comes out here yelling about no hot water again." He sauntered into the house with the wide-legged gait of a man who just got off a horse.

As if reading Claire's mind, Jack muttered, "Who said there are no more cowboys?"

Claire heard a movement in the bushes and turned to see Ralph staring up at her, eyes wide, a small grey mouse in his mouth. The mouse dangled limply, as though there were no bones in its lifeless body. Repulsed, Claire turned away, only to see that Jack was watching her.

"Not a pretty thing, nature, is it?" he said, then turned and strolled into the house.

Meredith went back upstairs to read, but soon fell asleep, sprawled out on the bed with Stephen Hawking's physics book lying open on her stomach. Claire put the book on the bedside table and spread a blanket over the sleeping girl. Meredith murmured and turned over in her sleep, then was silent.

Claire sat down in the wicker armchair next to the bed and picked up a manuscript. She glanced at the title: *Magic Societies.* It was a sociological study of the use of magic and ritual in different cultures, and Peter Schwartz, who intended to bid on it, wanted her opinion. Claire read a passage about human sacrifice in the Mayan civilization and then put the book down and stared out the window. A couple of sparrows were squabbling in the tree outside the window, chirping and fluttering their tiny brown wings at each other.

There was no formula, no magic, Claire believed; in the end, there was only physics. If there was reality other than atoms and molecules, she had yet to see it. Feelings were not to be trusted, and the vague yearnings you experience on a fiercely starlit night are still just feelings, the chemical reactions of an organism.

She leaned back in the chair and dozed off. When she awoke, the sun was low in the sky and Meredith was gone. Claire looked at her watch: it was after six, and Ted Lawrence would be arriving soon. She went to look for Meredith, but couldn't find her in the house. It occurred to her that the girl might be hanging around Two Joe, so she went to find him.

Claire found him in his studio, working on a sculpture of a miniature bronze buffalo. The animal was in midcharge, head lowered, its thick shaggy mane glistening in the sun pouring down from the skylight overhead.

"Have you seen Meredith?" Claire said breathlessly.

Two Joe put down his polishing cloth and looked at her. "Not since this morning. Is she missing?"

"I can't find her anywhere. Her father's supposed to be here to pick her up in a little while, and she's disappeared."

Two Joe shook his head. "I have a bad feeling about this. I will help you look for her."

They left Two Joe's studio and were heading across the lawn to Ravenscroft when they saw Liza coming out of her cabin. She waved at them.

"Have you seen Tahir?" she called.

"No," said Claire. "We're looking for Meredith."

Liza walked toward them. "I saw her about an hour ago."

"Where?"

"She was headed in that direction." Liza pointed to the trail leading to Rock Hill Road. Claire shuddered. It was the same path she had taken the day she discovered Terry's body.

"The woods is off-limits," Two Joe said sternly.

"I know; that's what I told her, but she said she was just going to pick some wildflowers that grow at the edge of the woods," said Liza. "She had been talking about doing that for two days."

Claire groaned. "She lied; oh God, what does she think she's doing?"

"We must go after her," said Two Joe.

Claire looked down at her flimsy sandals. "I've got to put on some shoes," she said. "Wait for me here."

She dashed into the house and tore up the stairs to her room. To her surprise, the door was open; she had cautioned Meredith always to lock the door. There, sitting on the dresser, was a note addressed to Claire in Meredith's untidy, sprawling handwriting.

Gone to the summit of Guardian Mountain. I think I've zeroed in on the culprit. Meet me there—and you might want to bring the police— M.

Claire's heart froze as she stuffed the note into her pocket. Kicking off her sandals, she pulled on her hiking boots, her fingers trembling as she struggled to tie the laces. She pulled the door shut behind her and ran down the stairs two at a time. Two Joe and Liza stood on the porch waiting for her.

"Get Sergeant Rollins and tell him to follow us up to Guardian Mountain," she said to Liza.

"What? What is it?"

"No time to explain," Claire said breathlessly as she bounded down the steps and took off for the woods, Two Joe loping after her.

Guardian Mountain was the highest Catskill peak overlooking Ravenscroft, and its summit was accessible only through a twisting, narrow hiking trail that began just off the wide path that began on Rock Hill Road. Claire remembered passing the entrance to the hiking trail the day

she discovered Terry's body. She ran down the path, Two
Joe just behind her, until they came to the hand-painted
wooden sign pointing up the trail toward the mountain. The
trail to the summit, Claire knew, was over two miles long,
a steep, crooked climb over rocky Hudson Valley terrain.
The trail was well marked with a white blaze, but the day
was growing late and soon the sun would sink. She cursed
herself for not having brought a flashlight, but it was too
late to turn back.

"Come on," she said to Two Joe, and they began the
long, arduous climb. Claire's lungs burned as they climbed,
stepping over fallen tree limbs left by the recent storms,
pulling themselves up over rocky ledges. As the sky darkened and shadows deepened, the bent and twisted trees
began to look like shape-shifters, dim and ghostly in the
dying light.

About halfway up was a rock ledge the locals called
Overlook Rock, a place where the scenic beauty of the valley was especially breathtaking. The Hudson Valley lay
below them, the river winding like a wide grey snake along
the foothills. A panorama of the entire Catskill range
stretched in every direction, the soft peaks purple in the
setting sun. They stopped just below it, Claire pausing to
catch her breath, totally indifferent to the beauty all around
her. She stood with her hands on her knees, breathing heavily, wondering how much farther they had to go. In spite
of his bulk, Two Joe seemed to be breathing no harder than
normal; he stood, head erect, sniffing the air.

Suddenly the sound of voices cut through the air. Claire
spun around to see Meredith standing on Overlook Rock,
her orange hair blowing wildly in the wind.

"Meredith!" she yelled.

Meredith looked down at her and raised one skinny arm,
her finger extended. With the sky turning grey all around
her, she looked like the Ghost of Christmas Past. "Here's
your murderer!" she called over the wind that whipped up
over the side of the mountain.

Claire turned to look in the direction Meredith was pointing, and to her surprise, there, standing almost out on the

edge of Overlook Rock, was Tahir Hasonovic. His usually mild face was contorted with rage.

"You stupid little fool!" he hissed. "You couldn't leave well enough alone, could you?" He lunged toward her, and Meredith gave a terrified yelp and scrambled away on her hands and knees, crawling along the sheer rock face as best she could.

Claire turned to look for Two Joe, but he had disappeared. Just then she heard voices coming along the trail, and Sergeant Rollins appeared, puffing heavily, his round face red as a tomato. Behind him were Liza and another uniformed officer.

Claire looked up at Meredith and Tahir on Overlook Rock; he had crawled after her and held her by the ankle. She clawed at the smooth surface of rock in an attempt to escape, but his grip was firm. He pulled her to her feet and dragged her over toward the overhanging ledge.

Sergeant Rollins heaved himself up to where Claire stood. "Stop!" he called. "Come down off the rock now!"

Tahir just laughed at him. "Are you out of your mind? I may die, but at least I can take her with me," he said, tightening his hold on Meredith, who whimpered like a frightened puppy, all the fight gone out of her.

"Let the girl go and no one gets hurt," Sergeant Rollins called, but Tahir laughed again bitterly.

"Do you know it's ridiculous that you American cops seem to learn all your speech from the policemen in your movies?" he said. "America—land of opportunity," he said sourly. "There is no such thing, a land of opportunity; that is just a myth. I came here to begin a new life, but you wouldn't let me, would you?" He looked at Meredith, shaking her. She was crying now from fear, the tears streaming down her face. "Well, that's too bad, because now you will have to die with me," he said, pulling her closer to the rock edge.

"No!" Claire screamed, and Tahir looked down at her.

"It isn't much to die, you know," he said bitterly. "I have watched many people die. Oh, yes, many people, more than you can imagine. At first it is hard, but after a while it becomes easier . . . after a while you stop thinking about it, stop dreaming about it . . . until you can watch a person die as easily as you would kill a rat."

At that moment Tahir stumbled and lost his footing, and Meredith slipped from his grasp. He lunged after her, but stopped suddenly in mid-stride, as if frozen. It was as though a film had suddenly stuck in the projector; he stood motionless, teetering on the brink of taking a step. He turned toward them, an odd expression on his face—not quite pain, not quite relief. It was only then that Claire saw what had stopped him: embedded up to the handle in his chest was a knife—a hunting knife, like the one Gary owned.

She turned to see Two Joe standing at the point where trees gave way to rock. She hadn't even seen him throw the knife, but she knew it had come from him—that he had thrown it with chilling accuracy. Tahir staggered, clutching his chest, as a dark red stain began to flower upon his shirt. He looked down at the knife in his chest and then at Two Joe.

"You," he said, and his mouth moved, but no more words came out. His eyes closed and his body swayed like a cobra. In slow motion, it seemed to Claire, he teetered on the edge of the rock, and then, his hands still clutching the knife, his knees crumpled and he plunged over the side, down into the valley below.

Claire buried her face in her hands as a low wailing sound filled the air. She thought it came from Meredith, and it was only after she felt Two Joe's strong arms around her that she realized it had come from her own throat.

Chapter 24

By the time they scrambled down the trail, it was dark. Two Joe led the way, nimble as a deer, warning them of protruding roots and loose stones. It was almost as though he could see in the dark. She was glad to feel his big rough hand clutching hers as she negotiated a fallen tree trunk or a gully in the trail. The sky had turned midnight blue, and the stars were out over Ravenscroft as they trudged up the front porch steps. Detective Hansom met them at the door, and a look of relief washed over his craggy face when he saw they were all right.

"Sherry called me and told me you'd all gone off to the woods," he said. "You are very foolish, young lady," he declared sternly to Meredith, but Claire thought she detected hidden admiration in his voice.

He decided to postpone the search for Tahir's body until the next day. It was some hours later, as the residents of Ravenscroft gathered around the big fireplace, that Meredith calmly explained how she had arrived at her conclusion that Tahir was the murderer. Claire was more than a little awed at the girl's *sangfroid*. She sat with her back to the blaze, a cup of cocoa in her hands, watching as Meredith explained herself to the amazed residents.

News had spread quickly, and everyone was gathered around the big stone fireplace. Detective Hansom and Sergeant Rollins sat on either side of Camille on the couch while the other residents crowded around, sitting cross-legged on the floor or in armchairs. Billy Trimble slouched indolently over the back of Gary's armchair, his long white hands dangling on either side of Gary's head, his fingers almost touching Gary's shoulders. Two Joe stood quietly on one end of the fireplace, one thick arm draped over the mantel. Meredith sat in her favorite rattan chair, knees pulled up to her chest, an untouched plate of Mint Milanos at her side. She was enjoying this, Claire thought; the girl was truly in her element.

"I was first alerted by the fact that even though he was supposedly a Muslim, he ate pork," she said. "In fact, he didn't seem to adhere at all to Muslim dietary laws."

"I'll say," Jack Mulligan said loudly. "He liked his pork chops." Liza glared at him, and he smirked and shrugged his shoulders. "Well, he did."

Just then the front door was flung open and Evelyn Gardner entered breathlessly. "I came as soon as I heard," she said, flicking a stray hair from the immaculate bun at the nape of her neck. She wore a red dress with padded shoulders and gold buttons down the front, black stockings, and a black-and-gold jacket. On her right wrist dangled a set of gold bracelets.

Liza looked at Sherry, who sat cross-legged at her feet. "I called her," Sherry whispered. "I thought she should know."

"Thank God you're all right," Evelyn said, seeing Meredith. "You must be so *proud* of her," she said to Claire.

"Well, actually—" Claire began, but Evelyn interrupted her.

"Please don't let me interrupt you; I'll just sit and be quiet." She settled her elegantly clad bottom in the armchair Jack Mulligan gallantly offered her, her gold bracelets tinkling.

Camille leaned toward Meredith. "What about the time

Tahir came back from the woods and said he was being followed? Did he make that up?"

Meredith shook her head. "Ah, that was to throw us off the scent. I was almost convinced, but then again I was certain this murderer was smarter than that, and wouldn't risk being seen or even heard."

Claire thought about her mad run through the woods, and wondered if maybe she was fleeing a deer after all. Now she would probably never know.

Meredith leaned back in her chair and took a cookie from the plate. "But what really got me thinking along the right lines was Stephen Hawking."

Evelyn Gardner crossed her legs, and Claire heard the swoosh of expensive fabric. "What do you mean?" Evelyn said.

Meredith turned to Claire. "Remember what I said about atomic theory—about particles not existing but having a 'tendency' to exist?"

Claire nodded.

"Well," Meredith continued, "I was thinking about the shadowy, hidden identity of the murderer . . . and then I was struck by the quantum theory of subatomic particles existing with *both the properties of waves and particles.*"

"Yes," Gary said a little irritably. "I'm familiar with quantum theory. But how does that relate?"

"I didn't realize that it did—until I had a conversation with Two Joe about shape-shifters."

"Shape-shifters?" said Camille, her dark, kohl-lined eyes wide.

"Yes," said Two Joe. "We have legends that speak of shape-shifters, spirits who can change their form at will. You saw the murderer as a kind of shape-shifter, then?"

"In a way," Meredith replied, taking a bite of cookie. "Also helpful was Einstein's theory of special relativity, which states that not only the object but the *position of the observer* determines how an object is perceived."

"I don't follow," said Sherry.

Meredith leaned forward in her chair. "Consider: what if the murderer had another property—an *existence,* if you

will—that we were unable to see? In other words, what if
we perceived him as a wave but he was really a particle?
In other words, an assumed identity of some kind."

"Hmm . . . interesting, but where does that get you?" said
Liza.

"Well, it got me thinking along the right lines," Meredith answered.

"But why did you suspect Tahir?" said Camille.

"Well, actually, the first thing that put me onto him was
when he didn't know it was his birthday."

"Really? When was that?" asked Sherry.

"Oh, wait—I remember," Claire said. "We were getting
ready for dinner, and someone wished him a happy birthday, but he didn't seem to realize it was his birthday. He
made some sort of excuse about not remembering because
of all he had been through, but it was a little strange."

"Right," Meredith agreed. "*Everyone* knows when their
birthday is. It started me wondering. And then I found this."
She held up a handwritten note.

"What is that?"

"It's a note he wrote to Claire saying she had a phone
call."

"And what's so strange about that?" Billy Trimble asked
languidly.

"Because it doesn't match the handwriting in the mar-
gins of the manuscript of his work," Meredith replied
smugly. "It isn't even close. Whoever wrote the notes in
the margin was left-handed, with that backward slant—and
the writing is really different. So that's when I figured Tahir
wasn't who he was pretending to be. So then I left him a
note saying that I knew it was him, and that he was pos-
ing as someone else."

"But how did you know he would follow you?" said
Gary.

"I didn't—and if he was innocent, then he wouldn't, of
course."

Camille shook her head. "I just can't believe you'd go
out in the woods alone with someone you knew—"

"*Suspected,*" Meredith corrected her.

"Okay—suspected was a murderer. Still, what on earth were you *thinking*?"

"Well, I figured if he were innocent, he wouldn't respond to my note; he wouldn't care. But if he *did* come, then . . . well, it was the next best thing to a confession."

"But why didn't you just call Detective Hansom?" said Liza.

Meredith frowned and rolled her eyes. "C'mon; I'm just a *kid*! Who would believe me?"

"I would, after tonight," Jack Mulligan responded. There was no hint of his usual cynicism; in fact, Claire thought she detected admiration in his voice.

"Well, whatever," Meredith answered with a shrug. "Maybe I acted rashly . . ."

"Maybe?" Claire exploded. *"Maybe?* I think we can all agree to that!"

Sherry shook her head. "You're a gutsy kid, I'll say that for you."

Meredith just shrugged, but she looked pleased.

"Gutsy or stupid," Claire muttered. Now that the danger was over, her concern for Meredith's safety was being replaced by anger at the girl's foolish actions.

Claire heard the sound of car tires on gravel and looked out the window just in time to see a long blue Cadillac pull into the driveway below the house. "Aw, damn," Meredith grumbled, putting down the plate of cookies.

Claire watched Meredith's father walk up the flagstone path, noticing how like him Meredith was in so many ways: the same lanky build, the ungainly lope of a walk, the same long head and high cheekbones. Meredith got up from her chair and opened the front door.

"Hello, Father."

"Hello, Meredith. Sorry I'm late. I got a late start and then I got a little lost on the way here." He stood there blinking at the assembled company, which, Claire realized, must have been a strange sight to a Connecticut WASP like Ted Lawrence. There was Two Joe in his black shirt and leather vest, his long black hair hanging loose around his massive shoulders, shiny as sealskin. And Jack Mulligan, in his usual camouflage-and-khaki getup, looking like a Hemingway wannabe. And Sherry, with her set of earrings running all the way up her earlobe . . . Claire wondered what Meredith had told her father about the place.

Ted Lawrence cleared his throat. Meredith responded as if she had been handed a cue. "This is my father, everyone."

"Hello," Ted Lawrence said stiffly.

Liza rose and extended her hand. "Liza Hatcher," she said warmly. "Pleased to meet you. Your daughter has just—"

Detective Hansom rose from his armchair. "Your daughter has just helped us find a murderer."

Ted Lawrence looked at Meredith. "Well," he said after a moment. "Has she really? Well." He shook his head, as if the words needed shaking up before he could really understand them.

Meredith looked at Claire and rolled her eyes.

Chapter 25

L iza persuaded Ted Lawrence to stay the night. He slept in Terry's old room; no one told him that it was the bedroom of a murdered man, but Meredith enjoyed what she called "the delicious irony of the situation."

The next day Detective Hansom showed up just as the residents were having breakfast on the porch. Sherry and Liza had gone into town and bought bagels for everyone. There was no sign of Ted Lawrence yet, but Gary and Billy had already retired to their studios for the day, and Two Joe and the rest of the writers were still sitting around the picnic table when the detective's car pulled into the parking lot. A flush came over Camille's face as the tall detective made his way up the porch steps. He accepted her offer of a cup of coffee and settled himself in one of the director's chairs, which, as always, looked too flimsy to hold his lanky body.

"Thought you might all like to know more about Mr. Hasonovic, as he called himself," he said, swinging one long leg over the other.

"Sure would!" Meredith exclaimed, leaning forward on her elbows.

"Well, I just spent most of the morning on the phone

with Amnesty International and the State Department," Hansom said to her. "You were right; he wasn't who he claimed to be."

"I *knew* it!" Meredith crowed.

"Then who was he?" said Jack Mulligan.

"Well, Mr. Mulligan"—the detective fixed him with a cold gaze—"it seems he was operating under an alias."

"Imagine that!" Jack exclaimed, and Claire couldn't tell if he was being deliberately insolent or if he suspected that she had discovered his own alias.

"So who *was* he?" Meredith repeated impatiently.

"Well, he wasn't Tahir Hasonovic, because the real Tahir Hasonovic was dead—because he killed him." The detective paused for a moment to let the information sink in. "Best as we can figure it, his real name was Stefan Razdan, and he was a colonel in the Serbian army."

There was another stunned silence, and then Sherry spoke.

"Wow. So that explains why he ate pork."

"So he came to this country under the assumed name of the man he murdered?" Liza said, her big face blank.

"Right," Hansom replied. "In fact, he was responsible for the massacre of an entire Croatian town—the same town Hasonovic wrote about in his story."

"Let me get this straight," Jack Mulligan said slowly. "This Serbian colonel kills Hasonovic after he writes about the massacre . . ."

"Right," said Hansom. "And then, assuming his identity, he comes to America to escape retribution for his war crimes. Tahir Hasonovic was something of a celebrity among his own people in Bosnia, but Razdan escapes before his deeds catch up with him. Now, Hasonovic has already applied and been accepted at Ravenscroft, so Razdan must have figured what was the harm in showing up pretending to be him? He somehow managed to steal Hasonovic's manuscripts, and it's free room and board for a while."

"Of course," said Jack. "All he has to do is lay low—"

"And he doesn't plan on running into someone who actually *knew* Hasonovic!" Sherry added.

"But Ms. Sorenson *didn't* actually know him, as best we can figure it," Hansom corrected. "She had visited the village and written about him, but evidently she never met the real Tahir Hasonovic."

"Then why kill her?" said Camille.

"Because she was close to finding out his secret," Claire answered. "For some reason, she was suspicious enough to confront him." She told the others about the conversation she overheard between Maya and Razdan shortly after she arrived.

Liza sighed. "When Maya confronted Razdan, she probably never dreamed that here, in America, he would resort to murder to protect his identity."

Sherry licked a spot of cream cheese from her paint-stained finger. "What about Terry? Did Razdan kill him because he knew Terry stole Maya's journal, then?"

Detective Hansom nodded. "Looks that way. Of course, there are some things we'll never know . . . why, for instance, he cut the brake cable on your car," he said to Claire.

"He must have thought I was onto him, too," Claire answered. The others stared at her.

"Claire!" said Liza. "You never told me!"

"He cut your *brake cable*?" Meredith said. "Why didn't you *tell* me?"

"I told Ms. Rawlings not to reveal the information to anyone, since we didn't know who we could trust," Hansom replied.

"But you can trust *me*!" Meredith grumbled.

"Well, I'll be damned." Jack Mulligan rose and stretched. "It all proves something I've always thought. Politics is almost always, in the end, personal."

Ted Lawrence chose that moment to appear at the front door, his eyes creased with sleep. "I apologize for sleeping so late," he said, yawning. "Usually I'm awake with the birds. It must be something about the air up here."

Maybe it was the release of tension after the stress of

the past week, but for some reason this struck everyone as funny, and they all burst out laughing.

A look of bewilderment came over Ted Lawrence's patrician face. "What? What did I say?"

This just caused everyone, even Detective Hansom, to laugh even harder.

"Oh, Father!" said Meredith, holding her sides. Claire had the sense that she was enjoying the chance to play the grown-up while her father stood there, barefoot, a look of puzzlement on his face.

Later, however, standing in the driveway in front of Ravenscroft, she looked vulnerable and childlike, dressed in one of Claire's blue oxford shirts and her only clean pair of jeans. Meredith had neglected to do much laundry during her stay, and borrowed a shirt from Claire so she wouldn't "embarrass her father" on the drive back to Connecticut. The shirt hung loosely on her bony shoulders, and clutched in her hand was Two Joe's small brass statue of the rearing mustang; he had given it to her as a going-away present.

"Good-bye, Ralph," she called to the cat, who was lurking under an azalea bush, sniffing at the ground. "He came to see me off," she remarked to Claire as she climbed into the front seat of her father's Cadillac. "Well, we're even now," she added, rolling down the window and looking out.

"What do you mean by that?" said Meredith's father as he put her knapsack into the trunk of the car. The knapsack looked so small inside the roomy trunk, and the sight of it lying against an immaculate tire iron gave Claire a hollow feeling.

Meredith squirmed in her seat and fiddled with the seat belt. "I saved her life once, and now she's saved mine."

"Oh, I see," Ted Lawrence replied, as though he were not quite listening to her.

"Okay," Claire said, closing the car door as Meredith snapped her seat belt into place. "We're even, okay?"

Meredith nodded. "Right. Even Steven. Good-bye, Redbird." Her pale blue eyes looked misty in the thin morning light. Claire wondered if she actually saw tears or if it was a trick of the light. She leaned over and kissed Meredith on the cheek. Suddenly the girl wrapped her arms around Claire's neck and pulled, hugging her so tightly that Claire had trouble taking a breath. Then, just as suddenly, Meredith released her and stared straight ahead, fingering the brass statue lying on the seat next to her.

Ted Lawrence closed the trunk and walked to the driver's side of the car as Two Joe came out of the house.

"Good-bye, Lightning Flash," he said, offering a large callused hand for Meredith to shake.

"Good-bye," Meredith said. "Thanks for . . . you know."

Two Joe nodded solemnly. "You are the one we all have to thank. Next time you must not take such a risk, however. Promise?"

Meredith sighed and shrugged her shoulders. "If there ever is a next time."

Two Joe laid a hand on her shoulder. "Promise?"

Meredith let her head fall onto the seatback. "Okay. I promise."

Ted Lawrence cleared his throat and extended his hand to Claire. "Thank you for . . . everything."

"You're welcome." Claire took his hand. It was smooth and strong, with perfectly manicured nails. She was reminded of Wally's beautiful hands, and was glad she was going to see him soon. Now, standing there saying good-bye to Meredith, she missed him with a sudden fierceness that surprised even her.

Ted Lawrence turned to Two Joe. "Thank you, too," he said, "for looking after her."

Two Joe nodded. "It was my honor. She is . . . well, you must know; you are her father."

Ted Lawrence cleared his throat again, and his mouth moved, but no words came out. He squeezed Claire's shoulder. "I'll be in touch," he said.

Claire watched the Cadillac pull slowly away, winding down the steep narrow curves of Guardian Mountain Road. A glint of sunlight flickered briefly off Meredith's copper hair, and then the car disappeared around a bend in the road. Claire turned to Two Joe.

"I'm hungry."

Two Joe nodded. "Me, too."

He put his heavy comforting arm around her and together they went back into the house. A spray of sunlight fell on the honeysuckle bush next to the porch, yellow on yellow, and on a pile of fallen crumpled brown leaves beneath it. Claire inhaled the sweet smell of summer giving way to the crushed-leaf aroma of fall, and felt that it was good.